SKY RIDGE HOTSHOTS

PROTECT

PAISLEY HOPE

Primary Dev. Edits : @Dev.edits.with.bri, @probablyalovestory

Editing : Caroline Palmier—Love & Edits,

Consult. Dev edits: Jordan Valeri

Hotshot consultant: S. (the superhero)

Proofreading and Book Design: Cathryn Carter—Format by CC

Cover @Whiskeygingergoods

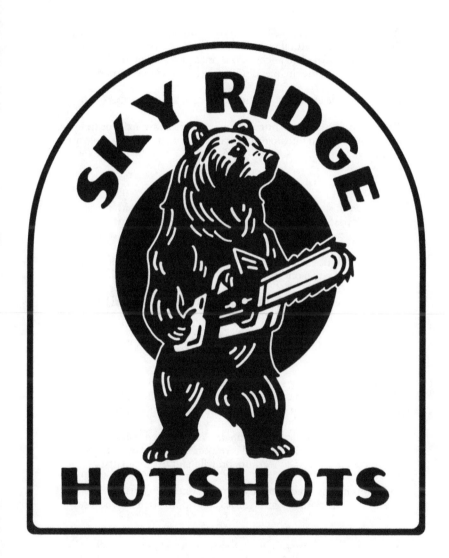

GLOSSARY

Anchor point: a strategic location from which to start building a fire line, starting at a natural unburnable area, such as rock scree, creeks, or trails. The goal of an anchor point is to prevent the fire from burning around the fireline, pinning firefighters from behind.

Ash pit: a hole in the ground filled with hot ash and embers.

Backburn, backfire, or burnout: terms for intentionally putting fire on the ground and burning vegetation against an active flame front to deprive it of fuel.

Black: the area that is already burnt.

Buggy: a transportation vehicle consisting of seating with no water supply. It has a total of 8 seats allowing for a large amount of crew to be transported to the fire.

Chain: a unit of measurement, commonly used in wildland fires. Eighty chains equal one mile, so one chain is sixty-six feet long.

Control or containment line: any constructed or natural barrier used to impede a fire's progress.

Crampons: a metal plate with spikes fixed to a boot for walking on ice or rock climbing.

Crown fires: when canopies of trees light with flame. These are often the largest, hardest to contain, and fastest-moving fires. When one canopy ignites, that fire can begin jumping from tree to tree.

Division: the person who implements xan assigned portion of the Incident Action Plan (IAP) and is responsible for all operations conducted in the division/group, on wildland fire incidents.

Drip torch: a handheld tool used to set controlled fires, or prescribed burns, by intentionally igniting fires by dripping flaming fuel onto the ground.

Ember wash: a shower of hot embers, carried by the wind, often enabling the fire to "jump" over control lines and spread by creating spot fires. Embers can travel over a mile before falling.

Engine: a truck or other ground vehicle that can transport and pump water, via hoses, onto a fire.

Engine Crew: a team of up to ten firefighters attached to an engine, tasked with initial, direct engagement of a wildfire. They use a variety of tools, primarily relying on hoses and water.

Escape route: a predetermined route to allow firefighters to get to safety, should the situation become unsafe on the ground.

Fire-chasing beetles or Melanophila beetles: insects attracted to forest fires because they use freshly burnt (and sometimes still-smoldering) wood to lay their eggs. They gather near the fire and have a vicious bite, often attacking wildland firefighters while working on a fire line.

Fire line: A line of ground without vegetation that will presumably stop or direct a fire's progress. Firefighters dig line by hand, using Pulaskis and other tools.

Green: fuel-laden area that hasn't yet burned.

Hand Crew: general-purpose wildland firefighters. Hand crews are typically eighteen to twenty people and work on digging line, clearing trees and brush with chainsaws, and setting controlled burns with drip torches.

Helitack crew: a team of firefighters trained and certified to support helicopters to fight fires.

Helibucket or bucket work: a bucket that hangs from a helicopter by a cable and is used to transport and apply water or retardant directly onto a fire. Helibuckets can be dropped into a lake or river to refill with water, holding as much as 2,600 gallons.

Hotshots: an intensively trained team of wildland firefighters primarily tasked with directly engaging a fire and digging hand lines.

I-Met: the Incident meteorologist.

Incident Commander: the leader on a fire and one of as many as dozens of people managing the complex planning, safety, strategy, and operations on a conflagration.

Ladder fuels: flammable materials, like small trees or low limbs, that allow a fire to move from the forest floor up into the canopy, increasing the intensity and potential growth of a fire. When those fires grow larger and "ladder" up trees, they can ignite crown fires.

MRE: Meals Ready-to-Eat. A self-contained, lightweight ration that provides a full meal for an individual.

Nomex or Yellows: the yellow shirt worn by wildland firefighters. Nomex is a trademarked term for a flame-resistant fabric widely used for industrial applications and fire protection equipment.

Osborne Fire Finder: a type of alidade used by fire lookouts to find a directional bearing (azimuth) to smoke in order to alert fire crews to a wildland fire.

Prescribed or controlled burn: a planned fire that is intentionally set to achieve specific management goals such as reduce wildfire risk and restore natural ecosystems.

Pulaski: a tool with a head that has an ax blade on one side and an adze on the other.

Roll: a fire assignment.

Scree: a mass of small loose stones that form or cover a slope on a mountain.

Ship: a helicopter.

Snag: a dead, often fire-killed, standing tree that presents a hazard for firefighters on the ground.

Spot fire: an occurrence when embers drift across control lines, and settle on vegetation or other flammable material, igniting new flames.

Stihl: a brand of chainsaw, used by wildland firefighters to cut brush, snags, and debris.

Torching: when one or more trees go up in flames.

UTV: a Utility Terrain Vehicle. A motor vehicle designed for off-road use that's typically larger than an all-terrain vehicle (ATV) and is often used for work rather than recreation.

Volly firefighter: a volunteer [wildland] firefighter.

ORGANIZATION FLOW CHART

THERE ARE THOUSANDS OF PEOPLE FROM
VARIOUS COMMAND TEAMS INVOLVED WITH
WILDLAND FIRE OPERATIONS, BUT FOR THE
SAKE OF KEEPING IT SIMPLE, WE ARE ONLY
LISTING THE ROLES MENTIONED IN THE
SKY RIDGE HOTSHOTS SERIES.

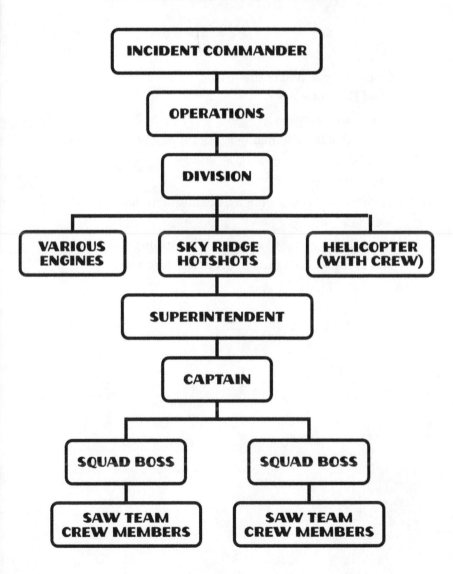

TROPES AND TRIGGERS

- Open door sexual content 18+
- Mild Degradation
- Mild Cum play
- Death of a family member (not on page-through flashback)
- Dealing with grief
- Anxiety and panic attacks, dealing with fear over a loved one's job
- Descriptive scene of injury while fighting fire
- Healing process of injury from fighting fire

PLAYLIST

1. Sleeping on The Blacktop by Colter Wall
2. Indigo by Sam Barber and Avery Anna
3. Angel from Montgomery by John Prine
4. Phoning Heaven by Waylon Wyatt
5. Break My Bones by Wyatt Flores
6. Burn Burn Burn by Zach Bryan
7. It's True by Gavin Adcock
8. Beautiful Lies by Tanner Ursey
9. Back In Back by ACDC
10. Jersey Giant by Evan Honer & Julia DiGrazia
11. Always Been You by Jessie Murph
12. I'm on Fire by Nate Fire

For those of you wondering if fire fighters are real life superheroes in more ways than one, I promise you they are. They're also hot as hell, and Rowan Kingsley is your proof.

Wildland Firefighters have an unwavering dedication to safeguarding our natural resources and environment, property, and communities. They wouldn't want to be called heroes, but they are. (Sorry, not sorry, S!)

Their selflessness, courage, and teamwork in the face of danger make them indispensable guardians. They sacrifice not only their family time, their entire personal lives and comfortable living conditions, but in many instances, they sacrifice their mental health.

Something I learned during this process is that these hotshots are primarily federal employees and they need more support! If you would like to donate monetarily to help advocate for proper job classification, better pay and or benefits for federal wildland firefighters please visit:

givebutter.com/GRWF

Nurses are angels on earth. They not only provide vital medical care, but also offer comfort, and emotional support to patients. Often, they must do so under challenging conditions, and without enough regard to their personal emotions.

The men and woman who take on these careers don't leave their work behind at the end of the day. They carry every single second with them everywhere they go and so do their families. For anyone who is brave enough to make these careers your life, I commend you, I respect the hell out of you, and I am grateful.

PROLOGUE
ROWAN

ALMOST 6 YEARS AGO

"You think he knew his time was up?" My best friend, Jacob, leans into me as he asks so no one else will hear him.

Such a loaded question pulls my attention from the multiple scuff marks on my boots. I scrubbed them as clean as I could last night. I was hell bent on getting them spotless for my sup. My *former* sup.

Fuck. There's nothing like swallowing the heaviness of that reality down.

"Don't know, man, but he went out like a hero," I answer somberly, taking a pull from a half empty bottle of tequila and passing it to Jacob. I don't normally make a habit of drinking in the middle of the morning—none of us do, but it's gonna take everything we have just to walk through those funeral home doors.

"Twelve weeks," my new captain, Callahan–Cal– says, shaking his head in disbelief.

"Just the rest of this season and he would've retired."

Cal looks like hell. We all do. Superintendent Garret

Macomb, our sup, was our mentor, our leader, our friend; and now he's just fucking gone. His old plaid jacket is still hanging on the hook at our base and he's never coming back to claim it.

I swipe the bottle back from Jacob and take another much-needed pull from it to stop the sting at the bridge of my nose. The tequila burns the back of my throat, but it's a burn I welcome.

The steady flow of cars and trucks through the rain seems never-ending, turning into the parking lot as my squad talks around me.

"Laney says there's a reason for everything. I say that's a pile of bullshit. Where was this rain last week? There's no reason for any of this," Jacob says, brushing the misty droplets from his sleeves.

We all wore our uniforms today—standard green Nomex pants and our yellow wildland fire shirts. We stand out in the crowd of dark suits and dresses but it's how we show our solidarity and respect.

"That's your girlfriend's job. She's just trying to make you feel better, trying to help," Cal says to him, patting him on the shoulder, already acting like our captain.

Jacob nods, fighting back tears. He's been my best friend since middle school, and I've only seen him cry once aside from now.

"Sup would have your heads for drinking at eleven a.m. over him, boys," Jacob's dad, Jack, says as he locks his truck behind him with a remote. He's a twenty-year vet and a squad leader with our crew. He's got more salt than pepper in his hair now but he's still a strong man. Jacob says he's thinking of retiring at the end of this season; he just wants to work at least one full summer with his son.

Jack's wife, Mae, walks in step beside him carrying a sympathy card. Her long dark hair is pulled back in a bun and it's obvious she's been crying. I scan the parking lot, knowing if

Jack and Mae Taylor are here, my biggest regret isn't far behind them.

"How's Molly, honey?" Mae asks Cal, giving him a motherly hug. Jack and Mae own the local bar *Shifty's* that we all hang out at more often than we should. Between that and basically growing up at their house, they've become like pseudo parents to all of us over the years.

"She's good, she's in there somewhere." Cal forces a small smile, gesturing to where his fiancée is inside.

I glance out at the mountains through the rain and listen to the group's chatter for a few minutes, forcing the last image I have of Sup from my mind for the thousandth time; he was sitting on the ridge, stuffing a turkey sandwich into his mouth like any other lunch break, laughing and cracking jokes, his eyes crinkling up into little crescent moons the way they did. I take another sip from the bottle of Patron and then pour a little out onto the grass beside us for the man that taught me everything I know.

Miss you already, ya sturdy fucker.

We're hotshots, wildland firefighters. Death and injury are expected in our line of work but that doesn't mean it isn't hard as hell to say goodbye. For today, tequila seems to be making this a little more bearable.

I take my final pull from the bottle at the precise moment I hear her smoky voice. Of course, I'm the one standing out here drinking mid-morning when she approaches.

"Never seen you boys so clean," she says to all of us as she steps up onto the curb, her pretty face still hidden by the black umbrella she carries, the ends of her long, honey brown hair are visible from under the brim.

I turn fully toward her, straightening up and passing the bottle to my crewmate, Caleb.

Violette Mae Taylor, Jacob's fraternal twin sister, looks stunning and somber in a black dress that fits her to perfection. It falls to her knees, tapering in at her small waist. The sleeves are long and cuffed at the wrist, and the neck is high, but it doesn't conceal that gorgeous body enough to stop me from swallowing. *Hard.*

Her light hazel eyes flit to mine, then quickly look away.

"King," she greets quickly. I wince.

Once upon a time, I used to be Rowan.

Her coconut scent fills my senses as she breezes right by me, smiling for the other guys, but not for me. It's been a long time since I've been on the receiving end of that pretty smile.

Violette hugs Cal and says something to him low enough that we can't hear before turning to face the rest of the crew to say her hellos. The ones who have known her a long time hug her as she gives her condolences.

"All right." Jack clears his throat as he checks his watch. "Time to get your shit together, boys. Let's send Sup off right."

Our crew utters various forms of *"fuck yeah"* and *"for Sup."*

Cal turns to lead us in through the dark wooden double doors as our new captain. Jacob and I follow with Jack, Mae, and Violette close behind.

The moment our crew enters the building all eyes are on us.

I nod to Xander, Sup's son, the moment I see him. He's taking over as Sky Ridge's Superintendent, effective immediately. The amount of people here to pay their respects to him, his brothers, and his mother is impressive.

Superintendent Macomb's yellow helmet catches my eye at the front. It rests at the foot of the podium holding his urn. Xander's mom stands beside it. I fight back the tears I know are coming as I wait patiently, willing myself to hold it together. Cal and Jacob shake Xander's hand before I extend mine. He pats me on the shoulder as if to comfort *me.*

"I'm so fucking sorry, man," I say. It's all I can manage to get out while choking back tears.

"My dad loved you, King. He was proud of you and Jacob."

4

He calls me by my nickname, gulping back sorrow of his own. "You know what he'd say?" A hint of a smirk plays in Xander's eyes even through his grief.

I fight the tears. "That I'm Rowan fucking Kingsley, and I should lock it up. Never let them see me sweat."

"That's right. You and Jacob are the new generation. He'd want you to be strong," Xander says, already following more in his father's footsteps than he realizes.

"I'll do my best, Sup," I tell him proudly, but his new title doesn't sit right with me yet.

"It's time to begin." The minister from our local church approaches us, gesturing to the seating area to our left.

I nod before moving on with our entire crew to take our seats. The first two rows are a sea of yellow and green.

Christ, this is only my second season. I can't help but wonder how many more of these memorials I'll have to attend over my career. I can't help but wonder if one of them will be for me.

Our job isn't for the faint of heart. We know the risks, but we take them with pride. I look around at my brothers, silently vowing to do everything in my power to protect each and every one of them, or fucking die trying.

CHAPTER 1

Violette

PRESENT

I stare up at the ceiling, singing the theme song to Hollie's favorite TV show in a fading whisper for the twentieth time tonight, willing her to fall asleep. After a few minutes, I'm pretty sure the twentieth time's the charm because her pretty blue eyes finally close. Her blonde curls settle against her pillow in tufts as I carefully watch her adorable little features, assessing the best time to make my escape.

We moved back to Sky Ridge almost a month ago and it's taken her this long to settle into a new bedtime routine. In her almost four years on this earth, Hollie has always been an incredible sleeper. I swear this child loved to lie down in her crib every night, cuddle in with her favorite stuffed animal, and drift off to dreamland. But one thing my Hollie doesn't like is change—*at all.* And the last year has brought us a lot of that.

I half roll off the toddler-size bed she sleeps in like a stealthy mom ninja and raise the guard rail, praying it doesn't do the squeaky thing it does sometimes and wake her up. Some nights I pass out with her but tonight I have to go to work, which is, truthfully, the last thing I want to do. After only two weekends I'm still not quite used to moonlighting at my parents' bar.

Did I picture myself slinging drinks for extra cash in the town watering hole at twenty-eight? Not a chance, but here we are. The thing is, I can't even use the excuse that it's to help my parents out, because it's not. It's to help *me* out. They were the ones gracious enough to let me work alongside their regular bartender Lou on the weekends for some extra cash.

Thankfully, it's not my only source of income. I'm also a nurse in the burn unit at Bakersfield Hospital, which is ironic, since fire and trauma are two of the reasons I left this town in the first place.

But oddly enough, working with burn victims over the last month has been sort of cathartic for me. My mother is convinced it will heal me of my emotional scars. I'm not quite sure if I buy that.

My career in nursing, unlike my bartending job, rewards me richly, but even with the child support I receive from my ex, things are a little tight having to pay for pricey daycare and what's left of my student loans. Sky Ridge, Washington is known to have a high cost of living to begin with, but in the nice, sought after area of town I wanted to raise Hollie in, homes have skyrocketed.

Our house at the corner of Pine Street and Maple is a 1920s one floor craftsman that cost me a small fortune, so the more tips the better. Hence my outfit tonight—my tightest, faded blue jeans and a ribbed white tank top that bears our pub's name *Shifty's* and shows a generous amount of cleavage. Ten years ago, I never would've been comfortable wearing something like this in public, but now I've grown proud of my curves and even feel confident showing them off a little. So, if a bit of cleavage helps my savings account, I'm here for it.

I hold my breath as I back out of Hollie's doorway, standing frozen for a few seconds just to make sure she's actually sleeping.

I fluff my long, golden-brown waves around my shoulders, thankful I got ready for work earlier so I wouldn't have to do it after Hollie fell asleep.

As I wander through my house picking up toys, I listen to the local news running on the TV. They've been covering the *Pinafore Creek Fires*, a series of wildfires burning in the mountains outside of Spokane for days. Normally, I'd shut it off, but I'm in such a hurry to tidy up before my parents get here to watch over Hollie, I just let it run.

"The Sky Ridge Hotshots, Central Washington's own Type 1 shot crew shared video footage of their fireline that redirected the Pinafore Creek fire from jumping into an unprotected conservation area. Which in turn, stopped the fire from spreading to an upscale neighborhood beyond the mountain late Saturday afternoon. The crew has been working with other crews from Arizona and Wyoming and they've managed to dig a line that Superintendent Xander Macomb says ultimately helped to bring the rapidly growing and potentially deadly wildfire under control. Just seeing the footage today has helped put nearby residents' minds at ease."

I flinch involuntarily at the reporter's words as I finish tidying. The familiar tight spread of anxiety creeps up my throat, the same feeling I've willed myself to push past, countless times since my twin brother Jacob's tragic death almost five years ago. Sky Ridge's deadliest summer to date. Two crew members, one season. I squeeze my eyes shut and try to take a deep breath, centering myself and willing the feeling away.

Tears are for another day, I tell myself repeatedly until the tightness subsides.

The handsome face of Superintendent Xander Macomb catches my eye on the TV, standing in the 'black'—the already burned aftermath of the forest—just as the sun is starting to set behind him. He's holding his phone up for his interview wearing headphones as his crew moves about behind him in the background. I can't help but scan the group of men—all powerful, muscular, and fit. They wear olive green pants, and yellow long-sleeved shirts, boots, helmets, and they're filthy from head to toe.

I look away quickly, berating myself for even searching for *him* in the first place. The reporter starts to ask Xander a question via video call just before I pick up the remote control to change the channel.

Nothing against Xander, he's a kind man who worked well with my dad and brother but hearing all about the deadly fire feels like too much for me when I have to put my best smile on and face the rowdy Saturday night crowd.

"Hey, Vivi. You look pretty," my mom, Mae, whispers as she comes through my front door. Bless her and the fact that she knew she needed to whisper.

She kicks her sandals off and sets her purse down on the bench in my entryway.

"So do you," I say, offering her a squeeze. My mom looks a lot like me—only older, of course. Her hair is still long, and dark. At almost sixty she's still in great shape, probably because she never sits still. My dad likes to say the devil shakes in his boots when my mom's feet hit the floor in the morning.

"Still not used to driving around the corner to visit. It's sure a lot nicer to pop in the truck and only be a few blocks away from my babies."

I smile at her. "I'm loving that too."

I've lived in Seattle, an hour and a half away for the last five years, and I've barely come home. My parents mostly came to us. My almost ex-husband, *Doctor* Troy Stafford and I have been separated for over a year. At first, I was determined to keep Hollie near him, but with his hectic schedule, Troy was the first one to agree that I needed to be near my family again. I needed a better support system, and he promised to make the trip on his days off to see Hollie. The only problem with that is he's hell bent on making Department Head and barely has any R&R time.

It took a couple months to get it all sorted out but now, after being back for a month I know it was the right choice, even though Troy hasn't really been keeping up his end of the bargain. He's only seen Hollie once this month. I'm hoping that will change as more time goes on. In the meantime, I'm adjusting to life back home, knowing I'll have to face the ghosts that wait for me here.

One living and one dead.

I pull the most comfortable pair of black boots I own onto my feet and follow my mom into my kitchen. As she flicks a light on, I remember.

Dishes. Shit. I forgot to do those.

My mom says nothing about the mess in the sink and rummages through my otherwise tidy space, pulling open the white cabinets and refrigerator, making a little cracker and cheese platter on my butcher block island.

"I don't know how late I'll be," I tell her as I move to the sink so I can at least rinse said dishes. "Depends on this crowd tonight."

Last weekend my parents ended up staying over in my spare bedroom.

"Where's dad anyway? I thought he was keeping you company tonight?" I pop a cracker from her platter into my mouth, before starting to fill the sink with hot soapy water.

"Stop messing with the dishes, I've got them, and your dad is in the truck on the phone catching up with Xander. He didn't want to wake Hollie. He'll be in in a minute."

I nod, fighting the urge to ask, shutting off the tap once the sink is filled. But my need outweighs my pride. Just like it does every damn time.

"Everything okay with the crew?" I ask as casually as possible, pulling a glossy pink lipstick out of my pocket. I use the microwave over my stove as a makeshift mirror, casting a glance at my mom over my shoulder. She smiles ruefully, knowing what my question really means.

"Yeah, baby, *everyone* is okay."

She turns back to her platter as I blot my lips with a tissue. I let out the breath I was holding as I waited for her answer.

CHAPTER 2
ROWAN

PRESENT

Somewhere southwest of Spokane, WA
Pinafore Creek Wildfire.

Most people get up every single day and go to a job they hate. Day in and day out, just dreading that 7 a.m. alarm. Maybe they're living for the weekend, living for their holidays, trying to make their husband or wife happy, all the while never really knowing true fulfillment, or what their purpose is.

I get why they do it. There's comfort in the expected. It's safe. Not to mention, the need to make a good living, pay for their kids' soccer, their dance lessons, the newest video game, that fancy car in the driveway.

But living that rat race?

Shit sounds like my worst nightmare. Give me my old pick-up truck, some vintage vinyl in my simple house, and the rush of being dropped right into the center of nature's biggest bonfire with the task of figuring out a way to shift its course.

It's not predictable. It's not safe, but I know without a doubt that it's my purpose. There's no bigger adrenaline rush on earth and I get paid to do it every single day.

"You're gonna head back up the other side and start a line there," Cal, my captain, calls to us over the noise of the ship we're riding in.

We're about to be dropped deeper up the mountains, a higher point than we've been working the last few days and I'm already exhausted. We've been at it sixty-five hours of the last eighty on the back end of almost a month away from home. The start to this season has been rough. It was 4 a.m. when our spike camp came alive for those of us who were sleeping, and the bosses told us we were moving up the mountain. Cal and Xander—my captain and sup—are smart as hell. I swear to Christ; Sup has a sixth sense with the weather. We say he can command the wind to work in his favor half the time, but this bitch of a blaze is mighty. It's burned up over nine thousand acres already.

"They're fighting me, want us to head northwest," Sup calls to Cal, talking about the federal powers that be. It's easy to guess the best course of action when you aren't the one on the ground. We aren't the only ones here either. There are two other hotshot crews working with us from out of state. Bitching about territory and protocol is always a thing. Sometimes it's easy to work with other crews, sometimes it's not.

Sup fiddles with the chin strap on his helmet as the part of the forest we're about to be dumped into comes into view. I can almost feel the heat from here.

"They want us up here for a reason. This blaze is acting a lot like the one in Oregon," Cal says, and we all nod, remembering.

I watch Sup as he nods and analyzes below.

"I just know it's gonna crown that ridge and head toward town," he says, looking out the window assessing the enemy.

"We'll burn out this side of the mountain so when she comes

over that ridge like a bat outta hell, there's no fuel for her to hang on to," Sup says.

We nod, the other part of our crew is in the chopper behind us, and they'll have to be filled in when we land.

"You good and ready?" Cal asks. He's asking me specifically because he expects me to keep the guys with me on task. I'm our lead sawyer today.

At twenty-eight, I don't have an official title yet, but that's my fault entirely. I've prolonged my promotion as long as I can. I've had my Firefighter Type 1 qualification to become a squad boss since the red card committee approved my task book in April. Becoming qualified isn't easy, so I should be proud, but I just haven't taken the plunge yet. Everybody knows it's a terrible middle management position, but it's a stepping stone.

Trouble is, the idea of being responsible for anyone but myself still torments me.

I lean my head back against the seat. The intense smell of smoke hits me as the ground gets closer. I reach my arms out in front of me, interlocking my fingers in a good stretch, willing my Nomex shirt to loosen. It feels like it's sticking to me already. The temperature will be 104 degrees today on the ground, and it's already hot at sunrise.

The choppers hit the earth and our boots are immediately on the ground, crunching the still roots and debris of the forest floor under them. Sometimes, the silence in the green—the area the fire hasn't touched yet—is deafening. Almost peaceful. The weight of knowing it's our job to keep it this way and live to see the other side rests on every single one of us. I look around and assess our surroundings. The sounds of wildlife are almost nonexistent, anything living was smart enough to get the hell out of here a long time ago.

"Let's get on it, boys, we'll start the line a hundred yards south. Anchor in the creek bed," Sup calls to us.

"Fucking rights," and *"let's fucking do this,"* mixed with

standard chatter ensues as we all begin our hike to location. The mood is always high energy but laser focused.

Twenty minutes later we're spread out and settling in to get our fireline going. I start pulling out my Pulsaki ax and my STIHL saw, so I can begin cutting brush. The embroidered patches that are sewn into all our packs catch my eye.

In memory – Jacob "Big T" Taylor. I reach back to pat it and nod reassuringly.

"We've got this one, brother," I mutter to Jacob, as if he can hear me while I start to work.

Some days it's less difficult to go up against the unpredictable flames of a wildfire than it is to battle the five years of blame and regret in my gut.

I fire up my STIHL and the adrenaline I chase fills my veins with the rumbling sound. I look to my left, facing the beast we're here to take on and smile wide.

Do your best, motherfucker.

"The blaze just…wasn't laying down. There was wide open grassland and tall dense junipers as far as we could see. Jacob went up to the ridge to look out. We were talking to him as he went on the walkie…" Xander, my sup swipes a tear from his face as all seventeen of us sit in the hospital waiting room with Jack and Mae Taylor.

Every one of us except Jacob. What's left of him is down the hall. A reminder that I failed. I couldn't protect him, and I couldn't save him.

Grief, disbelief, shame. It all weighs inside me, fighting a losing battle. Twisting and turning in a never-ending nauseating cycle. I've thrown up twice. Once when we pulled Jacob's body out of the ash pit he fell into, and once when they got him loaded up in the medevac.

Mae is a brick wall sitting beside her husband. She's either on the verge of a breakdown or in total disbelief that her son is being worked on and near death down the hall. His twin sister, Violette, is encircled in the arms of Jacob's girlfriend, Laney, as they cry.

I feel my chest tighten. It takes everything in me not to go to Violette and take her in my arms, but I know this isn't the time or place for that, nor would she let me. Hell, I can barely even get her to talk to me.

None of this is right. He was just supposed to be looking out, then a brutal wind none of us saw coming carried a tsunami of flames toward him. In the blink of an eye, it covered the entire ridge Jacob had gone up to. We assume he was running back down the ridge, to us in the black, when he fell into the pit. Medics said they thought it was a badger or coyote den. Jacob must not have seen its telltale signs, he just went through it, and it took us too long to get to him.

"You owe me a beer for this," he had said, looking over his shoulder at me as he started his climb up the side of the ridge. I had laughed and called him a cheap fucker.

I owed him a beer. Because I was supposed to be the one to go to lookout. But I wasn't quite done chipping a burning birch tree apart, so when he offered, I let him go.

Sup's words return over my thoughts as Jack cries openly across from him. Sup doesn't have any sons, but he knows what it's like to lose his dad this way. Fuck, our crew hasn't even gotten over that loss from a few months ago.

The sliding glass door opens to the waiting room. A doctor and two people with clipboards come through it. They don't even have to speak for me to know why they're here. Mae lets out a curdling scream that I'll never forget as long as I live, and I fall to my knees as they confirm what I already know. He never even saw one full season. Jacob is dead. My best friend is gone and it's all my fault.

I sit up, drenched in a cold sweat, smacking my knees on the seat in front of me. The buggy taking us back to base is disorientating and in complete contrast from my recurring dream. The mood is electric and celebratory for a bunch of men who haven't slept in almost twenty-four hours. It's not very often we're fighting a fire so close to home.

I pull my phone out. It's already early evening. My mom has texted me three times to check in. Aside from that, no one is worrying about me, but that's okay. That's the way I want it. No attachments. Hotshot life doesn't support relationships, which is why I don't have any other than my squad. Some of the guys make it work with girlfriends and wives, but it just seems like a fuck ton of work, and I haven't had a woman hold my interest for more than one night in a really long time.

I look over at Cal, he's currently sitting across from me texting his girlfriend, Scottie. Never seen him so obsessed with a woman. He's definitely one of the ones making this relationship thing work. I shake my head and chuckle as I take in the lovesick grin on his face.

Someone has "Back in Black" by ACDC playing. Caleb, a crewmate, is rocking a mean air guitar, Tex, Bobby, and Curly are talking football over the music, and two other crewmates, Dixon and Roycie are arm wrestling. Through all this chaos, I've been sleeping, oblivious to the commotion around me.

I try to take a deep breath. The char I feel in my lungs is worth it—we did our job, and once again, Sup was right, and the wind was on our side this time. We managed to mull out a perfect line, good looking enough for Mike Opperman—Opp as we call him—to take a picture.

"Twenty to home," Sup says over his shoulder to everyone. Some cheers go up.

Christ, *home*. I've barely seen it this month, I can't wait to shower, eat, and just stretch out on my sofa. I know I'll be awake for hours. My dreams about Jacob always come in spurts, so for the next few days, every time I close my eyes I'll see his face just before he headed up that fucking ridge. That vision and the same thoughts of blame rotate through my mind with a vengeance. The memories are like the embers of a fire that aren't fully extinguished. One gust of guilt and the whole thing tries to roar back to an inferno.

I should've gone with him. I should've been there. It should've been me—

"You all right?" Cal asks from across the aisle, setting his phone down. I realize as he asks that I'm breathing heavy. I wipe the sweat from my brow.

"Just hard to get Jacob's face out of my head sometimes," I tell him, running a hand through my knotted hair.

Cal sighs and looks out the window, a pensive look on his face as he scrubs a hand over the soot covered scruff of his beard.

"Probably always will be, it's hard to get ahead of that, thank fuck for grief therapy."

I nod. "Damn right."

Cal is a man who tells it like it is and doesn't feel the need to push, and right now I'm grateful for it.

"Hey. We got this one and we're all whole. One fight at a time, yeah?" he says, his face serious.

"Yeah," I say, taking a deep breath as the town limit of Sky Ridge comes into view. The land here is so green, so full of life and even though the night is warm, it feels cool after what we just worked through.

Our base is a shit shack—it's a large, glorified metal pole barn just outside of Sky Ridge but it's ours. The greenish paint is worn but there's lots of room for all our equipment and space to hang out. Sup's field office is here, along with a makeshift kitchen, a pool table, a decent gym, and common areas.

It takes us an hour to unload our gear and change. Sup pats me on the back as I'm hanging up my gear in the open room where all of our lockers line a white cinder block wall. Our motto is painted above them.

Fight for those who can't. Protect those we can. Honor the ones we've lost.

I turn to face him.

"You did good out there this week. You know you're ready," he says gruffly.

I nod and feel my body tense, avoiding his eyes.

"King. You're already doing the job; you might as well get paid for it."

I turn and pull a fresh black Sky Ridge Hotshots T-shirt from my locker and pull it over my head. I'm still wearing my green Nomex pants from the mountain and my boots.

"Yeah…uh, can this be a tomorrow conversation?" I ask Sup with a smirk.

"It's been a tomorrow conversation for months." He levels with me. "Look, I know the idea of an official crew of your own seems like a big responsibility. But we need you and the only way you get over it, is to *try* to get over it." He lifts a heavy boot up on the bench in front of me and tightens his laces as he talks.

"Cal said you had another dream. I still have them too, we all do. But Jacob knew the risks and he'd tell you just like I am right now that it's time. *He'd* want this." He gestures to the room of joking, light, and rowdy hotshots. The air in here is almost festive after putting down that line. Normally, I'd be as happy as they are with a job well done, but, fuck, sometimes those dreams take me right back to that moment I let him go.

I put my hands on my hips and look at my sup as he sets his jaw.

As hotshots we all have standards we have to meet regularly when it comes to physical fitness, so my Sup is a beast of a man.

Nothing really rattles him, so when he gets serious and emotional I know he means it.

"Don't dismiss the job because of him. Take it *for* him," he says simply. And for some reason, something in me finally clicks. I look around the room. This *is* my chance to make it right, to make losing Jacob worth something. But after I agree, there's no going back. This was supposed to be Jacob's job. He always wanted to make squad boss.

I blow out a deep breath and drop to the bench behind me. I know I can't drag this out anymore. I can't live in the past and not take on more responsibility because of my fear. Maybe being a squad leader will help me *save* someone. I can't believe I never looked at it that way until now. I can almost hear Jacob's voice telling me to stop being a pussy and to do his job when he can't. *You owe me that much after letting me die,* I imagine him saying.

"Shit, fine. I'm all in, Sup. Whatever you need," I say firmly.

He just stares at me for five seconds like he can't believe I'm finally agreeing, then pats me on the shoulder as his grin grows.

"Did I hear what I think I just did?" Cal asks, coming up behind me and gripping my shoulders, giving me a shake.

"Yeah, you did. Your boy here is moving up!" Sup adds, loud enough the entire room hears.

"Fuck yeah, that's the fucking spirit," Cal says, giving me one last pat on the shoulder.

"Now"—Sup looks around the room—"put on a fresh shirt, boys. Food and drink, it's happening!" Sup says to the room as he backs away. "We're celebrating our new Crew Boss." He points at me. The room explodes with my crew hooting and whistling for me.

I can't help it. I shake my head and smile wide.

Fucking hell, guess I'm gonna be a squaddie.

CHAPTER 3

Violette

"Every. Fucking. Time!" I hear Pete—a bar regular and local Sky Ridge medic—call out as he slaps twenty dollars down in the center of our worn pool table at Shifty's the precise moment I arrive with his beer.

"You take him again?" I ask Matt, his co-worker, with a grin. He clearly just beat him for the third time tonight. Matt's chuckling at Pete as he takes the two Budweiser's off my tray and passes one to Pete.

"'Course." Matt smirks. "I beat him every weekend and he keeps coming back for more," he says with a friendly wink.

I laugh. Matt's a good egg. And handsome. He's all pretty, wholesome smiles.

"Thanks, Vi." He pulls a five out of his pocket and pops it on my tray to tip me. He's been doing that all night, adding to my nice little stash behind the till.

"Good thing he's tipping, darlin', he's taken all my money," Pete says, looking crushed as he takes his first sip.

"Play nice, boys," I say, patting Matt on the shoulder. "Go easy on him; you know the more he drinks, the more he bets."

Matt leans in. "I'm counting on it."

I shake my head and cast them a smile over my shoulder.

"Double or nothin'." I hear Matt suggest as I start making my way through the crowd back to the bar.

A few of their buddies laugh. I had all but forgotten what Saturday nights at Shifty's were like. The smell of perfume and sweat fills the air, it's almost enough to overtake the stale beer and pub food smell.

We're packed full tonight with a bunch of townies and it's only 9:30. Some off-duty cops are huddled in a big group in one corner, lit up by the neon glow of vintage signs my parents have collected over the years, and a good-sized group of locals are line dancing to Luke Bryan in the back corner. The bar is lined up with a lot of people I've known most of my life. I make my way to a few tables, taking orders to help Lou out then venture back behind the bar to fill my tray. Lou always stays behind the bar. He's just plain faster than I am after doing this for so many years and he knows the drinks inside and out. I'm still learning, so server duty it is.

I'm just placing the last round of whiskeys down at the table closest to the door when it opens with a ding. I can smell them before I see them and grief swells in my chest. It's not their existence that hits me. It's that *smell*. Smoke, and the diesel mix that fuels their drip torches and…dirt. I'd know it anywhere. I take an extra few seconds placing my last whiskey down on the table in front of me, willing the tightness in my chest to subside, reminding myself I can always cry another day. I throw a silent prayer up that *he's* not here, then take a deep breath, turning to face the group of hotshots I know are waiting for me.

I immediately come face to face with those deadly navy eyes. *Shit.*

Rowan Kingsley. My other ghost, the living one I wish I could avoid.

His nickname is King to all of them, and he was my brother

Jacob's best friend. He was also the guy who absolutely decimated my heart when I was eighteen.

His six-foot-three frame looms over me. He wears his greens and a black Sky Ridge Crew T-shirt. He's much more muscular than the last time I saw him and of course, he's still gorgeous. Rowan has always had an all-American team captain vibe about him, like he was ripped right from the pages of *Men's Health Magazine* and dropped onto our local hotshot crew. His jaw is wide, strong, and right now, scruffy. His features are straight and rugged, and his right arm is entirely covered in ink. I notice a hawk, with its wings spread wide. They wrap entirely around so I can't see where they meet. It's the largest piece on his rippled, corded forearm. I spot the date above it. The date Jacob died. It's front and center and it hits me square in the chest. A wave of grief washes over me so hard I have to look away.

Fuck.

Before I can even say anything, or the tightness has a chance to set in, I'm swept up by one of them in a crushing hug. It takes me a second to realize the man hugging me is Mike Opperman.

Jacob loved him, he called him *"bear"* on account of his big, burly appearance. The guys call him Opp. He gives me a little spin and a "Fucking Christ, Little T, what the hell are you doing here waiting tables?"

I laugh, putting on my best brave face. It's been a long time since I've been called Little T. *Little Taylor.*

"Just living the dream, Opp." I laugh as Opp sets me down, gesturing to my serving tray. I've known him my whole life. In fact, I've known most of these guys my whole life. The image of their faces at my brother's funeral flashes through my mind. I squeeze my eyes shut to push the vision away. It was a lot easier to bury those memories when I wasn't here. But sometimes, it still feels like yesterday, not five years ago.

"Welcome home, Violette, your dad said you were working at Bakersfield?" Xander says, giving me a friendly side hug and a kiss on the top of my head. My eyes flit to King's for all of one second. The look he's wearing tells me he didn't know I was even home until he walked in here and saw me.

I look back at Xander. "Yeah. Almost a month now."

"That explains why we haven't seen you yet, we've been going non-stop for five weeks," Cal Woods, their captain, says, leaning in to give me a friendly hug too. "Anyone fucks with you in here, we've got you, lil' sis," he says patting me on the head.

I nod, knowing he means it.

That's how they all look at me, like I'm their little sister.

"I think I can handle them, but I promise, Sky Ridge's very own hotshots will be my first call." I wrinkle my nose. "Y'all could probably kill them with your stench," I say, letting my eyes move to King's again.

"Told you all it was a shit move to come in here so dirty," King says, looking at Xander. His deep timbre is as smooth as I remember it. My traitorous body must not recall that he's an asshole because as soon as he speaks, I get those familiar tingles up my spine.

"No time for showers when we're celebrating, 'sides it's gonna take at least two to get us clean anyhow," Opp says with a wide grin. He headlocks King and rubs his knuckles into the wavy dark blonde hair at the top of his head. They're the same height and almost the same size. "This one's making squaddie," Opp says proudly to me with a wide grin.

"Fuck, the whole bar doesn't need to know," King says, pulling away from him.

Another punch to the chest. That was what Jacob talked about before he died, and now he'll never have the chance. That pain I've really been good at holding in sifts like ashes through my carefully built walls. Talking to these guys is too close to home. Seeing all of them healthy and happy.

This is why I do my best to avoid these hotshots at all costs.

24

King pushes his messy dark blond locks back off his fore-head and looks at me.

"Got a spot where we won't dirty up your bar too much?" he asks with the half-smirk that used to make my heart race. I look away and gesture to the corner.

"The back tables are open. I'll send Lou over for your order," I tell them, secretly hoping Lou will actually do it for me. I don't want to spend my night serving him of all people.

They follow my suggestion and take up a few tables near the only window in this place.

I make my way back to the bar, trying to shake the way King's deep blue eyes stood out under his tan, or the way his wide jaw ticked when his eyes met mine. Someone with no heart shouldn't look like he could easily steal mine. It really isn't fair, but then, I guess life rarely is. If it was, I never would've been attracted to Rowan Kingsley in the first place, and my brother would be sitting at that table with them.

CHAPTER 4
ROWAN

"Earth to King." A fist hits my shoulder, and my eyes snap to Cal's

"You alright?" he asks.

"Yeah, just fucking wrecked," I say, leaning back in my chair as I take a swig of my beer.

"I hear that," Roycie, our rookie, agrees. This is only his first season, and *Pinafore Creek* is the worst fire he's seen so far. He's a good sawyer, but you'd never even know he was old enough to be a firefighter. Looking at him you would assume he's about seventeen not twenty-three, but he's a hard worker and he follows me around a lot as he learns. He's sort of like a stray dog. *My* stray dog, so I'm starting to feel responsible for him.

"Need to go home and shower somewhere I can't catch athlete's foot or step in jizz," Roycie says with a grin.

"We all had to learn the hard way, now you know it's better not to shower until you get home," Opp says to Roycie with a chuckle. Ain't that the truth. We all know better than to use camp showers, unless it's absolutely necessary.

"Don't fuckin' laugh. I'm traumatized, dude," Royce deadpans, which makes us all laugh even more.

"Hotshot training, lesson number one. Better to smell like ass than have sticky feet," Opp jokes, raising his beer, and Roycie gags.

It takes a bit for the rookies to get used to not showering. Some guys don't shower at all, no matter how long we're out there. At best, they may hose off or whore bath themselves with wet wipes. Camp showers are notorious for being the place where some real messed up shit happens, and for some guys, not showering is just a part of their superstition. When it comes to staying safe we all have our things. Like I only change my greens every four days and never shower until I get back to base or until I get home. I just hose off every few days. Opp takes it to the extreme. He doesn't wash his yellows all season. It's fucking rank but there's no shot he's changing his ways after five continuous seasons of living to see October uninjured.

"Been looking good out there, boys!" a female voice calls from two tables over. We all turn to meet the face the voice is coming from. A table of women. All locals. Dressed for the club, not for Shifty's. Roycie pipes up first, basking in the rookie hotshot glow, porn stash and all.

"Oh, *hells* yes" Dixon mutters under his breath taking them in. "Dibs on the brunette."

"You're fucking filthy, bro." I take my final sip of beer.

"I got a shower at home. If she wants it, she'll wait. A wise man once told me, 'gotta plant the seed, King, plant the seed,'" he says with a menacing grin, using my own words against me from when I was a rookie and balls deep in women just wanting to spend a night with a hotshot. In those days, I didn't say no very often either.

"Wanna join us, ladies?" Roycie asks, offering them an award-winning grin. "Could really use some company after the ferocious fire we just had to tame. Only been around these goons for almost a month straight." He smirks. He's sitting between me

PAISLEY HOPE

and Caleb and extends his arms out to grip each of our shoulders as he says it, then looks at me and waggles his eyebrows.

I chuckle. *Fuckin' manwhore.*

All four women nod and stand immediately, moving to come join us.

Cal doesn't even look up from his phone when the girls sit, Xander mutters something like "I'm getting too old for this shit," and even though one of the women keeps smiling at me. I'm just not feeling it tonight either. I learned a few years ago that mixing one-night-stands with locals is never a good idea. Roycie will learn that too in time.

I give the woman looking at me a tight-lipped attempt at a friendly smile. Friendly because that's all I've got for her. I'm fucking shook after coming face to face with Violette Taylor. I never thought I'd see her back in town.

Roycie plays the fake modest act with his audience. I half listen to him tell the girls that fighting wildfires is "all in a day's work," and that we're "just extreme landscapers." You'd think this fucker had been peddling this act for years instead of a few months.

I shake my head and laugh at our rookie, catching a glimpse of Violette through the crowd at the bar. It's been five years since I laid eyes on her last, back at Jacob's funeral. We didn't talk, she was with her boyfriend at the time and way too upset for that. Her face was the last thing I expected to see when I walked through those doors tonight, and seeing her when I'm in this shape?

Fucking humiliating.

I watch as she smiles at a local guy now—Matt. He's a medic who works with Cal's girlfriend. Violette laughs at something he says and passes him a beer from the cooler. The jeans she's wearing hug every curve she offers... and what she offers is perfection. Full tits filling out her *Shifty's* tank top, which I've never found attractive on anyone in here until today. A toned

28

waist that leads to soft round hips. Hips I could imagine rocking back and forth over me with my hands gripping them tight. And that smile, it curves up over her straight, white teeth as she tucks her thick hair behind an ear. Although she's too far away for me to see it, I know that glimmery sort of light she gets in her eyes whenever she smiles is there. I just really don't like that Matt is the one getting it right now. I scrub my hand over the base of my jaw.

Glimmery light? Christ, I need some fuckin' sleep, and apparently a cold shower, since I'm sporting a goddamn semi just from looking at Violette.

I pick at the soggy label on my near empty beer bottle, watching Violette while the guys chatter on about the line we cut in yesterday and how pretty it was. Roycie is showing photos to the girls at our table, one of them is already sitting on his lap.

I wonder why Violette's here and what happened with her husband as I continue to watch her. Her hair is longer than I remember, but still that same deep, honey sort of brown it's always been, hanging in shiny waves almost to her waist.

I watch her wipe down the bar in graceful swipes as she sings along to a country hit and I get lost in her again. She's still got the most incredible body. Curvy, but petite. That ass—

"We keeping you awake?" Cal chuckles nodding toward Violette. "Are you surprised to see her? Brings him back even more, doesn't it?"

"Yeah," I say, clearing my throat.

I contemplate asking about her for a few more minutes as the guys all talk.

Fuck it, I'm asking.

"So, is Violette, uh…her marriage—is she…you know, is it—"

"Over?" Sup asks, cutting me off, leaning forward, propping his thick forearms onto the table. "Yeah, it is, and she's doing her best to adjust, for her and *her daughter*. Jack says she's finally getting past some of those old demons," he adds. "In other words, you're gonna give her some space."

I scoff and look away. "Obviously," I say to my boss, annoyed he knows me so well.

Cal backs his chair out; it scrapes against the wood floor as he readies to stand. "Another round?" he asks the table.

I take my chance without thought, fully rising faster than he does. "Gotta stretch my legs anyway, Cap. I got it." I look around the table as I clap him on the shoulder. "Who wants?"

Dixon and Caleb ask me to bring them another, and Sup shoots me a look of warning, shaking his head.

"What?" I ask. "Just trying to give my hardworking bosses a break." I grin in defense, backing away from the table with my hands raised.

"Uh-huh, what part of *space* don't you get?" Sup's voice fades as I turn and make my way through the crowd.

I know Violette probably doesn't want to see me, and I can't say I blame her. In my defense, I was still a kid when I hurt her, and I had my reasons for both hurting her *and* not telling her why.

Now, it seems she's home *and* single. And that changes everything. It also makes me hope she might be willing to forgive and forget.

Memories, coupled with regret and the loss of Jacob, threaten to steal the breath from my lungs as I eat up the space between us with steady strides.

Violette looks up at me with those bright hazel eyes when I reach the bar and I decide right here and now that I'm going to show her the man I am today. I'm gonna fix this.

She leans one handed on the bar, propping her other hand on her curvy hip then cocks her head to the side, her waves tumble down over her shoulder.

"What can I get you, King?" she asks, clearly trying to make this a quick exchange, but I've got other ideas.

I drum my fingers on the bar and blow out a breath, glancing behind her at the liquor on the shelf and the framed photo of Jacob hanging behind the bar. I remember the day that photo was taken. Our third fire together in Utah. Jacob's in full gear, eyeing me down. If he was here, he'd be telling me to hurry up, get my beer, and stop trying to impress his clearly unimpressed sister. I ignore his imaginary scolding.

"What's good here?" I ask her, focusing intently on the labels.

She scoffs. "We both know that you probably know better than I do."

She's already annoyed with me, and it's been less than a minute.

"Oh, I don't know… If I know you, I'd bet you've memorized every drink in this place already," I say.

She sighs. "You *don't* know me anymore, King."

Now I'm really pissing her off, but at least I have her attention.

I maintain my focus on the bottles behind her as I speak.

"So, you settling in, Violette? Doing okay? Living at your parents or—"

"What is this?" she asks.

I move my gaze back to her. She's looking me up and down, her almond shaped eyes narrow, scrutinizing me.

"What?" I use my most offended tone. "I can't be curious how you're—?"

"We're not friends, King, you know it as well as I do."

I lean in, my forearms against the bar.

"That's the thing, Violette. I've decided I want to change that."

A few beats of silence hang heavily between us before Violette tosses her head back and laughs. She's trying to appear appalled, but her smile takes my breath away regardless.

"Seriously? After all these years?" she asks as she twists the top off a bottle of PBR and passes it to my left.

"Thanks, Violette."

I flinch because I didn't even notice Sup standing behind me. I make the mistake of glancing at him. He's side eyeing me like my grumpy older brother.

"Are you getting those beers, King, or taking up residence on Violette's nerves for the rest of the night?"

I look from him to Violette. "A little of both," I joke, doing my best to keep her eyes. She rolls hers and looks away, completely uninterested. *Ouch.*

"Well, hurry up, yeah? I'm sure she has other customers to tend to." He nudges me with his elbow and says it loud enough for Violette to hear.

"Sure do…" she answers Sup. "So, Budweiser then?" Her eyes move to me.

"Jesus, can't a guy just think of trying something new," I ask them both as Sup turns to head back to the table.

Violette cocks her head to the side. "With your drink or your personality?"

I chuckle, so does Sup as he walks away.

"Once again, both, I guess," I say honestly, scrubbing my jaw which earns an actual laugh from her.

"Look, truth is, I just don't want you to remember me as the asshole who hurt you, it's not who I am, at least not anymore." I blurt out, internally cringing as soon as the words leave my mouth. That's not how I wanted that to sound. As if she's some charity case I'm just trying to rectify. Her eyes instantly shut down and any progress I just made goes right out the window.

Real smooth, dick.

But Violette surprises me and leans in close, her eyes quietly explore my face. She's offering me a nice view of her cleavage if I chose to look. Of course I don't. I'm not *actually* a dick.

32

Her clean, coconut scent fills my nose as we stand suspended in silence.

"So, you want to do what then King?" She leans even closer "Just pick up right where we left off? Forget our history?" She asks, pulling me in with her eyes.

"Not forget, maybe start fresh though..." I say awkwardly.

"Maybe get some dinner?" she asks "Share all our secrets from the last decade? BFF's?" She adds. "And I'd be *so* quick to agree to that, because I've just been pining away over you since I was eighteen?"

She smirks and pats me on the cheek.

"I hate to break it to your *massive* ego, buddy, but you aren't as memorable as you think." She straightens up, breaking the trance she was holding me in and begins to untie the white serving apron from around her waist. "Did you ever think it might be possible that I just plain don't like you? Or that maybe you just aren't as charming as you think?" She shrugs.

I scramble, trying to get this train wreck of a conversation back on track. "Look, Vi, I—"

"*Violette*," she corrects, folding her arms across her chest.

"Violette," I echo. "It's been a lot of years, and I know we have some shitty memories between us, but maybe we can try something different, yeah? Just to get to know each other again? Who we are *now*. Maybe even become friends."

"It's not a good idea, we're nothing alike and I have no time for friends," she says with a laugh. "And I'm taking my break, so whenever you choose your adventurous new drink, you can give your order to Lou," she adds, nodding her head toward him at the other end of the bar.

I reach across the bar and grab her arm to stop her from leaving. The feel of her soft skin under my calloused hand is foreign but the connection ripples through me like a shockwave.

She looks down where I hold her delicate wrist then back up at me.

"You know what actually? Four Buds will be just fine," I answer quickly.

She narrows her eyes and her tongue comes out to wet her plush lips. I momentarily lose my entire thought process.

"Budweiser...America's beer." I shrug. *Did I just quote a goddamn TV commercial?*

Violette pulls her arm away and gives me the universal look for *what the hell is wrong with you?* then removes the caps off the beers before setting them in front of me.

I throw enough money on the bar to pay for the beers and give her a hefty tip, then grab two beers in each hand. I've definitely overstayed my welcome tonight and failed miserably in my attempt to get Violette to forgive me. But there's always tomorrow.

"Thank you, Violette," I offer her the smile that usually works for me.

She flat out ignores it and turns to fold her apron up on the counter, offering me a good view of her ass in those fucking jeans.

"Mm-hmm," she says without turning around.

"Oh, hey, uh. You look great by the way," I add over my shoulder.

"I know," she retorts, still not turning around.

I raise my eyebrows. Well, this Violette is certainly a little more confident than the one I knew when we were kids.

It makes me happy; she never saw her worth in her younger years.

I grin as I make my way back through the crowd. When I set the beers on the table, Sup is already giving me the hairy eyeball.

"Just can't listen, can ya, kid?" he asks.

I shrug as I take my seat. "No idea what you mean, just welcoming her home."

He shakes his head at me and mutters something as he sips his beer.

I glance at Violette when I sit. She's looking back, until the precise moment my eyes meet hers, then she looks away.

It's only a second but it gives me the tiny spark of hope I need. She's definitely gonna try to fight me, but I can be persuasive as fuck when I want something.

And if there's one thing I've learned, it's that you rarely get second chances in life, so if this is the universe giving me one, I'm taking it.

CHAPTER 5

Violette

AGE 18

Dalewood High, Library

"I gotta make this quick, got practice in an hour and I can't be late," Rowan says as he pulls the chair out across from me.

I feel the eyes on us from the table over, I know what they're all thinking. Why is Rowan Kingsley, the most gorgeous guy in school, captain of the rugby team, sitting with *Violette Taylor*? That's assuming they even know my name. Most of them are airheads who get drunk and party every weekend, but because I don't, because I spend my nights studying and mornings prepping our school breakfast club for kids who don't have enough food at home, I'm a social pariah.

I look up at him and my heart skips a beat as I smile. Rowan wears faded blue jeans and a white T-shirt with a black and white flannel over top, his standard Seahawks hat is on his head backward and a few stray dark blond waves escape it. God, he's gorgeous.

How I got lucky enough to be paired with him for our final biology assignment, I'll never know. Although, I did almost throw up in the girls' bathroom before I came here.

I see him all the time because he's always at our place. He's my twin brother's best friend and he's always been nice to me. I've sat quietly and read my books while he and Jacob play video games in our basement. I've watched the two of them play rugby since junior year, and I've washed the dishes while he's dried after many dinners at our house, but I've never been alone with him for any length of time, and that makes my palms sweat like crazy.

I pull my black hoodie away from my stomach a little to make sure it's not clinging to the wrong places while he sits this close to me. I've been trying to stick to my diet and exercise routine because I really wanted to lose ten pounds before summer came and Rowan was hanging around our pool every day. But it was mine and Jacob's birthday last week, so I'll admit I've eaten way too much cake, *and* I've had my period, so in turn I'm feeling super bloaty today.

"You look nice today, Vi," Rowan says as if he's battling my inner thoughts.

I feel the blush creep up my neck.

"You always look nice," I blurt out.

Rowan's eyes narrow a bit and he smirks, taking a sip from a bottle of water.

"All right, well, since we both look nice, let's get started." He chuckles.

I'm pretty sure I'm beet red, but I start talking anyway. Small talk with Rowan Kingsley may not be my thing, but biology? I'm confident.

"Well…I've already started laying the project out for us," I tell him, opening my notebook. I love science so I didn't mind getting it started, and besides, Rowan has a lot on his plate with his varsity rugby playoffs coming up.

"Of course you did." He grins. Butterflies take flight in my stomach. "I don't deserve you, Vi," he says.

"Hi, King," Kyleigh Miller, captain of the cheerleading squad, says as she passes by our table. Just looking at her lowers my self-esteem by about a hundred points. She's just one of those girls who is unfairly pretty. Every guy at Dalewood High thinks she's the hottest girl in school, and her two lackeys, Brittany Tucker and Carmen Smith, follow behind, trying desperately to be just like her.

"Hey," Rowan says without fully turning to face her. I watch his fists flex and his brow furrow, and I wonder why he doesn't look adoringly at her like everyone else does. He pulls his book out of his backpack as she stops behind him, placing her hand on his shoulder.

"We can't wait to watch you play Friday, you guys are gonna kill North Umber," she says, running that hand down his broad shoulder, touching him the way I've always wished I could.

"Yeah, uh, thanks," he says, shrugging her off.

She gives me the once over. Where she's all tall and thin with blonde, shiny hair and the world's most perfect body, I'm short and softer than I'd like to be, with wild curly hair that's neither blonde nor brown. It's a sort of in-between and never really straightens no matter how hard I try. And I'm plain. I don't have big blue eyes like Kyleigh. Those blue eyes drift back to Rowan now. I'm no match for her and she knows it. She looks down at my notes and our biology textbooks between us on the table.

"Didn't know you needed a study partner. I would've done that with you," she says with a pouty little look, showing her hurt.

"Thanks, but Vi and I got this," Rowan says, looking back at me with a grin "Don't we, Vi?"

"Yeah," I reply quickly, but to my horror, my voice cracks. I clear my throat. "Must be thirsty," I mutter.

"I'll say," Brittany says as the other two girls snicker.

My cheeks heat with embarrassment.

Why am I so awkward?

"See ya later then, King. Oh, and we're having a party after the game at Carm's. You should totally come," Kyleigh adds as she turns to walk away, purposefully giving him the view of her ass in her skinny, ripped jeans.

"Yeah, I'll see what the guys wanna do," he answers, picking up his phone to answer a text. "See ya," he adds, then sets his phone down and looks up at me.

"Sorry about that." His smile is genuine. "Kyleigh doesn't know how *not* to be invasive."

I laugh as I pull open my planner.

Almost everyone in this school acts like I'm invisible, but Rowan is always nice and treats me sort of like his little sister. He has all through high school, even though we're in the same grade.

"She obviously likes you," I observe as I tap the end of my pen on my notepad.

"Meh."

He leans in and the scent of his standard spicy cologne hits me. Sandalwood and mint. He holds a hand up to his perfect lips as if he's gonna tell me a secret.

"I'd have better luck pairing up with this chair as a study partner," he jokes, patting the back of the chair beside him. I give in and laugh too.

"Yeah, maybe, but she sure is pretty," I say, watching her and her two friends fully disappear through the library doors.

"She's alright, but trust me, I made the mistake once of thinking she was nice. She's not." He shrugs. "And that's kind of a big stipulation for me."

I didn't think it was possible for me to crush on my brother's best friend any harder than I already was ten minutes ago, but apparently it is.

"So, what do we have so far?" he asks, resting his forearms

on the table. For five long seconds his navy blue eyes transfix me, and I have to physically force myself to close my mouth. I look down to my notes.

"Pollutants," I fumble out awkwardly. "Types of mutations, artificial vegetative propagation…" I explain the basis of our project where we'll have to go find all the relative air, water, and soil pollutants common to our area.

We spend an hour going over the plan, places we'll visit for samples and how we'll lay out our presentation. It's worth 20 percent of our final grade and we have four weeks to do it. We map out a schedule of when we'll get together, and I'd be lying if I said spending three days a week with him for the next month wasn't making those butterflies in my stomach flutter wildly.

Rowan pulls his phone out and checks the time. "Shit, I gotta go." He stands and starts to gather his books, pausing to look down on me. "Hey, uh, Vi, thanks for doing this with me. I really need us to get an A on this…or, um…I might not pass this class. I hate science, if I'm being honest. I have a hard time even understanding protons and electrons." He laughs.

My mouth falls open. "You could *fail?* I had no idea," I mutter, leaning back in my chair. I don't tell him electrostatic connection is chemistry, not biology.

"Yeah, I don't exactly broadcast that shit. Give me trig, calculus, algebra any day and I'll ace it. This just isn't my thing, and the truth is, if I don't pass, I won't graduate. But no pressure," he adds quickly, probably seeing the worry on my face. "I'm gonna pull my weight and then some. I promise." He smirks at me, holding his hand over his heart. His full lips have a way of turning up in an almost lopsided curve that gives you the smallest preview of his gorgeous smile. It showcases the dimple he has in his left cheek.

"No problem," I say, a little starstruck. "I love biology. You can put your weight on me," I blurt out. "*The* weight!" I correct, feeling the heat of embarrassment creeping up my throat for the second time this afternoon.

He smirks even bigger, and the underside of the table is looking better by the second. "We're good to get together for this over the next few weeks?" he asks.

"I'm free every day but Thursday." I shrug. "Breakfast club prep," I remind him of the club I head up as part of the National Honors Society. It even gives me special access to the school so I can prep meals for kids who aren't lucky enough to have a good healthy breakfast at home. At least every Friday, they get one.

"Oh yeah, club pres, right? That's cool." He smirks. *It is?*

"See ya tomorrow, Vi." He chuckles, slinging his backpack over his shoulder waving at someone across the library as he goes. I watch him shamelessly under the curtain of my hair.

His walk is an easy steady stride, everything about Rowan just oozes swagger and confidence, and he doesn't even try; it's why everyone likes him and all the girls want him.

I sigh as he disappears out of sight.

I wonder if there will *ever* be a day that I don't drool over Rowan Kingsley.

CHAPTER 6

Violette

PRESENT

"Knock, knock. Who's there? Po-wer piggy! Knock, knock. Who's there? Tough little turt-le!" Hollie's sweet little voice wakes me up.

I open one eye then immediately close it. It's not even light out yet. The TV is still on because I fell asleep watching some cheesy rom-com. I was doing anything and everything I could to push Rowan Kingsley from my mind for the second night in a row. Trying not to remember the current that rushed through me when we touched. A current that just served to piss me off. Seeing him the other night at Shifty's left its mark, and I haven't been able to get that damn lopsided smirk out of my head since.

The audacity of this man isn't lost on me. I spent years building up my walls to keep him firmly out. And the idea that he now, ten years later, out of some sort of guilt, wants to be friends with me? No thanks.

Hollie is staring up at the ceiling in my bed, still singing the *SuperPets* theme song and moving her hands to the actions.

She's obsessed with all things superhero right now, especially *Power Piggy*, the resident super pig that flies. Clever, I know.

Gone are the days of the latest country hit floating through my mind. Nowadays, it's strictly Funhouse TV shows and Disney movies twenty-four seven.

"Mommy!" Hollie says with way too much excitement for 6 a.m., popping a chubby hand to my cheek. I grin, keeping my eyes closed.

"Mommy isn't here," I say in my best robot voice, which makes Hollie laugh hysterically. She was awake at five, so I gave in and brought her in here with me to get one more hour of sleep, and now I'm going to have to rush around like crazy to get us both ready and out the door within an hour. Thankfully, the daycare she goes to when I'm on the early shifts, is right in the hospital two floors down from where I work.

It's part of the reason I took the job. After our move, I still have some anxiety around leaving her.

"Can I have toast?" she asks with a big smile. Her chubby little cheeks are rosy, and her big blue eyes are the same almond shape as mine. "And gogurt," she says.

I giggle at the way we've just given in to pronouncing yogurt in this house.

"Let's go, gogurt head." I muss her golden curls and stand, pulling my big cozy Washington State hoodie on over my tank. She jumps up in her little pink nightgown and reaches her arms out to me.

"What have I said about jumping on Mommy's bed?" I ask as I scoop her up and pop her and her stuffed power piggy on my hip.

She giggles as we make our way to the living room. I turn the TV on and find her favorite episode of *SuperPets* while I grab her some juice, and toast, and of course, strawberry gogurt. After she's settled, my coffee is done brewing, so I fill myself a big mug full and pick up my phone off the kitchen counter where it's charging.

TEDDY

> Can we do a playdate this week? I need a conversation before this baby comes that doesn't start with Mooooom!

I laugh, as I take my first sip. *Sweet nectar of the gods, that's good.*

Teddy Hansen—Teddy Woods, as I've always known her—is Cal's younger sister. She's a few years older than me and just recently moved back to town from the next county over. We were never close growing up, but now we're both moms to kids that are almost the same age. Which means we basically live the same life. When I ran into her at the local park recently during Mom and Tot time, we instantly connected. Her husband was an EMT and he passed away last winter in a devastating accident while saving someone else during his shift. Another hero lost.

> Yes!

> Hols woke me up this morning singing about Power Pig, after I fell asleep dreaming about pigs. Send help.

I take another sip and wait for her reply. Teddy is almost ready to give birth to her late husband's baby, and she's all alone with two other children. Still, she is positive and funny as hell. She's a pillar of strength—I don't know how she does it. Befriending her was a no-brainer when it became apparent that Hollie worshipped the ground her eight-year-old son, Dalton, and four-year-old daughter, Penny, walked on. We chatted easily while the kids played, and I really knew we were destined to be friends when I saw a copy of the spicy romance book I've been wanting to read tucked between her kids' books, fresh from the local library.

TEDDY

> At least you didn't wake up stepping on a hot wheel land mine. My foot may never recover.

I laugh as I open the photo she sent. It is indeed a Hot Wheels landmine in the middle of her living room.

> Okay you win, I'm already late for work. Thursday? We can let the kids destroy my living room and eat pizza?

TEDDY

> It's a date.

I smile and check the time as I swallow the last of my coffee, realizing I have all of twenty minutes to get both myself and Hollie ready. I set my cup in the sink and round the corner of my kitchen. That's when I hear the words no mom wants to hear when she's already running late.

"Uh oh, Mommy."

The second I step foot in the living room I see it. Hollie, standing amidst an entire box of Cheerios spilled all over the area rug. The *shag* area rug and a plastic bowl peeking out from under the mess. I glance back at the kitchen cabinet where the cereal lives and see it's open. She snuck in while I was on the phone with Teddy and I didn't notice? I *must* be tired.

Her bottom lip starts to quiver when she thinks she might be in trouble. "Piggy was hungry too," she says.

I face palm and start to laugh. It's the last thing I need to deal with right now, but instead of getting upset I grab my phone and snap a photo, sending it to Teddy.

> You've been dethroned, I win.

Wish me luck getting this cleaned and out the door in twenty.

TEDDY

May the odds be ever in your favor.

CHAPTER 7

ROWAN

The veterans who taught me explained that in the world of wildland firefighting, no job is more important than your fireline. The all-important craft of creating a trench dug down to mineral soil, between a moving fire and unburned fuel.

I practiced digging with different hand tools and using different techniques when I first started this trade, the summer I turned twenty-two. I dug line on my first fires all summer and then picked up a saw for the first time about halfway through and found out it was something I was naturally good at. When the season ended, I walked away with a few new blisters on my calloused hands, some cuts on my boots, and a deep dark longing for the next fire season. The more skills I could learn, the better.

What am I getting at here? Fighting forest fires, standing up to mother nature, it's in my blood, but it isn't something I take lightly. None of us do.

We don't go into the bitch, ready to fight with our middle fingers raised, we fight with our heads down to show her we aren't worthy.

We know we can't stop the burning—that would be impossible. All we can do is try to create balance. We give a little and we take a little, carving out the path of least destruction. If we're lucky, she'll do what we want and let us out alive.

"King, what's your line anchored in back there?" Sup asks as I approach, my tread heavy. My Kevlar chaps are caked in mud, soot, and sawdust.

"Cold black," I tell him, wiping the sweat from my brow. My eyes are burning. We've been out here for five days after getting almost two off. We've been going non-stop. But it's good, I could use the distraction.

When we got called to head up here a few days after I saw Violette at Shifty's, I was just about to ask Mae, in the most inconspicuous way possible, if Violette still had the same phone number. I had no idea what I would say but I made the decision to either call or text her because for two days I couldn't get her out of my head. Couldn't stop wondering what happened between her and her husband. I also couldn't stop picturing the way her hazel eyes had turned just a little greener when annoyance for me flared in them.

"Where's Caleb?" Sup asks, writing notes in his phone and interrupting my thoughts of Violette.

I pull out my snips and clip some unruly brush.

"Finishing up with Opp and Roycie. There was a bunch of fern brush at the edge they're cutting down."

Sup pulls his glasses and gloves off to wipe his eyes with a semi clean hand. He's looking like a beastly racoon.

"Taking it to the deep?" he asks, making sure we're relocating our fuel to the deep green, furthest away from the blaze's path, where it's least likely to catch fire.

"Yep," I confirm. My arms are aching. I've been ax wielding, cutting brush, and digging for probably ten hours straight. Eating in between whenever I can because we don't really take breaks. We're supposed to, but the people who made those rules have no idea what it's like to be out here.

"Go scout a few chains up, make sure those boys are doing

their job, we gotta eat, it's gonna get dark soon. We've made some good progress today." He grins. "Squaddie."

"Fuck, still sounds so fuckin' weird." I chuckle. Resting my chainsaw on my shoulder, I grab a drip torch with my free hand bringing it with me in case the boys up there missed anything.

"Tell them to start tagging out for food a few at a time," Sup adds,

"On it!" I call back.

I glance over to the smoke on the ridge. The wind has died down a little and the forecast is calling for rain tonight. Hopefully it's enough to actually make a difference.

"Time to eat, fellas," I tell Roycie, Sam, and Gareth. They're working under the watchful eyes of our captain, Cal, to install a pump in an area south of the fire's hot edge.

"Just about done if you want to hop on this with us," Cal says. "We've been at it a couple hours just trying to pump some water in. There's still a lot of heat in those birch patches," he says, pointing toward the piles of dead and down and looking at Roycie.

"Deeper than my Pulaski," Roycie adds. "We just want to get a hose to the hottest area."

I nod. "Sure," I say, knowing the sooner we wrap it, the better chance we have of stopping deeper pits from forming.

Forty-five minutes later we have the area carved out, and we start spraying to cool it all down while Cal figures the best way to route the hose.

"We'll hold up and eat until this area has cooled, then we'll head down the ridge northwest," he calls to us.

We all stop what we're doing and take a breath. It's when my body stops that I realize I'm fucking starving. I listen to the guys banter as I scan the area and see some birch that could use a little more cleaning up. I chug some electrolytes before making my way over to quickly take care of it.

But I make the fucking rookie mistake of turning my head to

look over my shoulder while making a wise crack at them for missing it, when I lose my footing and I'm suddenly being sucked downward.

"Fuck!" I call out. My one leg lands in the ash while the other is still under me, contorted in a weird way. My arms are thrown over my head and that's when I feel it.

It feels like I'm moving closer and closer to a giant whistling kettle. Until I'm walking right through the heat of its steam, until it's like my face is in front of the spout and I'm inhaling all that steam with one deep breath. It feels like my insides are melting on contact. The white hot powdery ash from the pit singes every part of me and my left leg is burning.

I think I call out for help, but I can't be sure. Faces flash behind my eyelids and the burning continues as everything begins to fade to black.

Harsh realization hits me as I start slipping from consciousness. I'm going to die the same way Jacob did, because I've just fallen into an ash pit.

CHAPTER 8
ROWAN

"There are tadpoles in the water, it can't be that *polluted,"* Violette says, standing at the edge of the creek.

The end of May sun is hot, and it lands on her bare shoulders in a dappled pattern as it filters through the trees. She's got her long, wavy hair in a big ponytail, and she's wearing an oversized Green Day tank top. I can't help but check her out a little from behind. If she tucked it in it would show off her curves a little more. She always seems to want to cover them, and I can't for the life of me figure out why.

I chuckle and point to the edge of the Elk Creek. "There are also beer cans, so yeah, it can."

Violette wrinkles her nose. But she knows I'm right.

"Bush parties... kids come down here and party all the time," I tell her, knowing she has never gone to one. Violette is the quiet twin compared to Jacob's more ready for anything personality. "The town is talking about having security posted to stop the parties and the littering."

"They should," she says, like it genuinely bothers her. "I don't know why the crew you run with thinks they just own everything and have the right to mess with it. These woods and this creek belong to the animals that live here," she says in a heated tone.

In the two weeks we've been spending time together she's gotten a little bolder, but I can tell sometimes she still stops herself from saying exactly how she feels.

I raise my hands in defense. "I haven't been to one since New Year's. I'm too busy with rugby and trying to pass bio, but I'll be sure to note that at the next school shithead convention."

She laughs in spite of herself, trying to maintain that pissed off, tree hugging vibe. I never noticed how pretty Violette was when she laughed before. I mean, I've seen her a lot, obviously, it's not like being around her is a new thing. I practically live at her house with Jacob when I'm not playing rugby—at least, I did before he started hanging around that dumbass Max Peters all the time—but I've never really been alone with her before, not this often. I thought it would be weird, but it's actually been kind of fun.

The thing I think I like the most? We always have a lot to talk about. It's easy for us to have an actual conversation. A smart conversation, which is hard to come by at our school. Violette doesn't care about the latest trends or what she should say, it's like she can't help but be herself and that makes me less afraid to be myself around her.

"Double or nothing, Elk Creek has more pollutants than Petersburg Creek."

"You're on," she says, pulling a glass vial out of her backpack and filling it at the water's edge.

We've been betting all afternoon on which soils and water samples would contain the most hazardous pollutants, and we've had to go to some pretty unsavory places. Mainly, I've had to. She made me take a sample from the disgusting locker room floor at the local gym. Some weird shit goes on in that locker room and I had to wait for two bare assed older men to hit the showers to get it.

"*For someone who* 'doesn't even understand protons and electrons,'" *she says in a voice that I think is supposed to be mine, but it's a piss poor attempt. "You're pretty confident." She nudges me with her elbow and I get a crazy idea.*

"When—not if—I win this bet, we're going to see the new Annabelle *movie and you're keeping your eyes open the whole time," I say to her.*

Violette looks up at me, the smile falling from her full, pink lips.

Am I actually asking Violette on a date?

She looks up at me with those pretty eyes, and they widen in surprise. She's Jacob's sister and it's possible I'm reading this whole vibe between us wrong, so maybe I should take it back, but I don't. I just wait, curious to see if she wants to spend more time with me too.

"*Why would you want that as your prize?*" *she asks without hesitation. I give her points for being straightforward.*

I shrug and shape the brim of my hat, looking out at the water. "I don't know." I turn to face her. "Just thought it could be fun to hang out when we aren't scaling the fences at the waste station or trying to locate the town's deadliest soils, don't you think?"

Violette shrugs but it's like she's searching for a response. Something about catching her off guard is appealing to me. The hot, early summer sun shines onto her face, a thin layer of sweat glimmers on her cheeks and her forehead. A vision, that I'm in no way prepared for, of Violette getting sweaty in other scenarios, runs through my mind.

"*I'll go if you win, but there's not a chance I'll be keeping my eyes open the whole time, Kingsley. I could barely make it through that movie you and Jacob watched last weekend." Her words cut into my daydream of me pulling the scrunchie from her long hair and watching it fall around her shoulders.*

Fuck. *I blink to push it out of my head.*

"Jeepers Creepers *wasn't even scary.*" *I laugh, remembering her tucked into the couch like a little burrito hiding behind a pillow.*

"And you have to get your own popcorn, I'm not sharing with you. You eat way too much," she adds.

It's true, I do eat a lot.

"In my defense, I burn a thousand calories a day," I say, which earns another laugh from her.

"I'd love to have that problem. It would be nice to eat whatever I want and never worry about how many calories are in it. Your metabolism is enviable," she says, turning to walk toward the parking lot as she looks down at her figure.

The fuck?

"What the hell are you talking about, Vi?" I ask, shuffling in front of her. She stops walking and gulps as I invade her space. She says nothing, she just looks up at me in question, so I continue, "I just mean...you look great."

She laughs and starts walking again. "Thanks, but I don't wear rose-colored glasses. I'm okay with how I look, I'll never be stick thin like Kyleigh Miller or her crew of Barbies," she says as we make it quickly back to my mom's SUV that's parked in the conservation parking area.

We climb in and I turn to face her, really wanting her to hear this, so she remembers it in case some idiot doesn't appreciate the way she looks someday.

"Yeah, about that, just so you know, most guys want softness. Curves are a good thing, Vi."

She looks up at me, a soft pink blush creeping up her neck to her cheeks.

"Well, thanks, that will help me sleep better at night." She laughs, nudging me playfully with her elbow. The air thickens and I watch how she takes her plush bottom lip between her teeth whenever she's the slightest bit nervous. I think I like that I make her nervous.

"Next up, the sewer plant," Violette says, shifting the mood.

"My favorite way to spend a Friday," I tell her in a laugh as I start the SUV. But the thing she doesn't know is, this has been the most fun I've had in a long time. She reaches into her bag and pulls out nose plugs, holding one out to me.

"I come prepared," she says with a laugh. "King?" she asks. I try to answer but I can't.

"King...stay with me," she says, her eyes are growing concerned and her tone is off.

I try to speak but I can't—

"King, keep looking at me," I hear again but it's no longer Violette's voice. The light in Violette's eyes fades as another fills my vision. The sun? I think I'm moving. My arms are over someone's shoulders and whoever it is, is holding me, tight.

"Thank Christ he had those fire rated chaps on," the familiar voice echoes.

"The chopper will be here anytime. Think those are seconds?"

That voice is Sup's. He was three hundred feet away from me, how is he with me now? Seconds? As in second degree burns? The moment it registers, I feel it and howl. I try to focus on my left leg, it's dragging along the ground as the guys pull me forward, they're definitely taking me to the medevac site.

"My fucking leg…" I manage to get out, my teeth are chattering so fucking hard. I'm a trained medic in the off season so I know immediately that I'm in shock.

"I know, bud. Did yourself real good, but you're so fucking lucky. Stay with me here, you passed out," Cap says. "We're almost to site, chopper is already inbound."

"We got you out in less than ten seconds," Caleb says.

It's all coming back to me as I look down to where I can feel my calf and part of my thigh are burning. I look down at my arm, my yellow Nomex is burned through and there are blisters on my left upper arm, a fuck ton, but no black.

I let my head fall back, by the look of the burns they're seconds, Cap is right.

"Thank fucking Christ you were right there," I say to Caleb and Cap, and nausea washes over me with the stench of burned flesh and hair.

We make it to the site with my guys carrying me over the rocky terrain. The medic is waiting; he tells me his name, but I don't remember because the pain is fucking terrible. I'm set down on a small stool at the medic tent. Another wave of nausea washes over me. I turn my head as my stomach lurches and I vomit.

"Just hang on bud, you're going in real soon," Cap says gruffly as he pats my back. *Going in.* To the hospital. Looking down at my arm I know I have no choice, and right now I could use some fucking pain meds. I haven't been burned in a long time.

"Almost forgot the feeling," I say to the part of my crew that surrounds me—just Sup, Caleb, and Cap. Everyone else continues working, because even though I'm injured the blaze doesn't care.

The medic asks all the usual questions and gives me a shot of something for pain. *"How did this happen, what is my pain level on a scale of one to ten?"* I think I answer them. My vitals are taken. I've been in this game long enough to know they're monitoring me for how badly I'm in shock. My clothes are cut from me and I'm wrapped in a Mylar blanket to conserve my body heat. Over the course of the next several minutes, the nameless medic works to gauze me as I bite down on a rag Cal hands me.

Motherfucker.

The waves of nausea continue with the pain. Being burned like this feels like you're still on fire. Nothing and no one can stop it.

They wrap my leg and arm loosely with dry, clean gauze, my clothing hangs from me in tatters, but still in place where it isn't cut open and soaked through with water as the inbound chopper sounds. When it lands, I watch as it's loaded up. My medic designates Sup as my patient liaison.

I fade in and out as I'm loaded.

"Keep you posted, Tim," Sup calls out. *Tim.* That's the medic's name.

"We'll be there in less than fifteen. We're going to Bakersfield," Sup tells me reassuringly. "Seems like mostly seconds, you got a fucking horseshoe up your ass, boy," he says.

I think I nod, but I'm not sure. The moment the pilot's voice speaks over his comms to Bakersfield letting them know we're on route, I close my eyes. I will myself to fall back into the sleep where Violette's smile was all for me, and then I let the darkness take me.

CHAPTER 9

Violette

"We're going to send you for an echocardiogram, Mr. Rath. Your heart is still harboring a little arrhythmia. We just want to make sure it isn't something that needs a deeper look, okay?" I tell the fifty-something-year-old electrician who has been in my care for eight days. He came in with third degree electrical burns, and his heart has been acting up since, which isn't uncommon.

"Whatever you tell me, Vi." He grins. His pain is a lot better now.

"All right, someone will be in to help you into the wheelchair in a few minutes," I tell him, pulling the latex gloves from my hands and popping them with my disposable gown into the soiled bin at the edge of the semi-private room.

I duck out and enter in the meds I just administered into the rolling computer outside his door. It's a quiet night, I only have two patients in my wing right now, so I've been able to pay close attention to them, which is the way I like it.

I make my way to the nurses' station and sit down behind the desk, picking up what's left of my iced coffee. I don't normally drink caffeine at night but the first night of my six-night stretch is always the worst. I rotate through one overnight shift of six nights per month, which is better than my previous every other week cycle.

I'm hoping with this new schedule I won't be zombie mom half the time. I pull my phone out. 9:30 p.m. I quickly text my mom.

> How'd she go down?

MOM
Just fine, darlin.

I sigh in relief, hoping we're on the right track now with bedtime.

> Thanks.

MOM
At some point you're gonna have to stop thanking me for watching after my own grandbaby. It's my job and I love it.

I smile.

> Thanks.

MOM
☺

I laugh.

MOM
Besides I can catch up on housewives this way, your dad will never watch it with me.

I laugh and stuff my phone in the back pocket of my scrubs as the desk phone rings from the ER.

Casey, the other nurse on my floor, answers it. I semi listen as I add some notes to Mr. Rath's chart.

"They didn't ice him, did they? I've been telling the fieldies not to do that, it always makes it worse," Casey says to the other end of the line. That gets my attention. Fieldies means medics with the woodland firefighting crew.

"Fieldies did everything they could." A memory of hearing that when Jacob came into the hospital flashes through my mind. I blink and try to take a deep breath, it doesn't come.

Something happened on the line. I've been watching the fires burning in Skykomish all week. I know our local hotshots are on it because my dad has been talking about it. My blood instantly starts racing at the thought of someone I know being hurt or worse. The familiar crushing weight settles in my chest. I try to breathe and remind myself that Casey is too calm for it to be really bad. Whoever it is, he must be okay. Right?

Casey asks a few more questions as I listen intently. Her short red bob is tucked behind her ear. I catalogue the things she says in the conversation.

Second degree burns, patient's left leg, minimal to no third degree, scattered first and second degree to the upper arm and shoulder. Ten percent of his body surface is affected. Mild steam burns in various places, smoke inhalation. Male, Caucasian, twenty-eight.

My stomach drops as I try to remember the ages of all the guys on King's crew. Is anyone else twenty-eight but him?

I can't think. I get up and try to remember how to breathe as I move behind the chair to watch her open her screen, trying to get a look at his file. She hangs up and looks up at me before I can read his name.

"They're sending up a hotshot. It's Rowan Kingsley."

I physically feel the blood drain from my face as my heart pounds in my ears and my whole body grows hot.

"There's something else, Vi…he fell into an ash pit."

The tightness takes over my chest before the words have even left her mouth. Every vision I've had of how I imagined Jacob's last moments to be, plays through my mind. I will my knees and my voice to stay strong as I speak. I *knew* when taking this job that I could see this. I've been talking myself up about it for a month.

"We'll put him in 306-A, he'll be the only one in there. He may be up quite a bit through the night with the pain." I hear myself talking to her, but my voice has the same weird echo around it that I always get when I'm willing my head to stay straight, like I'm listening to myself talk, not actually commanding my brain. It's almost robotic.

"Vi? Are you okay?" she asks, standing.

My eyes flit to hers, they're lined with concern. I realize I'm still white knuckling her chair and panting. I let go and flex my hands. *Another day. This is another day's problem.*

"Yeah, I just...how are they saying he's doing?" I ask her, laser focused and intent on thinking of him like any other patient. I have a job to do.

She reaches out and rubs my arm. "He's stable." She knows I know him—everyone does. And she knows what happened to my brother was similar. Only he wasn't so lucky.

I breathe out a shaky breath and nod. "Okay, then. Let's get his room ready. How long?" I ask her

"Ten to fifteen minutes," she says, noting the room in his chart.

"I'll grab some supplies," I tell her, needing a second alone to compose myself before I see him.

I make my way to the supply room and close the door behind me leaning on it, begging my heart rate to come down.

I close my eyes, inhaling for five, exhaling for five. Too many memories of him wash through my mind in real-time as I grab a plastic bin to fill with some necessities, wondering what happened, or how he got out of the pit. I tell myself he's okay and that he's just like any other patient. I repeat it over and over until I almost believe it.

When I get to King's room, Casey is done making up his bed.

I set everything I grabbed onto his bedside tray, knowing we'll go through it quickly.

"I just need a few more minutes here, do you want to go down and meet them in the bay?" Casey asks as she finishes up, turning the overhead light on and closing the blinds.

"Yeah," I tell her "I've got it."

She nods. "When I'm through here, I'll go check on D Wing. Call me if you need me."

"Thanks," I tell her, leaving the room, I look down at my hands, shaking. I will them to steady.

The wait at the trauma bay seems endless. I fiddle with the drawstring of my pants, tighten my ponytail, drum my fingers on the desk, a million more questions and thoughts running through my head until I think I may drive myself crazy, and finally, I'm pacing. The noise around me is constant yet blends as I remember the last time I paced in a hospital like this.

I'm going to be his nurse. I'll do my job and do it the way I always do.

I look at the clock above the main desk. Shit, I think it's only been five minutes. I'm letting my past trauma over Jacob cloud this situation, I know I am. I don't even know King anymore, his being injured shouldn't affect me like this.

But it does.

If I can just see him... just get an idea that he'll be ok , then I'll be fine, I tell myself as I continue my figure eight around the bay.

The elevator doors opening is an almost deafening sound, kind of like a vacuum sucking the air from me. I'm not prepared for the way the sight of King laying on that bed rips my chest wide open and tears my heart into a million pieces. His blue eyes are closed. He's been changed into a hospital gown, but his face is dirty and covered in soot from the field, and his hair is caked in sweat, mussed and knotted. I can see the area on his good arm they scrubbed clean in order to get an IV in near his hand. His left arm is bandaged, mostly his upper bicep and shoulder. I take in where his burns are as I'm briefed by the ER nurse who accompanied him up. She walks with me as a porter pushes King.

"Dr. Grayson says your doc up here will want to assess him for skin grafts." She mentions one of the ER docs who must have treated King.

"Is she thinking he'll need some?" I ask.

The moment I speak King's eyes slightly flutter open, and that damn lopsided smirk, although a little dozy this time, appears on his face.

Someone's got some good pain meds in him.

"She didn't seem to think so but it's hard to tell yet," the nurse offers.

I glance down at King as we walk. His left leg is out from under the blanket, already having been wrapped and treated by the ER staff. There are spots the gauze doesn't cover, those areas look like they have patches of first-degree burns, angry and pink. His good arm even has some first degree burns on it. The ER nurse tells me his second-degree wounds have been cleaned and coated in Xylocaine jelly for pain.

"That must have been quite the job for you guys down there, getting him clean," I say, gesturing to his filthy appearance.

"Uh…ya." She laughs.

"Our doc up here will probably give it until tomorrow to assess," I say back to her.

King's eyes open a little more with my voice. Groggy, but just as blue as always. They're bloodshot, and I wonder when the last time he actually slept well was.

"Hey, Vi," King mumbles. "You look really fucking pretty."

The ER nurse stops talking and eyes me up, I feel my cheeks flush.

"He was my brother's friend," I offer awkwardly.

"I was your friend too, until I fucked up and—"

"Okay, let's just get you settled." I talk over him nervously, just hoping he'll shut up. If he wasn't already injured, I would smack him.

I look back at the ER nurse, she rolls her eyes and ignores our back and forth.

"He's good and stable, we just gave him some morphine."

That explains it.

"This stuff is the tits, Vi...I don't feel anything." Rowan gives me a very high thumbs up with his good hand, his eyes closed and his bottom lip between his teeth.

Christ almighty.

The nurse and I chat as the porter positions King's bed into place. I work to hang his IV fluids up, hoping if no one says anything, King will just keep his thoughts to himself until I can get her out of here.

King mumbles something, but I can't quite make it out. His tanned and soot covered skin is such a stark contrast to the gown and his good arm is propped up, strong and defined, even in rest. My brother's tattoo is front and center, causing my chest to tighten as I take it in, reminding me once again that Jacob didn't end up so lucky. I have a moment of sympathy rush through me thinking about King seeing Jacob in those moments and the demons he must live with.

I squeeze my eyes shut and take a breath in the dimly lit room.

"I'll leave you to it," the nurse says, a hint of a grin playing at the corners of her weathered eyes. "He's all yours."

I offer her a friendly smile. Outside, I'm the picture of composure, but inside, I'm wondering how the hell I'm going to make it through what looks like at least a week of me giving Rowan Kingsley close, personal care.

64

CHAPTER 10

Violette

AGE 18

My parents' living room

"You guys are going to take samples *again*?" Jacob pops a handful of Doritos into his mouth as he eyes me up. He's wearing his standard gym shorts with a tattered T-shirt and his short dark brown hair is wet from the shower.

"Why are you so dressed up?" he asks around his food.

I watch him as he shoves it in, bouncing his knee as he talks. He's been super antsy lately, something I can't quite put my finger on has been off. And maybe it's a twin thing but when he's antsy, so am I. I look away from him and down at my outfit so my nerves don't skyrocket any more than they already have.

"It's just a sundress," I mutter defensively, cocking my hip and placing a hand on it.

Jacob turns his attention back to the TV with what I'm pretty sure is a hint of a smirk. "Mmkay," he mumbles.

I grab my purse and sling it over my shoulder, not bothering to correct him on where I'm going. I'm already nervous enough, I don't need to hear him razz me about going out with Rowan… on a date. A fake date just because I lost a bet and he wants to see me sweat through *Annabelle*.

It took me way longer to settle on my white eyelet lace sundress and faded jean jacket than it should have. I never used to wear dresses but the self-confidence blog I've been following has really encouraged me to embrace my curves, so here we are, embracing my curves. Although I'm paranoid Rowan is going to get here, take one look at me, and say there's not a chance he's going to take me to the movies, even if he did win the bet.

Elk Creek had more hydrocarbons and pesticides than Petersburg by almost double. After some further investigation we determined that run off from a local farm was contaminating the creek. I think we'll get bonus marks for figuring that out.

"So, you're going to take samples for pollutants…in a sundress?" Jacob asks as my dad comes into the living room with his new iPad and a snack, ready to relax after having just come home from work. He's still in his clean Sky Ridge uniform, a black T-shirt and his greens. Fire season hasn't really got off to a busy start, but he still has to work a daily shift. Every day he comes home clean, I can breathe a little easier. When I was young, sometimes he'd take me with him to organize equipment or help him wash the service truck the guys use to stock the base, just to show me his job wasn't always dangerous. I've always had a fear of him getting hurt in the field, ever since third grade when one of my classmate's dad died. He was a hotshot just like my dad. It was the first time I understood that my dad was at risk and anything could happen to him.

"You look nice, Vivi," he says, kissing me on the top of my head. He smells like motor oil and heavy-duty cleaner.

"Cleaning the equipment room today?" I ask, wrinkling my nose.

"How'd you guess?" He grins.

I smile up at him, noticing for the first time a few threads of silver in his blondish hair. My dad is getting older, but he has to stay in shape as part of his job. He reminds Jacob every chance he gets that he could still kick his ass.

"She's got a date—I mean, homework—with King." Jacob snickers.

My dad looks at him, and as he does, I give Jacob the death glare. My dad is unfazed. He looks back at me and shrugs.

"I know."

My head snaps up from searching for my favorite bubble-gum lip gloss.

"You know?" Jacob and I both ask our dad at the same time.

He nods. "Yeah, Rowan called me and told me he was taking Vivi out. Said he won a bet and that she was gonna hate every second of it." Dad grins, and I want to die.

"What??" I groan at the same time a heavy knock sounds at the front door.

Dad and Jacob are still laughing when I swing it open to find Rowan wearing black jeans, a white T-shirt that fits him perfectly, and his staple black boots. His wavy hair sits perfectly, just touching his forehead and his tan is deep, making his intense blue eyes seem even more piercing. *Shit. What was I mad at him for again?*

His eyes rake over me slowly, from my strappy white sandals, over my dress to the snug fitting top, he pauses and swallows, and then his gaze continues to my face. Something about the way he looks at me makes me feel like I'm going to overheat. My hormones are just out of control around him. When his eyes meet mine his lips part slightly, and I'm wondering if I'm overdressed. Since I've never been on a date before, I have no basis for comparison and my only friend good enough to call for advice is away with her family for a week.

I clear my throat and Rowan blinks, then runs a hand through his hair.

"So…" He smirks. "Ready to hide behind your fingers all night?"

"You should take the blanket you hide behind when we watch scary movies here, Vivi." Dad chuckles from the sofa, turning up the Mariners game Jacob is watching.

Oh yeah, now I remember why I was mad. He called my dad.

"I looked it up," I say to them both defiantly. "It's not even going to be that scary. I'll be fine."

My dad, Jacob, and Rowan look at each other, and at the same time all of them start laughing.

I narrow my eyes at Rowan

"Whatever, jerks," I say awkwardly to my dad and Jacob, which makes them laugh even harder. As I storm out of the house past Rowan and onto the porch, I pause hearing Jacob speaking low to Rowan just inside the door. I turn back to them just as Rowan pats Jacob on the shoulder and nods.

Weird.

I hear him call out "She'll be home by ten" to my dad before adding, "Go M's."

"Got that right," Dad echoes. The one thing they always have in common is their love for the Mariners.

Ugh…if Rowan wasn't so annoying he'd be pretty close to perfect.

"Did you have to *call* my dad? I'm eighteen, I don't need permission to hang out," I bite out as I get into the passenger side of Rowan's mom's Ford Explorer.

"To *date*," he corrects as he closes my door with a smile on his face that I can't really be angry at. He gets in on his own side. "And yeah, I did. You aren't a stranger, I wanted to make sure your dad and Jacob were all right with it."

I roll my eyes. I mean, it was kind of sweet he told my dad he was taking me out, but little does he know I'll never hear the end of it from Jacob, and my mother will be asking me every five seconds what's going on between us.

I turn to face him, the scent of his cologne fills the space between us, and it's hard not to breathe it in. He smells so good. I will myself to focus and try to get my point out.

"It's 2014, you aren't 'courting' me, and you have no idea what happens in my family when you throw the word date around with my name like that—especially since I've never been on one! And also because it's only a date because I lost a bet. My family will hound me about this for years to come," I protest.

Rowan grins and starts the engine before looking back at me, placing his broad palm on my forearm, and I realize just how close we are. How close his face is to mine when he looks down at me.

"Vi, do you not understand that I've been having fun hanging out with you the last few weeks and that winning this bet was just an excuse to get you to go out with me?"

My mouth falls open and my eyes drift from his down to his full lips, then back up to his eyes. He *wanted* to take me on a date?

"*Why?*" I ask out loud before my brain tells me not to. Rowan's thumb grazes my arm as he speaks and my skin breaks out in goosebumps. He angles himself toward me a little more and leans in slightly, bringing that delicious scent with him.

"Lots of reasons…" He smirks. "You're terrible at judging scientific matter, you have a really hard time admitting when I'm right…about anything or that you even like me…but"—his voice grows softer like he's about to admit something—"the thing that seals the deal? You look really, really cute when you're trying to pretend that you aren't absolutely terrified of shitty horror movies."

I sit dumbfounded for all of three seconds before I scoff and swat at him for poking fun at me and also saying I looked cute, because he can't mean that.

"Uh-uh. Don't do that," he says, gripping my arm a little tighter, as if he's reading my mind. His eyes grow instantly serious. "For the record, when you opened that door tonight... you took my fucking breath away." He lifts his hand from my arm to twist a piece of my curled hair between his fingers then releases it.

We sit across from each other; the only sound is our breathing as his gaze drifts to my lips. Rowan is looking at my lips...like he likes them? I feel something start to heat between my thighs. I clench them together to stop it, but it only makes me feel it more.

"But I'm nothing like the girls you normally date..." I say, because I just can't make sense of it.

"I know. That's why I like you, Vi," He says it like it's the most obvious thing in the world, leaving me speechless as he turns and starts to back out of my parents' driveway.

I say nothing, because, well, I just really didn't expect that and I need a minute to process that this is my first real date.

With Rowan.

Internal panic mode activated.

So, it turns out *Annabelle* is that scary, and I did actually spend the entire movie peeking between my fingers, much to Rowan's delight while he chuckled and ate popcorn. He did tell me what was happening when I was too afraid to look and he did in fact share *his* popcorn with me. Every time I reached into the bag and our fingers brushed, those little butterflies swirled in my stomach. I keep reminding myself it's Rowan, but my body isn't listening to the logical side of my brain. My heart rate is almost normal again by the time we're leaving the theatre and there is a little more space between us.

"I think I might need to buy you some ice cream to bring

your heart rate down to a reasonable level. I can hear it from all the way over here." Rowan wraps his pinky finger around mine, pulls my hand to the center console and laughs.

I feel my skin heat with his unexpected touch, but I fight the urge to say no, I've been doing so well with my diet this week. I know one ice cream won't kill me, but I already ate popcorn and candy at the theatre. The familiar guilt creeps up and I do my best to push it down. How often do I go on a date? NEVER. I make the decision almost immediately to go with him. I'm sure there will be something of the healthier variety at our local ice cream parlour, *Licks*.

"Okay, but I can pay for myself, you know," I remind him, but he's already shaking his head.

"Not a chance," he says. "My mother would have my head for that," he adds.

"Well, when you put it that way, I'll do it for Liz," I say, mentioning Rowan's mom by name. She's always been so nice to me and Jacob, I've met her a lot more than I've met his dad because his dad is a long haul truck driver, he goes back and forth from coast to coast. He's only home for a few days every two weeks, but he does his best to make it to every one of Rowan's games he can.

When we get to the other side of town, Licks comes into view. You can't miss our town ice cream parlor, it's a staple in Sky Ridge. *Licks Dessert Bar* and a huge milkshake are painted in a bright, retro style on a large mural across the side of the big historic red brick building on the corner of Sky Ridge's Main Street and it's packed as it always is this time of year. There are people from our school sitting on the numerous picnic tables outside under the overhang and it features enough twinkle lights to brighten the entire patio in the dark. People who don't fit at the tables eat in their cars, or on their tailgates in the parking lot. I feel my palms start to sweat at the thought of going into this place with Rowan Kingsley and having to see all of these people from school. I look around nervously trying to talk myself into walking by all of them with confidence.

"Vi." Rowan chuckles as he sneaks into a free parking spot and cuts the engine.

"Yeah?" I ask, looking out the window. Kyleigh Miller, her cronies, and three of Rowan's teammates take up a few of the tables.

"You ashamed to be seen with me or something?" he asks, noticing my nerves.

"You're fucking with me," I say with a laugh.

He pulls his black Seahawks hat off the back seat and pops it on his head backward, then faces me. "Well, I can't help but notice you look like you'd rather rob this place than go in and get ice cream with me," he says.

I look back out my window. "I don't normally mingle with this crowd," I say truthfully.

"You aren't here to mingle with them, you're here to have ice cream with me." He smirks that lopsided grin and I know I've lost any battle I had of going in there with him. He's so relaxed all the time, nothing phases him. It's kind of contagious and I will it to give me courage.

Rowan gets out of the car and I follow suit, but he's at my side and towering over me before I even see him coming. He takes my hand in his, it feels warm and it's like I just...fit with him.

He leans down, my heart thunders in my chest as he does.

"Forget them, it's just you and me, yeah?" he says, his voice is deep and comforting in my ear.

His thumb strokes the inside of my palm. Okay, yeah, I'm pretty sure I'd do just about anything he asked when he's touching me. I nod and smile up at him.

To my horror, all eyes are on us as we round the corner, Rowan stays a step behind me and places his hand on my lower back. It settles me a little.

He doesn't get far before his teammates stop him, he does a little handshake with two of them and they start talking about some play they need to perfect for tomorrow night's game. I stand beside him, feeling so awkward and out of place. Kyleigh is sitting with Brittany and Carmen, of course. Every single one of them wears little crop tank tops that showcase their figures and cut off jean shorts. It's like they called each other and planned their outfits. The only difference is that Kyleigh highlights her very slender waist with a gold chain that circles her and dips below the top of her jeans.

"You all know Violette?" Rowan asks when there's a small break in conversation.

His rugby buddies turn to nod and say hi, looking between me and Rowan. One of them is taller than the rest, with a round, kind of baby face but he isn't chubby in the slightest, in fact he's built like a brick wall.

"Max," he says to me with a head nod. "You're Jacob's little sister."

I nod and smile. "Yeah, but we're twins, actually."

"Wait...no way, you're in our grade?" Max asks. We've had at least one class together every year, so my guess is if he doesn't remember that, he's probably never noticed me.

"Yep," I say, popping the p.

Kyleigh snickers, I'm sure just to make me even more uncomfortable.

"Awkward," someone says in a mock cough, and the rest of them laugh.

"You guys are dicks," Rowan says to all of them. "This is why I don't come out with you." He turns to me. "Ignore them, Vi."

"Ahh, come on, King...we're just joking, sit with us," Max says.

Rowan grabs my hand as he pulls the door open with the

other over my head, guiding me in. "Nah, we're good, see you fuckers at practice tomorrow."

I make the mistake of looking back at Kyleigh through the window, and discover her eyes are on me and she's holding her thumb and finger to her forehead forming an *L*, and laughing with Brittany and Carmen.

I look away quickly, doing my best to make conversation with Rowan to stop the bridge of my nose from stinging. They're all just out there laughing because I'm with Rowan.

"You should come to my game tomorrow," he says as we get in line.

"I am," I say, watching the way his face shows surprise. It only lasts a few seconds until he realizes.

"Of course, you're coming to watch Jacob."

I smile. "My whole family is coming. Playoffs are a big deal."

I scan the menu for anything remotely healthy. There is nothing.

"What are you gonna have?" Rowan asks, turning to face me while we wait in the long line. I blow out a breath.

Fuck it. I mentally block those girls out and decide to have whatever I want. I'm going to enjoy my date. I turn and smirk back at them over my shoulder, leaning in closer to Rowan. Mentally telling them, *"You can make fun of me all you want, but I'm the one who's here with him."*

"A scoop of rocky road, and a scoop of chocolate peanut butter with hot fudge and whipped cream," I say.

Rowan starts laughing. "Nicely done. Love that you didn't order a vanilla kiddie cone. You know what, I'm having the exact same thing." His face beams with pride over my sudden burst of confidence.

Rowan reaches forward and grips my open jean jacket tugging me toward him. I look around at all the people in the space, and he lifts a hand and curves his finger under my chin, tilting it up so I have nowhere to look but into his gorgeous blue eyes.

"Don't pay attention to them, Vi, I want your eyes."

My breath hitches and I'm pretty sure I gulp. What is this man doing? Half the school is here.

"You never stop surprising me, Violette Taylor. Now..." He pauses and looks up as if deep in thought, then brings his eyes back to mine with that damn smirk. "If only there was a way I could get you to admit you're *also* coming to the game tomorrow night to watch me..." he rasps, dipping his head low in front of everyone in the ice cream parlor.

They all fade away in a haze as Rowan Kingsley's lips meet mine.

CHAPTER 11

ROWAN

PRESENT

They must have the guy in the room next to me on some pretty heavy pain meds because he's been talking in his sleep all night.

My left side is on fucking fire. I press the button that slow releases the pain meds into my IV. It beeps back at me, telling me I'm at my limit for now. Basically, it's going to be a bitch and not give me anymore.

The pain is duller with the meds but it's still there. This is by far the worst I've ever been burned, and I can't help but think that every time I mentally complain this is what Jacob must have gone through, but a thousand times worse. The familiar pang of grief hits me as I try my best to sit up, squinting to focus on the clock on the wall with the fading sun coming through the blinds. It's almost seven, nearly twenty-four hours since I fell into that pit. I think I slept through Vi's entire shift last night and most of today. These meds are kicking my ass.

I know better. I've been trained better. I remind my guys better. I elevate the bed to a higher sitting position by pressing the button on the side, then pick up my phone to see texts in my group chat with Cal and my sup. GIFs of hot nurses from Opp. Well wishes and a mix of "Need anything?" from some of the other guys. I respond to them all one by one and leave my group chat for last. Of course, Cal and Xander are gonna bust my chops a little.

CAL

You know if you wanted a couple weeks off you could've just asked instead of pit jumping.

I chuckle and scrub the stubble along my jaw with my good hand. I know Cal has seen a lot. He struggles with not having been able to help Xander's dad the same way that I struggled with letting Jacob go up on that ridge. He watched Xander's dad die right in front of him. That shit messes with you. Not to mention, he had to be the one to tell Xander what happened, and overcoming that has been a struggle for him, so to put him through this sucks.

I would ask for a vacation but my boss is a fucking slave driver. Only two days off since May.

SUP

Sounds like the kind of boss that likes a hard worker and goes above and beyond when someone gets hurt.

You know, like carrying your heavy ass two hundred yards to the med tent above and beyond.

Still a hard ass.

SUP

Well to cut the shit for a second, this hard ass is fucking relieved you're ok.

Thanks Sup

SUP

Don't thank me, just get better, we need you out here.

CAL

Need anything? Scottie is running some errands this afternoon.

Nah man my mom is coming, bringing me clothes and stuff.

I don't even get the text sent before my mom's voice is echoing down the hall.

I can't hear what she's saying but I can hear the tone. I've always been a bit unpredictable, lived my life like it was an adventure, but my mom lives her life with a regiment of control. She's a worrier, and considering I just fell into an ash pit I'm sure she's about to spontaneously combust.

"...and they'll give him that med for how long? It's addicting, isn't it?"

"Yes, it can be, but I'll be here all week. I met with the doctor this morning and he said we'll be lowering his dose every day. By this time next week, he shouldn't need anything but naproxen or ibuprofen." The voice of the nurse talking with my mom is unmistakable—it's Violette, and now I know she'll be here all week.

I do my best to sit up on the edge of the bed as my mom rounds the corner with tears in her eyes.

She takes one look at me and loses it, coming toward me, unsure of where or how to hug me without hurting me.

"I'm okay, Mom," I tell her as she sits down beside me on my good side and hugs my neck. Her short blonde hair is messy, and her eyes are puffy under her glasses. She definitely looks like she needs sleep. My dad texted me and told me she wouldn't let him stop all the way home from their haul in California.

I shake my head. "I'm okay," I repeat, to make sure she understands.

"No, you're not. Oh, my baby," she cries. "Be honest," she adds, "what can I do?"

"Okay, if I'm being honest… I'm groggy from this shit they're giving me, and I fucked up my back when I fell, and my skin feels like it's on fire, but, Mom, *I'm okay*," I say, hoping she'll get my message.

I side eye Violette standing in the doorway, clicking away on the computer that the nurses roll from room to room. My heart breaks all over again as I realize Vi's mother never got this, the son who was injured but made it through. My mom instantly understands when she sees me looking at Violette. She sits up and sniffs.

"I'm sorry, it took me way too long to get here." She dots under her glasses with a tissue from her pocket.

Now that she and my dad are empty nesters, she sometimes travels with him on his long hauls so they can be together after so many years of being apart. He owns his truck and it's quite comfortable, with a little bedroom in the cab and storage. It's luxury on wheels. My dad says it's a nice way to spend his last few working years. They treat it almost like a road trip.

"Dad is getting the things you asked for from your house. He should be back real soon." My mom wipes her eyes as Violette finishes typing into her computer just outside the door and turns to face us.

"I'll let you have a quick visit and then I'll come back to check and change your dressings," Violette says with a nod.

My eyes flick to hers. Even after everything that happened between us and years apart, I still feel the need to make sure she's okay.

"Thank you, sweetheart." My mom stands and makes her way to Violette. "I'm so glad he's in your hands all week." My mom is a much taller woman than Violette, and she pulls her right in for a hug.

Violette tells her I'm going to be fine and hugs her back, her eyes meet mine over my mom's shoulder. I smirk at her and mouth the words *"thank you."* Her eyes don't soften like I want them to—like they used to. She simply pulls back from my mom.

"It's my job, you don't have to thank me, Liz. I'll be back in fifteen minutes," she says in a no-nonsense tone.

She turns to leave the room and because old habits die hard, I can't help but notice how great she looks in her scrubs, with her long ponytail hanging in graceful waves down to her mid back.

My mom comes toward me when Violette is out of earshot and gives me a barely there tap at the back of my head as if to give me shit.

"You might want to fix that. She's a gem. Remember when she used to like you?" she notes with a small laugh. Should've never told my parents what happened with Violette. They've never let me hear the end of it, they always liked her.

I chuckle and lean back in my bed, guess that sympathy from earlier is over. My mother chats my ear off about their trip down through Roswell, New Mexico. She rambles when she's nervous or worrying so I just let her go. Within fifteen minutes my dad is coming through the doorway with all my stuff from home. I'm basically a younger spitting image of him, only I'm an inch or so taller than he is. His hair has gone gray, but he looks happy, relaxed even. I haven't seen him since before fire season started, but I've talked to him over text almost every day.

"Hey, kid, looking better than I thought you would," he says, coming to me to give me a pat on my good shoulder.

"Thanks."

"Sorry, but I just gotta say it." He smirks. "What are the odds the one that got away is your nurse?" he says, hiking his thumb over his shoulder. My mother chuckles.

"Laugh it up, you two." I extend my good arm behind my head.

"Well, no time like the present to start fresh. And seems to me, you're already off to a good start," my dad says, taking a seat beside me.

"How so?"

"You made it outta that pit and she's here. You know, it might not be easy to make a friend out of her again, but nothing worth having ever is and you've got a lot of years to make up for."

I close my eyes, taking a breath.

"Tell me something I don't know."

CHAPTER 12
ROWAN

AGE 18

Teaching Violette Taylor science

Violette Taylor tastes sweet, like bubble gum or sugar. It isn't just one thing that has me desperate for her. The smell of her hair, the feel of her warm skin pressed against me, the sounds she makes when my hands trail under her linen shirt. She's incredible.

In the last four weeks I've spent almost every day with her, I've gotten to know her on such a different level than just as Jacob's sister. Not only is she insanely beautiful, but she's smart and she knows things about sports and music, and she beats me at every card game I throw at her, every goddamn time.

Even the nights we're just sitting at her parents' dining room table working on our bio project, listening to my iPod together, it's easy and feels good. We've discovered we both love 90's alternative music, and we've watched more scary movies in the last four weeks than I can even name. But my favorite thing is when I compliment her and that slow pink shade creeps over her pretty throat.

Since we handed in our biology project today, I've convinced her to come with me on a picnic to celebrate, which is where we are now. Food and music forgotten, laid out on a picnic blanket, tucked into a sand dune on Fraser Beach, with the sound of the lake lapping at the shore and seagulls overhead acting as our soundtrack. It's chilly tonight for late May, so the beach is empty.

I did my best to let her finish her dinner but the way she looked in the golden sunlight had me tackling her onto her back the moment I had my chance, and now my mouth moves with hers effortlessly. Every swipe of my tongue against hers has my dick aching against the zipper of my jeans. As the captain of our school's varsity rugby team, I've had my fair share of girls over the last few years, but I've never wanted someone the way I want Vi now. All we've done is kiss but, fuck, I can't get enough of her. The only problem is I have no idea what I'm doing with her.

It's been almost two weeks since I kissed her in the checkout line at *Licks* and I know I have to take things slow, but seeing her almost every day, seeing her in the stands at my games even though I know she's with her family, has made me fall for her—hard. Not only is she my best friend's sister, but I know I'm the first guy who's ever kissed her. She let that one slip the other day, which also means I'm definitely the first to touch her like this too. That is both a heavy responsibility and the worst fucking kind of torture.

A gust of wind blows the blanket we're lying on up around us, bringing sand with it. Violette pulls back and starts to laugh as her silky hair blows between us.

"The universe thinks we should stop kissing." She giggles.

"Not a chance," I say, swiping her hair from her rosy cheeks and diving back in. Moving my lips down to her neck.

Her pulse quickens, fueling me even more as she fists my T-shirt.

"You drive me crazy, Vi," I tell her, my voice husky, full of want.

She whispers, "I've never—I mean, I've never felt like this before...never *wanted* someone," she admits in a whisper.

I look down at her. The sun sinks over the water, shining its golden light on her silky skin. Even though the air is cool we're far from cold, wrapped up in each other.

My thumb strokes the soft skin of her waist under her loose tank top.

"Is this all we're going to do now that we have no science left to learn?" she asks with a soft giggle.

"Hmmm." I stroke the loose wisps of hair off her perfect face. "You wanna talk science?" I ask, dipping my head down so my lips trail her throat, her collarbone, she grips my shirt tighter.

"Maybe. Science I know...this is all new." She laughs as I nuzzle into her neck. Knowing that I'm the first one to touch her like this is incredible.

"Okay...chemistry...specifically autonomic structure. Protons and electrons." I dot a few kisses down her neck, slowly sliding my hand to her waist. "I learned about those fuckers," I tell her, "and I think they're a lot like us right now."

"Rowan," she moans as her eyes flutter closed.

I move back to drop my forehead to hers and kiss her lips.

"See, right now, this electricity you feel... here"—I slide my hand down, skimming the inside of her thigh—"it's attracted to me." I nip the skin at the base of her ear. "It needs my energy... begs for me to soothe it, balance it," I tell her. "Because I'm what you need. I'm the proton."

"That s-so?" she whispers, and I see she has a small smile playing on her lips.

"Yep. It's basic chemistry, Vi. Electrostatic attraction." I kiss her again.

"You learned that?" she asks.

"Yep, aren't I such a good student?" I smirk into her lips. Her eyes are glassy as she looks into mine.

I squeeze her thigh as I kiss her, she moans and "*Rowan...*" is wrapped up right in the center of that moan, with her eyes still on mine...it's too much.

"For my reward, I want to make you moan my name like that, over and over. Will you let me?" I whisper cautiously. My cock throbs even more, but I don't give a fuck about me. I just want to make her feel good. Her pretty hazel eyes open and the sun hits them as she drinks me in, trying to decide whether she should trust me.

She doesn't answer with words, she just lifts her head enough to start kissing me again, running her hands down my back.

I slide my hand down over her skirt teasing the lower hem of the fabric against her leg, pulling my lips from hers as the last of the day's sun dips below the horizon.

"I'm gonna need you to say it, Vi," I tell her gruffly, my self-control is slipping by the second.

"I want you to." It's a barely audible whisper.

My body takes over before my mind as my hand slides up under her flowy skirt, and I'm thinking of all the ways I'm going to take care of her.

CHAPTER 13

Violette

AGE 18

Learning about electrostatic attraction on Fraser Beach

Rowan's hands grasp the edge of my tank top and he peels it upward over my head.

I lie below him in just my white bra and my skirt, feeling so exposed to his hungry gaze. No one else is here, but it's his eyes I'm nervous to have on me. I instantly move my hands to try to cover myself a little. Rowan has been with a lot of different girls and all of them were probably thin and beautiful. Rowan gently grasps my hands and separates them, pushing them down so they fall at my sides.

"I never want to see you cover yourself, Vi, you never need to with me, got it?"

"I'm just nervous, I know the girls you've seen like this before. I don't look like them."

He makes a sort of grimacing face at me and an almost angry

growl leaves him before dipping his lips to touch the spot just below my ear.

I moan, unable to stop myself as heat pools between my thighs.

"You're beautiful, Vi…I've never wanted someone the way I want you right now. Let me show you…" He brings his fingers to my collarbone, tracing it, then trails them down between my breasts, over my stomach, until he stops and grasps my hand pulling it down, pressing it against the bulge in his jeans, hard and straining. More heat gathers between my legs just feeling him like this.

"See what you do to me?" he asks as his lips come down on mine.

I moan into them as Rowan lets my hand go and skims the hem of my linen skirt again. His eyes meet mine. The subtle minty smell of his breath, his navy eyes on mine and the heat from his strong, beautiful body overwhelms me. I have no idea what this is between us, maybe we are like protons and electrons, but I do know that I feel like I might explode just from his lips on my skin alone.

A million thoughts race through my head as he slides his hand up my thigh, taking my skirt with it. All the while, he kneads my flesh as he starts to discover parts of me nobody else has. The cool breeze blows my hair, and my nipples harden as he presses his fingers to my clit through my panties. He groans, and a tight feeling takes over my chest. I can't imagine wanting anyone more than him.

Rowan's kiss deepens as he skims the waistband of my panties and then slips his hand beneath. The moment his fingers meet the embarrassing amount of wetness waiting for him, he sucks in a breath between our lips and then he slowly lets it out as his fingers begin to move in circles against my clit. My eyes are closed but they still feel like they're rolling back as he kisses me gently. His middle finger moves through my slit with perfect pressure and precision, and I whimper into his lips. I think I hear the sound of one of our phones buzzing, but it does nothing to distract us, and we both ignore it while we kiss each other.

"Mmm..." he groans back into my lips. The vibration of the sound sends little shockwaves through me. "Feels good, yeah?" he asks, his voice is deep and low.

All he's doing is touching me and I feel like I could die from need.

"Y-yes," I mumble. I'm too far gone to care. I start to move my hips, pressing the ache I feel against the pad of his finger. He presses back and slips one finger into me. My pussy clenches around it. He knows exactly what he's doing and I'm helpless to stop him. I want whatever he's offering me right now. A tidal wave could wash ashore, and I'd beg him to keep going.

He gently adds another finger and I squeeze my thighs together to hold him there and show him I want it. He groans again.

"You're so wet for me, Vi, so fucking perfect," he murmurs.

These words. Why do they turn me on even more? My body feels out of control as he continues his gentle assault against me. My legs begin to shake as his mouth moves back down my neck, his lips dotting my shoulders, my arms, the tops of my breasts. Pressure builds low in my core as I remember how he felt in my hand, so hard and throbbing. A sweet, aching coil of heat flutters in me like I've never felt before.

"That's it, Vi, come for me," he whispers. "Open those pretty eyes and look at me."

I do and the sight that greets me tips me over the edge. Rowan's body hovering over me, his eyes full of lust and heat. The way he seems to be studying my every expression. It's too much. My vision goes blurry for a few moments as I come apart around his fingers.

"*Rowan,*" I cry out. Once? Maybe twice? I don't know because I'm lost. I keep my eyes closed as my vision slips.

When I open them to find him staring down at me, cheeks flushed, as his tongue trails over his lower lip and he gently pulls his hand from my panties and rests it against my bare stomach.

"Beautiful, Vi," he says as his phone starts to buzz again. My eyes snap from his to where I know his phone is lying.

"You can answer that," I say quietly. Now that my orgasm is over, I don't know what to do for him, and a phone call helps give me time to figure it out.

He shakes his head. "Fuck no, I just want to look at you," he says before his lips come down to mine.

"I don't know, I mean, I'm not sure what to do for you or what you'd—"

He chuckles as he strokes my face, kissing my lips softly, oddly starting the coil of heat all over again.

"Vi, I just wanted to make you feel good. Don't worry about me, we've got plenty of time for that." The buzz of his phone starts again, and my eyes meet his.

"It might be important." I shrug, not really knowing what to say to his "*don't worry about me.*"

Maybe I did something wrong, or something I wasn't supposed to—

"Stop." Rowan cups the side of my face, the pads of his fingers caress the back of my hair and his thumb traces my jaw. He kisses me.

"You're incredible, Vi, I just want to take my—" The buzzing of his phone cuts him off again.

"*Fuck,*" I hear him mutter under his breath as he flips it over and shakes his head, before finally picking up the call.

"Yeah?" he asks, annoyed.

I can hear a voice through the phone, frantic but I can't hear what's being said.

"Calm down, what do you mean? Where are you?"

More frantic mumbling continues as Rowan listens intently.

"Okay, I'll be there," I hear Rowan say. He looks over his shoulder at me.

"I'm with your sister, I have to take her home first," he says, keeping his eyes on me.

Jacob?

By the time he's hung up, I have myself a little more composed after my intense first orgasm, and my shirt back over my head, but now that we aren't tangled in the blankets I'm freezing. Goosebumps cover my arms.

"I'm sorry," he says as he tosses his phone.

"What's wrong with Jacob?" I ask as I shiver.

Rowan picks his full zip Seahawks sweatshirt up off the blanket and wraps it around me as he answers. "He's at Max's. He's got...some kind of issue, says it's girl trouble but he really needs my help."

I narrow my eyes, feeling like I'm missing something. But honestly, it's my brother so I'm not sure I even want to know. "I'm gonna go help him but I told him it'll be later, when I'm all done kissing you," he says, zipping the sweater up tight around me. The scent of him and warmth washes over me. I look up into his cobalt eyes.

"Fuck, it looks better on you anyway," Rowan says, leaning in again in search of my lips.

"He sounded upset. You should go to him," I say, not wanting to stop kissing him either. "I told my dad I'd be home by ten anyway and it's already nine thirty," I offer.

He nods, then looks down to the still obvious bulge in the front of his jeans.

"Yeah, okay, just need a minute." He chuckles as heat creeps up my throat with his admission. He leans back on the blanket and extends his hands behind his head, his muscular arms flex as he does. "Tell me all about the pollutants you found in that sample from the sewage plant last week." He grins. "That'll probably do it."

I lean back too, laughing with him, and begin listing the
pollutants we added to our project last minute as my arm brushes
against him. It feels nice so that I nuzzle in a little closer, but he
turns to face me, half serious, half joking, as he scoots away so
we're no longer touching.

"Uh, Vi, for the sake of me being able to say goodnight to
your parents without being bricked the fuck up...um, I'm gonna
need those few minutes to be *without* you touching me." He
grins wide, and I happily realize Rowan Kingsley wants me just
as much as I want him, and I know I'll never tire of that.

CHAPTER 14
ROWAN

PRESENT

SUP

You get our little care package?

I glance over at the window ledge where a huge basket of miscellaneous goods waits for me from my squad. All my favorite snacks, a deck of cards, a porno magazine and some lube—that was fun to pull out in front of the day nurse—and in the center, a children's book on fire safety and some Band-Aids. Not just any Band-Aid, but kid ones with little puppy firefighters on them.

Fuckers.

Yeah I did. Hospital porn is pushing it.

CAL

Maybe but my girl's a trooper buying that.

OPP

You realize by saying that you're actually just making me picture Scottie reading porn.

CAL

You realize by saying that you're asking for an
ass kicking

Cal sends through an image of himself and Roycie flipping
Opp the bird. Behind them it's smoky and charred. They're still
in the mountains near Skykomish, onsite still fighting the fire I
was on two days ago. Opp sends a pic back of him sitting on a
tree stump eating from a brown paper bag with a big old grin.
They're filthy, they look exhausted, and the pang of jealousy that
flows through me is unstoppable. Even burned and battered, I
wish I was there with them.

I hate that I'm not out there.

CAL

That's why we put some tissues in there, in
case you miss us.

I've cried so much I already went through
the box.

OPP

He's using the tissues for his tears? That's
what we're going with?

I call bullshit. You've got that copy of Wicked
under your covers, stop lying.

SUP

☺You know you aren't supposed to do that
when you're in the hospital right?

Optimal time to pop in, Sup.

OPP

I mean a guy gets bored. I get it.

CAL

You can only watch so much TV.

> Fuckers.

"How's your pain?" my day nurse, Bonnie, asks me. She's been here the last two days and she's the little grandmotherly type. Her eyes are kind and her deep brown skin is weathered. She told me she's been a nurse for thirty years and is about to retire. You get to know someone when you're one of only three patients in the unit.

"Could use a little more painkillers, if I'm being honest," I tell her

"We don't want to give you any more if we don't have to. Hydromorphone is no joke, we'll be discontinuing your pump and starting you on oral meds for pain soon," Bonnie says, pushing her big-rimmed glasses up on her nose with one finger.

I nod. "Yeah, I want to stay clear headed." I look at the clock. 6:45. I know Vi is coming in soon, if she isn't already here. I think she spent last night mostly checking on me when I was sleeping, and I'll admit that I slept through a lot of it. I was wrecked after being in the field for days.

"We'll start to wean you down over the next few days. The first five days are the worst."

"Yeah," I agree, but know firsthand that's not exactly true. I've been through this before. Not to this extent but I know my skin is still blistering as we speak. It won't be pain free for ten days at least, but it should get a little better every day.

"Looks like your dinner is here," Bonnie says, checking my saline and my drip. "Eat up and get some sleep tonight. It's pretty quiet in here right now." She nods to the space where the guy who was talking in his sleep used to be and she grins, knowing he was loud as fuck. He left last night, which is why I slept.

"How's our patient?" Violette pops her head in my door, avoiding my eyes and speaks directly to Bonnie. Bonnie looks at me.

"Well, he smells a little better, he got washed up and got one of those fancy new hydro baths today. We'll probably put him in that every few days or so. Good news is, Doc doesn't think he's gonna need any grafting at all."

I heard all about how lucky I was to get this new therapy when they took me down, apparently it's relatively new to this unit.

"Excellent news," Violette says professionally, still avoiding my eyes.

"We're gonna add some ibuprofen into his schedule tonight as long as Doc approves it. I'll go give him a call, but other than that he's in your hands, honey," she says to Violette as she pulls her gloves and yellow gown off, tossing them in the bio bin at my door.

This time, Violette looks right at me when she says, "Lucky me."

CHAPTER 15

Violette

"You all good for the night?" Bonnie asks me as she starts packing up her stuff at the nurse's station. "You seem tired. Hollie still having a hard time sleeping?"

I click the last button on my computer screen, checking in on the two other patients in our care before she leaves for the night. It's slow around here right now, which will make the night drag on even more than expected and I won't have as much to keep my head busy and distracted from thinking about King.

"Hollie's sleeping okay, it's getting better, I just have a lot on my mind."

I turn in my chair to face her, changing the subject.

"How was 306 today? How's his pain?" I say, asking about King. I have a feeling he wouldn't tell me how badly he was hurting if I asked him, but he might tell Bonnie.

Bonnie grins. "He blushed like a tomato when Kelly and I had to scrub the dirt off him and then help him into the hydro bath." She giggles, mentioning the large tub we lower burn patients into to help with wound cooling.

"He was fine after I told him that in my years, I've seen it all."

I can't help myself; I smile. Bonnie never filters her words and the image of King trying to appear unbothered basically naked in front of her is rather amusing. I thank my stars I'm working nights. Bathing is usually done in the morning and afternoon for patients. Although I've felt King's body against mine, *seeing* it in all its glory, would be something else entirely.

I am just about to speak when the call button goes off from none other than 306.

Bonnie looks down at the flashing green light on our desk.

"I'll tell ya one thing, he's sure a looker."

I look at Bonnie, my mouth falls open and I smile.

"What? I'm old, I'm not dead, honey. Ta-ta, see you in the morning," she says as she slings her purse over her shoulder with a wink.

I lean in and press the button to answer knowing full well it's him. "Nurses' desk, what can I help you with?"

"Vi? Uh—I was wondering if I could get some of that burn ointment, if you're not too busy?" King asks. "I'm just, kinda on fire here."

Empathy washes over me as I pull his chart up on the computer just to confirm the brand we're using and if the doctor's answered our request to offer him anti-inflammatory in conjunction with his pain meds. I know two days in, he's prob- ably still in a significant amount of pain. I note the brand and realize I'm going to have to actually apply it. Touching Rowan while he's awake is something I knew was inevitable but I was dreading it nonetheless. At least last night when I changed his dressings, he mostly slept through it on a hefty dose of meds. Tonight, he seems rather awake. I take a deep breath and press the button.

"Be right there."

CHAPTER 16
ROWAN

I hear Violette talking to someone outside the door before she enters my room, so I straighten up. The moment I do the side of the bed grazes my thigh and I grunt.

"What happened?" Violette is in my room and at my bedside faster than I can even readjust myself.

"Nothin'," I grunt again. I know my face is contorted, because, motherfucker, that hurt.

"Bill," Violette calls into the hall. The burly nursing assistant I've seen every day since I've been in here comes into the room. "Can you help me prop him up? We'll place that pillow under his knee to get the blanket away from his leg," she delegates to him, full nurse mode and pointing to an extra pillow on a chair.

"Sure thing," Bill says.

I nod to him as he lifts my leg up and gets it off the blanket. I couldn't have done it without using my bad arm so in this moment I'm grateful for him. The burn pain subsides a bit as Violette presses a button on the side of the bed to raise me up a little.

"Thanks," she says to Bill, then turns back to me, lifting my burned arm up to prop a pillow under it. I know this is probably awkward for her but she's gentle and her eyes show her concern. It's as if she doesn't like me being uncomfortable. Her soft hands touch the underside of my upper arm and I involuntarily shiver, like a teenager all over again.

Her eyes meet mine when she feels my skin turn to goose-bumps. This close, the hazel tone is light and her eyes are fucking hypnotizing.

"Better?" she asks in an almost whisper as she lets my arm go.

I look down and clear my throat. "Yeah, thanks," I say awkwardly.

"Don't try to change positions too quickly, the smallest touch can be excruciating," she adds as she moves back to her computer.

"No shit." I chuckle. She reaches into the drawer under the computer and pulls out a little packet of pills. Then clicks away, adding something into my file, I assume.

"How do you do this?" I blurt out without thinking. Violette's eyes snap to mine as she tears open the packet.

"Nursing in general?" She pours the pills into a little clear cup. "You have some water over there? This will help, it's an anti-inflammatory," she adds, moving back toward me.

I nod and try to reach over to my empty cup without flinch-ing. I fail. She's right, any movement right now is no fun.

Violette hurries to my side and lifts the cup, filling it with fresh water and passing it to me, I reach my good arm out and take it from her, doing my best to breathe her in.

"Yes, nursing, but the burn unit specifically," I add, hoping I didn't just open Pandora's box for her.

To my surprise, she doesn't tell me I'm being too personal. She just shrugs and says something so honest it takes me aback.

"I do it the same way you still fight fires. If we don't, it's like Jacob died for nothing, and I just can't live with that, I won't live with that."

I blow out a breath with the sound of his name. It's just not spoken out loud all that much anymore.

"Fair enough." I nod. I bide my time and take my pills while she washes her hands and puts on a fresh pair of gloves.

Violette moves with the kind of grace she's always had, only now she's more confident. She's changed a lot. She's been someone's wife. She's a mother, and I can't pinpoint why but I get the feeling she's been through a lot. What little interaction I've had with her tells me the woman she's turned into is really something. I try to imagine her as a mom. I'd bet my life she's an incredible one. If she can dislike me and still treat me like she genuinely cares about my well-being, she's definitely a great nurse too.

I try to keep my breathing steady while I wait. Contrary to popular belief, the last fucking thing I want is for Violette to see me at my weakest and help me apply ointment to my skin, or what's left of it. Yet when she offers me a small smile and sits down beside me, I'm glad she's here. I want to watch the way the light hits her hazel eyes, and the way the smattering of freckles that dust the bridge of her nose are only visible when she's this close. I want to breathe in the way her hair smells as she leans down to start her work.

Fuck. I scrub my scruffy jaw to get my shit together. This woman has me over a barrel, and I've only known she's been back in town for a week and a half.

Violette begins to soak my dressings in room temperature saline water to make it easier to get them off, then with patient expertise, she pulls back the dressings on my thigh working carefully but intentionally. "Let me know if it hurts too much, okay? We can do it in spurts."

"Yeah." I nod.

I keep my eyes on her face, deep in concentration and ignore the burn. Partly so I don't have to look at my leg blistered and weeping, and partly because she is just a much better view. Once the dressings are off, she stands for a moment and takes her gloves off, picking up a phone from her cart. She snaps a few photos, then puts the phone back.

"What's your pain level on a scale of one to ten?" she asks as she makes her way to the sink to re-wash.

"Six," I say honestly. It's not terrible—as long as I'm on drugs and I don't move.

Violette puts a fresh pair of gloves on and makes her way back to my bedside. What I assume is her own phone dings in her pocket as she does. She ignores it as she starts to clean my wounds. I grit my teeth as she works. Her phone dings again, once, twice, three times. Still, she ignores it.

"Maybe important?" I ask, curious to know who is texting her.

"It's just my ex," she says, not losing her concentration as she cleans.

"Ahh," I say. "Tom?" I smirk. That gets her attention. She pauses her work.

"Troy." She smirks but doesn't look at me.

"Right, right," I say as her eyes focus on the gory sight of my thigh.

"How do you know it's him?" I ask, curious again.

"I know when he texts. He has his own special message tone," she says, grabbing a tube of burn ointment and beginning to apply it. "In case anything goes wrong with Hollie when she's with him, I know it's worth checking."

I nod as she grazes one of my burns just enough to send a searing shockwave through my body.

"Fuck," I bite out. Her eyes flit to mine and her brow furrows a little.

"Sorry, do you need to take a break or should we keep going?"

"I'm good," I report, trying to be strong, and trying to

101

pretend that having her this close doesn't affect me more than the pain right now.

A long, drawn-out silence takes over while she does her thing, the only sound is the ticking of my IV pump, and my thunderous heartbeat in my ears as she touches me.

"So, you like being a mom?"

Her eyes meet mine.

Fucking lame King, Jesus.

"I gotta be honest with you, Violette," I add. "Being alone with you again, I'm—fuck—I just want to make this right here."

Her eyes stay on her work which makes me even more nervous for some reason.

"It can just be what it is. I'm your nurse, King, I'm going to take care of you the way I would any patient in my unit," she says with no emotion, using my last name. *Have I mentioned I fucking hate that?*

A few more moments pass as she finishes up.

"I'll be back to check on you in a bit. There are only two other people on the floor right now, so if you need me, I'll be close by. All you have to do is buzz, okay?" she asks, and once again her tone is kind but very professional. Visions of her laughing her real, genuine laugh fill my mind. Hell, even to see her angry at me would be better than this monotone type thing she's got going on. She tosses her gown and gloves into the bin and readies to leave.

I should just let her go. Quit while I'm ahead with her actually talking to me without looking like she wants to punch me, but I just want to keep her here for as long as I can, and I'm a sucker for punishment if nothing else, so I don't.

"Hey, Vi, you never answered my question."

She pauses and turns back to face me, for just a second the spark in her eyes as she rolls them almost gives me hope.

"Anyone ever tell you you're kinda needy, Kingsley?" she

asks as she places her hand on her curvy hip. Fuck yes, this I can work with. I give her my best, poor me face.

"Maybe I'm needy, but I can't help it—I'm injured *and* I'm high."

She tips her head back and laughs lightly, a small but genuine laugh that feels like a goddamn reward as she pumps some hand sanitizer into her palms and rubs them together. Her phone dings again in her pocket, the ex.

"Yeah," she says with a genuine smile, one I can tell is all for her daughter. "I really love being a mom, it's the best job I've ever had. Try to get some rest." And then she disappears out of sight. I lean back on my bed and grin up at the ceiling. It was *one* laugh, but at this point I'll take anything I can get.

CHAPTER 17
ROWAN

AGE 18

Crazy for Violette Taylor's lips

"I have to go…" Violette murmurs into my lips thirty minutes after leaving Fraser beach. The console of the SUV is digging into my ribs and I'm pretty sure my right arm is numb from leaning on it, but I'd take any amount of discomfort to keep these addicting lips on mine.

"Mm-hmm," I mumble, continuing to kiss her. I lick a slow trail across her plush bottom lip and my cock throbs. I'm used to it at this point. My cock may never forgive me for just getting rid of my hard-on and then spending the last fifteen minutes kissing and talking to her at the end of her street. I just couldn't drop her off yet. Jacob has been calling me on repeat and I know I have to go. Not to mention, any more of this and we're gonna fog the windows up in here.

Violette giggles as I nuzzle her neck and makes a throaty little sound that tells me she's just as turned on as I am. She's just as desperate for me as I am her. I can't wait for more nights just like this.

"Rowan," she half moans, "I told my dad ten."

I back up just to give myself a moment to compose myself, but the way her skirt is hiked up her thigh… she looks so good in skirts and dresses. She needs to wear them more often.

"Go to prom with me, Vi." The thought of how beautiful she would be in a prom dress is driving me to make it a reality, to make all these feelings for her official.

She sobers up and backs away from me. "What?"

"If you're not going with anyone, I mean," I add, realizing I shouldn't assume.

She grins just enough for the dimple to appear in her rosy cheek. "I'm not," she says in disbelief. "I don't get many prom date requests."

I'm just about to read her the riot act for assuming no one would want to go with her. I hate that she doesn't see herself the way I do, but before I can, Violette's phone rings in her purse, forcing me to keep my mouth shut about how incredible she is.

She pulls it out. "Jacob," she says, laughing, showing me her lock screen. She clicks the button to answer. "He's coming." Fuck, do I *wish* I actually was. I shift in my seat to soothe the ache.

"We're almost home," she adds.

I lean back and run a hand through my hair, realizing I really have to take her home now. I turn the engine over while she prattles onto her brother.

"What are you so desperate for?" she asks, but of course, I can't hear his response.

"Yes, he's dropping me off and coming to meet you." She sits in silence, listening while Jacob talks on the other end as I round the corner of her street and flip my signal on to turn into her driveway.

"You're going straight to meet him, right?" she asks, turning to face me.

"Put him on speaker," I tell her with a grin, and she does.

"Fuck, dude, you're needy. I'll be there in ten."

"Okay, hurry up," Jacob says, causing the grin to drop from my face. Whatever the fuck he's gotten himself into, he sounds worried. Violette doesn't miss it either.

"Are you in trouble or something?" she asks like a mother hen.

"No," Jacob answers too quickly. "Just cover for me with Mom and Dad, I need King's help. I'll be home by eleven, if you ever get here," he adds, directed at me.

"Okay," she says, not convinced but hangs up anyway.

"Will you tell me if he's in trouble?" she asks. "I worry about him. He's so…"

"Impulsive," she says at the same time I say, "Reckless."

We both laugh as I pull into her driveway and put the car in park.

"Yeah…" She giggles.

I look down at my slowly deflating cock, willing it to stand down so I can walk her to the door.

Violette reaches out and places her hand on my forearm, definitely not helping my cock with the feel of her skin on mine. "Yes, I'll go with you to prom," she says with a smile. "But I'm wearing my Chucks." She laughs. "I don't do heels."

I smile back at her. She could wear a garbage bag with cut out arm holes and still be the prettiest girl there.

I look up at her house, the light is on in the living room but there is no movement in the front window.

I take the opportunity to kiss her one last time, lingering for a moment to burn the feeling of her lips on mine into my memory to get me through the night.

"I don't give a fuck what you wear. I just want to be near

you, Vi," I tell her as the front porch light turns on. We both straighten instantly, and I let Violette get out of the car.

"I'll give this back to you next time I see you," she says, gesturing to my hoodie that she's currently swimming in— looking fucking adorable, I might add.

I pull my T-shirt down as far as it will go hoping I look put together.

"I had fun tonight," Violette says as we walk up the stone pathway to her front porch. Images of her face as she came around my fingers flash through my mind. She was fucking perfection.

When we reach the porch Violette turns to me, the rosy glow still in her cheeks, her pupils blown out. "You're making me like you, Kingsley," she says with a sexy little smirk.

I reach out and wrap my first finger around her pinky and pull her to me, not caring if anyone sees. "Oh yeah?" I ask her.

"Yeah, I think I'm even gonna miss seeing you tomorrow," she says, knowing I have a full day at my co-op placement and a final exam.

I bend down and kiss her on the cheek. "Don't need to miss me, Vi, I'm always with you," I whisper in her ear, letting go.

"Right, protons and electrons." She grins.

"Yep, see ya soon," I say, backing down her porch as she disappears behind the door.

I smile all the way back to my car. Thinking of every single thing she said tonight as I drive to Max's across town to meet Jacob. The drive passes in a blur of her lips, the smell of her hair, her voice, the way I almost came in my fucking pants when she did. I can't think of any time I've ever thought of a girl like this, or ever felt this way, and now I'm getting hard again. *Fuck.*

When I pull into the driveway, I see a white Toyota I don't recognize. I get out anyway and text Jacob asking him where he's at.

Jacob: Can you come in?

Me: WTF dude, if this is a prank I'm gonna kick someone's ass.

He doesn't respond, and when I get to the porch, the door opens before I can even knock. I blink, it's not the face I expect to see. It's not Jacob, it's not Max, it's Kyleigh Miller in a barely-there pink tank top and a jean skirt.

"Come on in," she purrs, reaching out to touch my chest. I swat her finger away, then push past her to get in the door.

"Where's Jacob? What are you doing here?" I ask her. She just smiles up at me.

I turn to see Jacob and Max sitting on the couch in Max's living room. Jacob is bouncing his knee and he looks scared shitless. I turn back to Kyleigh.

"What the fuck is going on?"

Jacob is the one that answers. "I fucked up, man. Big time. And I need your help—"

"He sure did, but don't worry…" Kyleigh cuts him off, smiling sweetly. "I have a proposition for you."

Fuck me.

CHAPTER 18

Violette

AGE 18

Outside Mr. Shoebottom's Biology class.

I look down at my phone for the tenth time in twenty minutes.

Nothing. Just like the last nine times I checked.

I blow out a breath and glance down the hall, willing Rowan to show up. It's been three days since our beach make out session and him asking me to prom. It's also the longest we haven't talked in over a month. He knows our bio teacher is posting the grades at three o'clock today. Mr. Shoebottom is very old school and refuses to do anything online, even though lots of teachers are starting to do that.

There's about ten of us standing outside the door, waiting to see our marks a half hour past the end of the school day. The majority of kids will wait until tomorrow to find out, but I just had to know. I'm not worried about my grade, just Rowan's. I know how important it is that he gets a good grade in order to graduate. Not that he seems as invested as me right now, since he hasn't even bothered to text me back. I know he's had intense practices for the rugby championship and Jacob assures me he's fine, but I'm not sure I believe Jacob—he's been weird the last few days too. I'd be lying if I said I wasn't panicking a bit. I mean, what are the odds I'd find the most incredible guy in my brother's best friend, and admit to myself that I'm falling for him only to have him drop me? I'd be lying if I said my insecurities weren't going crazy. I've never had anyone touch me like he did... Did I do something wrong? The same familiar sting creeps in as my eyes start to tear up. I've gotten too attached to him. I should know better.

Just as I'm about to head to the nearest bathroom I see him round the corner. He wears the familiar royal blue and yellow fitted shorts and T-shirt of our school's varsity rugby uniform. His matching socks and cleats aren't dirty yet, which tells me he's about to head to practice, not coming from it. My breath hitches as I wait for his eyes and that lopsided smirk I think I might be in love with. A few seconds pass before I get those blue eyes. When his gaze lands on mine I expect to relax, but something about the way he's looking at me makes me feel unsettled.

He moves in slow motion toward me with his long easy stride, catching the eye of every red-blooded girl in the hallway.

"I wasn't sure if you were going to make it," I manage to get out when he closes the distance between us, looking down at me and pulling all the air from my lungs.

"Hey, sorry...I've had some stuff and practice has been, uh—"

"It's fine," I say, looking away, not wanting the awkward excuse I can already feel coming.

He looks around and then grabs my arm, pushing me away from the crowd so we're standing almost right in front of the bio door.

"No, it's not, I have been busy...but, I'm just, uh, I'm going through something. Something I didn't expect."

"What?" I challenge.

He closes his eyes "I can't tell you. It's not my story to tell."

"Mm-hmm," I manage to get out. I can feel my palms starting to sweat and the tight feeling in my throat begins to take over.

"The prom...I am so sorry, Violette, but I can't take you. I have to help someone with something."

"Who? Why?" I ask

He just looks at me but doesn't answer.

Anger rushes to my center and I feel my cheeks heat but all I manage to eke out is

"I see,"

"Violette...I'm gonna need to cool things with us for a little while. It's not—" he whispers, low enough that no one else can hear.

"It's not you, it's me? Is that what's coming my way?" I interrupt him.

He says nothing, he just runs a hand through his hair nervously. "I'm sorry."

I knew it. I thought something special was happening between us...I thought he felt the same, and now what? He realizes I'm not the kind of girl he usually dates? He doesn't want to go to the prom with me because of how it will look? I can't figure out why he would change his mind now. Has he just been trying to figure out how to break this news to me for three days? I swallow down the raging emotion. No matter how hard I try, the words *"you just aren't good enough"* run through my head.

"Also, there's something else," he says, his tone defeated. "You're maybe gonna hear some things about me and Kyleigh Miller." *Kyleigh Miller? The girl who looks at me like I'm a joke every time she sees me?*

Rowan's eyes meet mine and I can't place the look he's wearing, but he's definitely serious as he reaches out and takes my hand into his. "I didn't fake this with you, Vi..." He gestures to the bio door, and suddenly it's all very clear. That look he's wearing? As soon as the words leave his mouth, I know what it is. Guilt. *Holy shit.*

He *used* me. He was the first guy I let touch me, the first guy I was ever remotely intimate with. I trusted him and he *used* me. I pull my hand away from him.

"How convenient this all came up right after we handed in our project. A project I worked on so hard just to make sure you would get a good grade," I spit out.

"It's not like that, Vi—fuck, I—"

"Alright, people, back up so I can hang this," our white haired, bushy-bearded science teacher says as he makes his way through the bio door with a single piece of paper in his hand, the pin already stuck through the top to be pressed into the cork-board. He walks right between Rowan and me. We back up to let him through, but we never take our eyes off of each other. Mr. Shoebottom pins the document up on the board and students clamour around it.

I force myself to pull my eyes from Rowan's and will myself not to cry. I move like a robot toward the board, not knowing if he follows me. I find our names immediately. 94 percent. How nice for him. I turn, numb to everything around me. I'm surprised when I see Rowan standing in the exact same spot that he was, looking down at the floor.

I don't stop walking. I just breeze by him desperate for the bathroom.

"Vi," he calls after me.

"Vi!" he says, a little louder this time.

I stop and spin around, anger and nausea washing over me. I fold my arms across my chest, waiting for him to speak. He runs a hand through his hair and takes a second, like he can't find the words he's looking for. He takes a deep breath and looks up from the floor into my eyes. Even from twenty feet away, they pierce right through me.

"I didn't want to hurt you, that's not what this was."

I scoff feeling the tears that are imminent.

"94 percent, Rowan. Seems it was exactly what it was supposed to be," I deadpan before turning on my heel and beelining for the bathroom without stopping. Even as I hear him call after me, I don't stop. I can't.

The only thing I have left is the shred of dignity I'm holding onto and I won't let Rowan fucking Kingsley take that from me.

CHAPTER 19

Violette

PRESENT

My living room looks like a tornado went through it, but the sounds coming from out there are of three happy, laughing kids who are five episodes deep into *SuperPets*.

"How long do you think we can successfully hide in here?" Teddy asks as she sips the mocktail I made. She shifts in the chair at my kitchen table, looking about ready to burst.

"Until they all realize we're gone or one of them needs food." I grin.

As if on cue, Penny comes running into the room, crying something about Dalton taking away her Barbie.

Her brown eyes are brimming with tears as Dalton comes running in behind her.

"She was throwing it, I told her she can't do that here because she might break something," he defends himself like the little caregiver he is. Teddy has told me since her husband died, Dalton has turned into the man of the house of sorts, and Penny has an adventurous side.

I take the opportunity to check on Hollie in the living room while Teddy settles the commotion. She's quietly sitting on the floor coloring and watching *SuperPets,* singing along with the music. I smile as I watch her, she is a naturally easy going child, always finding something to keep her busy.

The quiet moment of watching her ends as Dalton and Penny come back into the living room with Teddy. "Crisis averted." Teddy grins, tucking a strand of her blonde hair behind her ear. "I told Dalton we'd sit out here, so I guess our alone time is over."

I laugh, taking a seat on my comfortable sofa as Dalton gets a game of Candyland out for them.

"He's like having a built-in little babysitter." I nod toward him.

He explains the easy rules to the girls and Teddy smiles.

"He's changed a lot since Logan passed. He had to grow up so much faster than I would ever want." I see the pain in Teddy's eyes as she talks. It's only been six months, and I imagine being pregnant during this loss would be the most bittersweet thing imaginable.

"Will you have any more?" she asks, putting her swollen feet up on my ottoman.

I shrug. "I'd like to, I just… Who has time for that? Plus, I'd need a man I actually like and I'm not sure that exists."

"Well, technically, you just need one part of a man." Teddy blushes as she says it, the way she does anytime she says some-thing even remotely naughty. I laugh in return as she adds, "Well, actually, you don't even need that if you—"

"I get it," I say, tipping my head back to laugh.

"Well, that's it, I'm bringing it up. Are we gonna get to the point of why you brought my ready-to-combust self over here?" she asks. I feel the blush creeping up my neck. "Seriously, Vi, it took me ten minutes to do my sandals up. Out with it."

I laugh and groan at the same time.

"All right, well…Rowan Kingsley."

Teddy nods. "Hotshot extraordinaire, very handsome, currently residing in your burn unit."

"Yes," I say carefully, trying to decide how to word it. "Well, we have a history. He was my brother's best friend, always, for as long as I could remember."

"Right, I think I knew that," she says. Her history was always intermingled with mine but never really a part of it.

"And you hadn't seen him until you came home?" she asks, turning to watch as Dalton shows Penny how to spin for her next color.

"Drifted apart after your brother..." she trails off, not wanting to say it. Teddy, of all people, knows how hard it is to lose someone. I nod.

"We drifted apart long before that. He was the first guy I... cared about. My first kiss, my first"—I look to the kids to make sure they can't hear—"you know..."

Teddy's eyebrows shoot up in surprise.

"Oh, you were *with* him?" she asks, her pretty face is lined in surprise.

I shake my head. "No, not quite that far. If we're talking baseball, it was a third base type thing. First time to third base, if you know what I mean..."

She nods and sips her drink. "I think I got it." She giggles.

"But the thing is, I had feelings for him. Whatever it was back then, it was strong," I tell her, playing with a thread on my shirt. "I thought it was for both of us and I know I had those feelings for him, for years." I focus on the hem of my oversized T-shirt as I talk, relieving the truth for the first time in a long time.

"I think I looked up to him, even though we were the same age. We got really close when we worked on a school project together. He needed to do well to pass and graduate on time, and I was happy to help him because I was so crazy about him..."

I go through the whole story, half in code so the kids don't hear anything they shouldn't. Teddy calls that speaking "Momglish."

I tell her about our history, the way I wanted him for years, our time together, how effortless it felt and about him asking me to prom.

"I really thought he cared about me. He was the first guy I ever cared about. I was so happy, and then he just dropped me. He showed up to view our final mark a few days later and told me that he needed some space, and that we were done. It was obvious to me then that he had just used me to help him get a better grade. I was falling in love for the first time and he broke my heart, I was devastated." I swallow the rest of my mocktail. "I left right after and haven't really been back much since. It was too complicated, I knew he'd be around the house all the time. I didn't want to face him…"

"What a…poopyhead," Teddy says with a giggle. Dalton chuckles when he hears his mom.

"Mommy said poopyhead." Penny giggles.

"Total poopyhead," I agree as the kids continue playing.

"You two never talked about it?" she asks.

"No, I had to hold on to some pride, I was humiliated at the time."

Teddy doesn't say much, she just nods so I continue rambling.

"I compared every guy to him for a long time. I wanted to feel with someone else what I felt with him but I never did. The night of the prom I stayed home and cried in my room. I found out that he went with my nemesis, Kyleigh Miller. It was like the final nail in the coffin. I think I never let go of that because I got it *so* wrong. It really made me question my judgement in every relationship after. Maybe because I never knew *why*," I tell her as I eye the kids while they play. "Kyleigh was always so mean to me and he told me he didn't even like her as a person. But it made sense on paper for him to take her instead of me." I shrug "It just really hurt me back then."

"Why?" Teddy asks. "What made you think that?"

"She was popular, gorgeous, thin, everything I thought I wasn't."

Teddy purses her lips into a straight line, and I know she's mentally kicking my butt for the lack of self-esteem I had back then, especially since I always encourage her to boost hers.

"I had to see pictures of them all night long on social media. It was torture." I shrug. "I mean, it wasn't like we talked about being exclusive, but I know I was falling in love with him, I had been for a long time. We just had a crazy connection. I'm not sure I ever felt like that again, even with T-R-O-Y." I spell it out so Hollie doesn't know who I'm speaking about.

Teddy adjusts her position on the sofa. I remember being that pregnant, never comfortable for more than five minutes. "Despite your lackluster teenage view of yourself," she says, "I have to think you wouldn't waste your time now with someone who wasn't worth it."

I shrug, grateful to know Teddy and to have a sounding board that isn't my mother—who it seems is pro-Rowan at all times.

"He was always a great guy, that's why it never made sense. He was constantly at my house with Jacob and he never treated me like I was an outcast. But after that I had to get away from him. The summer after senior year I left for university. I was only home from school for a year before Jacob died, and when he did, I knew I had to get out of here. That's when I moved to Seattle, met Troy, and you know the rest from there."

"Something just doesn't add up, and"—Teddy looks at me in thought—"I never want to hear you talk about yourself like you aren't enough again."

I raise a hand in defense. "Speaking in past tense. I was an insecure kid then, you know I embrace who I am now, curves, crazy hair, and all," I say with a wink.

"Good, I was about to have to"—she holds a fist up, narrowing her eyes like she's about to clock me—"tickle you."

I laugh at her Momglish.

"You have to hear his explanation out, Vi." She sets down her empty glass on the end table.

"I think the last few days since he's been in the hospital, he's been trying. It's me who's hesitating…"

Teddy looks out the front window at the trees swaying in the early summer breeze.

"Maybe he was just a kid who made a mistake? Maybe there's more to it than him using you…maybe it has to do with you, but maybe it's not about him *or* you." She runs a hand over her very large baby bump. "The only way you'll ever know is by *letting* him explain. Of course, that means you'd have to admit he really hurt you and that you care enough to listen."

I blink in thought. "That's the hard part. I have this habit of brushing things under the rug. And I've definitely done that here. I buried it, but never really got closure. I don't know if that makes sense."

"Things aren't always what they seem, Vi," she says wisely. "And you can't truly get over things until you face them."

I shake my head. "I don't know why I can't get him out of my head. I don't even know him anymore. This is twelfth grade all over again."

"Because you like him. That much is clear," Teddy offers.

I shake my head. "I *can't* like him. I follow a strict rule. I don't date hotshots. Namely because the idea of getting close to someone who risks their life everyday by just going to work is too close to trauma I've already lived through. Add in that he didn't care about me *and* he hurt me once already? He's a double threat…" I trail off.

She nods, understanding all too well the risks that come with getting close to someone with a dangerous job.

"I get it, but, Vi, I have to say… for a guy who never cared about you, he sure seems to be making an effort."

The doorbell rings before I can answer her and I'm grateful for the distraction to just think.

"Pizza!" Dalton cries and the girls cheer. I get up and answer the door while Teddy gets the kids paper plates to eat from and gets them all situated at the kitchen table with drinks and napkins. We sit at my kitchen island.

"This is the last thing I'll say. People change, they make mistakes. I haven't really known you too long, Vi, but I can tell by the way you look all gooey when you talk about him that you owe it to yourself to see if you can forgive him." She takes a bite.

"I don't look gooey," I say defensively.

"Total goo fest." Teddy giggles with her mouth full. "Let me ask you this, is there tension between you? The good kind?"

I narrow my eyes at her.

"What? This is the only drama I've got going right now, aside from the daily fights over snacks or dinner." She giggles.

I blow out a breath and think back on how he looks at me, like no time has passed and it feels just like the time we spent together—

"So, that's a yes," Teddy says, standing up to grab another slice of pizza with a knowing grin.

I shoot her a haughty look for busting me daydreaming.

"I don't date hotshots."

Teddy laughs and rolls her eyes, swallowing the last of her drink.

"Yeah, you said that already. Got yourself convinced yet?"

CHAPTER 20

ROWAN

"So, Sup's riding his ass the whole time, and this poor kid is shitting his pants searching the equipment room, the tool shed, looking everywhere for a trench digger, not realizing *he* was the fuckin' trench digger." Cal chuckles, rummaging through the gift basket they had Scottie bring me, in search of snacks.

"Twenty goddamn minutes it took before it finally clicked in his brain that there's no fucking such thing." Opp leans back in his chair.

Cal pulls out two packets of chocolate covered almonds and tosses one to Opp.

"Shoulda' seen Sup, standing there with his arms folded across his chest and that fucking scowl on his face," Opp says, tearing into the package and pouring the contents into his mouth.

"Fuck, I miss it already," I say, scrubbing my jaw that I haven't shaved in almost two weeks.

Opp stands and pats me on the shoulder. "You'll be back, bro. Have you read the fire safety manual we gave you? Some useful shit in there for avoiding this next time." He smirks

"Been studying every night, ya prick," I mutter.

Opp digs through the basket and pulls out another sleeve of almonds.

"It was a bitch, though," he says, pulling his phone out of his back pocket and opening his photos then scrolls for a second, before handing me the phone. I stretch my left arm out; it's so fucking tight but thankfully it doesn't feel like it's still on fire anymore after four days of healing. I scroll through the pictures he has of the rest of their time in Skykomish, the last one of his drip torch in the center of a beautiful fireline. Blaze and smoke in the distance.

"So, no word on the next roll?" I ask. They've been home since yesterday.

"Fuck, I hope we get a few days," Cal says. "Be nice to take Scottie to dinner, get some hikes in, sleep in a bed…"

"How long till you can come back?" Opp asks, crinkling up his garbage and doing his best hook shot into the trash. "Kobe," he mutters as he lands it. I chuckle.

"At least another two weeks for this to heal up." I nod to my wounds. "Three weeks tops, I think I'll miss a couple rolls," I say. "Maybe get to go home in a few days, we'll see," I add.

"Oh, sorry." Violette's voice sounds in the doorway. "I didn't know you had company."

I sit up straighter in bed; fuck me, she looks gorgeous today. She smiles at the guys and makes her way between them to update my whiteboard. Her light chestnut hair is braided down her back, a few wisps frame her heart-shaped face, and she's wearing pale blue scrubs—the color on her is fantastic, and the way these ones fit her hips and are drawn in around her small waist—

"He always stare at you like that?" Cal chuckles, asking Violette. "What a hazardous work environment."

If I could hit him with my left arm I would.

"Christ…" I mutter. "I…was just thinking that color looks

122

nice on you, Vi," I say awkwardly to try to save myself from it looking like I was checking her out.

I mean…I was, but still.

Violette smiles then looks away, a pink blush starts to creep up the soft column of her throat. I love it.

"In his defense, he's on pain meds so that's why he's drooling," Opp adds from his chair in the corner.

"I'll be back in twenty, boys, my patient needs his dressings changed," Violette says, pointing at my guys as she disappears behind the door.

The moment she's gone they all start snickering.

"*You look nice today, Vi,*" Opp says sitting up straight doing his best mock impression of me. "*Can you give me a sponge bath?*" he adds.

I throw the cup on my bedside table at him.

"She could hear you, you fuck," I mutter.

Opp doubles over. "You might as well write '*I was staring at your ass'* on your forehead."

I look at Cal who leans back and folds his arms over his chest like the Godfather. Opp stands and grabs the whiteboard marker, writing in his messy scrawl "*Stop staring at Vi's ass*" under the "today's goals" section.

"Fucking erase that shit now," I tell him, gritting my jaw.

"Or what?" Opp coaxes, but, of course, he erases it. *Shithead.*

"What are you doing?" he asks with a head nod, more serious than the others.

I know how protective they all are of Vi.

I shake my head and run a hand through my hair. "I don't fucking know," I answer honestly.

"Look, I don't really know what happened with you two, aside from this weird kind of tension, but Jacob told me once you sort of dated." Cal leans forward in his chair. "I know she's single now, but she's newly single and she just moved back, so make sure you know what you're doing."

I look to the direction of the door where she last was.

"I don't think it matters anyway, she just barely started talking to me again, the chance of there being anything to worry about is slim," I say.

Cal laughs a real hearty Cal laugh, the one that only comes when he's thoroughly amused. My eyes snap to his in question.

"That fire burn your brain cells too?" he asks.

Opp snorts in the corner.

I look at them both with a blank stare.

"Violette looks at you like you hung the fucking moon. Has since she was eighteen. Even now that she's Violette *Stafford*, even when she looks mad at you, hell, even just five minutes ago when she walked in this room. That isn't changing anytime soon, so just be careful," Cal warns, like this is something I should just obviously know.

The guys stand and get ready to leave, I realize I should be happy to hear his assessment.

It should give me hope, but the only thing I can think of is how much I hate the idea of Violette—*my* Violette—with another man's last name.

CHAPTER 21

Violette

This isn't going to be awkward. I will not let this be awkward.

"I'm curious to see how good you're looking," I blurt out as I start to gather everything I need to give Rowan a sponge bath. "How the *burns* are looking," I quickly clarify.

Shit, this *is* going to be awkward. This is the universe testing me, I'm sure, because his daily sponge bath wasn't done this morning and he's on an alternate hydro bath schedule now.

"I'm going to wash you down now, they said they didn't do it this morning?" I ask, hoping maybe I misheard. The nurse before me said he slept most of the day, and she was short staffed, which means he'll probably be awake through the night with me. It also means I'm the lucky winner of sponge bath duty, because keeping the parts of him that aren't burned clean is so important.

"Uh, no, she was real busy and I was sleeping most of the day."

I nod. "Your body is healing. It's to be expected."

I can do this. I meet my reflection in the mirror above the sink and mentally give myself a pep talk as I fill the basin with warm water and soap. *He's any other patient.*

I soak the rags, and as I do, I wish it wasn't so quiet in here tonight. I can feel Rowan's eyes burning into my back as I work, and when I'm done, I carry everything over and place it on the table beside his bed.

He looks brighter today; his eyes are less glassy. From his chart, I know that they've significantly lowered the dosage on his pain meds, offering ibuprofen more frequently. Which is standard for four days post burn.

The only thing that's a little off about him is that his beard has grown out. I've never seen him with one, but it makes sense, I know the guys don't shave in the field and he was out there for over a week before his time here.

It gives him this whole lumberjack vibe that's only heightened by his perfectly unkempt wavy hair, his big muscular body and his tattoos.

I swallow and go for it. "I-I'm going to untie your gown now," I say softly, raising the bed up, then pulling down the blankets covering his thighs so they rest at the foot of his bed. His long legs are free of any clothing, save for the dressings on his thigh. I know he's only wearing the hospital gown, and I know there'll be nothing underneath it, so even as his thick muscular thighs draw me in, I remind myself again...

Patient. He's your patient.

I finish raising the bed up to waist height. His eyes meet mine and he nods as I lean in and reach up and around him to unite the gown at his neck. I don't know how he smells so good after being in the hospital but it's damn distracting. My fingers brush his skin, and I hear him suck in a breath.

"Sorry. My hands are cold," I apologize.

"No, your hands feel good—uh, fine. They feel fine." Rowan's voice is a close whisper, so close, and his breath comes shallow as I slink the gown carefully and slowly down, revealing his bare chest. Taking special care to make sure nothing brushes the dressings on his arm. I lay the gown across his lap, making sure he stays covered *there,* at least for now.

One test at a time, universe. I pump myself up to actually look at him, I *have* to look at him to wash him.

Good fucking God. He's beautiful.

I realize when I'm thoroughly finished my ogling that Rowan is watching me watch him. He looks down at his bare chest and then back up to my eyes. *Shit.*

I look away, closing my eyes as I turn and reach for my rags. When I have my back to him, I do my best to regain my composure from the vision of him. The terrain of ink, hard muscle, and scant trail of hair that makes up Rowan's chest. I take a breath and soak the rags way more thoroughly than I need to. My heart is thundering so loud in my chest it's like a soundtrack to my thoughts. The silence in the room is deafening, droplets of water hit the basin as I wring out the first rag, willing myself to get through this. I take a deep breath and turn toward him.

"Here. You can wash your face while I start." I offer Rowan a cloth in a feeble attempt to distract us both, and then turn back to wring one out for myself.

Get it together, Vi. He isn't that beautiful, you'll see, when you look at him next, you'll realize you're overreacting.

I turn back around and begin to carefully scrub little circles over his chest, I'm wrong. He's just as beautiful as he was the last time I looked.

Rowan washes his face as I smooth the rag under his strong jaw, down his neck, over his sculpted shoulder and then continue slowly to his muscled pecs. He sighs, and I can't fucking believe it, but I think washing him is making *me* wet, which has never, in any of my years of nursing, happened before.

I try to keep my breath steady, clenching my thighs together to stop the ache as I wash his other shoulder. I run the cloth over his good arm and the hawk tattoo that stares back at me. I do my best to avoid looking at it, before setting the used rag down and grabbing a fresh one from the basin. The ten seconds I manage to look away from him is the only way I'm holding it together right now. I need them to compose myself.

"You okay?" Rowan's strained voice cuts into my thoughts. "You just seem like you're having a hard time taking a deep breath or something."

Oh God. Was I panting?

"Fine, just concentrating."

On your body.

"I know it's hard to look at," he observes, glancing at his visible burns. I register that he thinks I'm grossed out.

"These?" I ask rhetorically, gesturing to them. "This is nothing, and I don't even see the wound. I only see the healing. The progress," I tell him as I finish washing his chest and waist, actually having to wash in the crevices of his insanely chiseled abs.

That's a first.

"As long as every day it changes for the better, then it's all part of the process," I breathe out shakily.

"Well, all right, that's a more positive way to look at it. All I see is damage," he says, his brow furrowed.

"Can you, um, sit up, and I'll...get your back?" I ask.

He grips the bed to lean forward, slowly, I assume to hinder the pain I know he's feeling and his arms flex, and as I watch him my mouth waters.

Another first.

I lean into him to reach his back, knowing at this point I just have to get this over with. I start thinking of anything I can to distract myself from the expanse of Rowan's wide rippled shoulders, as my phone dings in my pocket, once then twice.

"Trevor?" Rowan asks with mischief in his tone.

"Troy," I correct, knowing he knows full well what my soon-to-be ex-husband's name is. Very soon. Like three days soon.

Hmmm. That seems to be working. Troy, Troy not coming to see Hollie, Troy always putting himself first. Yep, definitely working to stop me from drooling over my patient.

"*Fuck,* that feels good, Violette," Rowan groans, his spicy sandalwood scent and the gravel in his tone floods my senses, bringing me right back to drooling. I back up and reach for another cloth as he leans back in his bed.

Just the lower half now, I tell myself.

"Do you two get along?" he asks, his jaw setting as I stare at his feet.

I realize a random conversation is the distraction he's looking for too.

"Yeah, you could say that," I mutter.

"That doesn't sound very convincing," he observes. I gently scrub his strong calf and the inside of his good thigh. I'm pretty sure I'm holding my breath at this point because his thighs are so thick and hard, they're just as enticing as the rest of him. I can't be sure, but I swear I hear him groan again, softly into his rag as he finishes washing his face.

I know it must feel good to be washed after a day in bed, but those groans are like little cherry bombs racing through my blood every single time.

"Troy was hard to be close to, hard to know. He's in a very prominent position at the hospital we worked for. He's always focused on work, so as long as I never wanted more than that or got in that way of his job, we got along fine."

"That doesn't seem very fair." Rowan's voice is deep as I carefully work on his thigh, taking time to work around his dressings. "To you or Hollie," he adds, tossing his face rag into the basin.

My gaze moves to his. I didn't even realize he knew Hollie's name.

"It isn't," I give. "He wasn't always like that, we had fun together before. But now, we've been separated for a year. It's why I'm here and why in three days we'll be divorced."

He nods but doesn't say anything else for a moment.

And I keep washing and talking, for *both* of us.

"I thought maybe once we split and he didn't see Hollie every day, he'd want to see her more often, or make more of an effort, but that's not the way it worked out."

Rowan makes a sort of a deep growl, and I wonder if I hurt him.

"It's his loss, Vi. He'll regret that someday. The one thing you can't get back is time."

"I know that, and you know that. I just wish *Troy* knew that."

Rowan gestures to his still covered wounds, I assume to change the subject, and then surprises me by his next honest words.

"I still don't know how you do it," he mutters so quietly it's barely audible. I watch a slow trickle of water drip down his thigh, through the dark hair there then onto the bed.

What did he say? "It would be like bringing his death back every day, wouldn't it?"

I make my way carefully up his other thigh, almost done with this sweet sort of torture. His leg flexes and I'm momentarily mesmerized by it. I blink and keep going.

"It actually helps me to know every story doesn't end like his. And this might sound odd, but I feel close to him here. This was the last place he ever took a breath."

He nods, his face filled with emotion. I do my best to lighten the heavy subject.

"You'll have some scars here, but eventually they'll fade." I pause to look at him, offering him a small smile.

"That so?"

"Yes," I whisper, returning my gaze to his damp skin. "The human body is an incredible thing."

I feel his gaze move to where I'm touching him, on the underside of his knee. And I make the mistake of looking up at him just as he looks at me. We both just sit in a suspended silence for a beat, staring at each other.

I can't pull my hand away or it will be obvious he's affecting me, so instead I do what I do best.

I ramble. My hurried voice cuts the thick silence between us in an almost whisper. "Our bodies, well, they're self-soothing." I move higher up his thigh. "Self-healing. They always know what they need, and they tell us in various ways." I watch Rowan's throat work to swallow, as I move inside his thigh. "All we have to do is listen to what they need and provide whatever that is without, um, overthinking it."

His deep blue eyes hone in on mine. Without breaking eye contact, he stops my hand by placing his over it. I look down and realize I'm mere inches from his very large, very hard cock under the gown that is doing nothing to conceal it. He holds me here, his thumb grazes mine, and a tingling feeling runs the length of my forearm.

I was not trying to make that sound sexual in any way but there's no denying that in this moment, I did. The room is a quiet hum and there's an almost electric connection between us. Inches away from him when he's practically naked feels way too close.

"I couldn't agree more," he says with that lopsided smirk that makes my stomach somersault.

He looks down to his obvious erection, not even trying to hide it. "I think I've, uh, got it from here." *Oh God.*

I move to let the blood circulate through my veins and the breath fill my lungs again the moment I break our gaze and hand him a clean towel.

"Okay, well, you can pat dry…I'll be back in a little while to work on those dressings—"

"Vi, you said it's not too busy here tonight?" Rowan asks.

"That's right, but you're not supposed to say that out loud. You'll jinx me." I answer honestly, moving to the bio bin and pulling off my gown, feeling the need to wrap this up and get the hell out of this room.

"I could, uh, really use a distraction from the fact that I'm lying here. I feel like I might go fucking postal," he adds, his eyes pleading. "Two handed Euchre?" he challenges, one eyebrow raised.

I start to answer, to say no, but he stops me before I can speak.

"Please? All I can think about is why I got out and...he didn't," he adds.

My chest fills with grief, and I let out a breath. If a sponge bath didn't break me, a game of cards isn't enough to make me want him again, right?

I nod in agreement, because I've also been asking myself the same damn question since the moment he was wheeled in here.

CHAPTER 22

ROWAN

"We don't exactly keep playing cards around here," is the only answer she offers me. It's so quiet it's almost a whisper.

I take a deep breath and do my best to will my raging hard on to go away after the sponge bath to end all sponge baths.

I nod to the window ledge without thinking, just grateful she didn't say no. "My crew brought me some," I say without thought, before I remember that there's a goddamn titty magazine in that basket.

Before I can protest, Violette starts to move toward it.

"Fuck, actually can you just pass it to me? These guys are a bunch of fucking d-bags," I say, my voice almost frantic. So frantic it piques her curiosity enough that she raises an eyebrow when she gets to it and sees the bottle of Liquid Silk and a rolled up magazine secured with an elastic.

She smirks as she grabs the latest edition of *Wicked Magazine* out of the basket and pulls the elastic off. I'm not sure whether I'm mortified or turned on as she starts flipping through it with interest...slowly, like she's studying the fucking thing. She gets to the centerfold and completely opens it up. I haven't even looked at it, but from here I can see the woman who's earned the coveted spot spread eagle, two fingers on her clit. *Fucking Christ*, that's it. I blew it. Violette is gonna think I'm just a fucking pervert.

She doesn't look at me like I'm a pervert though, or tell me what a jackass I am. Instead, she starts laughing. Really laughing.

"Wow, I admire the old school vibes here but, um…you realize your door is always open here, right?" she asks in a giggle. "At least try to keep your porn in your phone like a normal person, King."

I realize she's busting my balls here, but I still might fucking kill the guys anyway.

"Fucking pricks…" I mutter.

"Uh-huh," she jokes. "Whatever gets you through the day." Violette shakes her head and rolls the magazine back up, then starts digging though the basket in search of either more ammo or snacks, I can't tell which.

"Have you had any practice at Euchre since the days when I destroyed you?" she asks with a cocky little tone, reminiscent of another time that almost has me bricking up again on the spot. "Every single time we played?" she adds.

I like playful Vi. Fuck, I've really missed her.

"*Every* time is a bit exaggerated. And to answer your question, no. When you're naturally good at something, you don't really need to practice," I answer.

She scoffs at me. She did beat me and Jacob almost every single time.

"Hmm. My dad and I still play all the time online and now that I'm home, every Sunday," she says, as if to warn me of my impending demise. "I beat him too."

I chuckle.

"But I can't play cards with you while I'm working," she says, pulling out the deck of cards.

Oh.

"However"—she fishes out two bags of mini chocolate chip cookies—"on my break, I can offer you thirty minutes to remind you why you *shouldn't* play me."

Violette makes her way over to me, tossing the cookies on the tray beside my bed along with the cards. "Practice up while I'm gone." She turns and heads for the door. "You can find the rules at www.play-euchre.com, in case you forget them." She grins over her shoulder as she ducks behind the door.

"Just get your ass back here and get ready to lose," I call to her, with the world's goofiest grin on my face.

"Never lost yet, don't know why I would now, especially when you're weak, injured, and high." Her voice echoes down the hall in response, and I extend my good arm up, resting it behind my head as I lean back in my bed. I count the minutes until she gets back, pain, guilt and self-blame aside, this night is looking up, all because Violette is here with me and she's smiling.

"I'm sorry to beat you yet again and bring up all those bad memories of losing to me," Violette says, not looking the least bit sorry as she pops the last mini cookie between her plush lips and lays her card down on the tray between us.

We just finished our second game of Euchre. Somehow, even though I was in the lead five minutes ago, she just earned her final two points by picking up a fucking nine of clubs and making that trump with no bower in her hand. All she had in her hand was the king, a nine, a ten, and an Ace of Spades but she took every trick and just made me look like a chump. She giggles and swipes the cards up into her graceful hands and starts shuffling.

"How dare you come in here and have no mercy on me when I'm weak, injured, and high," I grovel.

"I see. I hurt your feelings too much?" she asks with her eyebrow raised and the prettiest fucking smile, the one where she's a little nervous and her bottom lip meets her teeth.

"Fuck yes, forgot you play dirty and make it on anything you turn up," I add to her.

Her mouth falls open in a gasp. "I do not play dirty. Rule number one, you *never* turn down." She tosses her braid over her shoulder, and I notice her toned arms and the silky waves of her hair as she does. "My dad taught me that, and he *always* won until I beat him," she says matter-of-factly.

She's right, no one else beat Jack Taylor at Euchre. He's won tournaments for Chrissake.

"Admit it." She stands checking the time on her phone. "Admit I've still got it and that you're not worthy." She giggles. I know it's been thirty minutes, probably longer, and she has to go back to work. I just don't want her to. I could sit across from her all night.

"I plead the fifth," I say, which earns me another genuine laugh.

"You need to get some sleep, and I have to go back to work."

"Violette?"

"Yeah?"

"Thanks. I don't sit still very well. It gives me too much time to think. Aside from physical therapy, I haven't done much. Mostly sit in this fucking bed with my demons…so, thank you for this. There are days when what happened to Jacob feels…too heavy, like it might crush me," I say honestly to her. I don't want to get into some intense conversation, but I do want her to know I appreciate it.

She nods, pursing her full lips. "I understand all too well what the weight of losing Jacob feels like. There are days it's still crippling, especially since I've been back."

"I can imagine," I offer, surprised she said something so personal. I don't even have time to register that moment before the walls go back up.

"Get some sleep," she tells me before she heads into the hall.

I lean back in my bed and let myself just remember her for the first time in a long time. I can almost still smell her beside me as I close my eyes. I think of the look in her eyes right before I kissed her all those years ago, the way her skin felt under my hands, and the sounds she made when I made her come for the first time. My cock remembers too, beginning to stiffen, and in this hospital gown there's no hiding it.

I know it's wrong to remember her like this when she's right down the hall, but I do. I catalogue everything she said to me in the last few days, grinning to myself when I think of the way her face looked as she pulled that magazine out of the basket.

Joke's on her if she thinks I'd even consider looking at that when I can still hear the way she moaned my name, or the sounds she made as my lips grazed her neck. I instinctively reach for my stiffening cock, Violette's face in my mind only makes me harder. *Fuck.* I will not jerk myself off in a hospital bed while the object of my quickly growing obsession is down the hall.

I force myself to think of every unsexy thing I can— unloading the dishwasher, filling my tank with gas, the way Opp's yellows smell. After a few minutes, I feel my hard-on subsiding.

Fucking Christ. Ten years of trying to forget how I let her go was just decimated by that stunning smile and a couple games of cards.

It's just because I'm desensitized to her after not seeing her for so many years, that's all it is. After a few more days, it will get easier…right?

Wrong. My obsession just gets even worse when, for the next two nights, Violette comes to my room on her breaks, always checking on me first, asking me questions like how my dressings feel, or how my pain is, but every time I somehow manage to keep her, and we talk more. About Hollie, her parents, my work, even a little more about Jacob. On her last night, when I know she'll be off for a few days, she tells me she's officially divorced as of today.

"The odd thing is, I don't even think I'm sad. How messed up is that?" she asks, popping her last bite of salad from the cafeteria into her mouth. "I almost feel relieved."

She's wearing baby pink scrubs today and the color just makes her look like a real life version of hot Nurse Barbie.

"I don't think it's fucked. If you aren't with the right person, if it's a struggle, then I would imagine there would be relief. You should never have to pretend." I offer.

"You seem like you're speaking from experience," Violette says, taking a sip of her sparkling water.

I laugh and scrub my face with my hand. "Fuck, I have no experience."

"None?"

"Well…" I feel my throat heat as I try to answer…fuck, am I blushing? "I have *experience*, I just…no one's ever, I've never— fuck, I don't think I've ever liked anyone enough to make it past a few weeks—"

Violette's laughing cuts me off, but it's more of a snorting kind of laughter.

"I was just fucking with you, Kingsley, I don't need the gritty details of your sexcapades," she says as she stands and throws her container in the garbage in the corner of my room.

Excellent, now she thinks I'm a manwhore. *Smooth.*

"Gotta get some work done, see you in a bit," she says before I can defend myself or say anything even remotely witty.

I fish my phone out and check the time. Only two hours left until she heads out for a couple days, and I'd be lying if I said I wasn't gonna miss her.

I pull up my contacts and take matters into my own hands, planning ahead. Because even though she won't physically be here, I'm not about to let that stop me. Not when she's finally starting to come out of her shell and I'm finally starting to see a glimpse of the old us.

CHAPTER 23

Violette

UNKNOWN

> My new nurse doesn't like to play cards, in
> fact she looks downright angry.

> I'm a little afraid for my safety.

> Maybe it's the drugs they've got me on.

> They're making me paranoid. Fuck. Maybe
> that's the point?

I roll over and rest my phone on my bedside table with a smile as
I shove my face back into my pillow knowing my early morning
unknown messages are from Rowan.

I should be keeping my distance from him but I just can't. I
grab my phone and start to text.

> Who is this?

UNKNOWN

> Your patient. Frankly I'm heartbroken you'd
> forget me that quickly.

> Hospital records are private. You shouldn't
> have my number.

> This is stalkerish behavior.

UNKNOWN

> She's coming back, I can hear her footsteps. If this is the last time we talk remember the only reason you beat me was because you play dirty.

I laugh in the dark of my bedroom. I know Tilly is his nurse tonight. She's a veteran nurse of almost sixty. She is gruff and handsy. Imagining her shooting down Rowan as he tries to win her over actually gives me pleasure.

> Just do what she says, don't make any sudden movements and you'll get out alive. I'll be back on Wednesday.

I open my group chat with my parents right away.

> Did you give King my phone number?

MOM

> Not me.

DAD

> I did, he said it was important, something about his care at the hospital.

I roll my eyes.

This is my second day off. From what I hear, Rowan may be checking out in a few days. Which means my time with him in the hospital will be over and as much as I originally tried not to let him get back under my skin, I think he might be starting to, and I really don't know what to do with that. Every night we talked a little more, went a little deeper. During my last night shift, I spent way too much time with him, granted he was only one of two patients I had to care for. I spent most of it eating the remaining snacks out of his basket and playing

Euchre. Where I beat him three games to none. When he suggested Euchre just wasn't his game and that's why he was losing, we switched to Gin, where I once again beat him. Twice.

It was comfortable. Too comfortable.

Much like it was too comfortable and enticing having his warm skin under my fingers as I was bathing him, but I know I can't ever let *that* happen again. Being turned on during patient care is a big no.

I roll over and quickly add him to my contacts because as much as I hate to admit it, I actually missed him yesterday. Fuck. *I am in total control,* I try to convince myself then blow out a breath.

I hear Hollie stir over the monitor. She's finally sleeping on her regular schedule now, which means I have exactly thirty minutes before she's up and bursting with three-year-old energy.

And before my coffee is even finished brewing, she's asking for cereal and *SuperPets*.

ROWAN
I want a rematch

www.euchre-tips.com

ROWAN
Savage.

I smile and set my phone down on the table, it buzzes seconds later.

DAD
Are you and Hols coming for lunch?

I look down at my side where Hollie is cuddled in happily munching dry Cheerios on the couch with me, and I feel the need to just stay close to home today and be with her. Troy is coming to take her for dinner tomorrow night. It will be the first time he's seen her in three weeks. I kiss the top of Hollie's sweet smelling head and decide to ask her.

"Do you want to go to Nani and Papa's for lunch?"

"Can I play with Bishop and Bentley?" she asks about my parents' two Yorkies.

"Of course."

"Then, yes," she answers immediately.

> Yes we'll be there.

DAD
> In case I haven't mentioned it enough, it's good to have you home kid.

> It's good to be home.

And for the first time since I've arrived, I actually feel like Hols and I are right where we're supposed to be.

"So, how is he?" my mom asks as she fries up grilled cheese. I watch Hollie through the kitchen window in the yard with my dad and their Yorkies playing fetch.

"Who?"

She turns to face me as I sip my iced tea.

"Your star patient who needed your phone number for medical reasons." She grins.

I sigh. "I think I'm just coming to the conclusion that it's just time to let past conflicts go, there's no reason we can't be civil or friendly even," I tell her.

"I think he's got a lot more hidden beneath that cool surface than you realize," my mother says, flipping the two sandwiches in her pan.

"Of course you do." I laugh as I drain my glass.

"What's that supposed to mean?" she asks, sounding hurt.

"Nothing, you just always defend him."

She turns to face me. "I don't always defend him." She points her spatula at me. "You know, since Jacob passed he comes here every time your dad needs something. Helped rebuild the shed. They clean the garage out, and do an annual dump run with all the dead limbs and brush from the property. Helps him open and close the swimming pool. Never forgets a birthday, or Christmas. He has his own parents but he's the son we lost, Violette. I know something happened between the two of you that you refuse to talk about. And I know there's a part of you that never recovered from that, but take my advice sweetheart, life is too short. If he's trying to make up for past mistakes, maybe try letting him."

As she finishes her little speech, a message pops up on my phone.

ROWAN

> My day nurse just helped me into the fancy hydro bath and I think she tried to sneak a peek. 😶

I laugh, and I hear my mom mutter, "Mm-hmm."

> Bonnie's seen it all.

And will fuck with him on purpose.

ROWAN

> Should I be offended or happy that she said it takes a lot to impress her? Am I impressive or not? I might not sleep without the answers to these questions.

I laugh out loud as my mother plates our lunch.

"Guess you don't need my advice, judging by the look you're wearing. But take my word for it, Vivi. He's a good one, give him another chance. He might surprise you."

I look down at the GIF Rowan has just sent me of Homer Simpson backing into a hedge.

I blow out a breath with my smile.

"So everyone keeps telling me."

By the end of the day, Hollie and I have visited with my parents and played for over two hours at the local park—which is Hollie's favorite thing in the world to do. I've caught up on all the laundry and tidied the house. It's been a full day with my baby, and normally I'd be ready to get her bath done and sink into my sofa with a movie, but today I've just been distracted.

Distracted waiting for the texts from Rowan that really haven't stopped since I opened my eyes. Most recently, a selfie of him at lunch when he wooed Betty, the grandmotherly lunch porter, to give him an extra plate of roast beef and potatoes. An update that Bonnie was nicer than Tilly, but she still wouldn't play cards with him. And finally by suppertime, an invitation to download an app so I could play online Euchre and various games against him.

Which brings me to where I am now; cuddled up on my couch while Hols and I catch what feels like our twentieth episode of *SuperPets*, as I beat the pants off him at cup pong while sending funny GIFs back and forth every time I do.

ROWAN

I'm really very good you know. I'm just letting you win so you'll keep talking to me.

Oh yeah?

ROWAN
Yeah.

I don't buy it, you're too competitive for that.
I'm just better, face it.

ROWAN
Wanna bet?

Depends.

ROWAN
On what?

The stakes of course

ROWAN
I win, you go out with me.

I don't date hotshots

ROWAN
I'm not a hotshot right now.

I don't date my patients.

ROWAN
Well, that's easy, I won't be your patient after
tomorrow either.

I sit up a little straighter.

They gave you the go ahead for release?

ROWAN
Yep.

As happy as I am, I fight the feeling of my heart sinking just a little.

ROWAN

Now, call it what you want, a simple hang out, date, coffee, whatever... but if I win, you agree to see me.

And before you get any smart ass ideas, I mean after I go home tomorrow.

And if I win?

ROWAN

What do you want, Vi?

I think for a second because I honestly have no idea what I want. The only thing I know is that I don't want to give him up just yet.

For our date to NOT be at Shifty's.

I wait as I see three little dots pop up, then disappear, then pop up again.

ROWAN

Holy fuck I can't believe you agreed. Deal.

You still have to win, you know that right?

ROWAN

Yep. I pick the game.

Agreed.

I wait a few minutes, trying to picture his face as he thinks really hard about what he could possibly beat me in.

I laugh out loud when a request to join him in a game of Wordbubbles comes through. It's a game where you have to spell words with your available letters over different colored bubbles that give you points based on their color. First to 250 wins.

> Seriously? Word games are my jam. I'm going to wipe the floor with you.

ROWAN

> I guess we'll see. 😉

The first word comes through from him. *GLOWING.*

I quickly scan my letters and spell the only word I can. HOLD.

A few seconds goes by, and his second word pops up. *PAST.*

I add my next word. FIRST.

I'm sure I look like an idiot sitting here staring at my phone when his next word comes through. *STRONG.*

I smile, slapping a word in, when more letters generate. SAFE.

He retaliates a few seconds later with: *LOVING.*

I feel the blush creep up my neck. I shift a little in my seat.

I check my board, and grin, firing back with: HOT.

I wait with bated breath.

EYES.

I feel heat creep up my throat as his next words continue to filter through.

I'm convinced that he's definitely got to be cheating somehow. *BEAUTY.*

I send back a real banger. BLUE, but it's a double point word.

When the next word comes through, I feel that last little thread of control I was holding onto begin to slip right through my fingers.

GRACE.

I shamelessly smile down at my phone like a lovesick teen and send him back: HANDS

I wait what feels like minutes for him to enter his next word, I'm just about to text him to see if he fell asleep when it pops up.

PERFECTION

ROWAN

That's game. I win.

Sure enough I look down and see that he's hit 250 points already.

I openly giggle, as I bite my bottom lip. What am I letting this man do to me?

I. Don't. Date. Hotshots.

"Mommy, why do you have a big smile like this?" Hols asks, smiling wide and looking up at me.

"I'm just happy, babe." I giggle as I bend down to kiss her head.

ROWAN

Also that was the hottest game of Wordbubbles I've ever played.

No idea what you mean.

ROWAN

You know exactly what I mean Vi.

I decide to just give in for tonight, not caring how much we text back and forth, not overthinking. I know if he changes his mind it's going to sting, but for tonight, I don't care, it just feels good to have him.

As I tuck Hollie in and our messages continue, I keep laughing and smiling until the early hours of the morning. So much so that when I wake up with my phone in my hand the next day, my cheeks hurt.

CHAPTER 24

ROWAN

"Any particular reason why you're looking like the fucking cat that ate the canary?" Sup asks, coming into my room just before breakfast.

I shrug. "Just finished a good physical therapy sesh and so fucking ready to go *home*."

I set my phone down from talking to Violette, she's just getting ready to head in for her shift and we've been talking since she woke up. We talked until she fell asleep last night too. At this point, the only thing I want to do is talk to her and I will stop at literally nothing to keep her talking. Even spending upwards of a hundred bucks for extra letters on Wordbubbles just so I could send her all the very particular words I wanted to in our game.

"You got a hot date when you get outta here or something?"

"Hopefully." I grin, giving Sup my full attention. "Fuck, Sup, you're *too* fucking clean," I say as he strides across my room and takes a seat.

"A day off will do that to a man. I think by my third shower I was actually down to my honest skin tone." He grins holding up an arm.

He fills me in on the things I missed on their last short roll and what the guys got done at base yesterday when they got back —all while I've been stuck in here. My breakfast comes, and I stand and walk to the server to take it off her hands. Sup texts with someone while I sit down on the edge of my bed and start to shovel it in. They don't feed me enough in here, and I'm desperate to get home so I can start eating right and working out again.

"You're looking good. You feeling good?" Sup asks as I set my fork down on my plate and place it on the table beside my bed.

"It doesn't really hurt much anymore, keeping a lot of it covered mostly, but just out of precaution so I don't irritate it. Aside from a few spots, it feels pretty good. My skin is healing up better than the doctor expected and she says the scars will be minimal."

Sup nods, his expression is pensive and concerned.

"I'm just ready to get back out in the field," I say, looking down at my arm and my thigh.

"It's been nine days. You need a little longer, bud," he notes. "You get heat anywhere near that right now and they'll be able to hear you howling in Oregon."

I nod. "Yea, I know."

"Listen, I'm here to tell you we're heading to Wyoming tonight to help out on a beast. Black Mountain Fire. Been burning out of control. It's taken 4000 acres in two days."

"Fuck," I breathe out.

"Yeah, just wanted you to hear it from me."

I set my jaw. It physically pains me to not be with my squad. "I wish I could come with."

"Soon enough, just heal."

I nod again.

"Something else." Sup looks at me, and I know that look, one that says he's about to have a heart to heart with me. "Your body is healing, but how are *you?*" He taps his temple with his first finger.

I shrug. "I'm okay."

"Yeah?"

I sigh. He knows me too well to bullshit him. "Sometimes, when I'm falling asleep, I'm right back in those woods, falling into that hole. I can feel the heat." I think for a beat. "But that's not what scares me awake."

Sup folds his arms over his chest, listening intently. It's what he's good at.

"It's the thought that I was in there for five seconds. *Five.* Jacob was in there so much longer, and I think about that. I think about your dad. It's just that...now, I can almost imagine what they went through in those last moments. If I had been stuck in there just a little longer—"

Sup nods and sets his jaw. "But you weren't. You're here. There's a reason for that."

"I have no fucking clue why," I say honestly. "Why did I survive and they didn't?" I blurt out.

Sup shrugs. "Who knows? But you did. You got a chance to go on. They didn't." Sup gives me his all-knowing look. "Kinda pressures you to make sure you aren't leaving anything off the table with people you care about, yeah?"

My gaze meets his and I wonder if he can tell I'm starting to have some pretty strong feelings, maybe feelings that never went away for Violette.

"Y'understand?" he asks.

I blow out a breath and nod. There's something so easy about Sup. He's like the older brother I never had.

"I hear you," I say to him.

"Good."

"Knock, knock,"

I hear Violette's voice. She's leaning in the doorway and when I turn to face her something in me just settles. It's only been two days since I saw her last but somehow, she looks even more beautiful. She's wearing black scrubs that hug her everywhere they should, and her hair is in a long braid that hangs down her back. I wonder briefly if she heard any of that conversation.

"Morning, Violette," Sup says to her with an easy grin.

"Your patient here is trying to get me to bust him out and take him with me to Wyoming."

She smiles, but there's something not quite right about it. "Is he now?"

"Fucking right," I answer. "Can't wait to get back out there."

Violette's eyes meet mine and I see something there I haven't seen yet—hesitation. And worry. Like the idea of me fighting fires worries her.

"You need...more time to heal," Violette says, averting her eyes.

Holy fuck, she's definitely worried...about me.

My eyes meet Sup's across the room. He gives me the two finger point from his eyes to mine, when Violette isn't looking, just to let me know he's most definitely on to me.

I don't care, I just keep smiling, because now I *know*. Whether Violette wants to admit it or not, she still cares about me...and *that* I can work with.

"Violette has shown you how to change your dressings?"

"Yep," I answer the doctor later that day. I've barely seen Violette since this morning and she hasn't really answered my texts either. There was a car crash on HWY 21, so new patients have been brought up who are more critical than I am.

"Okay, and you're going to want to change them just as

many times as they're changed here." She inspects the wounds that no longer have dressings on them. "These are looking good, leave them open to air," she tells me as I pull my sleeve down.

"Loose fitting shorts are best for a few days and cool baths."

I nod, I've got it all. I've read through the pamphlet Violette left me about leaving the hospital ten times already, and I'm already looking up foods and natural remedies I can take to help with healing.

"Alright, well, you're set to check out, give me a few minutes and I'll be back with your release papers."

I nod and shake her hand. "Thanks, doc."

No sooner is she gone than I hear the voice I've been waiting for all day.

"She springing you?"

I turn to face Violette. "Yep, looks like it."

"Well, I just wanted to check in on you before you left. You've got a ride?"

"Yea, my mom and dad are coming anytime."

She hesitates and a few seconds of awkward silence takes over.

"Okay, well, I gotta get back." She turns to leave, then stops herself. I can't place what exactly, but something in her has changed since this morning. "It's been nice talking again, King," she says.

"I agree," I say quickly.

"But…"

Oh shit.

"I have so much on my plate—Hollie, adjusting to this move, the date you asked me on—"

"*Won*," I remind her.

"Right." She smiles ruefully. "Well, I just think it's best if we just keep a little distance. You're going to be back out in the field soon enough."

"Vi—"

"Look, it's just that the last time we got close, it didn't end well. I'm past what happened with us. I'll admit, I didn't particularly like you when I came home, I was holding a bit of a grudge, but it's not like that now. I know you're a good guy, I just don't think I can trust you. That's the truth and it's all I have to give you right now, no matter what this is starting to feel like," she adds, gesturing between.

I analyze her expression. I'm calling bullshit because the way she's looking at me is very *un*-past it.

"Violette, you're lying to yourself," I say, desperate to stop her from doing this, just when I feel like we're getting to know each other again. "How I felt about you back then—"

"King, you don't have to. I said I'm past it," Violette interrupts.

"No," I say firmly. I know what this is, she wants to pretend there isn't some serious chemistry happening here. She wants to deny she has feelings for me, but I'm not about to let that happen. I'm too eager for her to admit the truth. I rub my temples, taking a second. I silently beg for forgiveness from Jacob, then take a deep breath. "Vi, I was falling for you. Like, *really* falling for you. When I left you after the beach that night and went to pick up Jacob, I walked into...a total fucking shit show." I move closer to her, until I'm right in front of her. "He needed my help."

She doesn't move, she just stands frozen, listening.

"Why?" she asks skeptically, with a look on her face that tells me she's going through her own memories of that night.

"Your chauffeur is here," my mother singsongs happily as she knocks on the door frame.

I flinch and Violette instantly backs up.

"Am I interrupting something?" she asks instantly, sensing something's up. *Fucking Christ.* I scrub my face with my hand. My mother has the worst timing known to man.

"No, I was just giving King instructions on his home care,"

Violette says, clearing her throat as my mother moves in to get a hug from her.

"Thank you for taking such good care of him, honey."

Violette smiles—a forced smile.

"You're welcome. He'll be just fine if he follows the doctor's orders." Violette's eyes move back to mine.

"I'll get you a few more supplies to take home," she says to me, and turns to leave.

My mother puts her hands on her hips, and I know I'm in for it.

"What, ma?" I ask.

"I told you that you need to straighten things out with her, but *not* in the middle of her workday, Ro."

Fair enough.

"Look, I've seen the way you look at her. If you've felt the same way about a girl for *this* long, it's worth fighting for. But you're lucky I came in when I did. Take your time, tell her how you feel, but not when she's at work."

I breathe out a sigh; she's right.

"I just have no clue how to make her trust me again, she was about to try to disappear, and I panicked."

"That takes time, but lucky for you, you both have lots of that. Now, say thank you to her and wait until the poor girl is done with her shift before you try to woo her." She moves toward me and smiles, patting her palm on my face. "And make it snappy, your dad is double parked," she says just as Violette comes back into the room.

"You know, I think I'll go thank the doctor quickly before we leave, I saw her at the desk." My mother winks as she walks out of the room.

Violette begins packing extra gauze, and ointment, and pulls a prescription from her pocket that the doctor left, handing it to me. She shrugs and it feels awkward as hell between us.

"I gotta go, my shift was over ten minutes ago and I have to

156

get Hollie ready. Troy will be at my place in an hour," she says, half to herself, flustered.

"Vi. I know you have to go but I just want to say this." I reach out and grab her wrist, gently turning her to face me. "You can be afraid of whatever was between us, and whatever still is between us…"

She looks so fucking beautiful and vulnerable that I fight with every fiber of my being not to tell her everything right here and now. Not only is my mother right, but I also need time to think about how I can get Vi to give me another chance without telling her things about her brother that will be too hard for her to hear. All she has left are her memories of Jacob.

"I know I'm asking for a lot, but the ball is in your court." I slide my hand down and take her pinky finger between my finger and thumb, tugging her closer. I can't help it, I tip my forehead to hers and breathe her in, just for a second.

"I just want you to let me back in, Vi. Give me a chance to explain," I whisper.

Her breath is warm, and she smells sugary and sweet. The feeling of any part of her near me is overwhelming and goes straight to my cock. I wish I could control it but it's unstoppable.

"Rowan…" she whispers, and, fuck, my name on her lips in any capacity for the first time in years, sends more shockwaves down to my already hardening cock.

I'm so goddamn desperate to kiss her. It takes a sort of superhuman strength not to. I swallow down the urge because I know I *have* to let her come to me.

"I need to go," she says, her voice shaky as her pinkie slips away and she backs up.

I nod.

She says nothing else as she turns on her heel and leaves the room with a last glance over her shoulder. I flex my fists the second I'm alone. I'm ready to hit something. I want with everything in me to go after her. I want to haul her back in here and press her up against the wall and kiss her until both of us are breathless, but I don't.

I let her go, because I should've told her the truth a long time ago and even though her being home now offers me the shot I never thought I'd get, that doesn't mean I deserve it.

I pull my phone out and open our chat. I know she's alone for part of the night tonight while Hollie is with Troy. The ball is in her court but that doesn't mean I won't make it easier for her to come to me.

I type out only my address, then I take a deep breath and send it to her.

CHAPTER 25

Violette

I don't even know how I managed to get home, pack a bag for Hollie, and get her ready. The address Rowan sent me stares back at me from my phone screen.

Avondale Road. Only a few blocks away. We walk down his street almost every day on our way to the park. My mind is full of his words from this afternoon.

He was falling for me...he walked into something with Jacob?

I want to believe him, and more than anything I think I want to know what happened because that time in my life has always felt unresolved. I also want to follow Teddy's advice and trust that people can change. I want to believe he didn't use me to begin with.

As I pop Hollie up on the counter in the bathroom and wash her face with warm water, I think back to that night on the beach and then the next day when Jacob was acting strange when he finally got home. He didn't talk, I barely saw him over the next couple weeks until school ended, but after those weeks he seemed okay.

"Will there be French fries?" Hollie asks me, cutting into my thoughts as I lift her off the bathroom counter.

I smile. "I'm sure there will be, and chicken nuggets too, I bet." I kiss her on the tip of her nose and she giggles.

"And I will come home to bed?"

"Yes, baby," I tell her. "After dinner and the Adventure Playland."

"But Daddy will go home, and we stay here?"

My chest aches with the idea of trying to explain the finality of divorce to a three-and-a-half-year-old.

"Yes, because Daddy has to work at the hospital, remember?" I tell her, just trying to keep it simple.

Hollie nods, her little brow furrows. "Can I bring Power Piggy?"

I smile at the only person in this world I would happily die for.

"Of course you can."

Just as I'm finishing up her pigtails the doorbell rings. I look at Hollie in the mirror over her shoulder and make a surprised face. "Who do you think that is?" I ask her, hoping she'll get excited. She snuggles into me instead. She's always been attached to me and a little more cautious with Troy but that's because we've been inseparable—aside from the times I'm at work—since the day she was born. I'm her constant, her safe space, and she knows it.

"Let's go see," I whisper to her, picking her up and propping her on my hip as I make my way to the front door.

When I pull it open Troy is on the phone. He nods at us but he doesn't hang up.

He laughs at something the person on the other end says, and Hollie sinks into me further.

I must give him the death stare, because he says, "I gotta go," and hangs up, then reaches out to Hollie expecting her to come to him. She doesn't.

"Hi, angel, are you gonna come see Daddy?" he asks, rubbing the top of her head.

Hollie looks up at me.

"It's okay," I tell her. I set her down. "Why don't you go get Piggy's special cape for dinner with Daddy, okay?" I ask her

She nods. "Is there gonna be French fries?" she asks Troy.

He gets down on his knees in front of her, and I'm happy to see he's giving her his utmost attention for the moment. I know somewhere in there, he's gotta be capable of being a good dad.

"I'll tell you what, I'll make sure there is, okay?"

She smiles finally and nods at him. "Okay." And then she runs down the hallway to her room.

"What's the matter with Hols?" Troy asks me when she's out of earshot, like I've done something to her.

I turn to face him with the fire of a thousand suns.

"There's nothing *wrong* with her, she hasn't seen you in over three weeks. That's a long time for her."

"I had to work." He shrugs.

"Troy, I don't need any excuses; I just need you to be patient with her. You've only got four hours with her. Make it count, she has to feel comfortable," I say as Hollie comes running back into the room.

"Of course she's comfortable. She's my daughter," he whispers before moving toward the living room to help Hollie finish packing her bag.

As I kiss her goodbye after tucking her into her car seat in the back of Troy's SUV, I make a plan for the night. I have four hours. I assume it will go by fast but in the end it only takes me thirty minutes to prep things for tomorrow and clean up the house.

I could change into my pajamas and settle in with a rom-com.

But I don't.

Instead, I find myself pulling out my phone in search of

Rowan's text. I toss on my sandals without a second thought and walk out the front door to head to the place the logical side of my brain tells me not to go, knowing once I have an explanation, I just might never get my heart back.

CHAPTER 26
ROWAN

I open the windows of my small ranch style house that sits dead center on Avondale Road to let the early summer breeze through the screens. My house is on a quiet suburban street in an older, historic neighborhood in Sky Ridge. These homes have been redone recently and a lot of families have moved in, mixed with older retired couples. I bought this place when I was twenty-five, and it suits me just fine. I've done some renovations to it over the last few years during the off seasons. Refinishing the kitchen cabinets, upgrading the counter tops, painting the entire place, and refinishing the wood floors. It's home. It's a place I like to be, except today it seems excessively quiet.

I turn on a vintage vinyl as the sun starts to sink a little lower behind the mountains in the distance. *John Prine Live* fills my house as I move to my liquor cabinet and pop the cork on a bottle of whiskey. I pour myself a shot, swallowing down two ibuprofens with it. It's the strongest thing I'm taking now, and I'm hoping the shot of whiskey will help me numb the edge a little bit.

I check my phone for any kind of notification that Violette

got my message but there is none. My message just sits delivered and practically serves to drive me crazy.

I've done everything I can, I've gone for a little walk around my neighborhood, got some mild stretching in, changed the dressings on the part of my thigh that still needs them, had the longest semi-warm shower that I could. And now I'm officially going out of my fucking head, whiskey in hand, pacing around my living room wondering if she'll answer.

Fifteen minutes later, I'm ready to get in my truck and go for a drive, just to clear my head. But when I open the front door, I suck in a breath because standing on my porch, arm raised and ready to knock is Violette. Faded blue jeans, black T-shirt that fits her perfectly, her hair is loose and swirling around her face in the summer breeze.

"Are you going somewhere? I can come back..." she says, lowering her arm and clutching the purse over her shoulder.

I grin and lean against the doorframe, looking up to meet her gaze and be as honest with her as I can, "I think I was coming to find you, Vi."

Her mouth pops open before she quickly closes it and the air between us thickens, both of us just stare at each other for a beat, our breaths heavy, knowing what this is. She's here because she couldn't stop thinking about me either. Images of taking her in my arms and kissing her run through my mind as the silence hangs between us, but of course, because it's Violette and I don't know what to expect with her ever, an almost annoyed look takes over her face, breaking my passionate daydreams.

"I'm just here to get some things straight with you," she says, inviting herself right in bringing the sugary scent of her hair with her. She takes in the space around her as she enters my living room. Everything in my home is simple and rustic. The walls are a deep gray, the furniture is a worn in natural leather, and the coffee tables are custom pieces I made myself with walnut tops. I follow her in and close the door, turning down my vinyl so we can talk.

"I didn't come here because I can't get you out of my head if that's what you think," she says, turning to face me.

"Whatever the reason, I'm glad you came," I tell her as I gesture to the sofa. She sets her purse down on the coffee table, but she doesn't take a seat. Instead, she puts her hands on her hips, looking sort of emotional and so goddamn stunning.

"I just came here to find out *why* you ended things and then we're going to put it behind us once and for all, because that's what I need, and I may not have been very good at voicing what I needed when I was younger, but I am now."

I just stand transfixed with her, because seeing her confidence, and the woman she's become is so fucking sexy and she doesn't even know it.

I make my way past her to the bar hutch she is standing in front of. I can almost feel her eyes on me as I pour myself another shot of whiskey, then one for her. She takes it with a shaky hand and knocks the whole shot back with one swallow.

I follow suit before setting the glass down on my coffee table. She sets hers on the hutch beside the still open bottle and begins to pace my living room.

"You know, I'm pretty sure you left me with some kind of relationship handicap," she says in a firm voice, almost like she's trying to convince herself that she's ready to tell me her deepest secrets. "Which seems crazy for the small amount of time we were...whatever we were, but I cared about you for so long before that. I built you up. I just never thought *you* would use me or hurt me." She stops and turns to face me. "I've never really given anyone my whole heart since, I'm sure of that now, even with my husband I kept walls up. I was blindsided by you and subconsciously, I just never wanted to feel let down like that again," she says, her pretty hazel eyes focusing on mine as she stalks toward me.

I let her. I want her close, I want her frustration and emotion. The only way she'll forgive me is if she tells me how she feels.

"You were the first man to break my heart, a woman never forgets that."

"I always planned to tell you how I felt, but you ran," I toss back. If she wants to talk truth, she's going to have to face some of her own.

"I didn't run," her tone isn't convincing. She *knows* she ran.

I move closer to her because now she's firing me up.

"You did run. You just believed right away that I didn't care about you… that I used you. You went to school and you never really came back. And then Jacob died and none of it made any fucking sense anymore. You got married, Violette! What should I have done? Should I have come to Seattle and told you that you're the only woman I've ever really had a connection with? That I compare every fucking woman I've met since to *you*?"

Her chest is heaving "No! I just lived for a long time after wondering *why* I wasn't who you wanted."

I tower over her, and unable to help myself I reach forward and grip her hips, tugging her to me, knowing I'm crossing a line but there's nothing that could stop me now. I'm too far gone for her, and whether or not she's ready to hear that her brother wasn't really who she thought he was, it has to happen. I tip my forehead to hers and breathe her in, bracing myself to tell her everything.

Sorry, Jacob.

"Let me explain." I nod my head toward the sofa. "Sit."

CHAPTER 27

ROWAN

AGE 18

Max's house, the shit show.

"Don't you want to hear my proposition, King?" Kyleigh bats
her false eyelashes at me, smiling sweetly.

I flex my fists, looking from Jacob and Max back to Kyleigh.
I'm still standing on Max's front porch.

Jacob is in trouble, I can tell just by looking at him, and he's
definitely fucking high again. He promised me after last weekend, when I had to pick him up and drive him home from a bush
party, that he was gonna cut that shit out. He was all fucked up
on Molly and booze. Him and two guys from the team thought it
was smart to try to rope swing into the shallow river. He sliced
his leg up real bad, I still think he should've gotten stitches.

All this shit has just gotten out of control over our senior
year. It started with weed, we all smoked it once in a while at
parties when we started high school, it was harmless, but he's
taken it too far.

Especially since he's been hanging around Max. Now, it's not just weed, more often it's Molly or Percocet, I'm sure it's been coke a few times too. It's been changing him, and I'm worried about him.

"Please, just come in, I—fuck. Please, King," Jacob begs, still bouncing his knee.

I push past Kyleigh and enter Max's small living room. Their house has always been a little on the messy side, they don't have much. His mother works a factory job, mostly nights, and his stepdad works the night shift at the lumber yard. They've both been known to drink a lot, so Max is just turning into a chip off the old block.

The Sports Network is playing on the TV, and a floor lamp from sometime in the eighties is the only light in the room. I take in the smell of cigarettes and some sort of air freshener as I sit down on the dingy old sofa across from Jacob.

"The fuck did you do?" I ask him only, blocking out the rest of the room when my eyes meet his. I hate this, feeling like his big brother instead of his friend.

His short brown hair is messy and his eyes are bloodshot. He leans back on the sofa and blows out a breath.

"They're trying to get you here so you can agree to my terms. I knew you'd never come to see me if I called," Kyleigh quips, sitting down right beside me.

I move so her leg isn't touching mine. I made the mistake of touching her once. I won't do it again.

"If you do, I'll keep quiet about what they did." She looks at them. "I found them in the math wing at school trying to steal the answers to their final—caught them red-handed, actually." She holds her phone up. "Got it on video." *Jesus Jacob.* "Wanna hear the best part?"

I look at her and wait. She's enjoying this way too much and it's pissing me off.

"They broke in, well technically I guess they were *let* in.

They used your new *girlfriend's* student ID fob to get into the building." She holds it up. I snatch it from her hand.

"It's pretty convenient for them that she has access to the school after hours, giving the card to her brother so he could steal, though." She makes a tsking noise.

"Breaking and entering with intent to steal school—well, technically, government—property when you're eighteen. I'm pretty sure of the rules, since my dad's the deputy sheriff. I *think* the county would charge them both as adults." She blows out a breath "Not the best look for a future WSU rugby star on a scholarship," she says smugly. "Also, not a good look for your girl, King."

"She would never and the school would know that," I fire back. She shrugs.

"Maybe. Sure would suck for her either way. Not the best for her college career either."

I stand up. "What the fuck, Jacob? You implicated *Violette* in this bullshit? Fuck's sake!" My voice is loud, and he knows I'm fucking pissed. *How could he? Oh, right, because he was high, that's how.*

"Oh, and add onto that, they've definitely been drinking and they're high, and he drove them both there." She points to Max with a scoff.

Fucking idiots.

I turn to her. "This is funny to you? Just fucking stop, Kyleigh, and let me talk to them. *Alone.*"

Kyleigh smiles. "Sure thing, King, it's fine, I'm gonna text my dad. He's coming to pick me up anyway. I'll be right back, boys, talk amongst yourselves." She looks pointedly at Jacob. "When they're done telling you about their piss poor life choices"—she glances back up at me and smiles—"come find me, we can talk about what I want to keep this quiet. For him and his loser sister."

I grit my molars to stop myself from shooting a slew of cuss words at her as she ventures out of the house, and I watch her through the window as she takes a seat on an old lawn chair on the porch, pulling her phone out.

I turn back to Jacob and sit down across from him.

"Tell me she's full of shit, you two."

"She's not," Jacob says, running a hand through his hair.

I've never wanted to hit my best friend before now, but I have to physically restrain myself. Violette is a model student, to use her like this sends a rage through me that I can't explain. Even in his less than sober state, I can see that he did exactly what Kyleigh accused him of.

"I'm failing trig, man." He looks over at Max.

"We both are," Max adds. "I just thought that if we could get our hands on the final, we could both pass, and…fuck, this is my meal ticket. My old man will fucking kick my ass into next week if I don't get into Oregon State. He's been bragging about it to all his buddies in the yard. My parents can't afford shit—this is my only ride."

I rub my temples. "Maybe you should be taking your classes more seriously then, instead of getting fucking high all the time." Max looks just as scared as Jacob, but I don't owe shit to him. "And what's your excuse? Why didn't you come to me?"

Jacob puts his head in his hands. "All you do is look at me like a fucking disappointed dad, and I fucking hate it!"

I fold my arms over my chest and eye him up, as if to say, *if the shoe fits…*

"Look, I know I have to stop partying. I figured you'd just give me shit for failing, and at the time I didn't want to hear it. I thought I had it under control and I'm in the same boat as Max. If I fail, I'm fucked. They're barely letting me in as it is with my GPA. Fail my final? I won't graduate, King, I'll lose my scholarship."

I know enough to know that getting into WSU on a rugby scholarship means everything to Jacob.

"That doesn't give you the right to bring Vi into this," I tell him.

"I know." A lone tear falls onto his cheek. "I would never want to hurt her. I wasn't thinking…. She goes there at night to bring food every week, they'd never even second guess the scan in logs with her ID, and there are no cameras in that part of the school."

"You never thought about what would happen if you got caught? It would look like she *gave* her pass to you, like she helped you, she would be taken off the national honors society, she could be expelled." I add, pacing the room. "And it would fucking crush her."

"We're fucked regardless. Kyleigh was leaving cheer practice when she saw us. She took a video through the window of us using our phones as flashlights to rummage around, she thought you might be with us. I slipped up and told her how we got in. I thought it would be better than her thinking we broke in," Max says, pulling a pack of smokes out of his back pocket.

"She just said to call you, you were the only one she wanted something from."

I look out at Kyleigh through the dirty front window under the porch lights, she's on the phone talking to one of her friends and she's *laughing*. Of course, she would want me to be here. She's been looking for payback for two years. One night. One fucking drunken night we hooked up and she's never let me hear the end of it. No matter how many times I apologized, no matter how honest I was with her. She even started a rumor that she was pregnant, which Jacob helped me squash by getting close to Carmen and getting her to admit Kyleigh was lying. I already knew she was, but this is a small town, if that got back to my parents? I was only fucking sixteen.

"What's she want from me?" I ask, turning back to face Jacob.

"Fuck if I know," he says, reaching down to take a sip of an open beer on the table.

I shake my head. He just got caught in this heap of shit and he's drinking. I have no idea what's running through his mind these days.

"Chick's fuckin nuts," Max says, lighting his smoke. "Said you owed her a favor."

Like fuck.

"Stay here and stop fucking drinking," I tell Jacob.

I don't know what Kyleigh wants, but I'm gonna find out right now. I'm done playing her game.

CHAPTER 28

ROWAN

AGE 18

I push through the flimsy screen door, leaving Jacob and Max inside, joining Kyleigh on the porch. She turns as soon as she hears me and smiles up at me.

"Did the dipshits fill you in?" she snickers.

"Enough. What do you want, Kyleigh? I don't fucking owe you anything."

She scoffs. "You actually believe that, don't you?"

"It was one goddamn night. We were both drunk. I told you the next morning how sorry I was. I've never even drank like that since."

"You took my virginity, King."

I sit down and blow out a breath. I've felt like shit about that for two years. It's one of the reasons why I'm taking things so slow with Violette. I would never want to take that from a girl again without it meaning something.

"You didn't tell me you were a virgin, Kyleigh. I barely even remember that night, but what I do remember is that I told you I just cared about you as a friend, but you were adamant sex was a good idea. *You* lied, You said you didn't like me that way either, that it was a one-time thing, that we were friends with benefits."

"Yeah, well, I figured you would change your mind," she says quietly. "We could've been great together, King."

"Why would I change my mind? All you did after was cause drama. You called my friends, my job, Kyleigh. You took it too far. You told people you thought you were pregnant when you weren't."

She looks down and tucks a lock of her long blonde hair behind her ear, and I grit my molars to calm down. I need to refocus here.

"This ancient history doesn't matter. I was honest with you, if you had told me you were a virgin, or that you wanted more with me, even as drunk as I was, I never would've slept with you."

I look up at the rotting wood ceiling of Max's porch. "Look, I can't take back that night. So what does any of this have to do with me? Why am I here?" I ask.

"When we hooked up it humiliated me, everyone knew we slept together that night, and I guess I forgave you, sort of, for a while."

"Well, you dated someone else for six months, so yeah, I assumed you were over it." I retort.

"I had to act like I didn't care. But then you started bringing Violette Taylor everywhere, and I don't fucking get it, King. She's bland. She's a fucking science nerd and she's fat."

I've never in my life, wanted to hit a woman, but I *wish* I could just reach across the space and give her a smack for talking about Violette like that.

"I don't want to hear you talk about Violette," I say through gritted teeth. "I can't believe you're making some sort of fucked up jealousy a part of this. And you still haven't fucking told me what you want!" My voice booms as I spit my words at her. I'm losing my fucking patience—fast.

"You want to keep this our dirty little secret? You're *mine* now," she says, leaning forward in her chair. "You're making up for all the times you ignored me, after we were together. You're going to go to prom with *me*. You're going to show the whole school that in the end, you chose *me*. I'm going to tell everyone that you came groveling back to me." She folds her arms across her chest. "If you do, I'll keep my mouth shut and after you keep up your end of the bargain, the video is yours." She shrugs. "It's that simple, and no one will ever know how fucking stupid your lowlife friends are."

"Not a fucking chance in hell, Kyleigh."

She shrugs, unbothered, and stands.

"Then I give the video to my dad, and oh... here he comes," she says, nodding down the street where headlights shine toward us. She leans down and tries to tweak my chin. I push her hand away. "I'm finishing my senior year with a bang, King," she says smugly. "I won't be the girl you stepped over anymore."

I just look at her, trying to understand how someone could possibly be so manipulative and so fucking bold as to try to blackmail me into dating her. For no reason other than to hurt Violette and prove something to friends that will probably mean nothing to her by this time next year. How fucking shallow is this girl?

I watch her walk down the porch. Her father's eyes land on mine when he pulls in the driveway. I stand. She smiles at her dad as he cuts the engine. The thing she doesn't know is that all my friends told me to date her. But she just has no substance. I didn't connect with her, or any other girl, the way I did with Violette. Kyleigh isn't brilliant and cool, she doesn't listen to my kind of music or kick my ass at cards. *She's* the one who's bland.

"Hi, Daddy, you remember Rowan?" she asks as her father gets out of his truck. My name on her tongue is like poison.

Jacob and Max push open the screen door and bring with them the heady scent of weed. *Fucking Christ, I was gone for ten minutes.*

"Deputy Miller," I say, extending a hand to distract him from my two obviously high friends.

He takes my hand in his. "Rowan, hell of a game you played last week"

"Thank you, sir," I answer as he looks around, taking in the surroundings his daughter is being picked up from.

"Rowan came by while I was tutoring Max."

If this situation wasn't tragic, I would stifle a laugh. Kyleigh tutoring anyone is just insanity. "And he just asked me to prom!" Kyleigh says excitedly, putting me right on the spot.

Deputy Miller gives me the once over. I know he's a single dad, Kyleigh's mom split years ago, and he gives Kyleigh whatever she wants.

"Well, I know Kyleigh will be pleased with that, seeing how you treated her less than favorable last year."

The fuck?

"I tell my dad everything," she says, looking at all three of us. "He's my best friend."

I repeat. The fuck?

"Lucky young man you are, son, taking my princess to the prom. And you've done good to not disappoint her *again*," he says, looking between Jacob, me, and Max. "I don't take lightly to *anyone* who disappoints Kyleigh."

"I'll text you, King, can't wait for the next two weeks," she says happily as she gets in the passenger side.

I look back at Jacob on the porch, he gulps. I flex my fists. I'm ready to fucking pummel him.

"You're putting me in the worst fucking situation possible!" I yell at Jacob as I drive his high ass home. "The fuck are you doing right now? I feel like I don't even know you. *My* friend would never risk his future, *my* friend would never risk his sister's future!"

"This is exactly why I didn't want to tell you!" Jacob says, his knee is still bouncing in my front seat as he looks out the window. "I know. I need to get my shit together," he adds.

"I could've helped you. I'm fucking great at trig, I have a ninety in that class." I look over at him in the dark. "Or was it just easier to steal it? Take the easy way out?"

My brain is going a hundred miles an hour. *I will find a way out of this. I will get that video.*

"I don't fucking know, man," Jacob says quietly. "I need help."

"You *need* to stay sober and stop hanging around Max. You need to let me help you study so you can pass, the honest way."

Jacob scoffs. "It's in two weeks."

"We can do it," I tell him, "I can help you if you straighten your shit out and you fucking *let* me."

I pull over as we near his street. I need to set this straight before I drop him off and I can't risk running into Violette right now. The thought of going to prom with Kyleigh makes me feel fucking nauseous. But the thought of Violette caught up in all this makes me feel even worse.

"I'll stop hanging around him, but I need you to do what Kyleigh wants. Please, man, did you see her dad? He knew. She said she told him *everything*. I'll be expelled, he could charge me! I'll have a record and Violette could get in so much trouble. What a fucking fuck up I am." He smacks a fist against his thigh as tears well in his eyes. He's paranoid, but he could be right.

"You don't understand," I tell him. "I care about Vi, Jacob," I say. "I'd be giving her up."

Jacob looks up at me like he had no idea I had real feelings for his sister. He's been oblivious.

"Fuck, man, I need you. I don't know what else to do."

We sit in silence for a beat, both of us catching our breath from this bullshit night.

"Look, even if you could just go with Kyleigh, get her alone and get her to delete the video. But for now, please you *have* to agree. You know Violette. She could never hate you, but, fuck, I don't want her to get in trouble. *Please*."

I hit my steering wheel, once, twice.

I look over at Jacob—my best friend, my brother— crying now in my front seat, and I know I have no choice. I have to help him and stop Violette from being dragged into this.

"No more drugs. You focus on rugby, school. We study— every fucking day—until the final."

He sniffs. "Okay, yea."

"I fucking mean it, Jacob, you have no fucking idea what I'm giving up here."

I'll think of something. I'll win her back.

"I didn't know you felt like that for Vivi, I thought you guys were just friends…" His face is contorted like he isn't sure how he feels about it, but I don't even give a fuck. My feelings are honest. Right now I'm so angry at him, but I don't want to see him get into real trouble regardless. I lean my head back against the seat and blow out a breath.

"I'll go in a group to prom, I'm not going alone with Kyleigh. I'll get the phone. I'll make sure she gets rid of any copies. But if you let me down after this I swear to fuckin—"

"I won't, man, this is rock bottom. I promise." Jacob sniffs again and swipes his tear-stained face.

"This is your future, man, and Violette's…" I tell him, hoping I'm making the right choice.

I look toward his house, knowing Violette is in there,

knowing this is going to break her damn heart and praying with everything in me that one day she'll understand and forgive me.

"There's one more thing." Jacob adds "You can't tell Violette. Not yet."

CHAPTER 29
ROWAN

PRESENT

Violette just sits, expressionless, and absorbs everything I've just told her. Tears stream down her face as she registers a side to her brother that I'm not sure she even knew existed, and I hate that knowing this about him hurts her.

"I was planning to tell you one day when it didn't matter, after Jacob went to school, maybe. Once he was on the straight and narrow and it was behind him. I was going to beg for your forgiveness. I just couldn't leave Jacob hanging, he was my best friend." I shake my head "And I cared about you too much. I couldn't risk you getting caught up in it or into real trouble, Vi." I take a deep breath. "You know, when you're younger you think you have nothing but time and everything seems like an existential crisis." I smirk.

She nods. "I understand that."

"You do?"

"Yeah, and you're not a bad person because you slept with Kyleigh, you were only sixteen. I know you wouldn't want to hurt her even if she's awful." Violette half smiles and looks up at me with understanding.

"She was fucking awful." I agree with a chuckle.

"I knew something was going on with him." Her eyes are a million miles away. "I figured it was girls, or the stress of going to university. I never would've imagined he was involved with drugs or that he could do something illegal, something to hurt me so easily." Another tear spills over her cheek, and I reach across the short distance between us and wipe it away, then tilt her chin up so I have her eyes again.

"He was good at hiding it. I was amazed he could play rugby the way he did and party like that all night."

She sighs and nods. "My parents never knew this?"

"No, I don't think so. He kept his end of the bargain, really laid off the drugs after that."

"I just wish you would've told me then. I wish he did. I wish he never died. I wish a lot of things were different," she says quietly.

"I'm sorry. I made myself believe you were better off not being involved until it was over, and Jacob and I spent the next two weeks cramming every day. Whenever we weren't playing rugby or at school, I was just waiting for the prom to come and go. I thought about you every fucking minute," I offer.

"That explains why he was gone so much."

I nod. "Yea."

"He passed trig," she adds, remembering.

"Yup, fair and square."

It takes everything in me to focus on anything but how fucking beautiful Violette is in the dim light of my living room.

"Of course, where Kyleigh is concerned I kept my end of the deal. I went to prom as you know, and she blasted her socials with every picture she could."

"Yep, it sucked," she says honestly, laughing now.

"I smiled for the camera and at the end of the night I pretended I was going to go to an after party with her. We got into the limo as a group, and I asked to see the photos she took. I knew she'd been drinking with her crew by that time so she let me, and the moment I had her phone in my hand I immediately went to her videos and deleted the one of Jacob and Max, then dumped it from her trash."

I blow out a shaky breath. "She admitted that it was her only copy. And then she said she didn't care anymore because I'd given her what she wanted. She had her photos, and the whole school watched me follow her around like a puppy all night. She told everyone the next day she dumped *me*."

"Including me," Violette says. "I ran into her in the girls' bathroom and she asked me how it felt being pushed aside for her. She said you asked her to the prom a long time ago. It only fueled my thoughts that you had used me even more."

That is something I didn't know. *Fuck.*

"She added that she didn't even like you, she just wanted to prove she *could* have you, that she could take you from me. And then she told me I was kidding myself for thinking Rowan Kingsley could ever want *me*."

"You have to believe that none of that is true, Violette. Please tell me you do."

Violette nods "I do but…." she surprises me by snorting, and then starts laughing—really laughing.

"She bribed you and she didn't…have a backup copy?" she asks through laughter.

I start laughing too because the sound of her laughter is contagious.

I shake my head. "No, she didn't use the Cloud yet. She really wasn't a very stealthy extortionist." I chuckle.

Violette laughs even harder, and for the first time since the day I let her down outside the biology room door, I actually feel good that she knows the truth.

"I told her exactly what I thought about her that night though before I got out of that limo. And I told her I was crazy about you."

Violette's eyes catch mine; it tugs on my heart the way she looks at me now—open, understanding even.

"Then she slugged me, and that night she hooked up with Dennis Bradman," I tell her, naming one of my teammates. I scrub my jaw.

"I knew what we had was special, I wanted to see you again and I hoped I could get you to forgive me without outing Jacob somehow, but I never got the chance anyway, you were already gone. You took that job at Pearce Summer Camp after you told me you turned it down."

"I called them and asked for the opportunity back. I had to get out of here. I didn't want to see you with her all summer or at my house all the time."

"I spent the night after you left pacing your house. I wanted to drive up to the camp, but Jacob *begged* me to let you go for the summer. He *begged* me not to drag you into it and he had been doing so well, he was staying away from everything, including Max. He was giving me hope that that phase in his life was over." I reach out my hand and put it over hers.

"He never wanted you or your parents to know how badly he had fucked up. And then you went to school... those years passed, you got *married*, had a child. I wasn't prolonging telling you, I thought I was protecting you and the more time that went by, the further apart we were. I always wanted you to know the truth but time and space, Jacob passing, it all naturally kept us apart, never giving me the chance. But now, here we are." I tilt her chin up so her eyes meet mine. "The moment I saw you in Shifty's, I knew. This might sound crazy, but I felt Jacob, like he was there, telling me it was my second chance, my chance to make things right. I wasn't about to let that pass me by, and now I don't regret telling you. It should've happened a long time ago, but maybe it wasn't *meant* to happen until now."

CHAPTER 30

Violette

"It doesn't sound crazy. I feel his presence too."

I stand and begin to pace his surprisingly cozy living room, the pull I have to him now is undeniable. Everything here smells good—like Rowan—and hearing how twisted my view was of what happened all those years ago is making me feel totally out of control right now. Knowing he didn't use me, that he didn't hurt me for no good reason, shows me I have no cause to stop these feelings I've been trying to fight.

"Jacob and I always had a silent connection. Even with him gone I can still feel it. The night you wound up in my burn unit, something about seeing you lying there, so many burns, so many marks, but his name and the hawk on your arm left untouched, made me think of him and I just *felt* you were there for a reason."

I run my sweaty palms over my jeans.

"And to find out after all this time that you felt the same way, that you didn't want Kyleigh over me?" I blurt out, Rowan scoffs.

"I *only* wanted you. You were just so quick to *believe I* didn't."

"Because we never made sense on paper. It was just easier to believe you used me," I whisper, before turning back to face him. Rowan just looks at me, hesitates for all of one second, and then before I have time to prepare, he's moving closer, dissolving the space between us in just two long strides. His hands circle my waist bringing our bodies together. A low growl leaves his chest as he leans into me, his lips only inches from mine. My breath hitches.

"Why wouldn't it make sense, Vi?" He whispers as he walks us backward slowly until I'm pressed against the living room wall, his thumbs grazing my waist. "Because you're brilliant?" They slide up my back and I shiver. "Because you're incredible? Sexy as hell?" He leans in even closer and I'd buckle if he wasn't practically holding me up.

"Because you're so beautiful that just looking into your eyes throws me completely off my game every damn time?" He lets go of my waist with one hand and brings it up to graze his thumb over my cheek. As he does something catches my eye on his inner forearm, the one that isn't burned. It's barely visible but I see it. Tucked right up under the wings of the hawk he has for my brother are two small symbols. A tiny p+ and e-. My stomach drops. I grasp his arm for a better view.

"The symbols for protons and electrons?" I whisper. "You got a tattoo? Of *our* symbols?

I look up to Rowan's eyes. His IV was in his hand in the hospital, and I tried so hard to avoid looking at that damn hawk tattoo that I never noticed...

"Jacob was my biggest loss, and you were a part of that, *we* were a part of that. When I added his tattoo, it was only fitting that you had a place under his wings. I wanted you there. You were always in the back of my mind. I didn't regret what I did for Jacob and for you, but I *did* regret losing you."

I suck in a breath. I'm not sure I've ever been as taken aback as I am now. He's had a representation of me? Of *us?* On his body for years? I run my fingers over it and my mouth turns to sand with his admission.

"How long?" I ask trying to keep my composure.

"Since he died," he admits, and I swallow, speechless.

"I never made it clear enough back then, so I'm about to now." Rowan tilts his head, his eyes roam over my face as if he's drinking in my expression, like he's studying my reaction to his touch. "For the last ten years, your face is the face I see. No matter who I'm with, no matter who I meet. When I fell in that ash pit, the last face that flashed through my mind was *yours.*"

"Please…" I whisper, but I can't decide what I'm asking for. If I want him to stop or keep going, because even though his words are heavy, they're also deeply satisfying.

"These eyes? The way they turn dark and needy like this when I'm so close to you… Goddamn, they downright torture me." He bends down and kisses me on the cheek, his lips linger there for a second and I shiver.

Rowan runs his knuckles over my jaw, then down to my neck as his thumb comes up to trace my bottom lip.

"And these lips, I fucking dream about how these lips taste." The weight of his stare on my mouth is heavy. "I've never forgotten. These lips are enough to make me hard all on their own." He kisses me on my other cheek, and I clench my thighs together in desperation.

Rowan presses his body into mine and I whimper as he brings both hands up to gently grip my face, his fingers sliding to the back of my neck, weaving into my hair. Every piece of clothing I'm wearing is weighted against my skin, the music from his vinyl has ended and the only sound is the crickets outside his window.

My eyes trace the features of his face and my breath is shallow as I watch his throat work to swallow. I move my gaze up to his lips, silently begging for them to be on mine.

This man who hurt me, who I thought used me, I find out

now after ten years that he didn't. He put mine and my brother's potential future before his own wants and needs? The truth spreads through me and I realize not only do I forgive him, but right now, all I want is to kiss him. *God, do I want to kiss him.*

"I don't know if you're ready to take another chance on me, Violette." His voice is low and full of gravel.

His words cause an unraveling. I drop my eyes to his lips, anticipating,

"*Fuck it*—I'm taking it anyway," he says just before his mouth is on mine. He groans into me the second our lips touch. The ten years between our last kiss and right now evaporate into thin air, like they never existed in the first place. The deep connection that's still between us is the kind of spark that risks setting us both on fire. He lingers for a moment, just tasting me as he grips the back of my neck and tilts my head for better access. I let him in, and the second that I do, I know the exquisite sink of his tongue into my mouth will be my undoing.

His kiss quickly turns from gentle to claiming and desperate, as if I might choose to push him away at any second. His tongue moves in a way that tells me he wants to savor me, and I move with him, searching his mouth as he searches mine. For the first time in ten years, I feel wanted and complete in a way only Rowan can offer.

He pulls his head back slightly and licks a soft trail across my bottom lip as I fist his T-shirt, pulling him in as close to me as I can. Another groan leaves his lips and I remember that he's injured.

"Did that hurt you?" I ask breathlessly.

Rowan chuckles before his mouth is on mine again, and several moments pass before we come up for air. His broad palms slide down and grip my ass through my jeans as he pulls me tight to him, so tight that I can feel him hard and pressing into my abdomen. I whimper when I feel his size, I knew he was big, I remember he felt big. But now that I've had some life experience, I know he would fill me like I've never been filled, and that thought is making quick work of soaking my panties.

"You could cut my fucking leg *off* right now, Vi, and I wouldn't stop."

"Noted," I murmur with a smile into his plush, delicious lips as he kisses me. His hands continue their slide over every part of me, kneading my body. My curves fit into his hands in a way that makes me feel confident, worshiped, and beautiful. I reach my hands up around his shoulders and lose my fingers to the strands of hair at the nape of his neck, tugging him even closer as I kiss him back. I'm half clinging to him, half clinging to the safety of the cliff where I've tucked my feelings for him away for ten years. My thoughts narrow to only two.

What am I doing? And, my God, please, don't let him stop.

Our hurried breath is the only sound between us, and it's steady and in sync as Rowan's hand slides up over my ribs to find my nipples hard and begging for his touch. He toys with one through my T-shirt. A deep groan rolls through his chest as his lips move to my neck, the spot under my ear that sends a shiver through my whole body. He bites me gently there as he plucks at my nipple. The slight pain mixed with pleasure causes me to jolt in his arms. Just as quickly as he nips at me, he kisses over the sting.

"These sounds you make...they're going to be the death of me," he whispers as he gently slides his hands under my shirt. I don't hesitate, I help him, wanting him as much as he wants me. Rowan doesn't miss a beat, he lifts my shirt off over my head and then backs up slightly, taking a moment to look over every inch of me in just my bra and my jeans.

"*Fuck...*" he mutters as he moves back in, his lips on mine, growing urgent, moving his tongue with mine in a steady, calculated pace that might make me come all on its own. "You're so fucking beautiful, Vi," he whispers as his fingers find my pebbled nipples again, teasing me through the lace of my bra.

I angle my hips into him, searching for any sort of friction as he pulls my bra down to expose my breasts. His mouth finds a nipple, and I grip his hair tighter, my head lolling back against the living room wall.

"Rowan..." I moan his name for the first time since we laid on Fraser Beach and it fuels him as he moves to my other breast and takes that nipple into his mouth next.

"Goddamn, I've missed the sound of my name on your lips...say it again."

"Rowan..." I whimper, grinding my hips to push my pussy into his uninjured thigh.

"So needy, Vi...fuck, I'd be lying if I said I didn't love it." He chuckles as he uses his thumb and forefinger to pop the button on my jeans, and then before I know what's happening he's on his knees in front of me, pulling my jeans from my body and tossing them aside. His lips move in a torturous pace up the inside of my thighs as his hands grasp any part of me that he can reach.

When I look down at him he's steady between my legs, looking up at me, watching the way my body quakes for him. Desire rolls through me with just that sight alone. I moan as his nose skims over my wet panties and he grips my ass tighter, pulling me closer, pressing his face into me and inhaling a long deep breath.

"Fucking Christ, Violette, everything about you is just as perfect as I always imagined." He breathes me in again, and I start to pant. "The way you sound"—he slides his hands over my skin—"the way you feel"—his nose skims my clit through my panties as he inhales deeply again, looking up at me like he can't believe he's holding me—"fuck, even the way you smell."

I grip his hair tighter and whimper as his words do something to me I can't quite explain.

"I bet you taste like perfection too, don't you, Vi?"

"M-maybe," I whimper as he dots kisses along the inside of my thigh.

"Fuck, I want to taste you," he murmurs with that lopsided smirk as he presses his lips to my clit through the thing layer of cotton.

"Pleeease," I beg, feeling like I'm on fire for him as he moves my panties aside, sliding his finger through my soaking slit.

"*Fuck,* yes," he groans when he finds me absolutely soaked for him.

His eyes move rapidly over every part of me.

My eyes roll back and I know I'm completely at his mercy. I want whatever Rowan Kingsley will offer me. And, oh yeah, that cliff I was clinging to? I just let go. I figure if I drown in him, so be it. At least I'll know I took the deepest breath I could before I went under.

"This pretty little dripping cunt, so fucking wet, so ready for my tongue." His tone churns my insides with want and need as he slowly pushes one finger into me, then just as slowly pulls it out and licks it clean. The groan that comes from his throat as he does has me pushing my pussy into his face.

I jump when my phone vibrates loudly in my purse. Rowan freezes as it stops ringing and then starts again. I can see the need in his eyes, the want. It reflects my own, he's barely even had a chance to touch me.

"Shit. Sorry, shit…" I whisper, breathing heavily as Rowan stands.

I pinch the bridge of my nose in frustration. "I have to answer it."

CHAPTER 31

Violette

"Hey, Violette, uh, are you coming home soon?" Troy asks the moment I pick up. I try to steady my breath after Rowan's face was just between my thighs, begging. Flipping from that to Troy's demanding tone is not an easy feat.

"Why?"

"I texted you." *He did? How did I not hear my phone?* "I had to bring Hollie home early."

"I, uh—I called your mom, she came over."

"*What?* What's going on?" I toss back at him, my tone stern. The way he thinks I'm just at his beck and call is crazy. He's been with Hollie for less than two hours.

I look back at Rowan, who hands me my shirt and my jeans, somehow knowing whatever we just did is now over. My eyes linger on his gorgeous face, his body, the way his arm ripples with muscle as he lifts my clothes—

"Hollie was crying, saying she wants you, maybe she isn't feeling well…I don't know. I got a call anyway; they could use me at the hospital tonight, so I was just going to drop her off early."

Right. Reality.

Rage slinks through my blood with Troy's words—not because I don't want him to bring Hollie home early, I'm happy to spend every second with her, but because he is such an ass sometimes. How does he ever expect her not to cry when he only sees her for an hour and a half every three weeks?

"So, can you come home?" he asks expectantly.

I turn my back to Rowan, not wanting him to hear me berate my ex over his utter lack of parenting skills. Mercifully, Rowan has dipped out of the living room. I see him open the fridge in his kitchen at the end of the hall. I take the opportunity to slide my jeans on and button them up, holding my phone between my chin and my shoulder.

"You can't just expect her to be your little puppet all the time, she's going to cry, she's going to have emotions, and that is okay. You can't just bring her home when she isn't perfectly behaved," I angry whisper into the phone.

"I know that, Violette. She just seems tired, and I already told the hospital I would be there a little early."

I look up at the ceiling and blow out a breath.

This is my reality. My priority. My life.

"I'll be there in ten minutes, I'm around the corner at a friend's," I tell him before I hang up.

I turn around to find Rowan coming back into the living room with two waters. He looks at me with concern in his eyes.

I toss my T-shirt over my head. For some reason—maybe it's because I don't want to get into the messy conversation about my ex, or maybe it's simply because if I tell Rowan what's going on —I have to mesh these two sides of my life somehow and I'm not prepared for that yet.

Whatever the reason is, I offer him no excuse. This phone call came to remind me that I'm a mom, and maybe this is a sign from the universe that I need to just unpack everything I learned tonight before Rowan ends up between my thighs again.

"I have to go, but I'll...text you later, okay?" I grab my purse and sling it over my shoulder.

Rowan nods. "Everything okay?" he asks easily.

"Yeah, it's just...I'm sorry. I got caught up in the moment, and you're, well, you're a really good kisser and learning all this truth is a lot for one night. And...not to mention all of this hotness," I say awkwardly, waving a hand over his incredible physique.

"Thanks?" Rowan says, one eyebrow raised.

"I think I just lost all control there for a few minutes," I say.

"Vi..." Rowan says when I turn to move toward his front door, but he gets to me quicker and stops me.

"Look, I'm not saying this isn't something, it's just that our lives are very different and...I—just have no idea how to be a mom and do...whatever this is."

Rowan sets his jaw with my shitty excuse. I know I'm panicking because mixing my life with his scares the shit out of me. But before he can really even retort, I reach up on my tip toes and kiss him. It sends a rush of want through me but I force myself to back away because I don't know what else to do or say.

I just about came and you hardly touched me?

I can't get close to you because I feel too much?

I have to go be a mom now?

He slides his hand down my forearm and squeezes just once, before I practically run out the door to my car like a kid sneaking home after curfew. As I back out of the driveway I go through everything he told me, and although it definitely changes my view on the past, I just need a hot minute to think.

I have Hollie to consider and I know the life of a hotshot. I know how quickly he could be hurt again—or worse. Am I really prepared to take that on? The closer I get to home, the less I know the answer.

"I am so sorry," I say to my mom as I come in the door. Hollie is running to me with a happy smile on her face, jumping into my arms like nothing happened, she clearly feels fine now.

My mom and dad are in the middle of my living room floor, puzzles and Guess Who? spread out like they were mid game, and *The Lion King* plays on the TV.

"Don't apologize, honey. Where were you, anyway?"

"With…Teddy. I had to help her with something," I lie. I'm just a big fat liar today, apparently.

My mom takes one look at me and narrows her eyes. Yep, she knows I'm full of shit.

"You two are getting a lot closer, aren't you?" my dad asks, wearing a trusting grin. He isn't as in tune with my lying face.

"Yeah, we get along really well," I say, tidying up the shoes at the front door.

I breeze past my mom not wanting to meet her eyes.

I keep myself busy by tidying up while they finish their game with Hollie.

I take Hollie and give her a bath when they're finished with their game, I just want a few minutes alone with her to ask her why she wanted to come home. She tells me the same thing she tells me every time. 'She missed me' and I know as I help her into her pajamas that this is her way of being cautious with Troy. She doesn't know him well enough to feel comfortable with him anymore. He isn't her safe space. I tell her it's okay and Daddy will come back and see her very soon. When I come back out into the living room my parents are reorganizing Hollie's puzzle shelf. I seriously don't know what I'd do without them.

Hollie runs to her room from the bathroom to pick out all of her stuffies to bring out to our snack party. I let her take her time and make my way back to the living room carrying her favorite pig. But when I get there I stop dead. I blink to make sure that I'm not imagining Rowan sitting on my couch talking to my dad. I drop Hollie's Power Piggy on the floor.

My dad takes one look at my face and grins.

"Don't blame Teddy here. Apparently, *he* thought you'd be on your own, Vivi," he chuckles as Rowan looks at me with nothing but apology and confusion on his gorgeous face. Until his eyes skim over me, taking in my outfit, then his face turns almost smug because I'm wearing black leggings, I've tossed my hair up into a big bun, and I'm wearing *his* Seahawks sweater. The one he gave me that night on the beach, the one I never gave back, the one I still wear all the time. The one I've kept for ten years. And then he smirks.

Well, shit.

I open my mouth to speak but don't really have any words before Hollie's singing and pitter patter fills the room, her little slippers thwap against the hardwood floor. She slows as she sees Rowan sitting on the couch. He's large and intimidating, taking up a cushion and a half sitting beside my dad. Hollie stops beside me and ducks behind my thigh, picking up her pig, then reaching up to grab my hand, she tugs. I look down at her questioning eyes and bend down so she can whisper into my ear.

"Who is that?" she asks in a soft little whisper.

Here goes nothing.

I pick her up and rest her on my hip, whispering back. "That's my friend, Rowan. He was very good friends with Uncle Jacob," I add. My eyes meet his.

"Rowan, this is my Hollie."

Rowan leans forward and looks at Hollie with an open, honest gaze.

"It's nice to meet you, Hollie, I like that your slippers have French fries on them," he says.

"French fries are my favorite," Hollie says, her eyes immediately move to the framed photo of me and Jacob on the fireplace mantel. Hollie is no stranger to Jacob's memory. We talk about him all the time.

"Mine too," he says with such a sincere smile that it melts my insides.

Hollie leans her head on my shoulder and takes in the sight of Rowan, he wears a black T-shirt and shorts, so the white gauze and tape is apparent, peeking out from his sleeve and on part of his thigh.

"Are you a superhero too?" she asks, which makes Rowan chuckle.

"We told Hollie all about Uncle Jacob being a hero and that's why he went to heaven, isn't that right, Hols?" I ask.

She nods. I see the pain flash across Rowan's face.

"Your Uncle Jacob was the best superhero I ever knew," he says, and Hollie smiles.

"Did you get hurt?" she asks, struggling to get out of my hold. I put her down and she walks over to Rowan, leaning on my dad's knee right in front of him.

"I did get hurt, and your mommy took care of me at the hospital, aren't I lucky?" He smiles at her and she smiles back.

"Did Mommy kiss it better?"

Rowan's eyebrows shoot up and he smiles at her.

"No, but she did keep me company." He chuckles.

She nods and looks back at me. "He got hurt like Rocky the Rabbit?" she asks about *SuperPets* resident rabbit. "He fell off Power Piggy's picnic table. He wasn't being careful," Hollie tells Rowan.

He chuckles at her, already enamoured with her cuteness.

"Were you being careful?" she asks.

"I was but I made a mistake, and I had a fall," he tells her.

"Do you like popcorn?" she asks him, switching gears the way a three-year-old does. She moves closer to him—obviously, she's enamoured too.

Rowan smiles at her completely at ease. "Sure do," he says. "With extra butter."

Hollie looks at my dad. "Papa, make some popcorn," she commands, and the room laughs, but my dad, who is totally putty in her hands, stands like there was never even a question of him not doing what she wanted.

"Okay, but only if you and Nana come and help me. Should we get Rowan his own bowl?"

Hollie nods, and my mom stands to follow them with a sly grin on her face.

"Teddy, huh?" she asks, passing between us.

"Mother," I whisper in protest, because she didn't need to point out the already obvious tension in the room.

The moment they leave the room Rowan is in front of me.

"I'm so sorry, Vi, you said—I thought you would be alone." Rowan pulls his hat off and runs a hand through his hair then replaces the hat, backwards on his head.

I sigh, taking in just how gorgeous he is. But it's not only that, it's also how much I like the idea of him in my living room. It's official, I'm hopeless.

I take a deep breath. "I didn't want to lie but I don't exactly know how to navigate being a mom and whatever this is."

"That was *him* who called you? He had to bring her home early?" Annoyance lines Rowan's tone as he moves closer to me, resting his hands on my hips.

I nod and then look into his intense blue eyes, facing the music. "I didn't want to tell you my ex can be difficult where Hollie is concerned. Sue me," I say, moving away to start folding the throw blanket on my couch. Rowan follows me and spins me around to face him.

"I wish you had. I would've understood. I think we've wasted enough time, and we have enough history to just be honest with each other. Which is why I'm here. I thought some-

thing freaked you out...now I see you had to come home for
Hollie, but I'm not *letting* you run from me anymore, Vi."

I open my mouth to retort.

"Here we go, popcorn for all," my dad announces like he's
going to walk into us making out or something.

I roll my eyes at my parents' theatrics as Rowan drops his
hands from my hips with the sound of his voice and takes a
step back. Hollie runs into the room and hands Rowan an over-
flowing blue plastic bowl of popcorn that matches her pink
one. He takes it from her and pops a big handful into his
mouth.

"Dewicious," he says to her, which makes her laugh.

"I think it's time for us to get going, what do you think,
Nana?" Dad asks Mom. My mom looks between us again and
decides to make a graceful exit, although I know she's dying to
stay.

"Can you stay?" Hollie turns her eyes up to Rowan who
looks at me. I nod, because I'm not going to say no, especially
when Hollie never takes to anyone this easily. Leave it to
Rowan's easy demeanor to charm her.

"Can I have all the popcorn I want?" he asks, taking a seat on
the sofa.

"If Mommy says so," she answers, practically with a little
shrug. "Do you like *SuperPets*?" The way Hollie asks sounds
like there's no way he wouldn't know what that is.

"All the other superheroes I know have told me about the
SuperPets, but I've never watched it," he says, his eyes moving
to mine.

Hollie's eyes light up at the prospect of adding another
SuperPets fan to her life.

"Can we, Mommy?"

I nod. "One episode, Hols, and then it's time for bed."

She smiles excitedly, scooting up onto the couch beside
Rowan with her popcorn. She holds her bowl up to him and says,

"cheers," which is something we do when we're having the same snack.

Rowan doesn't hesitate, he reaches his bowl out and taps it to hers. "Cheers," he says, looking down at her with an easy smile. I pick up the remote and point it at the TV because the way the two of them look side by side on the sofa like they're the oldest of friends? Well, there go my ovaries.

I put on Hollie's favorite episode as my mom kisses her on the head, and Rowan says goodbye to my parents. The theme song starts to play as I walk them to the door.

"Not one word," I tell them as they put their shoes on in my foyer. My dad holds his hands up in truce with an odd goofy grin.

"Why would we say a word? Just because you've been back in town for all of, what? Five minutes? And you two are already spending time together? Probably means nothing." He winks.

My mother kisses me on the cheek. "Have fun, Vivi," she says with a grin.

"Goodbye, world's nosiest parents," I say with a smile, closing the door to the sound of their snickers.

How do they always just know?

As I make my way back into the living room, I pause at the door listening as Hollie chatters on to Rowan, reminding myself that this is fine. I'm still in control here.

"He can fly," she tells him with a mouthful of popcorn while pointing to the screen.

"If I could choose a superpower, that's what I would do," Rowan says, like he's in discussion with any friend as opposed to a three-year-old.

"Why?" Hollie asks, using her favorite word.

Rowan shoves another handful of popcorn into his mouth and thinks carefully as Hollie reaches forward. He takes over, grabbing her sippy cup of milk off the table and handing it to her. She takes it from him eagerly and has a big sip.

"I'd want to fly 'cause then I could fly out of any place that wasn't safe and save anyone who was with me," he says as he picks up a bottle of water my parents must have offered him and opens it.

"Power Piggy can fly," Hollie says matter-of-factly.

"Then he's my favorite," Rowan says.

"He's my favowite too," Hollie says as she happily munches beside her new friend before reaching into the pile of stuffies beside her and pulling out one of her three Power Piggy's and handing it to him.

Rowan looks down at the tattered pig and takes it from her.

"You can't keep him, but you *can* cuddle him," Hollie clarifies.

Rowan laughs at her genuinely. "Okay, I'll just let him be my buddy while we watch, how's that?" he asks her.

"Power Piggy and Super Rowan!" Hollie says, giggling, holding up her cup.

"Cheers" she adds.

She smiles up at him and he reaches down and holds out his water bottle to cheers hers. I watch as he sets that damn pig on his knee and points it toward the TV as he asks her why Tough Little Turtle always gets to be the one to drive the *SuperPets* wagon.

Who am I kidding?

I am so not *in control here.*

CHAPTER 32
ROWAN

The only light in the room is the lamp beside Violette's sofa and the TV—that I currently have sports highlights playing on—while she puts Hollie to bed. I have no idea how to navigate this or any idea what I'm actually doing in Violette's living room, aside from the fact that I couldn't let her leave like that. The fear that rippled through me when she left like she might not come back punched me right in the gut.

I just wanted to come here and tell her I would wait—as long as she needed to feel comfortable. What I didn't expect to find was Jack answering her front door or Hollie being home. But I did what I always do, I improvised, and now after meeting Hollie, I'm not regretting a single thing. I glance at the pig Hollie gave me that I was privileged enough to hang onto when she left to go to sleep.

I don't really have any experience with four year olds, but she pretty much stole my heart the moment she handed me that bowl of popcorn and asked me to cheers with a cute little grin. It's obvious her mom is her number one fan—I can see why. Although, I might be a little biased based on account of how I'm feeling about Violette.

"She's asleep and judging by the way she talked about you, I'd say you're a hit," Violette breathes out as she comes back into the living room carrying the baby monitor, wearing yoga tights and *my* sweatshirt. I can't believe she kept it all these years. Her long waves are piled high on her head, her face is free of makeup, and she's wearing fuzzy pink slippers. I don't think I've ever seen her look so pretty.

Vi looks around her living room and shrugs.

"So, you just charmed your way into my reality without even trying. This is it. The messy, mostly sticky life of a single mom who was too embarrassed to say her ex can be a dud. It isn't romantic and it isn't your life, so I panicked. I didn't know how to make these two worlds meet when Troy called, so I thought it would be easier to just…bail."

I don't say anything. I just lean back on her couch and pat the space beside me. She makes her way over and takes a seat, and I do what I've wanted to do since she left my house. I move closer to her and without hesitation pull her into my arms and kiss her. Warmth spreads through me when I realize that, even though it's only been a couple hours, I've missed her lips on mine.

"None of this"—I gesture around her cute little house—"would ever make me change my mind, Violette. You're a mom, and it's obvious you're an incredible one, which only makes me want you more. You're not getting rid of me that easily, you just need to catch up to me here. I'm not letting you out of my sight until you give me a fighting chance." I kiss her again, because, fuck, I just want to. "I'm not making the mistake of letting you go again."

"And you're fairly certain I want to give you a fighting chance?" Violette asks in a flirty little tone. "Kinda cocky, isn't it, Kingsley?"

That's it. I pounce, grabbing her thighs and tugging her below me on the couch until she's lying flat looking up at me.

She gasps.

"Fucking right I am." I let my eyes rake over her, *slowly.* "You're wearing my shirt." I grin, hovering over her. I look deep into her eyes, just having her this close has my cock instantly waking up. I'll never get enough of her. She's so warm and she smells so good just inches from my face, I almost forget how to breathe.

"Maybe I just like the sweatshirt."

"Or maybe you just like me *and* the sweatshirt."

Violette giggles and bites her bottom lip. "Maybe."

"Violette. I was fucking crazy about you when I was eighteen, and I'm still crazy about you now. You just have to jump with me, let's see where we land."

"I'm scared," she whispers. I feel her grip on my shirt tighten as the smile drifts from her face. "What if I fall for you? I can't get over you twice."

My chest tightens with her words. I hate that I hurt her, but I can't go back, all I can do is move forward.

"I'll be right there with you, Vi, we'll fall together. We're protons and electrons, remember? We need each other." I stroke her face with my thumb. "Electrostatic," I add, "is there anything better?"

"I don't know," she answers honestly.

I brush a lock of hair off her forehead. "Neither do I. But, fuck, I really want to find out," I tell her, dropping my lips to hers. The kiss she offers me back isn't like the ones from earlier. This isn't gentle, it isn't sweet. It's demanding. It's her lips, hurried yet slow, her tongue searching my mouth, hungry and calculated. My hands sink into her hair and tilt her head. Violette meets me at every turn, kissing me until she's breathless before I pull away slightly to nip, and suck her bottom lip into my mouth.

She's fucking killing me with every little whimper, every little moan.

"All I want to do is take my time with you." I tip my forehead to hers. "But at the same time, I'm in the biggest hurry to make up for all the years I haven't been kissing you."

Violette's eyes focus on mine, the heat between us makes me want her so fucking badly I can hardly stand it, but on her couch while Hollie sleeps in the next room is not the time.

"Don't let me fall alone, Kingsley."

"Impossible. I'll be right there with you." I kiss her back. "And I have all the time in the world."

It's the most honest thing I've ever said to anyone, because I fell for Violette Taylor ten years ago, and I never got back up.

CHAPTER 33

Violette

ROWAN

That color looks nice on you.

I stare down at my phone, then at my royal blue tank top in total confusion, not because Rowan texted me, but because over the last week as I've split my time between working long shifts and momming, our texts haven't stopped. I'm only confused because I'm at the park with Hollie and he isn't so how would he know what color I'm—

"Super Rowan!" I hear Hollie call out running behind me. Clearly, their evening of bonding over *SuperPets* has stuck with her.

I spin around, and sure enough, Rowan's ten feet behind me, and he's clearly been out running. He's wearing black Nike shorts and a blue T-shirt that isn't much different in shade than my own. He's hot and sweaty and...really fucking *hot*. He swipes a hand through his damp hair and smirks at me.

"Are you here to play?" Hollie asks him. He closes the space between us in a few long, easy strides, still catching his breath.

"Sure, I can play, Hollie," he says, mussing the top of her

hair. She jumps up and down excitedly and runs toward the play equipment.

"Out for a neighborhood run?" I ask, raising a brow.

"Yep," he says as he squeezes my shoulder, walking past me. I start to follow him to the equipment where Hollie is.

"Mm-hmm," I comment.

"Rowan, push me!" she calls out as she climbs onto the toddler swing.

"Such a coincidence," I say a little louder, folding my arms over my chest.

Rowan turns, walking backward with his hands raised.

"I'm not saying it's a coincidence." Rowan turns to walk backward and talk to me. "In fact, I think *you* knew I'd be out for a run and *you* decided it might be a good time for a park visit."

"Is that so?" I ask, laughing at this man's ability to be so cocky and quick witted on a dime.

"So, this has nothing to do with me not going on that date yet?" I muse.

He shakes his head. "Can't talk dates, Vi, gotta go push."

I follow them, watching Rowan make sure Hollie is secure before he starts pushing her on the swing. He asks her what she had for dinner and she answers him, telling him about her macaroni and cheese and how many grapes she ate, as he listens with genuine interest.

Without even trying this man is tearing down my carefully built walls, one brick at a time.

Rowan's strong arms flex as he pushes Hollie on the swing, they've moved on to talk about which color of M&M's tastes better.

"Should mommy swing too?" he asks Hollie.

"Yes!" Hollie says. "You can go beside me, Mommy."

Rowan winks and offers me that lopsided smirk I can't get enough of.

"Well, come on, Mommy." He gestures to the open swing.

Something about the way he calls me Mommy just sinks into my soul as I take the next swing to Hollie. It is endearing and sweet. I definitely don't need any more reasons to fall for him, but it seems like almost every day he's giving me another.

> I'm convinced new baby smell is the fountain of youth.

I snap a photo of myself holding Teddy's sweet one week old baby, Bea, in my arms a few days later and send it to Rowan. I've already met this little bundle twice, but this is my first day off and I can't stop myself from snuggling her every chance I get.

ROWAN

> Bottle it up and bring me some. That workout just kicked my ass.

When I talked to him before lunch he was going to meet his personal trainer to help get him back into a decent workout schedule after over two weeks off.

> What do you mean? You've been pushing us on the swings every day.

Coincidentally, of course, every day for the last week, a gorgeous hotshot runner just happens to pass by the park at the same time as our daily play before my shift.

ROWAN

> You two are not a workout, a mild warm up at best.

207

> Tell the new mama I said congrats again. The amount of photos Cal has already is astonishing. He's a gushy proud uncle.

I stare down at Bea in my arms snoozing away as we sit on Teddy's sofa.

> How am I supposed to give her back and go to work tonight?

ROWAN

> Soldier on, I'm sure Teddy will let you sniff her baby like a total weirdo again tomorrow.

> And FYI I'm cashing in and considering tonight our first official date since you've yet to let me actually take you on one.

> I'm not the easiest to get alone for a date.

ROWAN

> Tell me about it.

I smile. Truth is, I would've let him but I haven't had a night where we could have been alone.

> FYI, It's not a date if I'm working at the bar.

ROWAN

> I can make any situation a date. Desperate times Vi. I'm out of patience.

> So what? You're just going to hang out at Shifty's all night?

ROWAN

> No, I'm meeting my friends, at the bar you happen to work at, if that takes your whole shift, so be it.

> You're crazy.

As long as we're clear.

A few seconds later I get a photo of him at the park bench making a funny face at me. He's sweaty again, he's been running. I know hotshots have an insane level of fitness they have to maintain, so of course, he's already running and getting back at it after being injured.

I zoom in on the photo. I can't help the blush creeping up my neck. He looks good, damn good, and enticing as hell. He's bandage free now and is healing up perfectly. He's expected to be cleared to work in the field in just over a week. I've had a lot of time to think and reflect on the truth he told me versus the way I've seen it for the last ten years. That shit messes with your head. Especially when he keeps proving to me with every passing day how great he actually is.

Truth is, Rowan and I have barely gone an hour without texting. Our chat is never ending, filled with random conversation, shameless flirting, and various online games.

My stomach flip flops at the thought of seeing him tonight, Hollie free. It feels like so much has changed since our talk the night he came home from the hospital.

"Are you smiling like that because you're in love with Bea or your phone?" Teddy asks in a tired voice taking a seat on the other side of the sofa. She's in loose pajama bottoms and a big hoodie, her blonde hair is piled onto her head, she's got that new mama glow and looks beautiful.

Baby Bea came fast, and Teddy was extremely lucky that Rowan's sup, Xander, lives right next door and was home when her water broke unexpectedly.

"Both," I tell her honestly as I gently run my fingers over Bea's feather soft dusting of hair. She yawns and her perfect little mouth forms a tiny O.

"You took my advice then?" she asks, popping a French fry

into her mouth then moaning with how good it tastes. I was officially declared Teddy's lord and savior when I showed up with kids' meals for Dalton and Penny and an order of her favorite fries.

I shrug and stand, patting Bea's tiny bottom as she makes the cutest little grunting sounds.

"Now that I know Rowan was just trying to help Jacob and me out of a bad situation, that he always had feelings for me…" I stroke Bea's soft cheek with the pads of my fingers while I talk. "It changes everything, but right now he's at home recovering so everything is easy." I continue to pace around Teddy's living room just needing to talk this through with her and myself. I didn't want to bombard her right after she gave birth, but she seems comfortable enough now and willing to listen to some of my drama.

"But reality tells me he's going to get called out again soon, which leads me to the other side of my coin. Even if I get through our past, I lived through years of my mother's silent anxiety, of her putting on a brave face when my father left. I know how it made *me* feel, the OCD tendencies it caused me as his daughter. The thought of being with someone where the possibility of that being my everyday scares the shit out of me."

"We cling to the fears we have because the possibility of reliving them terrifies us," Teddy says softly. My heart aches for her and the pain she knows, especially staring down at her darling new baby.

"I just haven't had five minutes of thought that don't include him since, and my head is a mess of hormones, all my fears, and history."

Teddy nods. "It's a combo alright." She yawns.

I sigh and reclaim my seat beside her.

"He sacrificed his own wants and needs to protect you *and* your brother, and he never wanted you to know after Jacob passed because drugs and breaking and entering leaves a stain on your brother's ghost? Vi, there's something so stand up and loyal about that. Kind of shows you who he really is."

"I know this, trust me. He's exactly who I always thought he was," I tell her.

She adjusts herself on the couch as she talks, she's sore for sure. Thankfully, Logan's mom is here for a couple of weeks to help out with the kids. Teddy may have lost her husband, but his parents are so supportive, and so is Cal.

"I have to say it's also kind of...hot. He sacrificed his feelings for yours," she says in a dreamy tone, munching on another fry.

"So you see my problem?" I sigh. "And there's more," I admit. "He really seems to genuinely like hanging out with both me *and* Hollie."

"I'm sure that doesn't help your hormones."

I sigh. "Yesterday, he brought both himself and Hollie snacks and juice boxes to the park," I deadpan.

"Oh, my goodness, he didn't?"

I nod. "He did."

"So, let's think logically about this. He isn't who you thought he was for the last ten years, turns out he's much, much better, he's awesome with Hollie." Teddy counts the items off on her fingers. "He is *clearly* crazy about you, he's a hard worker—a real hero, if you will—fighting fires out in the rugged wilderness, saving towns and wildlife from carnage," she says like she's writing his biography.

I laugh at her description.

"And he's easy on the eyes, to put it mildly. But you're still questioning because you have a fear of really putting yourself out there and losing someone you're close to again. Have I got all that right?"

"Dammit, Teddy, yes," I whisper, rocking her sweet new bundle. "I'm working on it. I want to let him in," I add, glancing at Hollie happily munching her own kid's meal with Teddy's kids as they watch a Disney movie.

"I'm sorry to tell you this, but the face you make when you talk about him? You let him in a long time ago."

I turn my gaze back to my friend. "Why you gotta be super mom *and* super right all the time?"

"I don't feel like super mom." She grins. "Maybe I will once this ibuprofen kicks in, still a bit sore."

We both laugh and I look down at Bea's sweet little scrunchy face.

"Thank goodness your mom's hunk of a neighbor was home to help," I say to Bea.

Teddy laughs. "Ugh…don't remind me."

I look over at her and smile. "I see the way you look at him when you talk about the sweet things he does for you. I think it was fate for him to be the one to come to your rescue."

Teddy blushes pink. "Whatever it was, I did not expect him to be catching my daughter."

I look down at sweet little Bea, already so in love. "Things just have a way of working out the way they're supposed to. I call it a bonding moment," I say.

"Yeah," Teddy says, popping the last of her fries in her mouth. "So then, Miss Things Have A Way of Working Themselves Out, are you ready to take your own advice?"

I stick my tongue out at her.

"I'll take that as a yes." She laughs. "So, it should be a fun night at work for you then?"

CHAPTER 34

ROWAN

I lean back in my worn wooden chair at Shifty's and watch Violette work the crowd.

The table around me is full of talk, laughs, and the general mischief typical of my squad, but, fuck, the only thing I can see, the only thing I can focus on, is this woman I've been talking to non-stop since I confessed my truth. We've texted all through her long ass work shifts, talked during our daily park meetups, that I definitely orchestrated on purpose, and late into the night while I ached to go to her and hold her in my arms. I'm quickly becoming obsessed with everything about Violette again and it doesn't help me fight my borderline obsession when she's a package deal with the cutest and coolest kid I've ever met.

I know her life is full, I know she's always on the go, but I watch her now, knowing that tonight I could possibly, if I play my cards right, have her all to myself. And that thought is making me almost electric with anticipation. It's like everything she does was made purposely for me, just to turn me on. The way she moves, the way she smiles, how her long wavy hair shines in the neon. And right now, how perfect her tits look in the low-cut tank top as she bends down to reach for something under the bar. Everything about her has me over a goddamn barrel. I've been fighting with this feeling for years, but telling her the truth only made me dive even deeper into this crazy.

Head first. Without a life vest.

All I can hope is that somehow, someway I'm lucky enough to convince her to jump in with me. Scratch that, she *will*—she just isn't ready to admit it yet.

"Look at her wrinkly little nose," Cal gushes to Sam and Caleb at my table. This is the first time in God knows how long we've all been both showered and out together. These champs just came back from a heavy sister blaze at the Wyoming border that sparked after their first roll. They're hoping for a couple days off, but they probably won't get it.

Most of the crew is here, only ones missing are Roycie—who already met a girl and left with her—and Sup, who's on his way.

"I think he might ditch me for Bea." Cal's girlfriend, Scottie, grins taking a swig of her beer. She's a trooper coming out with a bunch of scrags like us and putting up with the shit talk. Cal better not fuck it up, he's pretty much hit the jackpot with her. She's cool as hell and she calls him on his shit. Not to mention, she put up with his ass when they were lost together in a storm last fall and they weren't even on speaking terms. If they can get through that and come out the other side, I'd say they can get through anything.

Cal leans over and puts his hand on Scottie's jean clad knee. "Not a fuckin' chance." He gives her a squeeze and it almost makes me jealous. I've never wanted that with a woman before, but as I turn to see Violette working behind the bar, I wish she was sitting beside me with my hand on her thigh.

"You know the new girl?" Scottie asks me, catching me staring at Vi.

I turn to face her. "She's my girlfriend," I say with a wide grin, and Cal chuckles.

"That's Jack's daughter, the one I was telling you about," he says to Scottie.

"If you hit the bar at all and let her know her boyfriend sent you, she'll probably give you the special drink they don't serve to the regulars," I add.

"I didn't know you had a girlfriend." Scottie checks Violette out over her shoulder. "She's really pretty. Impressive for you." She winks, and I scoff in offense.

"The fuck is that supposed to mean?"

She just shrugs with a smirk.

"Scottie's real good at insulting you and complimenting you all at the same time." He leans forward and sets his beer down. "Does it better than anyone."

"Someone needs to keep you in check." She nudges him with her shoulder.

The song changes to "Friends in Low Places" by Garth Brooks as the front door dings amidst the noisy Saturday night crowd.

Sup comes strolling in, wearing his standard jeans and black T-shirt, and immediately my whole table stands and lets him have it, clapping like they're at a goddamn concert. Naturally, I stand and join them.

"Well, if it isn't Sky Ridge's favorite new doula," Opp cheers, and Sup just shakes his head. This is the first time we've seen him as a crew since he helped deliver Teddy's baby, but our group chat is a plethora of superhero memes and sarcastic jokes.

Cal approaches him and shakes his hand, patting him on the shoulder and saying something none of us can hear.

"Fuck you all," Sup says when he reaches our table. "Right place right time," he adds as he takes his seat.

"Yeah," Opp snorts. "Has nothing to do with how pretty your neighbour is." He chuckles.

Cal backhands him in the chest. "My sister. Guy. Fuck."

"Never fear, ma'am, help is here. Super Xander is on the

scene," I say in my best Sup impression, lowering my voice a few octaves.

"Don't worry, ma'am, I have very gentle hands," Opp adds in his best Sup voice, the rest of us, aside from Sup and Cal, follow suit.

Cal shakes his head at me. "Not cool," he mutters.

Scottie nudges Sup. "Need a beer?" she asks him, standing up. "I'm gonna go and officially meet King's girlfriend."

"I don't even want to know," Sup answers, his eyes on mine. "And please, I'm not making it through this night without one."

I lean back in my chair and glance over at Violette mixing up a martini. Her eyes meet mine as Scottie approaches the bar. I swear to Christ, everything moves in slow motion while we look at each other across the room. It's warm in here so the slight glow of her skin under those neon lights makes me want to hop the bar, press her up against the counter, and make her scream my name. She pulls her eyes from mine as Scottie leans in and whispers something to her. Violette looks at her first in surprise then directly at me with a you're-a-shit-head kind of grin.

I tip my beer to her and grin. Fuck, I can't wait to get her alone.

Violette

"He said I'd give you special beer?" I say to the pretty woman who's been tight knit with Cal all night. I'm guessing this is his girlfriend I keep hearing about. "And I would do this because I'm his *girlfriend*?" I ask in a higher octave.

She leans in, her light, coppery waves tumble over her shoulders.

"Yep, he said it with quite a bit of confidence too." She laughs.

"Thing is, I know you're not his girlfriend, I just thought maybe we could fuck with him a little?" she asks, eyebrow raised. "I'm Scottie, by the way. What's the girliest drink you've got in this place?"

I smile. She has an air of mischief about her. I like this girl already.

"Violette," I say, extending my hand. "You're dating Cal, right?"

"Still contemplating." She winks, and I laugh as I pull out a beer for the regular to her left, crack it, and hand it to him.

"He's a good guy—Cal." I nod. "A little hot headed sometimes, but good." I grin.

She turns and looks back at him. He's deep in conversation with Rowan. They're laughing and looks like they're busting Pop's balls over something.

"Yeah, he kinda keeps proving that over and over again." She grins. She has a pretty smile and she seems cool as hell. I can see why Cal is, as Rowan says, "borderline obsessed with her."

"So, what's the deal with you two?" Scottie asks, like we're already old friends, and for some reason I feel like we could be very easily.

I look at Rowan over her shoulder, trying my best not to notice how strong and relaxed he looks. His one arm is slung over the back of the chair next to him and the smile on his face is one that would bring any woman to her knees. He's easy, cool, confident, and so fucking hot it hurts. His strong upper arms strain against his gray Carhartt T-shirt and his dark blond waves poke out slightly from that damn backward baseball hat.

"Hmm, if I had to guess, Violette, I'd say you're contemplating too," Scottie jokes, her bottom lip between her teeth as she assesses my stare at Rowan.

It breaks my gaze, and I smirk at her and huff out a breath.

"Fucking hotshots." I giggle.

"Agreed." She laughs. "Now, you ready to fuck with him?"

I lean in so we can plan their demise accordingly. "Always."

ROWAN

"What the fuck is this?" I ask Scottie when she comes back to the table with beer for every guy here except me. In front of me she places Shifty's in house "No Shoes," their twenty-four-ounce strawberry cream daiquiri with layers of whipped cream and topped with a twirly pink umbrella and some fresh berries.

"Your special drink. So much booze in it you'll be losing your shoes and on the dance floor before it's gone, or so they say," Scottie yells over the music.

"So I've heard." I chuckle. Everyone in town has had this drink at some point or another. Except me. *Until now.*

"She said to tell you she knows her man, and her man likes his fruity little drinks," she adds, taking her seat beside Cal as every guy at my table busts a gut.

Scottie tosses Violette a grin over her shoulder, and I know these two vixens were in on it together.

Fuck it, I bring the sugary liquid to my lips intentionally and take a great big swig. *"Delicious,"* I mouth to Violette.

She laughs, and I feel like the joke's on her. I have her attention, her laughter, and even if it was fake, she called me her man.

Seems like a win-win to me.

CHAPTER 35

Violette

"Might have to start ordering those all the time," Rowan says, setting his empty daiquiri glass down on the bar in front of me.

I laugh. "Well, isn't it my humor that made you want to make me your girlfriend, darlin'?" I ask him.

He smirks at me, it's a bit of a tipsy smirk, but it should be considering I made his drink pretty strong. Rowan's a big guy though so it would take more than a daiquiri, even a good sized one, and a couple of beers to bowl him over.

He leans his elbows down on the bar, his face only a few inches from mine in the noisy crowd.

"Truth, Vi?"

I lean forward. "Truth, Kingsley," I challenge.

"I think you *like* that I called you my girlfriend."

"Oh yeah?" I ask, pulling out a shot glass and setting it on the bar, feeling a little free. With Hollie sleeping at my parents tonight, and Rowan in my space with his eyes on me for the majority of the night, I feel like a stiff drink is in order. I pour a double of Jack and knock it back, licking my lips as I do. When I set the glass on the bar and look back up at Rowan, he's staring, his bottom lip between his teeth.

"Never wished I was whiskey before so that's a first," he says. My core aches with just his touch as he tucks a piece of hair behind my ear. The stolen kisses when Hollie wasn't looking or after she's gone to bed have been the only contact I've had with him between my busy work days, but they're just enough to make me want more, to want it all.

He leans over the bar and brings his lips to the shell of my ear. The crowd is noisy dancing to Zach Bryan's Revival but all I can hear is him.

"You're so fucking sexy, Vi, and you're damn lucky this bar is full or I'd be propping you right up on this bar top."

"Oh yeah?" I ask. "Then what?" I taunt.

Rowan chuckles in surprise with my forward question, looking down to gather his thoughts. When he returns his eyes to mine, they're smoldering, like he's teetering on the edge of losing control. I never realized it until right now, but I think I *want* him to lose control.

His lips brush my earlobe and my neck breaks out in goose-bumps, as he rises to my challenge.

"Well, since you asked, I'd be pushing your panties aside, the ones I just know would be soaked for me, and then I'd fuck your tight little pussy until you were tired and spent from screaming my name." My breath hitches with his words. He slides his fingers up my forearm, and his voice is a hoarse whisper. "But, like I said, this bar is way too full for that, and I definitely don't share."

I tilt my lips up to his, feeling almost desperate and breath-less. I swear I hear a growl leave his chest.

"Pool?" Opp asks, wrapping his arm around Rowan's neck, breaking our connection.

"Hey, Little T," Opp says. "This fucker bothering you?"

I shake my head, trying to regain my composure and grin at Opp. "Not any more than usual."

Rowan knocks his fist on the bar once as he starts to back up. "One more hour until you're off, yeah, Vi?" he asks.

"'Bout that," I say without looking up to meet his gaze as Opp pulls him away.

"I'll be here. Just what kind of a boyfriend would I be if I didn't make sure you got home safe," he calls out, cupping his mouth through the crowd just as the music ends. The people in the nearby vicinity stop what they're doing and glance between us. A few of them start to laugh when they see embarrassment on my face.

"Let's fuckin' go, loverboy," Opp says, fake punching Rowan to the kidney, and I turn and smile to myself. I most definitely liked it when he called me his girlfriend.

As luck would have it, the last hour of my shift I end up taking over for Lou in the back for the rest of my shift—he can only enter in data so long before his arthritis kicks up.

When the noise has died down, I'm convinced Rowan has probably given up and gone home, but I can't be sure because I left my phone under the bar. I take a deep breath, I'm not a chicken, but the idea of being alone with him has made me, well, a bit of a chicken.

I tidy up my logbook and plug in the bar iPad, checking the time. It's just after 2 a.m.

Music still plays through the sound system as I make my way to the front, and I wonder why Lou left it on, he usually hates the noise after the bar is closed.

It's dark when I get out of the back office, the Christmas lights that hang from the ceiling are the only lights still on when I come through the long hallway at the back of the bar. I wonder briefly if Lou is even still here or if he left, but my question is answered the moment I round the corner and see Rowan, sitting alone in the dim light, waiting for me.

I stop dead in my tracks, not saying a word, just watching the easy rise and fall of his chest sitting at the bar, his large hands folded in front of him like he has all the time in the world.

I look around and try to appear like I have it together as he stands and makes his way to the front door.

"Are we alone?" I ask, already sensing that we are.

"Mm-hmm," he answers, standing and moving toward the one and only large front window. I watch frozen as he tugs the string of the blinds to drop them down to the bottom of the window. He grabs the handle and tilts them downward until they're fully closed.

Such a simple action shouldn't have my heart rate sitting at a cool 180, should it?

"I told you I was going to wait for you, did you think I'd just go back on my word, Vi?" he asks. "I sent Lou and the others off. Told them we'd lock up," he adds as he makes his way across the bar to the big wooden front door. His voice, normally full of flirty amusement, is different. Right now, it's deeper and steady, serious almost, and it's sinking beneath my skin, causing all the butterflies in my stomach to take flight.

"That make you nervous?" he asks.

"A little."

"Good, I like you a little nervous."

"I thought you'd just get tired of waiting," I say honestly as I remain frozen to my spot beside the bar like my feet are cemented to the floor.

Rowan raises a hand and places it in the center of the door as he uses his other to turn the heavy deadbolt, the click it makes almost echoes through the space as he locks us in the bar. He slowly reaches up and swings the latch guard over, then turns to face me, staring at me for a beat under the brim of his hat before he begins to stalk toward me in even strides. A look of surety lines the planes of his face and in this lighting, the square angles of his jaw and the intensity in his blue eyes is a sure fire way to anchor me here. Like I'm the prey, caught in his trap, just waiting for him to come and devour me.

He smirks. "If I haven't gotten tired of waiting for the last ten years, what would ever make you think a couple hours could deter me?" he asks as he takes his hat off and tosses it on a nearby table. He runs his hand through his hair as he approaches me. "Unless you're not ready to be alone with me…in which case, I'll go," he says. The flex of his arm is mesmerizing. I let my eyes trail down his skin, down the ink that peeks out from under his shirt and I remember just what Rowan Kingsley looks like naked. *Incredible.*

"D-don't go," I manage.

"What are you thinking about right now? The look you're wearing…I can't place it." He pins me with a concentrated stare as he moves even closer, until he's standing right in front of me.

Rowan looks down at me, the scent of sandalwood and mint fills my senses. His hands come up to slide down each of my shoulders, and I fill myself with as much bravery as I can muster. I tilt my head up to look him in his gorgeous navy eyes.

"Was just thinking about what you look like under that shirt." I know the moment the words are out of my mouth there's no going back.

Rowan drops his hands from me and huffs out a little chuckle before using one hand to reach behind his neck and grip the back of his shirt, pulling it off over his head easily and balling it up before tossing it behind him. My eyes move shamelessly over his body for a good ten seconds that feel endless. This man is goddamn perfection, he's packing some serious muscle under his clothes. Rowan's right arm, the one that wasn't burned, is covered in ink that fully encompasses his right shoulder with tribal lines and words that spread across the planes of his chiselled chest. Even his collarbones are sexy and defined. More ink spreads over his ribs, some sort of writing extends downward and disappears into his belt, and his abs…holy shit, it's like I'm just seeing them for the first time.

How does a person become *that* chiseled?

"Well, I work out a lot. I don't have a choice. Sup keeps on top of us." Rowan's words pull me from my trance.

My eyes flit to his. I blink.

Oh God. Did I just ask that out loud? I definitely did.

Rowan closes the space between us. "My turn." His voice is gruff as he slides his fingers under the hem of my shirt and pushes me into the bar, so my body is flush with his. He's already hard and pressing into me when he untucks my tank top and pulls it off over my head, my hair falls down around my shoulders as he drops my shirt to the barstool. He takes one look at me and mutters *"fuck"* before his mouth is on mine. His hands slide over my naked skin, grasping at every place he can as his mouth plunders mine with an unmatched hunger.

The other night felt like child's play compared to this. This isn't want, this is *need,* and the difference is enough to send my body into a sort of frenzy I'm unprepared for. I moan into his lips as he pulls back and looks me over

"You're a fucking goddess, Violette," he growls before lifting my body up onto the bar top. His hand moves to my back and he unclasps my bra with a one handed expertise that should concern me but right now I'm grateful for it. My bra hits the bar top as his mouth comes down to mine.

Our warm chests pressed together feels incredible. It's a closeness I'm not sure I've felt as he lets his lips trail my jaw, my neck, my collarbone. Rowan doesn't let one inch of my skin go untouched. I let my head fall backward as he moves to my breasts and trades between sucking my pebbled nipples into his mouth and offering light tugs with his teeth. A tightly bound heat aches through my core and I squeeze my thighs around him, searching for friction. Never have I wanted a man like I want Rowan now.

"Mmm," he groans into my breast and my eyes threaten to roll back. "So goddamn sweet," he murmurs gruffly against my skin. The warmth of Rowan's rippled shoulders under my hands feel just like I always dreamed they would. So powerful, so consuming as his arms encircle me. His mouth returns to mine and his kisses become languid and deep. The feel of our naked skin together spurs me on like little sparks from a flame as the back of Rowan's hand grazes the hardened peak of my nipple and slides downward, over my waist to the apex of my thighs.

I tightly grip the hair at the nape of his neck as his middle finger presses against my swollen clit through my jeans. I try my best to push against him. The denim is just in the way as I silently beg for more.

"I can practically taste you, Vi"—his lips trail my collarbone —"and I know I was right. I bet you're fucking soaked already, aren't you?"

How could I not be?

"Y-yes," I stutter.

Rowan kisses me deeply, like he may never stop as he pops the button on my jeans and lifts me with one arm to slide them down my body. They slide off at my ankle as he sinks back between my thighs, never once breaking the kiss, a kiss and a feeling I would get down on my knees and pray for.

"That's okay, you were right too…" Rowan whispers. "What you said to me in the hospital."

"Hmm?" I whisper as he presses his thumb to my clit through my panties and a zap of pleasure rushes through me.

"Our bodies *do* always know exactly what they need, all we have to do is listen…" He pinches my clit and this time I cry out. My eyes meet his, and he smirks. He knows he owns me. His pupils are blown out and full of lust, his hair is perfectly messy, and his strong arms are flexed as he holds me firmly in place.

"Yeah, I'm gonna give you just what your body needs." His voice is low and deep.

"Yes…please," I moan, not even getting the words out before my eyes roll back.

When I feel his first two fingers push the lace of my panties aside and he's met with my soaking core, he groans low and deep into my lips.

"*Fuuuuck,* Vi…" he mutters. "This all for me, love?"

It's a simple word, but the sound of Rowan calling me "love" is my undoing.

"Yes, all for you…" I mutter incoherently.

"You ready to be honest with me now?" he asks, pushing his first two fingers into my pussy. I whimper and clench around him as he stretches me. "See, I'm not afraid to admit that I've been thinking about you every waking second, since the moment I knew you were back in town. Now, you admit you've been thinking about me too."

I pant breathlessly as Rowan works his fingers in and out of my pussy, all while keeping his thumb moving against my clit in tight circles.

"Come on, Vi, be honest."

I tip my head down to meet his blue eyes just wanting to fuck with him.

"Not *all* the time," I say, trying my best to maintain control when really, I feel like I'm about to come all over his hand.

His fingers stop their gentle assault and he pulls back slightly to lay a tight little slap to my clit.

"I said, '*honest,*'" he commands in a deep timbre under the shell of my ear.

I shiver as the pain he just caused is erased by the slow sweep of my own arousal being spread through my slit and then over my clit, as if he's soothing the pain he just caused. *Fucking hell, that feels good.*

"I think of you, yes," I moan.

"When?" he asks, working his fingers back in like a reward for my honesty.

"When I want to…feel good," I mutter, lost to the way he's finger fucking my pussy.

"I see…when you want to come, that's when you think of me?"

"Yes," I admit, feeling just free enough as his fingers slide into me in a hypnotizing rhythm. "And I…think about you a lot more than that. A lot more than I should. It's goddamn frustrating," I add.

"Oh, yeah? Tell me more." I can almost feel his smirk skating across my neck with my admission. He loves that I'm at his mercy right now, but I'm too far gone to care, because the way he's touching me tells me my body is just an instrument and he's going to play me expertly, over and over again.

"I think of you…doing exactly this," I cry out. His words, the dirty things he says, his touch, all of it is too much. It's like a sort of sensory overload and I'm helpless to stop it.

"Just this?" he asks, adding more pressure to my clit. A zap of pleasure shoots up my body.

"And fucking me," I blurt out, but it's exactly what he wants.

"Do you want to hear my confession too?" he asks.

I nod in answer, barely able to keep it together, let alone answer him.

"This morning, I fucked my own hand, imagining this. Imagining making you *this* wet for me. Imagining doing unholy, depraved things to you. And I'm not ashamed to admit it. Do you know why?"

I mewl into him with his words. "Why?"

"Because you feel like my center Vi. You bring me peace, but Christ, all I want to do is fuck you like we're at war."

Oh God.

Just when I think I can't take anymore, Rowan curves his

fingers into me in such a way that has me writhing on the bar top. "And I think when you find someone you can have both with, you have to hold on to them as long as you can."

All at once everything I'm feeling rolls to my center and is heightened by his sweep against my clit.

"Now, give me a little taste of what I have to look forward to. Say my name, love. Show me you're good and ready for my cock."

"Rowan…" I cry without any thought, as my pussy clenches around his fingers and I come—hard. My legs shake as I see stars behind my eyelids.

"Again," he growls as he lays another little slap to my clit, and I continue coming in waves, the orgasm feels never ending.

"Rowan, please…" I trail off, burying my head in his shoulder, trying to regain my breath, trying to come back down from such an intense orgasm.

"Attagirl, I knew you could be honest." Rowan pulls his fingers from me and sucks them clean, even sucking what he can from his thumb.

He stands between my legs, a shirtless god, his eyes full of want and I decide this vision of him is hands down the sexiest thing I've ever seen.

"I've waited so long for you," he says, sliding my arousal back over my still so sensitive clit. "I'm going to fucking devastate this pussy, and when I'm done Violette, you'll be thanking me for giving you exactly what you've missed for ten years."

CHAPTER 36

ROWAN

I bite back a groan as I take in the most incredible view sitting before me on the bar top, glistening and needy. Violette's eyes are full of desire, her cheeks are flushed, and her breath is quick and shallow. Her hair hangs down in thick waves over her perfect tits. The soft dip of her waist begs for my hands, she's all mine for the taking and, fuck, have I waited. I've never wanted a woman more, and I know I never will.

Violette Taylor is the salvation I seek, and I want everything all at once as I unbuckle my jeans and back up, trying my best to savor this view.

My cock bobs free and I take it in my hand as Violette's cheeks pinken with the sight, her eyes grow wide.

"Holy shit," she blurts out as I move back toward her.

I chuckle as I continue my stroke. She squirms, and the sight of the prettiest pussy I've ever seen, ready for me to lay claim to it, causes pre-cum to leak from my tip.

"You failed to tell me you had a twelve-inch cock," she says, fear lining her voice. My ego likes the idea of Violette being a bit afraid.

I chuckle. "Not quite, love." I shrug. "Nine, and on a real good day, maybe nine-and-a-half."

"This is going to hurt," she mutters, yet her eyes are full of want.

"It might," I tell her honestly. "But I'll make sure it feels so fucking good."

I drop a chaste kiss on her lips, anchoring myself between her soft thighs. Thank you, Shifty's bar top for being the perfect height to fuck.

"Promise?"

"Promise. We'll be a perfect fit, you and me."

She moans when she feels my cock slide through her soaking slit, up and down, slowly.

Fuck, I'm dying to be inside her. So warm. So *wet.* So fucking *tight.*

"We're really gonna do this? In the bar?" she asks with a smirk, looking so beautiful and breathless, pulling me closer as I toy with one of her nipples.

I stop with her words and slide my hands up to grip her face, kissing her gently.

"There isn't a part of me that cares where we are," I tell her as I pull her hand down and place it against my chest. She breathes a little slower when she feels the steady thunderous beat of my heart.

"All that matters is this—how we feel—and I feel so much for you, Violette. All of this is for you," I tell her before sliding her hand from my chest down to my cock. "And all of this," I mutter before my lips are on hers again.

She moans into my mouth and her voice is a whisper. "I really want you, Rowan."

Her eyes focus on me and I can't take one more second. I press into her just a little, just enough to make us both stop breathing for a second and look into each other's eyes.

"I'm on the pill," she says quickly. "And I'm clean."

I nod. "I'm clean too, I've never gone without a condom, but I don't want to wear one with you, ever." My cock throbs against her. "I want to feel every inch of you, Vi."

"Me too." She tilts her head to kiss me. It's a gentle kiss that makes it feel like time has stopped, because as she kisses me she's pulling herself closer, just enough that I sink into her the first inch or so. Her kiss tells me she trusts me, she wants me. That after everything, she's *choosing* me, and that feels over-fucking-whelming. It's giving me the kind of feelings I have no clue what to do with, because I've never felt them before.

Violette breathes out in tiny pants as I push myself into her a little more. It's definitely going to be a tight fit.

"Breathe with me, love," I tell her.

"Breathing isn't going to help me here." She shivers as I push in a little further. I kiss her plush pink lips and smirk down at her.

"You'll get used to me. This pussy will be begging for me to fill it every fucking day. Now, breathe."

Violette does what I tell her, sucking in a breath as I grip her pert ass in my hands and pull her down onto my cock a little more. Goddamn, even this threatens to ruin me.

She grips my shoulders as I continue my sink, one inch at a time. I pause when I get halfway and stroke her cheek with my thumb.

"I'm so fucking proud of you, Vi, you're doing so good."

"*More,*" she says with a bit of sass, and I do what she commands, this time not quite as gently. Violette whimpers with pleasure, and I know there's a side of her I'm going to love uncovering.

"Fuck, the way your soaking cunt stretches around my cock is so goddamn perfect," I groan, losing myself to this pussy that was made just for me.

"Rowan," she whimpers. "Please...those words, I want more."

I lose all control with her dirty admission and bury myself in her almost to the hilt, staying here for a second, stilling my hips until there's no telling where I end and she begins. Violette wrapped around my cock with nothing between us feels fucking otherworldly.

"Own it, Vi. Take that last inch, show me how desperate you are for it," I tell her.

She moans and her head falls back against my hands. I grip her hair in my fist as she tightens her legs around my waist and pulls herself down on my cock, filling herself with the last inch until I'm fully rooted in her. We both huff out a breath.

"You're fucking *killing* me," I groan.

"Same," she whimpers as I pull out of her slightly and then bottom out inside her again.

"Oh *God*." She shivers as she meets my depth.

I press my finger to her plush lips, her eyes open, meeting mine. I shake my head. "Rowan," I correct. "I told you. I don't share. My name only, *always*."

Violette looks right at me and fucking smirks. "*Rowan*," she says in a sexy, deliberate moan, as she moves her hips, taking control. "Like that?" she asks with a tone that encourages me to properly fuck her until she can't walk.

"Fuck yes," I tell her. "Little brat," I add with a smirk, pulling out and slamming back into her. Her eyes flutter closed.

"Fuck...*Rowan*," she moans again, louder this time, almost loud that enough anyone on the street outside could hear her.

"You feel...I'm so full."

"Goddamn," I groan as I set my pace, fucking into her with the deep, claiming strokes I need after years of waiting for her.

With every single thrust I threaten to unload in her. She feels too good. There will be time to be tender, time to take things slow and times when I'll fuck her from sundown to sun up, but this isn't that time.

This is a savage need we both can't control. This is something I'd be willing to bet neither of us has ever felt. Glasses hanging under the bar top start to rattle as I fuck into Violette without restraint. Her pussy clenches my cock as her legs squeeze my waist and heat licks up the base of my spine. I take hold of her thigh and I don't stop. *I never want to stop.*

"Your pussy has been waiting so patiently for *me*," I tell her as I bury myself in her then pull out almost to the tip, trying to savor every single second. I slam back into her again and again, I don't know for how long and she cries out. Every time, I almost come on the spot.

"I was the first man to make you come?" I ask her, already knowing the answer.

"Yes...you were," she whispers breathlessly, lost in the perfect rhythm of us moving together.

"Mark my words, love. I'll be the last," My voice is low and commanding. "Now look, Vi," I tell her, glancing down to where we connect. "Look at how well you take every goddamn inch I'm giving you."

"Your words...I'm going to come." Violette's legs shake as I continue driving into her and I can't wait to see the unhinged side of her. I can't wait until she's comfortable enough with me to voice all those dirty thoughts in her head.

"Come for me, Violette, show me what a pretty sight it is when you drip down my cock."

"*Fuck,*" she cries as the orgasm crashes over her, her nails digging into me.

"You come too. You come for *me, Rowan,*" she commands, and Christ, I'm done for.

Violette's pussy clamps down around my cock and I grow inside her as a deep growl rises from my chest. My release barrels up my shaft and I grip her so tight I know she'll be marked tomorrow, but I want it, I *love* it. The evidence of me having claimed her being left behind is intoxicating.

I want to completely own her and destroy her for every man aside from me.

"Fuck, *Vi*...you're incredible... take every goddamn drop..." I breathe out as I spill into her. My cock jerks and static lines my vision until both of us are panting, falling into each other in a boneless heap of tangled limbs and sweat. Her whimpers are the only sound.

Moments pass before I slide my hands up her slick back and kiss her lips, gently, sweetly, swiping her soft brown waves off her neck.

"Rowan?" she whispers my name and it hits me square in the chest because us, like this, I'll never tire of it.

"Yes, love?"

"I'll go on that date with you now."

I grin into her lips, this woman. She doesn't know it yet, but I'm never letting her go.

"It just took some convincing?" I chuckle.

"Something like that." She answers as I kiss her again.

"That's my girl."

CHAPTER 37

Violette

"Does that happen a lot?"

"Well, I mean, it's been…hmmm…forever since I've had a one-night-stand," I say, leaning into my shower to turn the hot water on for us. Rowan smacks my ass, and I yelp.

We've made it back to my house to clean up and order pizza. I have the day off tomorrow but I'm going to pay for staying up this late when I have to keep up with Hollie. Troy has just postponed tomorrow's visit, so my quiet afternoon alone isn't going to happen anymore, but regardless, I'm not ready to give Rowan up just yet. Us together, was unlike anything I could have ever imagined. At least *I've* never felt like that with anyone, before. It felt like we were made for each other.

"Brat," he comments. "I meant your ex bringing Hollie home early or cancelling on her altogether. What's up with that? If you want to tell me," he adds with a shrug. He has a different air about him now than he did before. He's calm, warm, and *very* affectionate. I don't think more than two minutes have gone by since we put our clothing back on at the bar that Rowan hasn't touched me or kissed me. I'm realizing giving in to Rowan is kind of like opening the floodgates and that one of his love languages is definitely touch.

I take a deep breath and decide to be honest with him as I grab us towels from the small closet in my bathroom.

"Troy loves Hollie, he just really has his priorities messed up. He, for some reason, seems to think his time with her is unlimited and he's always put his job and the hospital first. It was the biggest problem in our marriage after Hollie was born." I set the towels on the teak shelf beside my shower.

Rowan doesn't say anything, he just nods and pulls his shirt off over his head. My mouth turns to sand and I lose my train of thought for a few seconds. The deep V that flexes as he pulls it off, the strong chest—

"You're staring, Vi." He runs a hand through his wavy hair, then skims the tops of his fingers along the slight scruff that lines his jaw and smirks. He's so naturally fucking sexy and he knows it. "Not that I mind; you can stare anytime."

I kiss him lightly. "Whatever, I was just noticing how well your burns are healing," I say in half- truth, pointing to his arm that *is* healing up nicely.

He scoffs. "Uh-huh." Rowan's hands slide down to my tank and pull it off of me, tossing it to the floor. "Fuck, let's get you cleaned up so I can make another mess of you, yeah?"

He grips my ass tight with both hands and my core comes alive again. I let out an involuntary moan. Rowan chuckles.

"I love that you're so needy. It's the hottest fucking thing," he says, as we climb into the shower and let the water run over both of us, before Rowan leans in to kiss me.

"To be serious for a second though, I don't understand how he could be a father and only have those few hours a week, but then he gives them up the first chance he gets? I'm sorry that's how it is, Vi." His brow knots as he swipes the water through his hair. I almost don't register his words because I can't stop staring at his naked body in my shower.

"He's going to regret that one day," he adds.

I blink and regain my train of thought, letting the water warm my skin. "I don't know how you can see that so easily, but he can't," I say honestly.

Rowan shrugs and looks me dead in the eye. "I just know how quickly life can change, to waste one second not spending time with the people you love is...crazy."

His words hit close to home because I agree so completely. I watch as tiny droplets of water cascade over him, while he washes his skin and I feel my heart rate increase. It's like I'm getting my own up close and personal firefighter pin-up show in my shower.

His eyes never leave my naked flesh. There's already a hunger brewing there and I wonder how long we'll make it in this shower together.

"I did my best to explain to him that Hollie's only young once. I already have to be someone's mother. I couldn't be his too." I add shampoo to my hair and Rowan turns to massage it into my scalp, then detaches the shower head to rinse it. When he's done, he puts it back in place then pulls my loofah down from my caddy and adds some of my body wash to it.

"My turn to scrub you clean, and maybe I'll torment you a little. When you washed me in the hospital, I ended up with the worst blue balls I've ever had in my life." He chuckles, swiping my hair to the side, he begins to wash me.

"Definitely the hottest sponge bath I've ever given." I smirk as he cleans my skin. I normally have a very hard time accepting help from people, but Rowan makes it easy, natural. I sigh, everything he does, every little bit of care is genuine. It makes so much sense to me why he fights fires. He's a man of action.

"You're a really great nurse, Vi, and a really great mother. I don't know how you do it all. You deserve to have someone take care of you too," he says, squeezing the puff and the last of the suds onto my back. I swallow back the lump in my throat because I'm not sure anyone has ever really said that to me before. I don't speak as Rowan finishes washing every part of me, slowly.

My nipples are peaked and begging for his touch already. The steamy air between us fills with the scent of coconut and I do my best not to let my eyes flutter closed as he touches me, running the suds over my waist, then reaching further to the front of my thighs. Even though there is nothing erotic about his actions, any way he touches me just ignites me. Rowan leans forward to kiss me on the shoulder, the neck. It feels like nothing short of worship.

His fingers trail the valley of my breasts to the center of my navel and I shiver, partly from his touch and partly because the water is beginning to cool. His eyes follow his fingers, taking in every single part of me. I would've thought I'd be self-conscious being this exposed, but with Rowan I feel beautiful and strong as his hands slide over my hips.

"The curves of your body fit my hands like I was put on this earth to hold you. You're so fucking perfect." He drops a chaste kiss to my neck, and I break out in goosebumps.

"I used to be self-conscious about my curves," I admit. He shakes his head and turns to shut off the faucet.

"You were self-conscious, and I couldn't keep my fucking eyes off of you."

He steps out of the shower and grabs a big fluffy towel from the shelf and wraps it around me, then grabs one for himself, beginning to dry himself off.

Rowan runs a hand through his soaking wet hair and droplets cascade down his rippled chest.

"Keep looking at me like that, Vi, and we won't even make it to the bedroom," he says.

I offer him a little smile. "Of course, you would be just perfect enough to *make* me stare, Kingsley," I tell him as I brush past him into my bedroom. The soft glow from my bedside lamp is our only light in my quiet space.

"Oh look, we made it," I joke sarcastically as he grips my arm and spins me around. It almost feels choreographed as he pulls me in close. Everything about Rowan is confident and open. He didn't even put a towel on, he just followed me— completely naked—into my room.

"Almost didn't make it," he says gruffly, pressing his body to mine. Goosebumps break out across my skin with just the lower tone of his voice. Rowan's lips come down to whisper beside my ear.

"Do you have any idea what you do to me? What you've always done to me?"

"No..."

"Let me tell you." He doesn't break my gaze as he reaches up with the smallest flick of his wrist and unhooks the towel between my breasts. It falls to the floor and my nipples pebble when the cool air hits them.

"Just the look you get in your eyes when you focus on mine like that, makes me want to do ungodly things to you." His knuckle ghosts my nipple, and I shudder. "Every damn time."

"And what look is that?" I retort as Rowan's hands slide down to my waist and grip it. I feel his warm, swelling cock pressed against me.

"The look that tells me you want me and that you don't understand the way this thing burns between us any better than I do."

"Is that right?" I try to sound as confident as I can, but I'm crumbling because his soft pinch of my nipple is making quick work of turning me to putty beneath his hands.

"That's right," he says as he bends down to kiss my lips gently. "And *this* look? The one that says you *want* me? The way your cheeks flush when I touch you?" Another kiss comes as his fingers slide downward, over my stomach then between my thighs through my already dripping slit. "That look begs me to *claim* you."

My eyes flutter closed and my lips part.

"Rowan…" I whisper.

"And *that*? The way you say my name when you want me?" His fingers enter me, and I bite back a moan with my bottom lip between my teeth. "I've waited ten years for that. It's like my own fucking brand of kryptonite, Vi, I'd do anything for it."

His hard, naked body presses into mine and I slide my hand down to palm his cock. Rowan groans the moment I connect and kisses me deeply as I continue to stroke over him. Feeling spontaneous and freer than I've ever felt, I do something I've wanted to since… I think always.

I drop to my knees, and grip his cock, looking up at him through my lashes.

"And now? What happens when I look at you like this?"

Rowan slinks his hand into my damp hair and grips a handful of it, before tugging tightly, I suck in a breath.

"This sight is enough to make me come undone, Vi," he says as I lick a slow trail up the underside of his shaft. He's so thick and so solid, just the memory of him filling me has me squeezing my thighs together to try to soothe the ache between my legs.

"*Jesus Christ,*" he mutters between breaths. I watch his chest rise and fall as his teeth sink into his bottom lip.

"That's not *my* name, Rowan," I whisper as he tightens his grip on my hair in response, "I don't like to share either," I tell him. The sound he makes is almost feral but I don't miss the hint of a smirk playing on his lips. He *likes* it when I challenge him back.

What he doesn't know is that when he looks at me like this? Out of control and needing me? He's *my* kryptonite too, and all I want to do is please him.

Rowan's thumb strokes my jaw and skims my bottom lip,

pulling it down, then letting it bounce back into place. He groans.

"You make me feel powerless, Violette, in ways I've never felt with anyone else."

Something dark and delicious begins to coil inside of me at the thought of him wanting me more than anyone else.

"Give it all to me then Rowan," I challenge, swiping pre-cum off the head of his rigid, veiny cock then swirling my tongue against him, taking in the first couple inches. He sucks in a sharp breath and his head falls slightly back with the feeling. "Never hold back," I tell him.

His cock pulses in my hand.

"All right then, dirty girl. *Spit.*"

Wait, what?

"I …what?" I ask.

"Spit on my cock." He commands gruffly, tugging my hair. I've never done anything like that before. Troy was straight silence in the bedroom for five years; in fact, no one has talked to me like this since Rowan. But my body loves it. The ache between my thighs intensifies, unprepared for the way those words hit me. I sit back on my heels, and shift, wishing for friction.

"*Now*, love." His voice is deep and commanding and it fuels my every move.

I let my body take over, spitting onto his cock and using my hand to slowly stroke him. Rowan groans in approval, his grip on my hair tightens, and I moan as he angles my head so I can take him into my mouth.

"You like the idea of pleasing me? The idea of sucking my cock the way I want?"

God, yes. I've never been more turned on from being on my knees in my life. I let my tongue flick his crown.

"Mm-hmm," I mumble.

He reaches down and pinches my nipple and I buckle. "Yes…" I whimper as I pop my mouth open for him, desperate.

"Good girl, then eyes up here while I fuck your throat." His voice is gravel as he drops his rock hard cock on my tongue, sliding into my mouth slowly and keeping my eyes as he does.

I welcome him, as my pussy throbs, doing my best to take him deeply, but he's too big and the moment he hits the back of my throat I gag. That doesn't stop him, he just grips my hair tighter and holds himself there for a beat. The groans that leave his throat tingle right through me as my core aches to be touched. I get out of my own head and just let go, I want to be *this* woman with him—wild, dirty, free. He makes it feel erotic and special.

Rowan pulls his cock out to the tip and drives back into my mouth. I look up at him and the vision I see is something I'd sell my soul for. His jaw tics, and the knot between his brow is concentrated as he focuses on me.

With every move, I keep my eyes on his. They're so dark and full of lust. I try to relax my jaw to take him deeper.

"That's it, open up for me. Let me all the way in."

I moan against his cock and it vibrates through him. Rowan's growl is a savage sound as he grips my hair and I adjust my hips. I'm desperate to touch myself, desperate for him, more desperate than I've ever been.

I squirm, letting one hand fall on my lap and he notices right away. It's at this point I realize he's watching every single thing I do.

"Touch yourself, show me how wet sucking my cock makes that tight little pussy."

I slide my hand between my thighs and let out a little whimper the moment my finger meets my aching clit.

Rowan gets himself into a rhythm, his own pleasure taking hold as he hits the back of my throat over and over, and I love it. Pre-cum and drool drip down my chin as I try to keep up.

"Fucking Christ, I wish you could see what I'm seeing right now," he grunts out as he continues to fuck relentlessly into my mouth. I stroke with my hand what I can't cover with my mouth as I swallow him down. Every time he hits the back of my throat I gag, but the look he gives me in return makes me want to do it again and again.

"You *want* to choke on my cock as much as I want you to, so be my good little slut and do it, Violette. Take it all."

Holy shit, why are these degrading words so fucking hot?

I take him deeper. My gagging and sputtering only makes him harder, makes his groans more frequent.

"Mmm…I knew these lips were made for me." He thrusts in again, and I feel him stiffen even more. "I want you to swallow everything I'm about to give you, understand?"

I look up at him and nod with his cock in my mouth and he completely loses control, groaning my name as warmth fills my throat. I swallow down his cum as his cock jerks in my hand. He pulls himself from my mouth and hot ropes of cum jut out onto my lips and my neck.

I lick my lips as he uses his thumb to swipe his cum back into my mouth. I dutifully suck it off, grazing him with my teeth as I go.

Rowan stares down at me, catching his breath for all of five seconds before he's pulling me up by my elbows and kissing me deeply. He still feels hard and ready as he crushes himself to me. I am completely on fire for him.

He shocks me by letting me go and moving to my bed. He lies back against my pillows, extending one muscular arm behind his head.

His gaze moves over me as I stand before him, naked and desperate. I have no idea what he's going to do but, my God, he looks good in the middle of my bed. Rowan smirks at me, an easy smirk of a man who has all the time in the world. He taps his lips twice.

"I'm hungry."

Christ almighty.

I stalk toward him. "If I must," I say with a small smile, which makes him chuckle as I crawl to him on my bed. He helps pull me up so his tongue can meet my dripping pussy with a light flick over my clit.

"Grab the headboard tight. And Violette, *sit*. I got interrupted last time and I'm ready to fucking drown in this pussy."

CHAPTER 38
ROWAN

Every goddamn part of Violette Taylor is perfect. Just like I always knew it would be. Her skin beneath my hands, the softest dip at her waist before her full tits rise and fall as she breathes in little pants. Her pebbled pink nipples on display and begging for my mouth. I can't touch her in enough places all at once. She's fucking glorious, hovering over me with her sweet, soaking pussy against my tongue.

She cries out as I pull her down by her hips, roughly. I can feel her tense like she's hesitant to sit, but I'm stronger.

"*No*, you sit, all the way down," I tell her before my tongue licks a firm trail up her slit. She instantly relaxes and does what she's told, letting me pull her down onto my face. I groan as I breathe her in, this time I'm not letting up.

"Mmm, *fuck*, I'll be either eating or fucking this pretty cunt until you're wrung out and begging for me to stop." My words are the only warning I give her before I bury my face between her legs.

"Fuck!" she cries out as I squeeze her thighs tight.

I close my eyes and live in the taste of her, sucking her clit into my mouth. It takes all of a minute of me tongue fucking her pussy for her legs to shake violently. The sounds she's making already have me hard as a rock again and ready to fuck.

"Good girl, Vi, make me messy," I command just as she falls apart.

Violette cries out and grips the headboard, rolling her hips, quaking above me. She could suffocate me right now and I'd be okay to die, my face buried as deep as possible between her legs.

"So fucking sweet," I groan into her as she soaks my face. I lap up every drop of her, I can't get enough. I'm addicted to her pussy after just one hit.

"That was like…a religious experience," she mutters, coming down.

"As long as I'm the one offering you salvation, I'm good with that."

I lift her off of me and flip her easily down on the bed so I'm hovering over her. She looks up at me like she thought we might be done. I chuckle then gently kiss her lips, lingering there long enough for her to taste herself on me.

"Ready for the next one now?" I ask gruffly.

She kisses me back, wrapping her legs around my waist, already wanting more.

Guess that's a yes.

"Attagirl." I grip her thigh and lose myself to her tight soaking pussy, making good on my promise, worshiping every part of her until the sun begins to rise.

CHAPTER 39

ROWAN

The sound of someone's truck starting wakes me up, and I can tell before I even glance at the clock that it's late morning. The kind of late where the sun streaming through the crack in the curtains feels hot already and so does the breeze that comes with it. I don't even remember passing out last night. I'm pretty sure it was after five but it was the best sleep I've had in a really fucking long time.

Violette's small room is brimming with comfort. Even her headboard is like one big stuffed cushion. The wallpaper in here looks like something my grandmother would've had. It's navy blue with tiny little flowers on it but somehow all the pillows and antique furniture just works. It's soft and warm and makes me feel at peace. It's Violette, in a space. Off her bedroom there's a little patio door that leads to an old, covered deck overlooking her square, but private yard. It's flanked with trees and has a little swing set.

I angle myself on my side to watch her as she sleeps beside me, we're both still naked and I wish we never had to get dressed.

Violette's skin is golden in the morning light and I take in the tiniest of details that I never thought I'd have the privilege of seeing.

Like for one, when Violette lets her hair air dry, it gets super curly, reminding me of when we were younger. It's splayed all over the pillow and my forearm, so soft. Her face is upturned, and she breathes in a quiet, even pace. Her lashes flutter in a dream, they're thick and dark, even though any makeup she was wearing has long since been washed away, and the dusting of freckles over the bridge of her nose is like a little constellation.

I've been with my share of women, though Violette was always in the back of my mind. I've unabashedly compared every single woman to her and every single one of them has come up short.

I glance at my phone to check the time. It's 10:30 and there are a dozen messages in my group chat with my squad, mostly memes and videos, Opp asking me if I got home okay with a laughing face—he knew I was going to wait for Violette. I scan through the rest and find one serious message from my sup; a crew member on the Montana shot crew we've worked with went to the hospital with third degree burns last night after a fire in California. Sup asks us to keep the squad in our thoughts.

I hate seeing it. Even though it's not us, every single time someone is injured, we all feel it.

I slink out of bed and pull my boxers on without waking Violette up and head down the hall, one more minute of laying with her and I'll be sliding my fingers into that perfect pussy again and I know she was sore last night. I didn't exactly take it easy on her.

The sun is covering everything in her bright kitchen as I begin my search for coffee and food. We never did get that pizza last night and I'm fucking starving. I find coffee easily enough and start brewing a pot for us, then I pull the makings of some scrambled eggs and pancakes out of her cupboard and decide to make some breakfast. She'll either think it's sweet or be pissed at me for messing around in her kitchen, but when she *tastes* my pancakes, she'll forgive me. I might not be the best cook, but I make a mean stack of pancakes, I use my dad's recipe, and it never fails.

I've got Colter Wall playing through my phone and I'm singing along, halfway through my second cup of coffee as I cook. Just as I'm pulling my first three pancakes off the griddle, Violette makes her way into the kitchen wearing nothing but my T-shirt. It falls to the curve of her upper thigh, barely covering her ass. Perfectly placed to drive me insane. Her hair is loose and full of curls as it falls over her shoulders, and she's yawning as she looks around and takes in the work I'm doing in her kitchen. Our eyes meet and she smiles at me, it spreads across her face slowly and it takes my goddamn breath away.

"You *better* be making me breakfast, Kingsley, your dick is huge, and I think we burned a thousand calories last night," she says, coming over to where I'm working and pops a strawberry into her mouth.

I chuckle as I hand her the piping hot plate of pancakes.

"Good morning to you too," I tell her, kissing her on the lips.

She happily hums as she tosses her hair in a big messy bun on top of her head. She helps herself to a mug of coffee and places the maple syrup in the middle of the counter. Every time I think I've seen Violette at her most beautiful she proves me wrong.

If you asked me now, I'd say that this version, first thing in the morning, spewing random profanity, and freshly fucked is my favorite.

CHAPTER 40

Violette

What's hotter than a gorgeous shirtless firefighter in your kitchen? A gorgeous shirtless firefighter making you breakfast.

I pop the last bite of the world's fluffiest cinnamon pancakes into my mouth and take a sip of my coffee. Rowan's hoodie is slung over the back of my kitchen chair so I can still smell his cologne that clings to it as I eat.

"So, about that date…" Rowan says as he sits down to my left with his own plate of pancakes

"Last night *was* a date." I lean back in my chair and propping my feet up on the one across from me.

"Like fuck," he says as he shovels in a bite.

"Hollie is going to *SuperPets* live with Troy on Wednesday," I offer.

Rowan doesn't look up as he shakes his head. "I'll take it but that's too far away."

He looks up at me. "What are you and Hollie doing for dinner tonight?"

My mouth pops open and my chest warms at the idea that he would want to spend time with both me *and* Hollie. So of course I do what I do best.

I panic.

"Um…I'm not sure." I stand and take my plate to the sink, setting it down and then focusing out the kitchen window.

Rowan stands and brings his own plate to the sink, spinning me around so I'm facing him.

"Yeah, this isn't going to work for me."

"What?"

"This thing you do where you get scared and hide like a little turtle in its shell. I want to see you *and* Hollie. I've waited too long to have the chance to spend time with you. Hollie is a part of you, and she's my little buddy. I'm all in, Vi." He kisses my lips. "No turtling."

I laugh in spite of myself then wrap my arms around his neck, brushing these feelings I'm having off for another day.

"You think you know me or something, Kingsley?"

He bends down and kisses my lips gently. "Not nearly well enough, love."

The sound of my front door opening has both of us jumping back from each other. I didn't lock it last night? I look at the time. It's only eleven, my parents aren't due with Hollie for at least another two hours.

"Hello…" Teddy bellows into the hall as she enters. "Sorry to barge in but I got stuck waiting at a train and I'm about to pee my—" I scramble for the hall but I'm not fast enough. The moment I come around the corner I'm face to face with Teddy wearing baby Bea.

I stand straighter, a little breathless, and tug Rowan's T-shirt down my thighs as if doing so could somehow turn it into a full outfit, preferably one that belongs to me.

"Well…" Teddy blushes looking back and forth between us. "I think I just have to say it like it is here…um…" Teddy says, looking from me to a half-naked Rowan. "This is just awkward."

Rowan chuckles and leans against the counter and smirks. "Morning, Teddy. Coffee?"

My eyes shoot to his, how can he be so calm?

"No, I can't, I'm the food source, but thank you," she says, pointing to Bea. "I'll just take some juice if you've got it." Teddy drops her diaper bag on a nearby chair with the most puzzled, uncomfortable look on her face.

"Why are you—" I start. "You know what, hold that thought, I'm going to get dressed."

"You're not dressed now? I hadn't noticed." Teddy winks at me and giggles, she's normally not this forward but it's like she can't help herself and she's answering my question that yes, this situation could get more humiliating.

"Thought you had to pee?" I call out.

Rowan laughs and pops a strawberry into his mouth.

Five minutes later, I'm back in the kitchen to find Rowan, now wearing his hoodie, holding baby Bea. I don't expect the sight of his strong arms cradling her to affect me but, my God, he looks incredible like this, smiling down at her like she's the greatest thing since sliced bread. Bea fits right into the crook of his arm and he uses a finger from his free hand to stroke the top of her head. I've died and gone to perfect daddy material heaven as I watch them.

He's leaning against the counter chatting to Teddy about Xander helping her with Bea's delivery as if she didn't just bust us after obviously spending the night together. He's completely at ease, like he just belongs here, like he just belongs with Bea in his arms.

I clear my throat and both of them look up at me. I move nervously to the sink and grab the dishcloth, starting to wipe down the kitchen counters.

"So, to explain this…" I say.

Teddy raises her hands as Bea starts to squirm. She makes her way over to Rowan who hands Bea to her with an easy grace.

"I don't want to know anything. As far as I'm concerned,

Rowan felt like cooking you breakfast, he was hot coming over here, so…he had to take off his shirt?" She shrugs.

Rowan chuckles, picking up his coffee mug and swallowing the last sip before loading it into the dishwasher.

"So, Vi, uh, did you forget we were going to go for our little walk? Bea's first outing in her stroller? Ringing any bells? I only have an hour before this little peanut will have to eat again," Teddy says, smiling.

I blink.

"No." Y*es.*

Rowan takes that as his cue.

He leans down and kisses me on the cheek before heading to my room. The moment he's out of earshot Teddy is gushing.

"When did this happen?" She moves closer toward me. I take the opportunity to get a glimpse of sweet little Bea all nestled into her mom.

"Teddy."

"Oh my goodness, Vi, I had no idea you went from '*I'm working on it*' to '*this is my bed, sir, let me introduce you.*'" She giggles and I can't help but laugh with her. "His truck isn't in the driveway; you should have told me. You know, since you didn't forget we were going for a walk."

I toss her a side eye as I remember him parking on the road in front of the house next door and she snickers.

"Look, I don't need to know anything, but you two seem to fit together, take it while you can—happiness, I mean."

I look at her and smile, feeling more comfortable and just needing my friend.

"I'm not really at the place in my life to be taking it while I can. I was married, I have Hollie."

Teddy makes a face at me and picks up a strawberry from the bowl still on the counter.

"And that didn't work out, life is about adapting. Trust me.

And Troy and Rowan are nothing alike. Do you want my honest opinion?" she asks softly, fixing Bea's little bonnet.

I finish pretending I care how clean my counters are, ringing out the dish cloth and resting it on the edge of the sink before turning back to face her.

"I don't know, but I think you're going to give it to me anyway."

"Troy was the safest option, and the furthest thing from every man you've ever known. I know a thing or two about worry, Violette. But safe doesn't always mean better, it just means *safe*," she says, giving me a true look of knowing on her end and mine. A million other things are left unsaid, namely that I ran from this town and the people I loved who risked their lives for this job, and I am trying not to do that again.

"This was just one night, I have no idea what will happen now, don't get so invested," I fire back at her, downplaying what I *know* is more than one night.

Before she can say anything more Rowan is coming back down the hall, in his clothes from last night, yet somehow, he's still devastating, and he's left his hoodie for me. My heart skips a beat when he doesn't hesitate for one second, approaching me and tucking a piece of hair behind my ear before kissing me intentionally right on the lips—twice—then backing away slowly taking in the look in my eyes.

Teddy clears her throat and Rowan smirks.

"It's been fun, ladies. I'm gonna meet my crew then head to the gym." He turns and begins to move toward the front door, stopping only to grab his keys and wallet from my kitchen island. He gives Teddy's shoulder a friendly squeeze.

"Good to see you, Teddy, Bea's adorable. Hey, uh, if you see my sup before I do, say hi," he says.

"Pretty sure he's seen enough of me for a while," Teddy says way too quickly then averts her eyes from his. "But good to see you too, King," she says back, fussing with Bea.

Rowan toes his shoes on and cracks the front door before turning back. "Oh…and I'll see you tonight, Vi," he says with a smug look on his face.

I say nothing. I just nod, because who am I kidding? I want him to come back; in fact, I'll probably be counting the minutes until he does.

The moment the door closes Teddy is doubled over, her words come in between snorts.

"One night, *my ass!*"

CHAPTER 41
ROWAN

"So, basically, you're bullying the poor girl into dating you?" Cal asks, dipping a few fries into ketchup before popping them in his mouth. The lunch crowd at Shifty's is noisy so there's no fear of anyone around us hearing these two busting my fuckin' balls for the last fifteen minutes.

"Come on, that's not really fair, man," Sup says, picking up another chicken wing. "He doesn't have to bully her—he's milking this injury for all it's worth. She feels *sorry* for him."

I shake my head and take a bite of my burger. "Fuck you, both" I mumble around my bite.

My phone dings in the middle of the table, I wipe my hands on the napkin and grin down at it when I see it's my girl.

> **VI**
>
> Gave Teddy quite a show this morning.

> I think you planned it. Trying to show me off.

> I'm a person Vi, not just a piece of meat.

> **VI**
>
> I forgot she was coming, that never happens.

I'll take that as a compliment.

VI

Cocky.

Precisely.

"I'll say one thing, if you're looking at her with that fucking dopey grin on your face, that girl is going to get a restraining order on your ass." Sup takes a swig of beer, chuckling at his own joke.

I return his grin, leaning back in my chair and nodding.

"Saw Teddy this morning, she said to say hi."

I meant it as a joke just to razz him, but Sup's face goes from fuckery to crimson in one second flat.

"She doing okay?" He avoids my eyes, concentrating really hard on his wings.

"Seems like it, she was going for her first real outing. A walk with Violette."

"That's the other thing," Cal says, leaning back in his chair. "Just remember where Violette is concerned, this doesn't just affect her," he warns.

"You think I don't know that? Hollie already has a dad who doesn't come around. Trust me, the fact that Vi comes with another little person is at the forefront of my mind. I am taking it seriously, and besides, Hollie is awesome," I tell them.

"Just sayin', I see it with Teddy. Her priority is her kids, I can't imagine how cautious she'd be if someone was trying to date her," Cal adds.

Beside him, Xander chokes on his beer. "Wrong tube," he says, clearing his throat.

I look back at Cal. "It's taken me a decade to get here, I'm not letting her push me away because she's afraid."

"It's not her I'm worried about, it's what happens if you do some kind of fuckboy thing."

"Not gonna happen," I tell them, annoyed that neither one of them has faith in me to be serious. "I haven't been a fuckboy, as you call it, for a long ass time."

I finish my burger listening to the two of them bitch about the California crew they worked with in Wyoming and where they're heading back to tomorrow for a few days.

"Fucking guys just go rogue any chance they get, especially their cap, just show boating," Cal says. "Shit is dangerous."

"I'll talk to Jackson if we work with them again this season," Sup says, mentioning their own leader.

I'm just putting my last fry into my mouth when Violette's dad approaches our table.

"Boys," he greets, patting Cal on the shoulder.

"Jack," we all say in unison.

"Good lunch?"

We all nod as Jack turns to me. "You feeling good, son? Ready to get back out there?"

"Was ready a week ago." I grin.

"I get that, I got some third degrees in '99. Had six weeks off. Was so damn hard not to get back out there at the end, but this is when you need the rest the most. The beast will be there when you're healed," Jack says, folding his arms over his chest.

"All right, I gotta be on time meeting Scottie for our hike or she'll kick my ass," Cal says.

I'm ready for my workout so I chuckle and move to stand.

"One second there. What's your week like, King?" Jack asks. I'm not sure, but I think the look of a school kid getting in shit from his principal just took over my face.

"Uh…not too busy, what can I do for you sir?"

He nods. "Stop by the house sometime over the next couple days, just want to catch up."

"Sounds good," I say to him before he offers his goodbyes to us and heads back to the stockroom.

Sup starts to chuckle as he stands, putting his phone into his back pocket and pushing his chair in. Cal follows suit.

"He's on to you, you're in shit now," Cal says as he throws a twenty on the table.

"He probably wants my help with something," I retort. It's not uncommon for me to help him around the house since Jacob died.

"Keep telling yourself that, bud," Sup says with a big grin as he pats me on the shoulder.

"My guess? You're about to get the '*hurt my daughter and I'll be kicking your ass*' speech," Sup says.

Apparently, they think they're pretty funny, laughing as we leave Shifty's. It's about halfway home when I realize Jack does know pretty much everything that goes on in this town. He would fiercely defend his daughter and while I have the best intentions with Violette, I do have a bit of a reputation from my earlier years.

By the time I've pulled into my driveway I realize that they're probably right. I am about to get the talk.

Well, shit.

I meet Opp at the gym and move through an intense workout. Probably the hardest one I've had since my injury and I'm feeling it by the time I leave. My muscles are tight and sore but the only thing I can think of is getting home, showering, and heading to Violette's.

Only thing is, she hasn't answered me since lunch, but I know she's busy with Hollie.

I quickly shower and do my best not to brick myself up while thinking of Violette's wet, warm body in the shower with me.

By 5:30 p.m., I've got my truck packed up with snacks, drinks, and my grandfather's custom Euchre set for after Hollie goes to bed. As I get into my truck, I worry that Violette still not answering me is her way of doing her turtle thing, hiding on me. All I want is the chance to show her how I can add to her life, how I can help, not take away her time with Hollie. I go over everything I'm going to say to her tonight as I drive.

We can go as slow as you want.

I wouldn't even think of rushing anything with you or Hollie.

You deserve so much. You deserve it all.

I've got it all figured out by the time I pull into her driveway, but the moment she opens the door and holds her finger to her lips to *shhh* me, I understand why she hasn't texted me back. She looks awful. Still beautiful, but awful.

"Fuck, love…" I whisper, bringing her into my arms, resting my wrist to her forehead. She feels hot as fuck.

"I didn't have a chance to text you. I'm sorry you came all the way here," Violette says into my T-shirt. She is wearing tights and the vintage Sky Ridge hotshots hoodie I left her this morning. Her hair is loose and wavy, but she looks…wrong. Pale and clammy.

"Hollie started with some kind of stomach bug after lunch, she was sick every twenty minutes all afternoon, but I think she's over the worst of it, she's sleeping now," Violette whispers as we come through the front door. "Except now, I think I have a fever and I feel really nauseous."

She holds a hand to her forehead, then reaches out to run her hand down my forearm. "Save yourself," she says with a weak sort of smirk. How does this woman have the stomach flu but still look so goddamn enticing?

I don't tell her that there isn't a shot in hell I wouldn't have come here, even if she had texted me. I take the cards, drinks, and snacks I brought into her foyer, knowing we won't be touching them. "Seriously, Rowan, I don't want to get you sick."

"Don't worry about me, Vi, I never get sick."

"I have nurse immunity, yet I'm still sick," she deadpans.

I chuckle softly as I take my shoes off.

"If I could guarantee you that I wouldn't get sick, would you *want* me to stay?" I enter the living room and see little Hollie laying on the couch all snuggled up, her cheeks are rosier than normal, and a plastic Tupperware bowl sits beside her on the floor. It tugs at my heart, and the feeling to do whatever Hollie needs to help her feel better almost overwhelms me.

"You can't guarantee me you won't get sick—" She stops mid-sentence and looks at me with the strangest look on her face, clamping her hand over her mouth. Neither of us move for a beat and then she's gone, darting down the hall to her bathroom. I follow her in as she drops to her knees in front of the toilet, grasping for her hair to keep it back before she gets sick, but I'm quicker, scooping it into my hands and grabbing a clip off the bathroom counter, securing the strands back.

Yeah, there's not a shot in hell I'm leaving this house right now.

"I'll be right outside the door if you need me, Vi," I tell her.

She nods and I make my way outside, closing the door and making my way down the hall to double check that Hollie is still sleeping and then I keep busy. I can faintly hear Violette getting sick and there's not much I can do about that. There's no way I'd want her in the bathroom if the tables were turned. I can only be there for her after, so instead, I clean up her place one toy and dish at a time.

I use my wrist again to press it light as a feather to Hollie's forehead, the same way my mother always used to do for me. She's cool, but covered with sweat, sleeping comfortably, like Vi said, probably through the worst of it.

When I'm done tidying, I head to Violette's hallway linen closet and grab a fresh washcloth, then lean my head against the bathroom door.

"I have some electrolytes and a washcloth if you want them," I tell her.

"Okay…" Violette says meekly. I cast a glance at a still sleeping Hollie and then make my way in.

"Is Hollie—"

"She's asleep, and cool," I say.

Violette's bloodshot hazel eyes snap to mine.

"You checked her temp?"

"Well, it was just the wrist test, but she doesn't seem feverish anymore."

Violette leans her head back against the tub. I run the cloth under hot water then ring it out.

"Thank you…but, Rowan, you don't have to stay," she says as I make my way over to her and pat her forehead with the cloth for a second. She closes her eyes.

"Let's just get this outta the way right now. I'm staying," I tell her.

She must be tired, because she just nods.

"Feel good?"

"Mm-hmm," she says. Her eyes snap open. "I'll sleep on the sofa."

"Nah, you sleep in bed. I'll stay up and watch over Hollie. Gotta catch up on my sports highlights anyway," I tell her.

"If she wakes up, come get me, there's toddler electrolytes in the fridge and—"

"I told you, I'm here. I'm on it. You just need to rest; we'll be right in the next room."

I fold the cloth and place it on her forehead then sit down across from her.

"And just to remind you, I'm a trained medic, you'd have to do a lot worse than a little stomach bug to get me to leave. Even if you did sound like a boot came out of you." I smirk, handing her a Gatorade. She takes it right away, and sips from it.

"Shut up," she says, closing her eyes again. We sit like this for all of five minutes before that look is crossing her face again, and I know it's my cue to give her some privacy.

I huff out a breath when I close the bathroom door behind me as I make my way back to the kitchen, taking some time to wash my hands. I'm not *actually* superhuman, I could get sick.

I spend the next hour checking between her and Hollie. Violette doesn't move from the bathroom floor the entire time. When she finally does move, she gets lightheaded, so I pick her up and carry her to her room, tucking her into her bed. I pull the blankets up over her and kiss her hot forehead.

"I've got Hols, you just get some sleep," I tell her.

She nods and her eyes flutter closed. "Thank you, Rowan."

A tight twinge centers in my chest. The idea that Violette trusts me with Hollie hits me a little harder than I expected. I make my way to the bathroom and give it a quick clean. By now, Violette is asleep and doesn't even notice what I'm doing.

I finish up and make my way back to the living room to check on Hollie, wondering what Violette would've done if I wasn't here, but I already know the answer. She would've trucked on through and wouldn't have let herself rest.

Fuck, being a mom isn't for the weak.

I just sit down on the loveseat and take a breath when a matted haired Hollie sits up on the sofa across from me, rubbing her eyes with the heel of her palms. I check my phone, 9:30 p.m.

I make my way over and sit down beside her, brushing a piece of hair off her clammy but cool forehead.

"How are you feeling, Hols?"

"Where's Mommy?" Hollie asks.

I point to Violette's bedroom.

"You know how your tummy was sore before?"

She nods, hugging Power Piggy and then reaching into her nest of blankets and pulling out the one she gave me the first time I came over. She hands it to me, I take it and set him in his spot on my knee.

"Well, now Mommy feels like that too, so would it be okay if I sit with you for a bit? We can watch anything you want."

"Okay…I got all my yuckies out," Hollie tells me matter-of-factly." I went blahhh," she says.

I chuckle. "Well, that's good."

"I'm hungry," she says in a yawn.

I nod, because that's a great sign, especially since it's been quite a few hours since she got sick.

"Tell you what," I say, moving to the kitchen and grabbing some electrolytes from the fridge. I rummage through Violette's kitchen in search, remembering where her dishes are from this morning.

I crack the seal of the bottle and pour some into Hollie's sippy cup and then screw on the top.

"You drink some of this and if your tummy feels good after an episode of *SuperPets*"—I rummage through the pantry and find what I'm looking for—"you can have a couple crackers, okay?" I bring the box of salted tops crackers with me.

"Okay I'm firsty," Hollie says, reaching her chubby hands up to me. "Can you sit with me?" she asks, looking up at me with those big hazel eyes the exact same color as her mom's. "Bring your pig too," she adds, pointing to my pig on the other side of the couch. "He's friends with my piggy."

"Piggy, right," I say under my breath, grabbing it and sitting down beside her. I pick up the remote and turn on *SuperPets*.

"Do you feel sick?" Hollie makes her pig ask my pig in a high-pitched voice.

"No, we're Power Piggies, we don't get sick, right?" I say in my best pig voice.

"Right," she says with a weak little smile.

"Do you get scawed?" she asks.

"Sometimes." I make my pig tell hers.

"I was scawed when I blahhed," Hollie tells me.

I look down at her and raise my pig's little hand, patting her pigs head. "That's okay, everyone gets scared. But you feel better now?"

"Yes," she says.

Hollie sets her pig beside mine on my knee, satisfied with their chat, I suppose.

I turn my attention back to the TV, picking out an episode.

What I don't expect to happen part way through the first episode is Hollie scooching over to me and snuggling right into my arm, before smiling up at me.

"My tummy feels better," she says with the cutest little grin when the first episode is over. I look down at her and realize that in this moment, *I'm* her comfort. This little piece of Violette. One little smile and I'm a complete goner for her too.

"That's great, Hols. Want some crackers?"

"Will you have some too?"

"Sure," I tell her, realizing I didn't even eat dinner.

I take some out of the box for myself too, and Hollie holds up her cracker and says, "cheers." I grin and cheers my cracker with hers. And this is how we spend the next little while, chatting and watching her favorite show until she's finally ready to fall back asleep sometime around eleven, and I carry her in, placing her beside Violette before tucking them both in tight.

I check Violette's temp, she's definitely a bit cooler than earlier. I look down at them for a few minutes, both sleeping peacefully side by side. I don't know about fate, or about life's twists and turns to get you to the place you're supposed to be, but I wouldn't trade my journey for the world if this is where I get to land. The vision of them sleeping soundly, safely, fills me with a kind of peace I've never known, as well as an overwhelming need to care and protect them both fiercely.

When Hollie snuggles close to Violette and winds her chubby little hand in her mother's hair, I know I'm not just falling for Violette.

I'm falling for them both.

CHAPTER 42

Violette

Water

Need water.

My eyes flutter open to the sight of said glorious water and a Gatorade on my bedside table, and it hits me square in the chest that Rowan really came through for me last night. He could've left but he didn't. Instead, he took care of me and Hollie, and he must have slept in my living room.

I sit up at the edge of my bed and get my bearings. The sound of Hollie's laughter echoes down the hallway along with the sound of *SuperPets*. The episode where Power Piggy leads the crew in a dance party on the beach to celebrate World Nature Day.

I pick up the glass and chug my water. The faint growl of my stomach tells me I'm done being sick, and by the sound of Hollie's energetic chatter, so is she. I grab my fleece robe and put it on, noting that my fever has broken too. I take my time washing my face and brushing my teeth, making myself feel semi human, then I approach the kitchen.

"Not like that!" Hollie giggles hysterically, and I slow my pace just to listen when neither of them knows I'm here yet.

"I'm not doing it right?" I hear Rowan ask.

More giggles from Hollie.

"No, *you* say, *'everybody stomp your feet!'* and *I* say, *'come on, pet friends, jump up for the earf.'*"

I suppress a giggle as I peek around the corner and see Hollie in little miss bossy mode wearing her superhero cape and glasses, and Rowan wearing a pair of Hollie's sunglasses and one of my throw blankets secured around his shoulders like his own makeshift cape. Hollie has her toy microphone and Rowan has a wooden spoon.

Rowan rewinds the show a few minutes and the two of them stand side by side. Rowan looks down at her. "Okay, I got it, you ready?"

Hollie nods. "I was ready before."

I snort back laughter as Rowan chuckles and presses play.

"Come on, everyone, clap your hands as loud as you can!" Rowan sings.

"Evewybody, do your part, find the love in your heart!" Hollie sings.

Both of them jump to the side, put one arm out just like the TV pets and sing together "Shout out for the earth, now LET'S GET LOUD!" they call out, pumping their fists before they both start to jump around.

Hollie jumps up onto the ottoman. "Come on, pet friends, jump up for the earf!"

"Everybody stomp your feet!" Rowan sings, and both of them proceed to stomp until Hollie falls over in fits of laughter as Rowan improvises really, really terrible dance moves.

It's fucking adorable.

I start a slow clap as I enter the room with what I'm sure is a fairly lovesick look on my face.

Rowan spins around; he looks ridiculous, but this might be the sweetest thing I've ever seen. I start to laugh at the adorable sight that greets me, Rowan makes a surprised face at Hollie.

"Mommy is awake!" he says, reaching his arms out, she jumps into them and he carries her toward me with the same kind of ease I do, propping her on his hip.

"You're quite the duet," I tell him with a slow smile. He shrugs and looks down at Hollie.

"Just getting ready for her big night," he says.

Troy is picking Hollie up in two days to drive to Seattle for *SuperPets* so I'm relieved she's feeling better.

"We cut you up some fruit and Hollie said she's going to make you peanut butter toast fingers." He comes toward me and Hollie reaches her arms out.

"It helped her tummy last night," he says. "Just a twelve-hour bug or something," he adds. I swallow down my emotion as I take her from him and she clings to me in a tight hug, Rowan stops in front of me and takes his neon orange glasses off then traces a thumb over my cheek. "Glad you're feeling better, Mommy." He smirks then nods, starting to walk toward the kitchen.

"Toast time, Hols!" he says.

Hollie struggles free from my arms

"Coming!" she says, and I oblige, setting her down. She runs to Rowan and grabs his hand as they enter the kitchen together.

As I sit at the table and watch them make my toast together, chatting easily about Hollie's favorite Disney princesses, I realize how *good* this man is, good to his core.

As he and Hollie place my breakfast in front of me, it hits me that I've been lying to myself. I can tell myself whatever I want but I *am,* in fact dating a hotshot and worse than that? I'm definitely falling in love with him.

CHAPTER 43
ROWAN

"Come in, son," Jack says when I knock on his door a couple days after Violette and Hollie's bout with the stomach bug. Luckily, I do seem to be Super Rowan and I haven't caught it yet. I have a million things to do before Troy comes to get Hollie at three. I'm finally taking Violette on that date we keep trying to plan but I wanted Jack to know I'm always available for him.

The Taylors' house hasn't changed in years. The furniture still sits in the same spot as it did when I was a kid. Their house isn't unlike Violette's, warm and comforting and full of a lot of love. It's just missing one thing and that still hits me five years later as I look around the room.

"Hey ya, baby." Mae waves from the kitchen. She's got country music going and it looks like she's making her world-famous potato salad.

"Barbequing today?" I ask, trying my best to not let this visit be awkward as fuck.

"Yep, got the Smiths coming over," Jack says of their long-time friends.

"Great day for it," I answer, hoping he can't tell how nervous this visit is making me.

I decide to just ask the question I've been dying to know since he asked me to come over the other day.

"I'm always up for a visit, but did you want to see me for something specific, some help with something?" I ask.

He nods and grins at me. "Let's sit on the porch, you want a coffee?"

"Sure."

Jack nods and pulls two mugs out of the cupboard, pouring us each a coffee.

"We'll be out back, Mae," he tells his wife. She doesn't even look up; she just nods as he hands me my steaming mug.

I take a seat on one of the Taylors' cushy outdoor chairs and look out at their swimming pool.

"Well, there's no beatin' around this bush. I've known you for a long time, kid." He takes a sip, and I nod.

"We've seen some shit together," I agree.

"We have. And that's why I invited you here. I know Violette is a grown woman and you're a grown man, and I know there's always been some kind of tie or what have you between the two of you. I just want to be sure you understand what she's been through."

A little confused, I look and wait for him to continue.

I take a sip. Goddamn, that's good. Mae always makes good coffee.

"Not just her divorce. I mean, that was a lot for her to go through, yes." He leans forward a little. "But I'm talking about how she changed after losing Jacob."

"I can understand that. We all changed," I tell him, focusing on my mug.

He nods. "True."

I wait as Jack thinks for a moment.

"Twins have a bond and losing him was like losing a part of her, she's never really been the same since, but she won't let herself recognize it. She was getting panic attacks before she left, she says they stopped when she moved home but now that she's back and spending time with you…it might trigger some old, deep wounds."

His words tug on my heart.

"I understand," I tell him.

"I know you, King."

"You do," I affirm, taking another sip of my coffee.

"I just wanted to talk to you. Man to man. You care about her."

I nod. "More than I think I've ever cared about anyone."

"Then be patient with her, yeah?" He sighs. "She has walls around her, but she needs someone like you in her life, someone who will bring her out of her shell."

I smirk at his words. I keep referring to her in the same way. Hiding in her shell.

"Violette has a way of keeping people at arm's length since he passed."

I nod because I've noticed it too. I watch Jack's brow knot as he talks about his only son. I take another sip, swallowing the lump in my throat. I can't even imagine the kind of pain he felt losing Jacob.

"Mae doesn't think she was even in love with Troy, but he was safe, predictable," he adds. "So, getting to the nitty gritty, I believe that you do really care about her, and I know that there's no way if you're spending time with her that you don't care about Hols too."

I grin and focus on the mug before meeting his gaze.

"It's impossible not to care about Hols." I set my mug down, just wanting to have an honest conversation with him. "If I can be as straight as possible, Jack, even after having her home for this short time, I know I'd wait as long as it takes where Violette is concerned. Vi, Hollie, the three of us together, it's just comfortable and right. There's no other way to explain it, aside from that. And Hollie's definitely the coolest kid I've ever met," I tell him, meaning every word.

"I'm sure you understand that being a hotshot brings up a lot of bad memories for Vivi. I always came home, just make sure you do too." He nods.

"I'll do my best," I say. "Not planning on landing myself in the hospital again anytime soon." I pick my mug up and take my last sip.

Jack takes the final swallow of his coffee and chuckles as he gazes out to the yard.

"Fucking prick!" Mae hollers so loud it makes both me and Jack turn toward the house where she's coming through the back door, phone still in hand.

Jack makes a move to stand but Mae is outside before he has a chance, her eyes blazing not unlike the way Violette's do when she's angry.

"Troy canceled on Hollie. I have half a mind to call the asshole myself."

I set my mug down on the table beside me and rub my temples with one hand as Mae starts to rant having just got off the phone with Violette. She fills us in. Troy isn't coming to take Hollie to *SuperPets*. The poor kid has been looking forward to it since before I met her. I don't think a day has gone by where she hasn't talked about it.

I pull my phone out and text Opp. Fucking Christ, letting down Violette is one thing but letting down Hollie?

That's just a hard fucking no.

CHAPTER 44

Violette

TROY

She's 3, Violette.

This was YOUR idea!

She knows it's today, Troy. She's been looking forward to this for weeks.

Can you transfer the tickets into my name?

TROY

I tried that, it's not possible. TicketHub is adamant now about this sort of thing. Apparently, it's to stop the resale of tickets.

What am I supposed to say? You're leaving me in the worst possible scenario. She's going to be crushed.

TROY

They're coming to Tacoma in October. I'll take her then.

Great I'm sure she'll be satisfied with that only being three and a half months away.

I grit my teeth trying hard not to scream into my pillow. How could he do this to her?

How could he just blow her off like this? Any thread of hope I had for Troy being able to not be selfish just went out the window.

> Don't bother. Hollie is a person and I'm done with you pushing her aside.

TROY

> Violette, you knew what you were signing up for when you married a doctor. I'm trying to do my best for this hospital. They need me for this promo and this is the only afternoon the film crew can be here. I'm sorry I forgot when I said yes yesterday.

> I might've signed up for it, but Hollie did not.

> Don't come around until you're ready to start putting Hollie first.

I swipe the tears off my cheeks and toss my phone on my bed. I don't want to see his snarky reply that I know will be coming. Of all the shitty things to do three hours before he was supposed to pick her up.

I make my way to Hollie's bedroom door. She's halfway through her daily nap and when she wakes up, she's supposed to start getting ready. I glance to the closet where her Power Piggy costume hangs and feel the tears creeping up. I'm not prepared to break her heart.

I spend the next hour while she naps combing the online re-sale websites and it turns out Troy is right. TicketHub has a whole new policy that stops people from using tickets in other people's names which basically means I'm totally screwed. I start tidying up my kitchen and text Rowan explaining what happened and to let him know that our date night he's been planning will have to be postponed.

While I wait for his reply, I start to run through every fun thing I could possibly do for Hollie tonight to make up for this. Take her to the toy store and spend a shit ton of money I don't really have on *SuperPets* toys and then going for ice cream seems like the best plan I can come up with. By 1:30 p.m. I hear Hollie start to stir and the feeling of dread settles deep in my gut. For the first time since she was born, I feel hate towards Troy for letting her down. These moments shape her little mind and create core memories and being a doctor, he should know that.

He does know, he's just selfish.

"Mommy, can I put my Power Piggy dress on now?" is the first thing Hollie asks when she wakes up. I smile, her wanting her to wake up a little first or this is going to be so much worse.

"Why don't we go have a snack first, babe, and a drink? Did you have a good nap?" I ask, picking her up as she yawns.

"Yep." She smiles putting her chubby hands on the sides of my face. "Can we watch the one where Power Piggy saves the baby fox?"

"Sure, baby." I kiss her and bring her out to the living room glancing at the clock. It's two, she's supposed to be leaving in an hour. I make her a quick snack with some fruit and cheese and carry it out to the living room where she happily munches it and watches her show. When she's done, my time is limited and I know I have to tell her.

"Hols, Mommy needs to talk to you about today," I tell her, snuggling right up beside her.

We both jump when a sharp knock on my front door interrupts me. We look at each other for a second before I get up to open it, Hollie following behind. Rowan isn't due here for another couple hours, I had asked him to come over anyway even though our date night is out, and I'm hoping doing something with the three of us together might help cheer Hollie up after I break the news. I pull the door open and stand dumbfounded. I'm pretty sure my heart may burst as I take in the sight

275

before me because it's Rowan, in an adult version of a Power Piggy costume—glasses and all.

"What are you doing?" I whisper. "Didn't you get my text?"

"Yeah, I got it." He smirks. "No comment on my incredible find?" Rowan gestures to the cape and glasses that Power Piggy wears. He's also wearing Power Piggy's magic yellow gloves. If this day wasn't devastating for Hollie, I'd probably be laughing.

"Super Rowan!" Hollie calls out to him. "Can I put my Power Piggy outfit on now too, Mommy?" she asks me again.

Here goes nothing.

"Actually, babe, Daddy—"

"Can't make it, so he wanted me and Mommy to take you to see *SuperPets*. Would that be okay with you, Hols?" Rowan interrupts me, looking at me to go along with him. "He really didn't want you to miss it, so what do you think?"

Hollie starts to jump up and down in excitement and runs for her bedroom to change. "Come on, Mommy!" she calls, running to her bedroom. The sound of her humming the theme song from her room is the only sound as I turn to Rowan.

"You can't get tickets. I've tried—"

Rowan reaches into a bag and holds up three printed tickets. "Already got 'em. Lucky for us, Opp's sister works at the Paramount in hospitality. She hooked me up, we're in the staff box so not on the floor like Troy's tickets, but at least we'll be there."

I look up at him, registering what he's telling me. I think I'm in shock.

This man.

"You...did that?" I ask in disbelief, on the verge of tears. "For Hollie?"

"'Course," he says, leaning in to kiss me on the cheek. "She's been talking about it since the day I met her, there's not a fucking shot she's not going." He taps me lightly on the ass. "Now, you're burning daylight, love, time to get ready. Got a costume for you too," he says, handing me a bag with a grin.

I open and look inside it's Tough Little Turtle's costume.

"Perfect, right?" He smirks.

I don't hesitate, I can't. I throw my arms around his neck and kiss my own personal superhero with everything I have. He chuckles and kisses me back.

"Thank you," I whisper to him, not knowing what else to add. There are no words. The fact that he not only went out of his way to get us tickets, but to also make Hollie believe Troy didn't let her down, is more than my heart can take at the moment.

He kisses me once more, smirking into my lips.

"Never thought you'd be wearing a turtle costume for our first official date, but I gotta tell you, I think you'll still find a way to make it look hot."

I back up and stick my tongue out at him. It feels like a weight has been lifted off my chest, and I realize this is what it feels like to be a team. To be able to count on someone other than yourself where your child is concerned.

I let the night ahead of me register as I make my way down the hall to help Hollie get ready.

We're going to *SuperPets* with Hollie for our first official date and there's no other way I'd rather spend it.

CHAPTER 45

Violette

My cheeks hurt from smiling so much. I glance down at the photograph in my hand, myself and Rowan with Hollie and Power Piggy during intermission. Rowan and I look ridiculous in our costumes, but Hollie is smiling bigger than I've ever seen her smile.

I turn to peek at her now, snoozing in her car seat.

She's worn right out and probably won't even wake up when I transfer her from the truck to her bed, but she had the time of her life dancing and singing for two straight hours.

"She said this was the best day of her life." Rowan smirks as he passes the county line thirty minutes outside of Sky Ridge. "I just—fuck, I'm just so grateful I got to be there," he says as he reaches over and squeezes my thigh. His cape is no longer around him; it's between us in the console with his glasses, but he's still my hero for the day.

I reach down and place my hand over his in the dark as the radio croons to us softly through the truck speakers. The moment my hand touches his, heat slinks up my arm. Whatever I was feeling for him before has grown tenfold now, and I'd be lying if I said it didn't scare the shit out of me. But that voice saying I'm afraid is being drowned out by the voice that's telling me to notice the ripple of veins and muscle in his forearm, or the way he somehow looked hot in his over the top Power Piggy costume. I think back to the way he sang with Hollie tonight, how he picked her up and pointed things out to her at the show, and the way she snuggled into him as he carried her back to the truck.

I look out the window and feel my phone buzz in my pocket.

TEDDY
That man deserves a reward, blow job?

It's not always about sex.

TEDDY
Maybe not, but gosh Vi, a man who puts your daughter first? Without hesitation?

He's pretty great...

TEDDY
blow job great?

I giggle at my phone as Rowan glances at me just before he turns onto my street. "What's so funny?"

"Teddy," I tell him. "And that's all I'm saying."

Rowan side eyes me. "Fair enough, not sure I want to know anyway. That woman has a habit of saying things with no filter."

I laugh, because he has no idea.

"You carry Hols in, I'll bring everything else," he says as he parks in my driveway.

I turn to face him.

"You want to stay for a while? I could beat your ass at cards?"

Rowan grins. "Prepare to go down, Vi. I've been practicing."

"Oh yeah?"

"Yep, added your dad on *Game Room*, been playing every chance I can."

I laugh and pat him on the shoulder. "I'm afraid it won't be enough, but you can have fun trying." I wink.

Rowan chuckles and runs his hand along his jaw just looking at me like he can't get enough before he simply says, "Never looked forward to getting my ass kicked more, Vi."

CHAPTER 46
ROWAN

"You're cheating," I say, tossing my nine of clubs down on the table to meet Vi's ace. "I don't know how you're doing it but you're cheating."

Violette laughs as she swipes both our cards from the center and glances down at the score— nine to six for her.

"One more point and your ass is mine, Kingsley," she says, taking a sip of her homemade sangria.

We're sitting on the outdoor sofa on the patio attached to her bedroom playing cards as we wait for Hollie to settle into a deeper sleep, and I'm taking in the way the moonlight hits her face every chance I get.

Violette shuffles the cards and glances over at the monitor. The sound of Hollie softly snoring at the other end of the house makes her smile.

"I should be letting you win after the day you gave, Hols," she says as she starts to deal our cards out onto the cushion between us. "But I've never been known to hold back in a competition, so I'll just say thank you again instead."

"Wouldn't dream of it," I say just as she flips up the trump card. It's a Jack, the highest card she can turn up. Of course.

"And you don't have to thank me." I reach across the table and grab her hand. "Whatever this is between us, Violette, it's not just you I care about. When I heard Troy wasn't coming...I knew I had two choices. I could drive all the way to Seattle and beat his fucking ass..."

Violette laughs. "That's how I felt."

"Or I could make it possible for Hollie to go, and understand that Troy is the one who loses, because he didn't get to experience that with her." I graze her knuckles with my thumb, wanting her to understand. "The more time I spend with you, Vi, the more I realize these feelings I have for you *and* for Hollie, they aren't temporary."

"Rowan."

I move closer to her and enclose her small hand between my much larger ones.

"Don't Rowan me. Anytime I want to talk to you about anything even remotely real, you brush me off. I'm not letting you anymore, Vi." I pull her hand up and kiss the inside of her wrist, just breathing in her sweet coconut scent. I drop another kiss because I can't help myself. I look into her eyes. "I know you've been through a lot, and maybe you aren't ready to tell me how you feel but I want you to know, I've never felt like this before—with anyone. I know enough to know that when the right person comes along, there's no other choice, it just *is*. I was too young to understand it before, but I get it now."

Violette reaches her hand up to press her palm to my jaw. I turn my head to kiss it. "What I'm saying is, you're my only choice, Vi, you *and* Hollie, and I'll wait as long as I need to for you to be ready to accept that, but what I won't do is pretend I'm not fucking crazy about you for one more second, because I am."

"I'm afraid," she says quietly. I place my hand over hers and bring them both to my lap.

"After Jacob...passed..." I can tell she still has a hard time saying the word, like it affirms he's gone. "I had what my doctor said were panic attacks, but it wasn't just that. I've had those before in my life and this didn't feel like that. It felt like I was experiencing a glimpse of what Jacob felt when he died. We've always been so connected. Once I was at school, and this is going to sound crazy, but my arm just started hurting out of nowhere. Right at my elbow, I couldn't even bend it. When I got home, my mother told me my dad had taken Jacob to the hospital —he had fractured his elbow." Tears begin to well in her eyes and my heart feels like it's breaking. "I get these auras, like everything around me is hazy, I feel almost faint and the weight on my chest, it's crushing, like I can't breathe... like I'm inhaling smoke..." Violette swipes a tear off her cheek. "It hasn't happened in a long time but the thought of you out there, and something happening, it's like I can feel the prickle of that heat just waiting to overtake me." She shivers and goosebumps break out over her arms. I squeeze her hand and look into her eyes, offering her some of my own truth.

"I'm afraid too. I still see him before he cracks a joke and then heads up that ridge, it wakes me up in a cold sweat, and I've always felt like I suffered that loss alone, until you came home. You're the only person who's more connected to him than me. But I feel it too, Vi, I feel him pushing me to do things, pushing me to make choices. He's always here."

I take a deep breath and tell her something I've never even uttered out loud before.

"When I fell in that pit, I was burned in so many places. The powder in there is white hot, and I remember, in those seconds right before I blacked out, seeing it land all over me. When I got to the hospital and I could really see the damage, I had little singes and pink everywhere on this arm." I reach down and pat my tattoo for Jacob. "But not here, not one ember, not one singe, and I felt like..." I blow out a breath. "Talk about crazy, but I felt like I was meant to be there with you. Like he was putting me there with *you*. I know it's scary, but what if we're scared together?"

Violette smiles up at me and it takes my breath away even though I've seen it countless times. "They say misery loves company." She shrugs.

I chuckle and pull her hand up to kiss the top of her knuckles.

There's something heavy pulling me to her at this moment— a need I can't explain, a need to taste her, to feel her body against mine. I lean in and kiss her, losing my hands in her hair. Violette kisses me back. I let her take over. This kiss is all her. Languid and sure. Her soft lips move with mine and her tongue sweeps into my mouth to meet my own. It's a perfect kind of harmony, one I've only ever felt with her. It's a feeling I'm starting to crave to feel whole. Violette moves closer, cards fall off the couch onto the concrete below, our game forgotten, a whole new one beginning. As Violette's hands move to the hair at the nape of my neck every cell in my body races. After that talk her mood has shifted. She's lighter, almost playful.

"Follow me," she says breathlessly against my lips, and a carnal instinct to claim her takes over. Violette pulls back from me and stands, picking up the baby monitor. She moves toward the door to her room and when she gets there she turns back and smirks at me. Her eyes beam when she smiles at me over her shoulder. Again, it's fucking breathtaking.

"I'm just letting you off the hook, you know you were about to lose," she says in a cocky little tone. One that has me on her heels and walking her backward with barely enough time for her to set the baby monitor down on the dresser.

My mouth is on hers and she's moving, stopping only when her thighs hit the bed. Violette's nails dig into my skin through my T-shirt, which is just in the way. I reach behind me and yank it off, only breaking the kiss to let the fabric pass between us before her lips are back on mine and her nails are biting into me again in a slow delicious drag. I take her juicy bottom lip between my teeth and bite until she whimpers. There's an intoxicating balance between the sweet, playful way we are with each other in everyday life and the carnal depraved way we need to own each other in the bedroom. It's obvious to me that those two worlds colliding and somehow meshing perfectly, could only mean that Violette Taylor is it for me.

She's my twin flame.

Pulling herself free in a breathless pant, Violette looks up at me. I place my fingers at the center of the flannel shirt she wears, pulling it open with one sharp tug, buttons go flying and hit her wood floors as I press my naked chest against her. I revel in her kiss, her warmth.

We lose the rest of our clothes in a heated blur, tugging and pulling at them until they land on the floor in heap, and I'm pressing against her, rock hard and leaking pre-cum against her abdomen. She moans and reaches her hand between us to stroke me, my cock throbs and I groan into her mouth. Violette sits down on the edge of her bed and looks up at me, taking my thick cock in her hand and licking the tip. My eyes roll back with the feeling.

"Fuck," I grunt as she wraps her soft lips around me. She licks a hot trail from my base to the tip and swirls her tongue against the underside of my shaft. This view of her pretty eyes looking up at me through her lashes and my cock in her mouth almost does me in. I slide in deeper and hit the back of her throat.

Violette gags but I don't stop, I use my knee to notch her thighs apart. She spreads them wide enough for me to sink between them and slide just my middle finger through her soaking slit.

"Mmm." I take my bottom lip between my teeth as I fuck her pretty face for another few seconds, before pulling my cock from her lips and resting it there. I want to burn this image in my brain, and it makes me even more desperate to be inside her.

"Get up on the bed, on all fours, and spread these thighs, love. Show me how wet this pretty pussy is. Show me how ready you are for my cock."

Violette moans and her eyes flutter closed but she doesn't hesitate. She crawls up onto the bed before me, her dripping cunt on full display. The room is dimly lit but seeing her soaked like this, so ready for me, has me losing all control. I climb onto the bed behind her, swiping her long hair off her back, tracing her spine with my fingers. The way she moans as I touch her feels like she's releasing the weight of everything that sits on her shoulders, like only I can offer her that relief. It's a reward I'll seek over and over.

"Rowan," she whimpers as I slide my hands down to her hips, stroking the globes of her ass. Fucking hell, I'm ready to blow my load all over her just from looking at her like this. I drop my lips to her upper back, her shoulders.

"I…" she moans

I slide my hand downward between her legs, running my finger along the insides of her thigh, toying with her for a beat, never touching her exactly where she wants.

"You what, love?" I ask her.

"I…just…" she says almost incoherently before her head falls down and she mumbles, *"fuck,"* because my first two fingers have just slipped into her pussy and my thumb is toying with her swollen needy clit.

"Having trouble getting your thoughts out?" I grin, pulling my fingers out of her and sucking them clean, just for a taste. I push my fingers back into her and the two of us catch eyes in the mirror over her dresser. I watch her face as I work my fingers expertly into her. The slope of her shoulders, the curve of her back as she rocks into my hand. The way her eyes slightly close and her teeth meet her bottom lip so she can stay as quiet as possible.

Fucking stunning.

"Yes, I…I just…I think you're really great," she mutters in a moan.

I smirk. "I think you're great too, Vi…" I kiss below the shell of her ear. "The greatest," I whisper to her as I center myself. When I pull my fingers from her, she whimpers. "And I'm here to take care of you, Vi."

She nods and shivers as I force her thighs open wider and hike her ass up to meet me, taking my place behind her. My cock presses between her ass cheeks, and she whimpers again, rocking into me more.

I'm so fucking ready to own her body the same way she owns my soul.

"Look at us, right there," I tell her, reaching around to pull her face up so she sees us in the mirror.

"Look at this body, so fucking beautiful…so needy and eager. You're good and ready for my cock, aren't you, love?" I ask, as I slide my cock through her slit, coating myself in her arousal. Fuck, even that feels incredible.

She looks at me over her shoulder in the mirror and moans, nodding quickly, desperately, begging. But I'm not giving in yet. Not before I've made a meal of her perfect pussy.

"I…please, Rowan," is all she offers, but it's enough. I know all the words she can't say. They're irrelevant because I can *see* them just by looking into her lust filled eyes, and, fuck, if that isn't the most beautiful sight.

CHAPTER 47

Violette

I think you're really great? In the number of moments I've said something stupid in my life, that one takes the cake, but Rowan doesn't seem to mind and that might be the thing I love most about him.

He never makes me say more than I can and that's the greatest gift he could give me. My heart is damaged and skeptical, partly because of him, but I'm trying. *I really want to try.*

Rowan moves his hands around to my front, paying close attention to each nipple, driving me to the brink of insanity, his lips and tongue trailing the skin of my back, and my spine. Every nip, lick, and kiss is like throwing little cherry bombs into the blazing heat flowing through my veins. He holds my legs apart so I can't squeeze my thighs together and all I want him to do is bury himself in me.

I clamp a hand over my mouth to stay quiet as Rowan crouches behind me and traces the inside of my thigh with his tongue. The closer he moves his mouth to the ache between my thighs the more desperate I get. When he settles there, running his flattened tongue over my dripping slit just once from behind, I grip my sheets and push my hips toward his face, begging without words for anything he'll offer me. He drops little kisses to my pussy and chuckles as I pant, grinding my desperate pussy toward his face.

Finally, he lets me really have what I seek. His mouth. Flicking his tongue over my clit only teases me and I'm a mess as I wait for him to fully bury his tongue in my pussy. Heat creeps up my throat, my cheeks, as I breathe in shallow breaths.

Rowan pushes two of his fingers inside me, to the place that will be my undoing, as he leans in and groans before he firmly sucks my clit into his mouth. I gasp as quietly as I can. Rowan doesn't stop, timing his tongue with my bucking hips, trading between sucking my clit into his mouth and fucking his tongue into me as I struggle to breathe and rock into him more, taking exactly what I want.

"Attagirl, Vi, I want every drop," Rowan says as he hooks an arm around my waist, pulling me even closer, holding me tight so I have no ability to move.

This is where I come undone, doing just as he orders. My legs quiver as I soak his face, biting into my pillow. He doesn't slow until I'm a panting heap. I've dug my nails so deep into my sheets I'm sure I've shredded them. His mouth makes a slow sweep up my center until he raises up behind me, I watch him in my mirror, the look in his navy eyes is out of control. Starving.

Rowan grips his cock, sliding it through my slit from behind. My heart beats faster and my core tightens as he begins to push into me, one inch at a time.

"Every second I had to wait for you was worth it, Violette," he says as he continues his slow intentional sink. I swallow a deep breath and feel my pussy clenching, adjusting to his size at this angle.

The feeling that washes over me as he continues losing himself to me, it almost makes me feel faint as he grips my hips, moving agonizingly slow. I grab my pillow again and push my face into it to keep from crying out.

"Better bury your little face and bite the pillow, love. I'm only giving you half."

Half???

"Fucking perfect little cunt..." Rowan groans, tipping his head back. He gives me more, then pulls out slightly before sinking back in, squeezing my ass so tight. I lean back to take more of him as his hips move, he fills me like I've never been filled and though it hurts it feels...so fucking good.

"See what I mean?" Rowan slides his hand around my throat again and angles my gaze back to the mirror. "Look at how pretty you are stuffed full of my cock," he mutters, pulling out and driving back into me again, his eyes trained to mine in the mirror. I begin to meet his thrusts, as he moves in and out of me, fucking me like he wrote the damn playbook.

He brings his hand back to my side and grips my hip so tightly as he falls into a rhythm that has me biting into my bottom lip, trying not to scream.

"That's it..." Rowan groans as his pace increases and his gaze moves to where we connect. Watching him in the mirror is oddly erotic, the way he bites his lips as he takes in the view of my pussy working to accept him.

"Look at how your body begs. Sucks me right in, begging me to fuck you deeper." Rowan pulls almost all the way out and then slams back into me again with a rhythm that lines my vision with static. "Begging me to fuck you harder." He bites back a groan, his bottom lip between his teeth again.

"The sight of you like this leaves no room for control." Rowan sinks his hand into my hair and winds his fingers through.

I white knuckle the bed sheets, the pillow, anything I can, rocking backward into him, meeting each thrust. My pussy spasms around him as he gets rougher and faster, and then slows his pace. I can't keep up with him. I'm not out of shape, I walk every single day with Hollie, I do yoga when I can, but I am no match for this man and his hotshot stamina. Rowan fucks me like he could go for hours and barely breaks a sweat. Slow to quick, calculated to unruly. Rowan unleashes his desire like he's wanted me forever, and maybe he has.

In turn, I meet him with every deep thrust because maybe this is what I've always waited for too, someone to be messy and uninhibited with, someone I can truly be myself with.

"Fuck, Vi, I'm not ready to come yet," Rowan groans as he reaches down and pulls me up, my back to his front. "Neither are you." I shake my head and whimper. I wish I could stay like this forever. "But your tight little cunt is begging to milk my cock."

He kisses every part of me that he can as he brings me to the edge one more time. He tells me how beautiful I am, how well I take him, as my head falls backward onto his chest and every word of praise feeds me in a way I've never known.

"You've got another one, Vi, don't you, dirty girl?" He reaches down to circle the pad of his middle finger against my clit, and I reach my arm back behind his neck and turn my face up to kiss his lips because I'm definitely going to come again, but I want him to know.

"Rowan..."

"Yes, love?" he groans as buries himself in me to the hilt.

"I-I think I'm falling..." I whisper into his neck, digging my nails into his skin, anything I can to stop myself from crying out and waking the whole block.

"It's about time you caught up, love. I fell a long time ago, and I've just been waiting for you to catch up," he says as my orgasm centers through me and I'm coming. I reach back and grip his hair tight, his movements and kiss become hurried and deep as he bites down on my bottom lip, and I let him so it stops me from crying out.

"Fucking *Christ*, Violette," Rowan growls as he spills into me.

I feel him everywhere all at once, his warmth consumes me.

Both inside and out, I feel his praise, his words, his kiss, his cum —all of it. His muscled arms wrap around me tightly, slowing his pace but staying inside me for what feels like an eternity. We still, tangled up in each other and this moment, neither of us wanting it to end.

"I've never felt anything like you," he whispers.

"Me either…" I say, still breathless.

"Electrostatic connection." He leans down and kisses my sweaty forehead. The air is heavy and full of emotion.

"Attraction," I correct.

"Yeah, that too." He smirks, kissing me again as he pulls out of me, leaving me feeling hollow.

I fall down onto my bed, my arms in an outstretched U above my head. I smile up at the ceiling as Rowan lies down beside me and kisses my shoulder.

"You know you can tell me anything right?" I ask. His eyes are puzzled as I giggle. "If you were afraid to lose at Euchre to me and wanted out of the game, you didn't have to get all mushy on me. You could've just forfeited," I say as my grin grows to blissed out proportions.

Rowan pounces on me with a growl. I flinch then softly giggle as he nuzzles my neck.

"Brat," he mutters against my skin. "Now, spread these thighs, I'm nowhere near done with you yet."

CHAPTER 48

ROWAN

"You're definitely bringing Scottie, right?" I ask Cal as I keep an eye on my portion of the line where my sawyer is cutting down a snag. We've spent the day an hour outside of Sky Ridge near Benny Ridge National Park prepping for a prescribed burn near a highly developed area. We take away heavy fuels in an area that is highly susceptible to fire, especially when we haven't had any rain the entire month of June.

Sup was tickled when we were tasked to it. He says it's a really good opportunity to "team build" and get the newbies learning. We have three new crew members this season, bringing our squad to a record high since I've been on board.

"Yes, for the tenth time," Cal mutters, wiping his brow before turning to the team.

"Your arms are on fire, but will you stop digging?" Cal calls to the newbs behind us.

"No, Cap," the crew calls out as they dig.

"Making this hole your bitch?" Dixon asks, working with them. I shake my head and grin.

"That's what she said," Roycie calls out to Dixon.

"Well, your mom has a way with words, what can I say?" Dixon fires back.

Roycie pauses long enough to give him the Ross Geller flip off.

I chuckle at their typical bullshit.

"Reason number 101 why I don't want Vi to be the only woman there with this group of miscreants." I hike my thumb over my shoulder as I say it.

Cal chuckles. "Point taken. Scottie likes Vi, said she wants to get to know her better."

I nod, liking the sound of that.

The moment Sup comes up from the base of the hill to check on our crew, everyone instantly becomes a little more serious. Cal won't ride them quite as much about fucking around a little. It's 90 degrees out here and we've been mucking for four hours already. I've been back to work for five days and we haven't been called out to our next roll yet, which never—and I mean *never*—happens. I think the longest I was ever off after mandatory R&R was two days. So, five? That's unheard of. But I'm not complaining. It means I've been spending almost every night with Vi and Hollie, and for the first time ever in my seven years on this crew, I'm actually dreading going out on my next roll.

If I'm being honest, the memory of falling into that pit is still fresh in my mind, although I'm doing my best to stay above it, and the other reason I'm dreading going? I just don't want to leave Violette, not when I feel like something deeper is really starting to happen between us.

"This getting serious?" Cal asks like he's reading my mind. "Hold that thought," he adds before shuffling over to correct Roycie on something.

He's gone for more than ten minutes so when he gets back, I don't expect him to remember to ask me the same question again, but he does.

"So…Little T, that serious?" Cal asks again.

"I'm just trying to get used to the idea that she actually wants to spend time with me."

"And she does?" Cal asks, genuine concern lines his tone.

I nod. "Yeah, seems so."

"You in love with her?"

I let the question sink in for a beat as I toss my chain saw over my shoulder to move up the line. I take a second to wipe the dirt and sweat from my brow. "I wanna be with her every chance I get," I say honestly.

"That's a start." Cal smirks.

I shrug. "I'm all in with her, I can't explain it. It's like I'm picturing things I've never pictured before."

Opp moves a little closer to us as he digs. "Like what?" he asks with a grin. "Talking about T, right?"

"Fuck," I mutter. "This doesn't need to be a PSA."

"You know what, bro? Don't even worry about it, bring her around tonight and we'll all be able to tell you if it's true love after five minutes." Opp grins.

"Absolutely fucking not. You assholes better be on your best behavior tonight." I point to Cal, Opp, and Dixon, who all start chuckling.

Opp raises his hands in innocence. "I'm fuckin' hurt King, whaddya take us for?" he asks with a grin that says I'm fucked.

By the time I get to Violette's I'm still re-thinking taking her out with the boys. They're a bunch of unhinged apes when they drink, and the last thing I need is them putting her on the spot or spooking her.

I know Hollie is already with Mae and Jack for the night, and even though I'm starting to get attached to mine and Hollie's little *SuperPets* ritual, the thought of having Violette all to myself has me already getting hard on her goddamn doorstep as I knock on the door.

I wait not so patiently for Violette to answer. Knock again, wait again. Five minutes on her porch and I start to get worried. Her car is here so I know she's home. I turn the knob to find it unlocked, and now I'm really concerned. Nothing seems out of order in the foyer. There are no lights on in the kitchen or dining room to my right, but a soft lamp glows in the living room to my left. I kick my shoes off.

"Vi?" I call. No response so I make my way through the living room, she could be in the shower—

The sight that finds me mid thought sends a warm, twisting feeling through my whole body. Violette is curled up on her sofa, still wearing her navy blue scrubs, her thick hair in a high messy bun. She's wrapped up in a fleece blanket and she's out fucking cold. Dead on her feet after the week she's had. She's had back-to-back rotations and a busy burn unit after a bad barn fire on Highway 4 earlier this week. I know it's been a rough one, particularly because one of her patients is a kid not much older than Hollie. She even shed some tears over him the other night.

Suddenly, the last thing I want to do is haul this exhausted, incredible woman, mother, and nurse out onto the town.

CHAPTER 49

Violette

A calloused thumb stroking along my cheekbone wakes me from the deepest sleep I've had all week. One that is still clouded with dreams of six-year-old Timothy Feldman, covered in third degree burns and crying for his mother. A mother who might not make it.

My eyes snap open to find Rowan, sitting on the floor, one arm propped up on the sofa beside me watching me sleep. He's turned my gas fireplace on, I realize as I shiver. I left the windows open and it's gotten cool.

"Hello, love." He smirks.

I sit up and look for the time on my fireplace mantel.

"Shit, I was just so tired, I just wanted to rest my eyes, what time is it?"

"Shhh." He smirks at me, sliding his hand down my arm. "It doesn't matter. Change of plans tonight. I didn't want to subject you to that group of miscreants and their twenty questions anyway, and you look exhausted, Vi."

I'm supposed to be getting ready right now. I lie back down and take a breath, looking up at the soft shadows from the lamp on my living room ceiling.

"I am," I admit. "It's been a long week on our floor, and of course, Hollie has been bursting with energy. I just need a minute and I'll go get in the shower, let them know we'll be an hour late?" I mutter with a yawn.

Rowan shakes his head and leans in to kiss my lips. "Nah, I've got a better idea."

He stands and makes his way into my kitchen. I look over my shoulder trying to figure out what he's doing as I rub my tired eyes with my palms, willing myself the energy to get up and get going.

I love nursing. It's the most rewarding part of my life aside from Hollie, but there are days— weeks even—where it's really fucking hard. Truth be told, the last thing I wanted to do was go out for drinks and food with a crowd of people at the end of my shift, but I'd do it for this man who keeps showing up for me and Hollie again and again.

A few minutes later Rowan returns, a glass of red wine in one hand and a bottle of coconut lotion in the other. He pulls his phone out and puts his bluegrass playlist on, low enough that we can still talk.

I grin at him. "Wine and lotion? Things about to get interesting?" I ask with a little laugh.

He just smirks, making his way to the wing back chair in front of my fireplace and sits, setting the bottle of coconut oil down on the fireplace hearth. Looking at me expectantly, he spreads his legs and points between them. "Come sit," he says, "and lose the clothes from your waist up."

He holds the wine out for me and I understand immediately what he's offering. I have no idea why, but I begin to tear up as I walk toward him, pulling off my shirt that still smells like hospital, then my cotton bra next. By the time I'm taking the wine from him and sitting topless on the floor between his legs, I'm desperately gulping back all the feelings that are crushing me. Gratefulness, adoration, fear of him leaving anytime to fight the next fire, *want.* I take a long sip from the glass of red he poured me as I sit and relax between his thick jean clad thighs.

"Why are you so good to me?" I ask, as my favorite cab sav coats my lips, and, damn, it tastes good right now.

"Do you realize how good you are to everyone around you?" Rowan asks as drops of the sweet-smelling lotion hit my shoulders before he begins to massage it into my skin.

"I don't think about it, I guess. It's my job as a mom and a nurse."

"It's a lot of peoples' job to be a mom and a nurse, but you do it with everything in you, Vi, with your whole heart. You deserve to have someone give you everything in return."

Rowan's broad palms smooth the oil over my shoulders, and I can't help it, a soft moan escapes me as I feel my entire body start to relax.

"You deserve to have someone take care of you."

"No one has ever tried," I say without thinking.

"Well, then it's a good thing I'm here then, because I plan to every single day."

I sit, sipping my wine to try to swallow down the thick emotion as Rowan takes his time, working his magic fingers into my aching muscles, ridding my shoulders, my neck, and my upper back of every single knot.

"When we fight fires, we always look for the next part of the blaze coming up the ridge. There's never just one, there's almost always two. Twin flames. One feeds off the other, they support each other, they help each other grow."

He bends down to kiss my shoulder, then pulls the clip from my hair. It all comes tumbling down and it feels so good to be loose.

"They connect on a level so deep they just *know* what the other needs, rolling through the trees together. That's what I want to be for you, Violette, but you have to let me…" Rowan's hands slide up over the nape of my neck, massaging gently, and I feel the tears fill my eyes. Even now, after he's shown me time and time again how amazing he is, the pang of fear still holds me back.

He bends down to kiss my neck. "Let me be your twin flame, love."

"I'm trying," I whisper.

"I'll do all the work; you just need to get used to someone being a place you can land."

I have no idea how long we sit here in silence for but through it all, his hands never tire. The breeze and the glow from the fire give my living room a magical feel. I let my head tip backward, nuzzling even deeper between his thighs, barely grazing his cock and I can feel he's hard. I smile with my eyes closed when I notice.

Rowan chuckles. "You're topless in front of me in this light, what do you expect?"

A lot has been said tonight through his touch and our words, and suddenly all I want is to be in his arms. I brush my shoulder against his cock again and I feel him shudder.

"Turn a bit," he says, and I oblige, angling my body so I'm nestled right up against him. My shoulder brushes against the rock-hard bulge in his jeans, as I look up at him. His eyes are dark; the way they get when he wants me. He massages my scalp through my hair even further, his heavy hands feel exotic as they work. I shift again, keeping my eyes on his as he works without relent, moving downward to my neck again, to my collarbone, to the front of my chest as he lightens his touch so the pads of his fingers gently sweep across my neck. I instantly break out in goosebumps, my breath quickens, and my lips part.

"Careful, Vi," he warns. "I'm doing my best to make this all about you but I'm one touch away from pulling you right into my lap." He smirks that addicting lopsided grin, and suddenly I'm feeling just relaxed and tipsy enough that I want nothing more than to push him past his breaking point. I nuzzle in more, offering his cock some attention with my shoulder and drop my gaze, licking my lips at the sight of him so hard and ready to please me. The lethal look in his eyes is a shot straight to my core.

"Maybe I want to be in your lap."

His mouth is instantly on mine, and before I can see what's coming, I'm being hoisted up and he's pulling my pants from my body, unbuckling his own jeans and freeing his hardened, aching cock before pulling me onto his lap. I yelp as he strong arms me and a low growl leaves his chest.

"You asked for it, woman," he says gruffly as he slides his hand down and yanks my thong out of the way. His cock slides through my arousal and he groans before he kisses me deeply. We stare at each other for a few moments as "Wanna Be Loved" by The Red Clay Strays begins to play. The slow twang of the guitar fills the air and both of us breath hot and heavy.

These few seconds feel significant, like we're speaking with touch instead of words. I lean down slightly, licking his bottom lip, and it tips him over the edge. I watch his shoulders flex as he reaches up to palm my face, pulling my lips to his. His tongue slips between mine and I meet it with my own. We kiss, uncontrolled, urgent. The taste of wine on my lips mixes with him and he tastes like home after this hard day, this week, forever.

Rowan's hands slide around me, running the length of my back to my hips where he kneads my flesh, before gripping my ass and slowly sliding my wetness all over him. He never breaks his kiss as he lifts me just enough to push the tip of his thick and solid cock inside me.

I know without a doubt, as he begins his slow sink into me, that I will never want a man the way I want Rowan Kingsley, the way I've always wanted him. This feeling overwhelms me. The feeling of being whole when he's inside me. Rowan bites the skin along my shoulders, kissing over the sting he leaves in his wake.

"I have a hard time deciding whether I want to be gentle with you or fucking claim you…it's almost fucking impossible to decide," he mutters into my neck. "I've never needed someone like I need you, Vi. Never wanted someone…like I want you."

"I want you too…so fucking badly," I moan as the last brick in the wall I've spent years building around me crumbles.

Rowan takes the peak of my nipple into his mouth, and my core throbs with pleasure. All the while his hands never stop moving, feverishly, like he's learning every part of me for the first time as he inches his way inside me, stretching me. I'll never get used to the way he fills me.

"Claim me and kiss me…I want you. I want it *all*."

"I'm already yours and you're *mine,* Violette. In every way that matters, you *always* have been."

He groans with his next thrust *"Mine."*

Things begin to move in a slow haze around us, the light from the fireplace casts shadows on our skin that make the whole space around us feel magical and the breeze blows through the open window. The only sounds are the soft music and us. Rowan trails kisses down my neck, and I lose my train of thought, thinking only of his hands, his lips, and our bodies moving together in the dimly lit room. My chest heaves as we swallow down each other's sounds while Rowan lays his claim to me. Our lips part and I suck in a breath while we both adjust to the heavy feeling in the air. As Rowan sets his pace looking up at me in his arms I feel it, stronger than I've ever felt it. In his arms, I'm home.

CHAPTER 50

ROWAN

I wait patiently as Violette finishes getting ready, we're heading to Shifty's late because Violette is hungry and her shower took way longer than expected because I had to have her one more time. It's not my fault her naked body dripping wet is the most incredible thing I've ever seen. I've managed to keep my hands to myself, barely, while she dries her long hair into waves. We're already an hour late to meet the guys, and if she doesn't put something on besides her panties and a tank top soon we're going to be even later.

"Stop looking at me like that, Kingsley, I am not having another shower before I eat," she tells me, setting her straightening iron down.

I take the opportunity to wrap my arms around her and slide my hands down to palm her heart shaped ass as I kiss her lips. "Maybe I don't want you clean, hmm?" I ask, nuzzling into her. "Maybe I want my cum dripping from you, waiting for me when I tear your clothes off later."

She wraps her arms around my neck and I'm about to devour her when her phone rings on the bathroom counter.

I groan into her mouth, and she laughs, patting the side of my face before looking down at it, then showing me. It's Mae Face-Timing, which means it's Hollie calling to say goodnight. I back out of the bathroom and make my way to the living room as Violette follows behind me tying her fleece robe around her while she answers the call.

"Hi, Mommy," I hear Hollie say as Violette sits at the other end of the couch. They talk for a few minutes about Mae and Jack letting Hollie swim with Bentley and Bailey. They bought her new goggles, and they're going to have a campfire now.

"Is he there?" Hollie whispers. Vi smiles and nods.

"Mm-hmm, he's here, we're going to go out for dinner," Vi says.

I chuckle, wondering if talking about fire reminded her of me.

"Will you have chicken nuggets?"

Violette laughs. "Maybe, but I bet you Rowan will." She moves over beside me so I can see Hollie's cute little face on the screen.

"Should I have nuggets, Hols?" I ask her.

She's all cuddled up on the couch beside Mae and she nods. "And French fries." She giggles.

"Deal," I tell her. "I'll eat extra nuggets just for you."

Hollie smiles wide and a pang of warmth moves through my chest as part of me wishes it was just a 'stay at Violette's and eat snacks' kind of night. As much as I love having Violette to myself, I think I *miss* Hollie.

"Mommy, can he have it now?" Hollie asks Vi.

I look at Vi and she smirks then looks back at Hollie. "I thought you wanted to wait until it was his turn to fight a fire?"

"No, now, please," Hollie says, clapping her hands, sure of her choice and seeming way older than just shy of four.

Violette stands and hands me the phone. "I'll be right back," she says.

I look at Hollie through the screen. "What are you having for your snack?" I ask her.

"Popcorn," she says, showing me her bowl. "Papa put butter on like you do."

"Yes, Hollie wouldn't stop talking about your perfect popcorn," Jack says from somewhere in the room.

"Will you have some when you watch *SuperPets* tonight?" Hollie asks, and I chuckle at the way her little mind just assumes I'll be doing that even when she's not here. Maybe I will, just for her.

"Sure, Hols, if I have room after all my chicken nuggets." She giggles into the phone as Violette comes back into the room carrying a brand new stuffed SuperPet and hands it to me. "This is from Hollie." She smiles sitting beside me. "Tell him, Hols."

I look down at the little stuffed Power Piggy, still with the tag in my hands. I have no idea why, but just knowing she wanted me to have it settles with me right in the back of my throat. I swallow down my emotions as I smile for her.

"Mommy said you have to fight a fire soon."

I smile at her, knowing Vi was going to have this talk with Hollie to prepare her for me not being around a lot this summer.

"Yes, I will have to very soon," I tell Hollie.

"You can't take my Piggy, because he's mine, but you can take that Piggy to your fire," she says before leaning in and whispering, "He will help you fly to the safe spot."

Vi's hand squeezes my thigh, and a feeling I can only describe as love settles in my chest.

"Thank you, Hols, this is, uh...the best present I've ever gotten," I manage through the lump in my throat. "I'll bring him over and he can play with your piggy as soon as I get home, how's that?" I ask her.

"Okay," she says happily.

I flank my mouth with my hand and lean into the camera. "I bet he will help me fly," I whisper.

305

She just smiles and nods and then Violette turns the phone back on her face to say goodnight.

But me? I just sit here and stare down at this stuffed pig in my hands. Because I've faced death countless times... I've watched people get hurt, I've said goodbye to friends, and I've been afraid—really afraid—but the funny thing is, all it took was a little stuffed pig to bring me to my goddamn knees.

As Violette hangs up and finishes getting ready for us to go out, I realize that this is what it feels like to have something to come home to. A family.

CHAPTER 51

Violette

"How have we let this happen?" Cal asks, leaning his hands on the edge of the pool table as he shakes his head.

I look at Scottie and grin. She winks and raises her beer in salute. We just kicked their asses for the second time at snooker, and since they're technically on call we're drinking and they're not—which makes it even funnier. I wouldn't normally, but after Hollie and Rowan's little bonding moment I needed a drink. Hollie is getting attached to him and already worries about him fighting fires, even at her young age, which just serves to fuel my anxiety around the subject.

"Best three of five? Or are you boys ready to admit defeat?" Scottie asks Cal. He chuckles at her.

"As always, Vi, you're playing dirty," Rowan says with a furrowed brow. He doesn't like to lose any more than I do, especially in front of half his crew, but so far, he's been a good sport about Scottie and I pulling out all the stops. Bending over in front of our men when they're ready to take their shot, or when Cal just went to sink an easy shot that could've won them the game and Scottie leaned down on the pool table on her elbows, offering him a good view down her v neck T-shirt. Needless to say, he missed.

"I don't have a clue what you mean. I grew up in this pub, I'm just good at pool. I'm sorry but you guys never stood a chance." I look at them both with a look of mock pity.

"Why doesn't it work if we bend over in front of them?" Cal mutters to Rowan.

"I think they're ready to admit defeat," I affirm.

Scottie tips her head back and laughs. "Whaddya say, boys? Should I wrack 'em up? We'll play fair this time. Scouts' honor." She holds her first two fingers up.

"Nah, I'm not getting sucked into that trap, I've had enough humiliation for one night. Let's get some food. You two were over an hour late for some reason, so you missed nachos." Cal chuckles, wrapping his pinky finger around Scottie's as he calls Rowan and I out.

Scottie follows close beside him and makes her way past us to the tables we've pushed together where eight other hotshots from their crew sit. But when she passes by me, she holds a hand up to her mouth and whispers, "Chicken shit."

I begin to laugh with her just as I feel two strong arms wrap around me from behind. Rowan leans down and kisses my neck. "I know we haven't officially told everyone how crazy you are about me yet," he says. "But you were already tempting me in these fucking painted on jeans, add in kicking my ass like a sexy little pool assassin, and I'm about to pull you into the stock closet." I reach my hand up and push his face off my shoulder in a giggle.

"Oh, baby. All I'm hearing is that you just admitted you lost."

Rowan tips his head down and kisses me. "Call me that again," he says into my lips.

"Okay, baby," I murmur with a grin, spinning out of his arms and taking his hand.

When we reach the table it's full of animated chatter. Opp, Dixon, and Roycie have some local girls sitting with them, and Xander is in deep discussion with the local sheriff at the table behind ours.

"I don't think I can clean another piece of equipment or run another drill for one more second," Opp says. "It's fucking June, we should be in the field."

"I feel like I've been out of the game for months after missing the last few rolls," Rowan says, leaning back in his chair.

"Don't worry, we'll hold your hand on the next one, King," Caleb says with a smirk, not even looking up from his phone, Rowan tosses a fry at him. Caleb doesn't miss a beat. He picks it up from where it landed on the table and stuffs it into his mouth

"Thanks for the free food, bitch." He chuckles. The table laughs but I gulp back the feeling of dread that I've been telling myself for weeks I wouldn't let out. I pick at the label of my beer as they talk about the crew that came in from Missouri to help on the last fire in Wyoming.

Rowan must sense my worry with my silence because he leans in a little closer and settles his broad palm on my thigh under the table.

"This is where we're headed," Dixon says, raising his half-eaten wing to the TV hanging on the wall behind me. I turn to look and notice the local news is playing footage of a fire close to home near Knox Mountain just at the edge of town, it just started in the early hours of this morning.

"Such a fucking shame," Dixon mutters taking in the burning mountainside.

"Oh shit, I'm coming for you, mama." Caleb points his fry to the TV. "Haven't fought a beast *this* close to home in ages."

"Sup says it's gonna be a rager, says he'll be surprised if we aren't called out there by tomorrow," Roycie adds.

They all seem excited to get out there, but something else is happening to me. The familiar weight is sitting on my chest and suddenly I feel like I can't take a deep enough breath.

I look up at Rowan because even though the entire table seems to know this threat was a possibility, he hasn't mentioned it to me, not once today. I do my best to smile up at him, but fail. He sets his beer down.

"We'll be safe," he says quietly.

I nod, and he squeezes my thigh. I do my best to join the conversation over the next half hour as I drink the rest of my beer, but I keep getting distracted by the footage on the TV, playing the fire news that is way too close for comfort. I know about triggers, I understand the concept of them, but I don't think I've ever really felt one crash into me quite like this until I focused on the flames on that damn screen and the weight sitting on my chest intensified.

I watch in what feels like slow motion as Xander stands from a few tables over and hangs up his phone.

"All right, just got the call, boys. Time to wrap this shit up, we're headed for Knox."

Conversation around me halts with his words.

"We report ASAP. Pack up and head out, let's meet at base in an hour."

I know that Knox is only twenty minutes away and if it's spreading as fast as they say, there will be a layer of ash on my porch by morning.

Heat begins crawling up my throat. *Rowan will be fine; it won't be like Jacob,* I tell myself to calm down. *This is another day's problem. Breathe, Violette.*

He *will* be like my dad. My dad came home safe every time. *Get it together,* I will myself, trying to breathe.

I've had time to process this, I walked into this. I knew this day would come, and yet as prepared as I thought I was, I could never anticipate how I'd feel the moment Xander said they were going. White hot fear creeps up the back of my neck and no matter how hard I try to stop it, it keeps coming for me. My fingers start to tingle and I feel lightheaded. I glance at the blaze consuming the west side of the mountain at the edge of town and I brace myself.

What am I doing? This is *why* I shouldn't be dating a hotshot. This is why I shouldn't be letting myself fall for a hotshot.

I stand and look around the table, my eyes landing on Rowan last. "I'll be right back," I say softly, but I haven't even finished the words before I'm moving.

I don't want him to see me like this. It's not fair to him. I *need* to be brave for him.

My palms are sweating, and I feel almost dizzy as I get to the long hallway that leads to the restrooms. I bend down and rest my palms on my knees, trying and struggling to take a deep breath but it doesn't come. Static starts to line my vision.

I hear Rowan speak, but his voice has an echo around it as I look up at him. He doesn't hesitate. He drops to his knees in front of me.

"Vi...fuck, love. I'm here, baby, I'm here."

ROWAN

"Okay, baby, sit down, I need you to do two things for me, okay?"

She nods, still struggling to breathe. "It's okay," she pants, "it's...another day's problem—"

"I need you to take a deep breath through your nose and exhale through your mouth. Can you do that for me?" I tell her, ignoring her rambling. She's clearly having a panic attack and she doesn't want me to know.

Violette nods, listening and doing her best to breathe deeply. "Now, I want you to focus on my words. Take another breath and then tell me three things you can hear." I rub her shoulder gently and she tries to take one. "Good girl," I tell her, wondering how many times this has happened to her before. I could see it all over her face the moment Sup announced we were heading out.

"I hear the sound of a pool cue breaking a rack," she manages to say.

"Good girl. Another breath now," I continue, doing my best to distract her long enough to stay with me. "Hear that Keith Urban song they never stop playing in here?" I ask. "What's it called?"

The hint of a smile spreads over her beautiful lips as she nods. "Blue," she answers as she takes another breath.

I hear Opp laugh, his deep methodic laugh. "Hear that chucklehead laughing?"

"Yes," Violette answers, speaking steadily for the first time.

Relief washes over me.

"Good, that's it, Vi, another breath. Okay, now let's focus on three things you can see."

Violette looks around, her eyes land on a chip in the wood floor in front of me, the neon signs in the hall that says *Buck* over the men's room and *Doe* over the ladies, my hands over hers. I don't need her to tell me what she sees as long as I know she's looking.

"Good, one more breath and then try to tell me three things you can feel."

She breathes deeper this time; the pink I love returning to her face. She looks down to my hand on her thigh. "You," she says, followed by, "this floor is uncomfortable to sit on, and sticky."

I chuckle and squeeze her hand, keeping my thumb over the pulse in her wrist. Her heart rate is almost normal now.

"Good, Vi, that's it. How do you feel now?" I ask.

She takes a breath, this time like it's actually filling her lungs.

"The ringing in my ears is gone, so…better," she says.

I tuck a piece of hair behind her ear and lean in to kiss her on the forehead.

"That's my girl," I say as she brings in another deep breath.

"Has that ever happened to you before? Vi, you just had a panic attack."

She nods and worry lines her face. "It used to happen all the time after Jacob died. I'd dream about him and wake up in a cold sweat. It stopped after a while."

"What did you do to make it stop? What helped?" I ask

"I moved away and promised myself I would never get close to a hotshot again." Her eyes turn up to mine, and I realize what she's saying without saying it.

A hotshot like me.

I don't acknowledge it because I'm not prepared to have that conversation, not when I have to leave her to go to fight this fire for God knows how long.

"I didn't intentionally keep the possibility of us going out on this fire from you," I tell her, wanting to be totally clear with her on that.

"I know," she retorts simply.

"I just didn't want to worry you until it was set in stone. I know this is hard for you, Vi. I know it brings it all back—the worry, the fear."

Violette looks down at her palms, tears in her eyes.

"I thought I could do this," she whispers, and now this time, it's me who's filled with panic. Because I can tell by her tone that she's protecting herself, and that she might be trying to run before she can get hurt. Well, I'm not having that, protecting her is *my* job.

"Vi, this is extra hard because it's the first one I've been called to since this started between us and since I was hurt. Hell, even I'm a little nervous if I'm being honest."

More than a *little* nervous.

"But I know the moment I get out there it will all come back to me. I have a lot of training, I'm going to rely on that, especially after my injury. And I can promise you that I will do everything in my power to make sure it doesn't happen again. But, Vi, that's all I can offer you because the truth is, it could. I won't lie to you and say it *won't* happen again."

"I would never want that promise," she says, surprising me. "I know, logically, that you'll probably go off to this fire and be okay." She takes another deep breath. "I just can't help it. I cling to these deep feelings and anxieties that I've never really let myself admit to because it's *too* painful."

I set my jaw and listen, the idea of her in pain torturing me.

"It's the *fear* of something happening to you." A tear spills over her cheek, and I instinctively reach out and brush it off her cheek. "Rowan, Jacob was my best friend. He was the only person who knew what our house was like when we were curled up with our parents watching TV when we were young, or what Christmas morning sounded like, the way my mom would always turn on the fireplace channel and hum Christmas music as she handed out presents," she says, lost in a memory.

Fucking hell.

I bring her right into my arms. "I'm here, love, let it out," I whisper into her hair as a sob escapes her throat.

"He was the one I went to when my dad was in the field and I was petrified that he wouldn't come home."

I stroke her hair and fight back the sting at the bridge of my own nose.

"I wasn't ready for him to go. I wasn't prepared. The last time I saw him, he told me that when he came back, he'd help me build my new bookshelves. I didn't even hug him. I was on the phone and he just stood in my door and waved." She looks up at me and wears a look of instant regret, knowing my last vision of him was a lot worse than hers.

"I'm sorry. I can't even imagine your memory of the last

time you saw him," she whispers. I grip both sides of her face as I speak, stroking her cheek with my thumb.

"Vi, I've had *three* years of talking to someone to help me deal with that and I still think about it every single day."

Almost every time I close my eyes, but you and Hollie make that better.

"You did the right thing and got help. I didn't. I ran," she whispers like she's admitting that to herself for the first time.

"You did what *you* had to do to cope. We all did." I swipe a piece of hair off her forehead and kiss her there.

"It's never too late to talk to someone, never too late to deal with those ghosts," I tell her. "I'll help you anyway I can."

Just don't push me away, please don't push me away.

"The fear is inevitable, Vi, but so are we, we're in this together."

Violette looks up at me, her eyes look different, hardened. Reserved, even.

"I can breathe now, thank you," she says. She begins to stand and I rise with her, helping her. She looks at me in a way I instantly hate. With a fake sort of smile that says she's about to pull away from me. "This is a problem for another day, I don't want you to leave to fight a fire like this," she whispers.

"You said that already, but, Vi"—I stroke her cheek—"how *long* has it been a problem for another day? "

She looks down at her boots and her answer is barely audible. "A really long time."

Fuck, she's breaking my heart.

"Maybe it's time to make these feelings a 'today' problem?" She nods and fights more tears. "I promise I'll be there to help you every step of the way." It's all I can offer her.

I bend down to kiss the top of her head as she nods.

"I can't change this, Vi, this isn't just what I do. Just like you're called to be a nurse and a mom, it's who I am—"

"I don't want you to change," she says quickly. "I love that you're a hotshot, Rowan. I just don't know if I'm prepared to handle the constant risk of losing you. I know it's shitty to say that now, but I think I was in denial that it would happen. I just can't lose anyone else." She lets go of my hand and I ache to bring her into my arms.

"There you are, bro—" Opp says as he rounds the corner.

"You okay, Little T? Scottie offered to take you home," he tells her.

"I'm taking her," I say firmly.

Opp nods and Violette pats him on the shoulder. "Be safe, Opp."

"Always," Opp replies, ruffling her hair. "Don't worry, girl, we'll bring him back," he says, nudging me, probably more serious than I've ever seen him.

Violette smiles at him but something is off, and it settles with me deep in my gut. I won't let her run this time.

The drive to Violette's is way too quick and when I pull up outside her door, there are a million things running through my head,

I don't want to leave you either, but I have to.

You and Hollie are the brightest part of my life now.

It's not my fate to die out there, you are my fate.

Violette turns to me and I can tell she's doing everything she can to make it seem like she's strong, ready for me to go.

"Don't forget your pig, I'll tell Hollie you have it."

"Give her a hug for me, tell her I'm sorry I'll miss Wednesday's new episode," I say, feeling choked up myself. Just over a month of Violette being back in my life and the whole thing is turned upside down.

Violette nods and then leans over to kiss my cheek. I unbuckle my seatbelt and turn, wrapping my arms around her. I kiss her full on the lips, reminding her what we have and why she shouldn't be afraid. She kisses me back, but it's a kiss that feels like forever and goodbye, all at the same time. I can't help myself.

"I love you, Violette..." I whisper. "I love you so goddamn much it physically hurts me to leave you. But I promise, right this moment, that I will never leave to fight another fire without telling you that before I go, even if you're not ready to say it back, even if it takes you ten more seasons."

Violette sucks in a breath and her eyes fill with tears as she backs away. Maybe I've pushed her too far, but, fuck, she has to know.

"Just come home, Rowan." She gulps back more tears with a small smile. "And maybe it will be the first thing I say to you when you do," she says in a whisper. Squeezing my hand one last time as a tear spills over her cheek, she's out the door, leaving me feeling like I could put my fist through something with the amount of frustration I have from leaving her and the pull from the need I feel to do my job. I want to run after her and tell her I'll stay with her, but I can't.

"Fuck," I say under my breath as I slam a hand on the steering wheel, giving one last glance to her door before taking a breath and then forcing myself to drive away.

I have *no* choice. This fire is in our backyard. I *will* protect this town, and I *will* protect my girls.

"You gotta tell her," Cal says, clapping my shoulder forty-five minutes later when we're packing up the trucks.

"What?"

"Little T, you gotta tell her you love her. She needs to know, but first you have to fully admit it to yourself."

My brow furrows as I think. "I have admitted it. I did tell her, and I know she loves me too, but she has years of trauma surrounding Jacob's death. She's only been home a couple months, and all her fears came to a head tonight."

"You're right though, she definitely does love you too." Cal looks at me. "Always has."

"How can you be so sure?"

"Because the only reason she'd push back like this is if the thought of losing you was too much for her to handle. And you don't have those kinds of feelings for someone you don't love with your whole heart."

I nod and scrub my jaw with a little chuckle.

"Christ, when the fuck did you get so philosophical?" I ask him with a chuckle.

"Rom-com 101, bro." Cal smiles wide.

"Now, let's do this fucking thing right so you can come home and tell the woman you love that you love her over and over until she gets sick of you, yeah?" He turns with another laugh and moves to the next truck to help pack it up. His words register, along with everything I've been feeling.

Instead of thinking of all the things that can go wrong, I think of coming home to her and Hollie, and coming home to more babies one day. Lazy Sunday mornings making my girls breakfast, stolen moments tangled up with Violette in our bedsheets, not wanting to come up for air.

This is love, the deepest kind. The kind that's always been there, just under the surface smoldering for ten years, waiting for the spark to breathe life into it again. A love I never let go of. A love that shaped me.

I fucking love Violette so goddamn much it hurts, and I love Hollie. They're my future and telling her that tonight was right.

This affirmation is the boost I need to finish packing up because the moment I get home, I'm going to tell her that even when she tries to push me away, I'll be there, waiting for her to come around. Because that's what I owe her, to always come home and to always be her safe space.

I pull the Power Piggy Hollie gave me for good luck to the top of my pack hoping it offers some.

"See you soon, Hols," I whisper, patting the top of the pig's head.

"Y'all packed up here?" Sup asks, seemingly appearing out of nowhere.

"Yes, Sup," I tell him, heading to board the buggie with most of the crew.

I look out the window as the Sky Ridge town limits pass us by and we head for the mountain.

Now, all I gotta do is make it through this beast.

CHAPTER 52

Violette

The Knox Mountain fire is the worst fire we've seen in ten years. They've had to evacuate homes on the west side, a few homes have even burned with the blaze. Thick smoke and ash has the air quality around us thick, and for me, torturous.

My days pass in a sort of blur, I keep as busy as possible. I work, I play with Hollie, I sleep, I dwell on all the things I should've said to Rowan before he left, and then do it all over again the next day...all while I wait for the possibility of a text from him, if he has service. From the news I'm told, crews are deep in the mountains in spike camps so it's been radio silence, which makes my anxiety feel even more crushing.

I did learn one thing from the night he left. I learned I needed to finally talk to someone. So the very next day, before I lost my nerve, I got on the phone and found a grief therapist, and after two sessions with her I already feel a little lighter. Just being able to talk to someone who will listen without judgement or ties to my family has been like taking a deep breath for the first time in years. Someone offering coping mechanisms has me feeling better already somehow, and I wonder why it took me this long to do this.

Yet still, my days pass in worry while Rowan is gone. The only connection I have to him is the live footage of the blaze. When I hear at the end of every day that no firefighters have been lost or injured, I feel relief, but I know I won't fully breathe right or sleep properly until he's home.

If I could go back to the night he left I would've flung my arms around him and told him I loved him too, but I can't. All I can do is never let him leave again without telling him, and that every day that passes I just feel empty without him. I *miss* him, so much so that the next day I did something long overdue. I went to visit Jacob. I just needed my brother.

I know I can't be out here long. The air is thick with humidity and smoke. I swipe the ash off Jacob's headstone and the crushing feeling of loss spreads through me like I lost him yesterday.

"I know you're thinking I suck because I haven't been here," I tell him, taking a seat on the grass. "I've been busy, but it's not an excuse…" I proceed to tell him all about Hollie and Troy and our move back, and even Rowan coming to tell me the truth about everything.

"…sending Rowan into my burn unit? That was some trickery. And I can't help but wonder if it was your way of giving me your truth."

I picture the way Jacob would smile when he was up to something or denying the truth and it makes me smile in return.

"I know it wasn't a mistake, and I'm glad I know what happened, I just wish you would've told me at the time. I wish you would've trusted me with that," I add, imagining him saying, "You would've flipped out."

"True." I sniff through my tears as I pluck a clover from the grass and twirl it between my fingers.

"It's never been the same since you left, and I've been pretending it's all okay and burying these fears and this grief for five years. It was easier to leave rather than face the fact that

you're gone. But now, I feel like you brought me back here, and you brought me Rowan, and for that…" I choke out a sob. "I could never thank you enough because he's the only one I've ever loved. He's a good man, Jacob, and I just wish you were here with us. I wish you could see Hollie…" I sniff and blow my nose, trying to find the words I know have been holding back for a long time.

"I'm getting help, finally. I know I need it. I've got an appointment tomorrow," I whisper so quietly I barely hear it myself. The moment I do a gust of wind blows some ash into the air and my hair swirls around my face. I suck in a breath and close my eyes. I can feel him all around me.

There are moments, even in death, when I know Jacob is trying to tell me something and when I hear the words "I wouldn't bring him to you just to take him away, Vivi" echo through my mind I know without a doubt it's been Jacob guiding us together, guiding me to learn the truth, and guiding me to face my past this entire time. That feeling alone tells me everything will be okay, that I'm right where I'm supposed to be and that through all of this, he's never really left me. He's in my heart, always.

More days pass, and by day ten I'm about to go out of my mind as I'm packing Hollie up to go with Troy to dinner and to see the new Disney movie. It's the first time he's seen her in over a month, since before he canceled on her for *SuperPets*, and the only way I'm getting Hollie to go is because he's promised to buy her ice cream after the movie. I've also decided in Rowan's absence that I'm going to carve out some time to have Troy settle a schedule with me. It's only been a few months since we've been home but this will no longer work. Hollie needs to know she can count on her father, and I won't tolerate him popping in and out of her life. If he doesn't like it, he can see me in court.

"Will you be here to tuck me in?" Hollie asks as I add some snacks for the movie into her backpack.

"Of course, babe. You're going to have so much fun with Daddy tonight."

I've told Teddy I'm coming over while Hollie is gone and made her promise to feed me pizza and wine, which she happily agreed to do if I watch all the kids long enough for her to have an uninterrupted shower.

"Knock, knock," Troy says as he knocks while walking right into my house.

"I was coming," I say, letting him know that's not cool.

"Daddy!" Hollie calls as she runs to him. He picks her up, dotting little kisses all over her cheeks and tells her she's grown so much and she's so big.

"I want to have a cheer burger," Hollie says. He nods and sets her down. She makes a beeline for the back of the house when I ask her to be my helper and get her pink sweater from her bed. Troy makes his way toward me and leans in with an awkward side hug. *This is new.*

"I got the promotion," he says with a big handsome smile. It only serves to annoy me.

"Congrats?" I say to him, not understanding what that means exactly.

"All my overtime paid off, you're looking at Seattle Sinai's newest chief resident."

"That's great, Troy," I say as I turn and head into the living room where Hollie is holding her sweater while watching the tail end of a TV show.

"That means I'll have more regular hours so I should be able to come out every other weekend, maybe even bring Hollie back with me for a night."

That's nice that he's fitting her in now. Until the next big promotion.

"That will take some time, after a few months of you coming regularly she might be ready for that," I tell him, doing my best to sound in control and authoritative.

"What's this?" Troy asks, standing in front of my fireplace staring at the 8x10 *SuperPets* frame of Rowan, myself, and Hollie at the concert. My mouth falls open because I was not prepared to explain Rowan to a man who's barely been around.

"You went? How? Who is this guy?"

"Super Rowan!" Hollie calls out as she runs back into the room.

Troy looks from me to Hollie. "Super Rowan?"

"He's my friend and Mommy's. He is in the forest with the fire!" she says, and I internally flinch.

"He's my friend, yes. My good friend." I look pointedly at Troy to make sure he understands I'm not hiding my relationship from him but talking about it in front of Hollie isn't appropriate. "He knows someone who works at the stadium, so they gifted us last minute tickets in the staff box, *thankfully,*" I add.

"And he's a firefighter? Hotshot?" Troy asks, looking back at the photo. I nod.

"Like Uncle Jacob," Hollie says. "But he's not in heaven."

Troy and I lock eyes for a few seconds as it registers with him that I have someone in my life, someone close enough to have spent time with Hollie too.

"Come on, Hols. You're all packed up," I say, handing Troy her bag. He takes it but says nothing before looking back at the photo on my fireplace.

I almost feel bad as a knee jerk reaction, and then I mentally slap myself.

Troy has a way of always trying to be the victim, but I stand tall now, we're divorced, and we've been separated for over a year. Did he think I would stay single forever?

I hug Hollie and walk with them to Troy's SUV at Hollie's request.

When I buckle her into her car seat in the back, Troy already has the air conditioning running and her favorite music playing through his speakers. I kiss her goodbye and shut the door, and Troy is waiting beside me.

"Have fun, have her home by seven, okay? I need to get her in the bath and to bed on time," I say, moving to walk past him.

"Violette?" he says, grabbing my arm. I pull away, he lets me. "Just...is this serious?" he asks, and I instantly know he means Rowan.

"Troy, we're not having this conversation. We've barely spoken in over a year, what difference does it make?"

"I don't know...I guess, just somewhere in the back of my mind I thought there might be another chance for us someday."

I think, but can't be sure, that my mouth falls open in shock. Because why Troy would ever think there was a possibility of us getting back together is *beyond* me.

"Troy, that ship has sailed," I say gently.

He nods. "You're right. We can talk more another time."

Or not.

He starts to move to the driver's side of the truck.

"Violette?"

I stop and turn to face him when I'm halfway up my porch steps. "Yeah?"

"What are you doing tomorrow? Could I, uh, come get Hollie again?"

Okay, that time I know my mouth fell open. I blink.

"I could take her for an early dinner. I'll go home after my shift, have a nap and then drive back up for three—"

I blink again. "Uh, sure, I switched with Bonnie tomorrow so I'm taking her afternoon shift. I work till eleven so Hollie will be with my mom if you want to pick her up there. I'll let my mom know to expect you."

"Awesome. I've been missing Mae's disapproving glances so that should be fun," Troy jokes.

"She just doesn't like it when you cancel on Hollie any more than I do," I fire back.

He nods. "I'm going to do my best to change that, and Violette?" he says as he climbs in and closes the door.

"Hmmm?"

"Thanks," he says, shutting the door. I almost believe him.

I walk up the steps, waving to Hollie as they drive off. Once I'm inside the safety of my house I close the door behind me, and leaning on it, I blow out a breath.

Troy wants to take Hollie two days in a row? Why?

Troy isn't the jealous type, but he is the type that lives for the way things look. My guess is the idea of me having a boyfriend who knows he's barely shown up, would bother him more than the act of not showing up.

One of two reasons come to mind regarding his sudden interest in spending time with Hollie. One: he's trying to dig a little further into my relationship with Rowan, or two: hell has frozen over. Since it's Troy I'm dealing with—I'm betting on one.

CHAPTER 53
ROWAN

When a forest fire is at its worst the sound is unmistakable. It's almost like a rushing river. You never get it out of your head when you're in the field. Not when you're working, not when you're sleeping. You simply live with it, knowing it's the kind of river that can swallow you whole. We knew this fire was going to be bad, but it has been a hundred times worse than we expected.

For ten days we haven't showered—at best we've been hosed off when we needed relief from the heat—we've barely had time to eat, barely slept, barely had time to talk. For days, we've dug, we've chopped, we've sawed, we've climbed this damn mountain foot by foot, digging down to mineral soil while our arms ached, then we kept fucking climbing. Thing is, I would be lying if I said I didn't love it. There's no greater high than going up against nature and redirecting its carnage.

Even with all our work, more than two thousand properties on the west side are under an evacuation order, and more than a thousand more are under an evacuation alert. This mammoth has grown to almost twelve thousand acres and the only thing between it and the homes and businesses of our town and the neighboring ones, is us. Crews from Utah and Oregon have worked alongside us tirelessly, and finally, the air cooled and the wind died down for the first time in over a week. We're seeing flames turn to black, and the lines we've dug in are doing their jobs, and I'm finally sitting to eat and take a proper break for the first time in ten days.

"Holdin' that thing up in the air isn't going to make it work any better." Sup winks as I hold my cell to the sky hoping for service. I don't know why I'm still trying. I haven't been able to get any since I got here, I don't know why I'd think I would today. We're too deep in the woods. We're sitting in the black eating beef jerky and trail mix. Lunch of fucking champions.

"Fuck this is depressing." I chuckle, taking another bite. Sup grins.

"The secret ingredient is misery."

"Pretty much."

"You'll get dinner. Probably stir fry again, but it's hot food," Sup says, scrubbing his dirty face with his hand.

"Hey, at least this caterer is better than Pickler Mountain." Caleb chuckles, ripping open an Uncrustable peanut butter and jelly sandwich. The thing looks like it got run over by a truck.

"What happened on Pickler Mountain?" Roycie asks, taking a seat. He wipes his face with the back of his sleeve, and it turns his black soot and ash covered face to a lighter, smudgy gray.

"We all got food poisoning," I tell him. "We were all excited because they said they had a caterer for us, it wasn't a very big fire so that's abnormal. Someone from town wanted to be kind."

"Plain boiled chicken with a bit of teriyaki. Fucking traumatizing." Caleb says.

"*Fuckkk,*" Roycie says, opening a bag of Skittles.

"We all saw it again later that day...in various ways," Sup adds. Our entire small group starts to laugh.

"Double fuck," Roycie says. "Then I'm not complaining about our sixth night of stir fry then."

"Right?" I say, dumping my trail mix into my mouth.

The group quiets for a minute, everyone in their own exhausted thoughts.

"With any luck, we'll be heading out tomorrow," Sup says. "Y'all outdid yourselves. That first night was—"

"A hundred fuckin' years of fightin' fires in one night?" Roycie asks, and the rest of us laugh.

"Yeah," Sup says. "But you killed it."

I swallow my last bite of shit jerky and lay down in the black, looking up at where the sky should be. We did it. We kept the county safe. Of course, I still can't see it, all I see is smoke but, fuck I know it's there somewhere. I hold my phone up trying to get a signal again. Nada.

If I could just talk to her, hear her voice. I'd give just about anything right now.

I look to my left where the smoke is the thickest. *I own the rest of you, bitch,* I tell the flames. Not long now. I'm ready to go home.

The sound of thick mud under my boots is comforting as we make our way down Knox Mountain, through the last of the foothills into the clearing where the site is a frenzy of packing and loading. This is the first green I've seen in days, and after last night's rain it's soaked. The sun is out and the sky is actually blue. My eyes burn after almost two weeks in the thick smoke.

I pull my phone out of my back pocket. My pack is heavy on my back after our trudge from the spike camp we called home for the last eleven days. I have service but it's three in the afternoon and I'll be home before four.

I know Violette's on days this week, so by the time I get

home and spend an hour in the shower scrubbing until I can see my actual skin, she should be home. I'm struggling with the decision to tell her I'm coming or surprise her. A thought occurs to me as I wager it.

"Anyone talk to Jack today to let him know we're coming home?" I ask as I help the boys pack up the trucks and wagon.

"No, I'm gonna call him tomorrow and go for a beer with him, give him the lowdown. He still likes to feel connected," Sup says with a tired grin. "But tonight, I just wanna veg."

I nod. *Perfect.*

Opp nudges me as we climb into the back of the uncomfortable green buggie that will take us home.

"What do you think Jacob would say about you and his sister?" he asks.

I look out the window. "I've thought about that a lot," I tell him honestly, instinctively rubbing my thigh, it's been aching all night. "He knew I cared for Vi, we only talked about it once, but he told me he thought I'd end up being an actual part of his family somehow and to not fuck it up."

"Was that after you took Sheriff Miller's daughter out for him and stole the video of him breaking and entering off her phone?" he asks, still looking out the window. When I don't respond, he turns to face me and starts to laugh.

"He may not have told you this, but he told me. Said it to me one drunken night a few months before he…you know." He trails off without saying "he passed." Five years, and we all avoid saying the words still.

"Said the only reason he was a hotshot was because you saved his ass once and it gave him a get out of jail free card."

I gulp.

"Said you gave Vi up to do it and that he always regretted asking you because he thought you two belonged together."

"Why wouldn't he have said that to me?" I ask, not really expecting an answer.

Opp shrugs. "We all live with regrets, who knows?"

He flicks his gaze back out the window. "Just make sure you do right by her, or we'll all kick your ass."

I chuckle and backhand cuff him in the arm. "Listen, if I fuck this up, I'll welcome any ass kicking." I pull my phone out and check the time as I say it; not long now.

I can't fucking wait.

CHAPTER 54

ROWAN

I rest my eyes most of the drive back, my body finally relaxing after days in the field. I've already heard we may be heading to Montana after our mandatory R&R which means I only have the next two days to spend some time with Violette and Hollie.

It takes me over an hour and every drop of hot water in the tank to get myself clean. I make a few stops on the way, so when I pull up to Violette's house at six thirty my mind is already full of kissing her. I think about taking them to dinner, maybe playing Candyland with Hollie, and curling up on the couch with them. I'm desperate for that feeling of peace only being with them gives me. So when I immediately notice that Mae's car is parked in the driveway and Violette's car isn't, my heart squeezes in my chest.

I look over at the little gifts on my passenger seat, all the girls' favorite snacks, a new pair of slippers to replace the worn ones Vi wears around the house after a long day on her feet, and a souvenir stuffed moose from Knox Mountain for Hollie.

I make a snap decision to make sure Violette isn't here and say hi to Hols and Mae anyway. I make the short trek up her front walkway and I'm just about to climb the front steps when the door opens and a polo wearing, clean-shaven guy comes out calling back into the house, "Thank you, Mae."

"Don't thank me, I always want to spend time with my granddaughter. Maybe next time *you* could stay longer," I hear Mae call back.

The guy mutters something under his breath that I can't make out as he closes the door behind him, and I instantly know this is the infamous Troy.

Troy almost walks right into me before he realizes I'm standing here. He jumps back a beat, and his eyes grow wide as he looks up at me, then down to the gifts in my arms. I'm only a few inches taller than he is but I'm quite a bit bigger. I don't move, I just grip the gifts in my hand tighter.

"Shit, man, you scared me," Troy says, running a hand through his hair. He looks at me for a second and then straightens—like he knows who I am, almost—folding his arms across his chest.

"Violette's not here, she's at work until eleven."

I nod in disappointment, realizing she must have changed her shift.

Troy looks me up and down but doesn't say anything. *That's right, she's mine,* I think as I extend my free hand

"Rowan Kingsley."

He takes it and gives me a measly shake, then tries to stand up straighter, like a rooster puffing his chest.

"Dr. Troy Stafford, I'm Violette's husband, Hollie's dad."

A silent rage seeps through my blood, hearing him call himself Violette's husband. I know they've been officially divorced for weeks and apart for over a year.

"Violette has mentioned you," I say. Violette, and not Hollie, because realistically, in all the time I've spent with them I haven't actually heard Hollie mention Troy on her own, not even once.

"Huh, and yet she only just mentioned you yesterday," he says back with a sort of smug glint in his eye. *Prick.*

"Maybe if you'd been around more since she's been back in Sky Ridge, you would've heard more," I retort, doing my best to stay calm while wondering what the hell Vi ever saw in this guy. In the two minutes I've known him, I can tell he's pompous and cares way more about appearances than anything else.

"Well, that's true I guess, isn't it? Well, I've been around a little more lately, had some more time to talk to Violette, spend time with Hollie while you've been off in the woods."

My blood boils but I remind myself this is Hollie's father and I'm outside her house. Punching him in the face in the middle of the front lawn is probably a bad idea.

"That's nice for Hollie," I lie.

"Oh, hey, thanks for taking them to *SuperPets,* that was real kind of you, man," he says, but it doesn't sound like he's grateful. It sounds like an afterthought. "I was working toward becoming Department Head for Orthopaedics at my hospital. Now that I've secured that position, I'll be making some more time to get up this way, spend extra time with Hollie and Violette."

I grit my molars and flex my fists.

"I guess that will be up to Violette," I say, doing my best to keep calm.

He shrugs. "She seemed pretty open to it when I asked her last night. I guess time will tell." He brushes past me on the concrete walkway and miraculously, somehow, someway, I don't actually hit him. "Lots of history, you know they always say a little girl needs her mother *and* her father."

This fucking chump.

"I think a little girl needs people who constantly show up for her," I grit out. "Put her first," I add, not able to help myself. I move closer to him and speak low.

"I'm gonna fucking level with you, Troy. There's only one

reason I'm not beating your ass right now for bringing Hols back early—like the complete douchebag you are—*and f*or calling Vi your wife. That reason is inside those four walls." I point toward Vi's house. I grit my jaw and continue. "But I swear to Christ, if you let Hollie down one more time or you take it upon yourself to call Violette your wife…"

He gives me a smug smile, he knows I won't hit him with Hollie inside, and it takes everything in me not to knock him right the fuck out.

"I'll put you through the fucking ground. I may not be perfect, but I know that little girl in there deserves a fuck of a lot better than you."

"You don't know the first thing about being a dad," Troy says, backing away from me.

I fold my arms across my chest and shrug. "Maybe not but trying is a good start. You just remember what I said, Troy. Unlike you, I'm a man of my word," I call to him as he backs away, then scurries into a Mercedes SUV parked in front of the neighbor's house. It's flashy and black and doesn't belong here.

Once to the safety of his SUV he calls over to me.

"Don't bother knocking, hero," he calls back. "Mae was going to get Hollie's overnight bag packed and then take her back to their place right away. Poor kid's exhausted after our fun day together. Guess you'll have to give her those trinkets another day," he says before he starts the car and takes off down Violette's street, leaving me standing in the middle of her front yard wishing I had hit him.

I make a beeline back to my truck, needing a minute to just think. I take a deep breath and talk some logic into myself. There's no way I've been gone less than two weeks and Vi has let this guy back into their lives after he'd let them down so much. Not a chance, he's definitely full of shit. She would let him see Hollie, but her?

No fucking way. I white knuckle the steering wheel for a few minutes and blow out a deep breath. I start my truck. Even though I know he's full of shit, I need to vent this out as I wait for Violette to finish her shift. One thing is certain. When I find out this guy was lying to me, I'll be having more than words with him the first chance I get.

I check the time, it's not even seven.

Me: Does meeting for a beer count as vegging? I could use some company.

Sup: Sure thing. Twenty?

I reply with a yes and start to head to Shifty's, grateful my sup is always there when I need him.

"From what Jack says the guy is real showy and shiny, he never really understood why Violette married him, aside from he was the furthest thing from us… from here. He offered her a steady, predictable future…and most importantly, he had no connection to Sky Ridge or Jacob." Xander sips his beer. "Or you."

I nod. "Does the entire squad know we had something between us when we were kids?" I ask, stuffing a fry into my mouth.

"Roycie doesn't know much." Sup grins.

"Fuck." I chuckle.

"There's no way she's working things out with him, kid."

"I have no doubt about that. I don't know if it's the haze of being gone, but I just needed to hear it from someone else, so thanks."

He nods and we chat for the next half hour about the Montana fire we're going to be heading to this weekend if it gets any more out of control over the next twenty-four hours. By nine, I can tell Sup is exhausted and I decide to let him go home.

I take to driving around Sky Ridge to bide my time because going home to my empty house is not an option. I feel like I'm going out of my skin waiting for her shift to end. I think back to the last time I saw her. It feels like so goddamn long ago. I'm lost in remembering the way we kiss as I follow an old pickup truck onto the highway and cruise out of Sky Ridge into the countryside.

It's just getting dark and the sky is beginning to come alive with a thousand stars. As I drive and listen to the country station, I think of all the ways I'm going to tell Violette I'm madly and deeply in love with her. I'm so distracted by my thoughts that I don't see the elk running out onto the highway from the field beside us until the old truck in front of me is swerving to miss it. The sound of tires screeching is deafening through my open windows. The SUV in front of him hit the tail end of the elk as it veered wildly off the road into the ditch, it punches through metal fencing before it settles.

I slam on my breaks and come to an abrupt stop. Thankfully, there's no one behind me, and the truck is still standing right side up on the wrong side of the road, but the SUV is a fucking mess. The elk is gone; either its injuries aren't life-threatening and it took off for safety, or it's going to get a hundred feet into the field and die.

I go into medic mode. I'm not on duty during fire season but I have a Samaritan duty being trained to help, and I know any doctor at Bakersfield will back me. I pull my phone out of my pocket as I get out of my truck and dial emergency simultaneously. I dart across the road to get a better look at the SUV and to make sure whoever is inside is still alive, because fuck, this thing is face planted into metal fencing and the front end is non existent. It isn't until I get closer that I realize I've seen this black Mercedes SUV before.

About three hours ago, parked in front of Violette's house.

CHAPTER 55
ROWAN

None of this makes sense, Troy was leaving town at six thirty. What the fuck is his SUV doing in a ditch beside the highway a few miles outside Sky Ridge three hours later?

I rush across the road.

"911, what's your emergency?"

"Hi, Laurel, this is Rowan Kingsley. I'm off Route 12, just past Yarmouth Line near the Pinery Motel. There's been a car accident. One vehicle swerved to miss an Elk, hit a metal guardrail."

"They okay, man?" An older man comes darting across the road from the pick up that was in front of me.

"I don't know. I'm a medic, are you okay?" I ask him. He looks fine, the vehicle sustained no damage.

"Yeah, I'm good, man. Holy shit, look at that front end..." he rambles on as I get back to my phone.

"Okay, Rowan, we're going to send a team out right away, can you see the patient? Will they need an airlift?"

"I'm just approaching now, I'm not sure yet," I tell her as I notice the smoke coming from under the hood.

"Stay back, okay? I have an ambulance on the way," I tell the man from the truck.

He nods and says something about waiting with me in case I need him. As I get closer I can hear yelling for help. But it's not Troy, it's a female voice. My heart rate spikes, and I break out in a cold sweat as I rush to the vehicle. I swear to God if it's Violette who's injured, I might fucking pass out. I run the last fifteen feet, getting close enough to see that, thank Christ, it's not Violette.

"There are two patients, vehicle is front loaded against the rail, smoke is coming from the hood. One male, early thirties, unconscious," I check his pulse, it's steady. "but alive, bleeding from the head. His injuries, I'm unsure of at this time. One female late twenties, significant bleeding from her forehead and her right arm. Looks like fencing from the roadside has punched through the window and given her a deep gash."

Actually, it looks like she's damn lucky she still has an arm.

Metal fencing is embedded in the front end, the windshield is shattered from the impact, and it's obvious that the broken glass has cut them both to shit.

"Can you hear me?" I ask the woman in a calm voice as I approach. I search for any immediate dangers surrounding the vehicle, and aside from that smoke, I see none. Her door is mangled and part way opened and she's clinging to her bleeding limb but her fingers are doing nothing and she's losing blood, fast. She's moving her head without trouble but she's hysterical.

"Don't move," I tell her as I rip off the bottom of my shirt, creating a tourniquet of sorts to wrap around her arm and slow the bleeding. "What's your name?" I ask her

"Angela," she answers crying.

"Okay, Angela, I'm Rowan, I'm a trained emergency responder but I'm off duty. Help is on the way, but every move you make exerts you and causes you to bleed more, and right now we don't want that, okay?

She nods as she sobs.

"Are you hurt anywhere else?" I ask, pushing aside the deflated airbag.

"I hit my head. I don't know where." I look her over, her pupils are okay. If they can get here and get the bleeding stopped, she should be fine.

"You're going to be okay, but you can't move. Help is on the way. I need to go to the other side of the car now and check your driver," I tell her, picking my phone back up and moving to Troy's side of the vehicle.

"Laurel?"

"I'm here, Rowan, the team is less than five minutes out," she confirms.

"Female is bleeding. A lot, but stable, no neck fractures, no loss of consciousness. Just checking the male now."

"Right place, right time, Rowan," Laurel says. She's been the dispatcher for years and the whole crew knows her.

"Yeah," I mutter, going around to Troy's side of the SUV. When I get there he's coming to, groaning.

"Troy, I need you to stay as still as you can, okay?" I let it register that of all the car wrecks I could pull up on it would be Vi's ex. I just threatened to kick this guy's ass three hours ago.

"I don't even know his name," the girl says. "We just met at Barracuda," she adds, mentioning the only strip joint in Sky Ridge, tucked in an old warehouse downtown. "I tend bar there," she adds. "We were going to the Pinery Motel."

Troy opens his eyes as I'm making sure his door is safe to open. I don't like the amount of smoke coming from the hood, it's growing thicker by the second and is likely to catch fire any minute. Hot metal, combustible fluids…never a good combination. I try to reach in and shut the car off in hopes of stopping the smoke but I can't. The front dash is pushed right up against Troy's body. He doesn't appear to be bleeding anywhere but from his head, and that cut is deep above the bridge of his nose.

"My neck is fine," he croaks out, assessing himself. "My arm is fractured, possible broken ribs," he adds. At least him being a doctor is coming in handy a little.

"You're a firefighter," he says.

"I'm also a trained medic. It's one of my jobs in the offseason."

"Fuck, my head" he groans. The way he's sandwiched in, they'll be lucky if the team doesn't have to cut the roof off to get him out.

"You've got a broken nose and a nasty cut at the bridge." I tell him as I check my phone. "ETA, Laurel?."

"Less than one minute, Rowan." she replies.

"I need to get out." Angela says in a panicked voice.

"Let the medics get here first. They have equipment that I don't, and they'll be here any second." I tell her again.

"I'll keep my eye out," says the truck driver.

I nod at him and then look back at Troy. He looks at me. Understanding clicks between us. He didn't have to go for a shift. He went to the strip club to hook up and he left his daughter to do it. And he could've just died.

"I'm sorry," he says, fear in his eyes.

"Just stay still," I order.

"Here they come!" the man from the truck calls out. I glance up to see their lights.

"Okay, they're here. You guys are going to be alright," I tell them both as I lean back on the door frame and wipe my sweat covered brow.

Fucking Christ, of all the accidents to land on.

I'm here, Jacob, I hear you.

Ten minutes later both Troy and his new friend are loaded into separate units. Troy is slipping in and out of consciousness. He's got himself a pretty good concussion.

"Can you ride with us? Let us know what happened so we can prep the ER?" As luck would have it, one of the EMT's is Scottie, Cal's girlfriend.

"Yeah, sure thing," I tell her.

She nods and gestures for me to get in the back with Troy. I give her the run down and she radios in the details to Bakersfield.

While she talks with them, Troy reaches out and weakly tugs at my shirt.

"You think I'm an asshole," he says.

I look at him and wonder why such a thing would even matter to him right now.

"I'm the guy who dropped my daughter off to go meet some-one…to serve my own needs," he mumbles semi-coherently to himself.

That's one way to put it.

"What I saw tonight doesn't shape my opinion of you one way or the other. My mind was made up about you the moment we met," I tell him, leaning back against the ambulance wall.

He coughs and then cringes; he's definitely got some broken ribs.

"Always the hero, I guess. Eh, hotshot? Would've been easier for you if you just kept on driving and let the car catch fire."

I look down at him and shake my head. There's something different about him, like he's realizing what a shitty excuse of a human being he's been. Near death will do that to you, I suppose.

"It still is easy for me, Troy. I love Violette, and she loves me. Nothing you've done or try to do will ever change that." He grimaces and grunts as he tries to shift his weight. "And you know, I didn't save you to be kind, or to fill some sort of hero complex. I saved you for *her*," I tell him pointedly.

Scottie is off the radio now and pretending like she's busy doing anything but listening to us.

When Troy doesn't say anything, I continue, knowing in his condition after this experience my words might actually fucking sink in. If they don't now, they never will.

"Hollie deserves to have you be there for her, even when it isn't easy. She deserves to have you put her first and she deserves to have you remind her every goddamn minute that she can count on you. You can't be there enough, understand?" I ask as we pull up in the emergency entrance of Bakersfield and the EMT's climb out.

I give him one last look, noticing the tears in his eyes. "Do better, Troy."

Troy doesn't say anything; he just sets his jaw and nods once before letting his head fall back against the gurney.

The doors open and the medics pull Angela out of the other ambulance first, then Troy.

When I get out, I'm surprised to see Cal waiting on the bench at the front doors.

"Scottie said you'd need a ride back to your truck."

I look at where Scottie is wheeling in Troy. She winks.

I clap Cal on the shoulder. "She's a keeper," I tell him.

"Don't I fuckin know it." He chuckles back. I take a deep breath.

"So, uh, that was Vi's ex. You want to explain what just happened out there?" he asks as we walk through the parking lot.

I suck in a deep breath and shake my head, running a hand through my hair.

"Not a fucking chance."

I get into Cal's pickup and lean my head back against the seat. This has officially been one of the longest days I think I've ever lived through. I watch the hospital disappear as we pull onto the road and head back outside of town for my truck.

"I gotta be honest, I'm surprised you didn't go inside and tell Little T you're home," Cal says, nodding in the direction of the hospital.

"Thought about it but she's working and, after eleven days without seeing her or talking to her, I don't want to share *that* reunion with anyone but Violette."

CHAPTER 56

Violette

My feet are aching, and I haven't stopped since I got here. Offering to take Bonnie's ER shift has been a flashback to my Seattle days. The ER here is a far cry from Seattle and the slower pace of the burn unit. Working in the ER reminds me why I like doing what I do now. But I work with Bonnie frequently on my floor so when she asked if I would swap with her, and in turn she'd take my Saturday shift I jumped at the chance. I'm not working at Shifty's this weekend and a whole Saturday off with Hollie is rare.

I'm not even regretting it now as I wolf down a turkey sandwich from the vending machine on my first break seven hours into my shift, but I will have had my fill of the ER by the end of the night, I'm sure.

I plop myself down in the breakroom and pull my phone out only to find it's dead. The charger I use at work is sitting comfortably at the nurses' station on the 5th floor which is just too far for my aching feet. I decide to go the old-fashioned route, picking up the receiver in the break room, I call my mother's cell only to find out that Troy brought Hollie back early, saying he had to head back to Seattle. I shake my head and make a mental note to call that lawyer on Monday and get the ball rolling on custody.

"That ex-husband of yours is a real piece of work," my mom says.

I sigh and rub my temples.

"I thought after we talked yesterday that maybe he was actually going to make it through today's visit without bringing her back early," I tell her, taking another bite of my dry sandwich.

My mom scoffs. "Leopards don't change their spots, honey. My thoughts? He wants something from either you or Hollie. Best thing you did was come back home," she says.

"I know," I say as one of my colleagues pokes her head into the break room.

"Sorry, Vi, I know you just sat down."

"Mom, I gotta go," I tell her, then hang up.

"We need you, MVA off Yarmouth coming in any second," she says.

I stuff the rest of my sandwich into my mouth and rise on my aching feet before heading back out into the busy ER. But the moment those doors open I stop dead in my tracks and feel like I might pass out. The face on that gurney, bloody and battered, is Troy's.

My eyes meet his from across the room but I don't have time to talk to him because I'm being told to assist the girl who came in with him. Her right arm is going to need surgery for the deep lacerations.

I get one glimpse of Troy's eyes as he's pushed to the opposite side of the ER, and I go through the double doors with his passenger wondering why the hell he's still in Sky Ridge.

CHAPTER 57

Violette

Thirty minutes later I still don't have any answers as the girl we just brought in—Angela—is taken away to be prepped for surgery. And I'm taking matters into my own hands to find out what the hell just happened.

I find out that Troy is stable and is having his fractured arm casted, his minor burns treated and his head stitched up as we speak. He'll have to stay the night but will probably be released tomorrow.

I wait for the go ahead and then, just as my shift is finishing, I find his room and push the door open. It's dark and he's hooked up to saline and a drip for pain. When I enter, he turns his head and faces me, and I swear I see his eyes turn glassy.

"You're a sight for sore eyes, Violette," he says as I come closer to the bed and sit down in the chair beside him.

"What happened?" I ask. He looks broken, and according to the reports from the medic team he and his friend were damn lucky.

"What happened is… in a span of ten seconds, I realized that I have been a really shitty husband and father for the last two years."

I recoil with his admission and stay quiet; I just don't have the words.

He moves to reposition himself and his face scrunches up in pain.

"You know how they say your life flashes before your eyes? That's true, Violette. Mine did and I didn't see anything but work." He holds his side where he has three broken ribs.

"I left Hollie tonight because I'm a lazy fucking father. And your guy, the one you're dating…" he says. My eyes move to his. "I lied to him."

My mouth falls open as I try to figure out what he's talking about. "I don't understand."

"He's back, freshly back from Knox—I assume that's where he was. It's all anyone was talking about at…the club. He came to see you and Hollie tonight when I was dropping her off with your mom. I told him we were… you were, open to maybe trying again… with us," he says.

I grip the sides of the chair *"What?"* I ask too loudly for this quiet space. "Why would you—"

"Because even though we're over and I let you and Hollie down, the feeling of being replaced hurt my ego," he says honestly. "I realize now we would never work, Violette. I'm a selfish asshole and it's my own fault you replaced me. I was never good enough for either of you."

My mind reels. All I can think about is getting to Rowan wherever he is right now and telling him Troy lied to him.

"But your guy—"

"Rowan," I correct him.

"Rowan. Funny enough, he was driving behind me when I hit that elk, and he called 911. He even rode in the ambulance with me. He could've left me there; he had no reason to help me, but he did."

Everything around me starts to go hazy and I feel lightheaded. That's why Scottie said she'd talk to me on the next run. She was going to tell me Rowan was home.

Oh my God. Rowan is home and there's nothing stopping me from finding him right now other than this conversation, which I'm done having.

"He helped you because he's a good man, Troy, a better man than you. I hope you learn from him." I stand and move to leave the room. "We'll talk about this when you're better, but your daughter isn't a pawn, and if you really do realize that, you're going to put your money where your mouth is. She's a person… and going forward if you want to see her, we're going to have a set in stone schedule. One you will abide by, or I'll be taking you to court and having an order mandated. You *will* show up on your scheduled days and you *will* treat her like she deserves, or you won't see her," I tell him, finding the fire inside me.

"Violette—"

"No, Troy. I'm going home now, but you have a couple days to think. Decide what you want to do and let me know," I tell him with a shrug as I push through the door feeling freer than I've ever felt. I don't have to overcompensate for Troy. Hollie has me and she has Rowan. If Troy wants to know her, he's going to do it in a way that works for Hollie or not at all.

The moment I get into my car I'm plugging my phone in, I know it's going to take a few minutes to come alive. I ponder as I drive. Suddenly, everything is clear, and I feel like the heaviest weight has been lifted from my shoulders. Tears are streaming down my cheeks as I drive. All of my fears, all my anxieties about Jacob's death and about Rowan's job dissipate along with any feelings or any obligation I ever felt for Troy, and all I can think about is getting to Rowan. I turn onto Main, knowing I'm minutes away from the only arms I've ever really felt whole in.

As I'm pulling into my driveway I'm telling myself that he knows me better than Troy's words. That he knows how I feel about him even though I've never really told him clearly.

"Almost forgot how goddamn beautiful you are."

My body is instantly covered in goosebumps as the deep timbre I've missed so much for the last eleven days washes over me. My eyes search in the direction I heard Rowan's voice and find him rising from my outdoor sofa. He looks fresh from the shower; his dark blond hair is still damp and he's wearing gray sweats and a black T-shirt. He looks like he was prepared to camp on my porch all night.

I stand frozen, just drinking him in, the broad expanse of his shoulders, the deep navy of his eyes and the subtle scruff of his jaw. His arms seem even more powerful than before he left and I can't remember seeing anything so beautiful. He smirks at me and starts to make his way off the front porch until he's towering over me, looking down at me from his full height.

"You look damn good, Vi," he says and then his mouth is crashing down on mine in the dark. His arms wrap around me and move over me, and I, in turn, wrap mine around his neck and pull him closer, not caring if anyone drives by, not caring if a meteor lands in my backyard. I fist his shirt, and I lose myself a little more with every languid sweep of his tongue. Rowan kisses me back like I'm the breath he needs to fill his lungs.

"I'm not getting back together with—"

"Shhh…of course I fucking know that." He kisses me again. "We had a deal." He smirks. "Those weren't supposed to be your first words to me, Violette." His lips coming down on mine again in a desperate kiss is settling. An affirmation. Like I'm his need to survive. Moments pass like this and when he pulls his lips from mine, I whimper with the loss.

"I love you, Rowan," I whisper, reveling in the easy way it rolls off my tongue.

"I love you, Violette, so much," he murmurs. "I've fucking loved you since I was eighteen years old. It's taken us a long time to get here, and there are times I feel like everything and anything has tried to keep us apart, but I know I'll never stop loving you. I love you and Hollie, and I want to be with you both —always. I want to be everything for both of you." He kisses me on the cheek. "I'll wait as long as I need to for you to come to terms with my job, I know it's dangerous, I know it brings up terrible memories for you—"

"No, Rowan," I say as a tear spills down my cheek. He kisses it away. "I'm not afraid of us anymore, and I'm working on not letting the fear of losing you cripple me. Jacob wouldn't want that; he'd want me to love free of fear," I say in a whisper.

Rowan strokes my cheeks with his calloused thumbs as he looks into my eyes.

"I'm working on it." I repeat, "Troy was the *safe* choice. The doctor, the man who takes zero risks in life. And he could've died tonight. Simply driving down the road. Our jobs don't matter; how careful we are doesn't matter. The only thing that matters is fate, we end up where we're meant to be and with the one person we're meant to be with. And I'm meant to be with you." I grip my hands behind his neck.

"It's always been me and you, Kingsley. An electrostatic attraction. Fate." I grin. "I love you so damn much," I say, sliding my hands up to press my palms to either side of his face. I reach up on my tip toes and kiss him.

"Say it again," he says, his tone full of gravel.

I grin. "I love you, Rowan Kingsley. You've always had my heart."

I'm answered with another kiss as Rowan scoops me up into his arms like he's about to carry me over the threshold. "I *need* to get you inside before every piece of clothing you're wearing ends up at your feet in the grass."

CHAPTER 58

ROWAN

I cannot get this woman to the bedroom fast enough. I push through the front door and kick my shoes off, all the while my lips are on hers, wanting her, just needing to feel her, this woman I've loved for so long, who just told me she loves me back.

"I need a shower. I'm covered in hospital." Violette giggles into my lips.

That I can fucking do.

A low growl leaves my chest as I push open her bedroom door and make my way through to her bathroom beyond. I set Violette down and pull my T-shirt off. Violette backs up and pulls the clip from her hair, holding a finger out to stop me when I advance on her.

"I don't know," she says as she pushes open the shower glass. "Can you be good while I clean myself?" she asks, one eyebrow raised.

"Yep." *Nope.*

"I don't believe you." *You shouldn't.*

Violette looks like a walking wet fucking dream pulling the drawstrings on her black scrub pants loose and sliding them over her full hips. She turns, just to torture me more, and turns the shower on, feeling for the water to warm up. Her long wavy hair hangs down her back as she reaches inside and that perfect pert ass is on display in her lacy panties. They're the kind I love that only cover half of her cheeks and they make me want to bend her over the nearest...anything.

Violette slinks out of her panties and climbs into the shower while I pull my sweats off outside. I instinctively grip my cock through my boxers as she lets the water run in ripples over her beautiful body and her pretty pink nipples harden when the water hits them. I just stand back and take in the sight that I dreamed about every second I was in those woods away from her.

"I just need a minute and I'll be all clean," she says with a grin, and it's in this moment I know she's fucking with me. I slide my boxers down and grab my cock.

Moving toward the shower, I'm not wasting one more second not touching her. I can play her game. We can clean her up first, but I'll be doing the cleaning.

I spend some time washing her hair, the thick soapy strands cling to the curves of her back. It's fucking mouth-watering.

"Pay attention, Kingsley. This hair can't go without conditioner," she tells me, pointing to her tresses.

I let out a laugh but do what she tells me, squeezing the excess water from her temporarily straight strands before smoothing them with a good amount of conditioner, all the while planting as many kisses on her as she'll let me.

"What was it like out there?" she asks as I smooth her hair.

"Terrifying," I answer honestly. "Exhilarating," I add as I pull my fingers through her hair before angling the shower head to rinse everything out.

"I think what you do is incredible," she says, leaning her freshly conditioned head back on my chest and looking up at me. "Admirable, and I never appreciated it like I should've. Even when my dad did it, I let fear take over and never took a moment to realize how truly amazing it is that you go out there and risk your life to save nature, homes, people. I just wanted to tell you that."

I set my jaw as I stare at her, looking so fucking beautiful. I kiss her lips. *My* lips.

"Thank you," I say simply, because there's really nothing more to do than show her I appreciate her saying it.

"I'm learning that in therapy. To put a positive spin on it," she says, and I bend down and nip at her neck, her shoulder. Knowing she's talking to someone makes me happy. When she's well, I'm well.

"Talking to someone is the first step to really healing, I'm so proud of you, Vi."

She smiles as my thumb traces her perfect bottom lip.

"I can still smell the diesel on you." She grins. "I don't hate it."

"Yeah…it'll go away in like…October," I taunt, bending down to kiss her again, wrapping my arms around her waist in the process.

She laughs and it echoes through the bathroom. The urge to consume her washes over me as her ass presses against my already rock hard cock and the mood instantly shifts.

I angle her face up to kiss me. Violette moans into my mouth and I lose it. It's been too many days, too much emotion and I'm done playing her waiting game.

CHAPTER 59

Violette

Before I can even set my soap down Rowan is pinning me against the shower wall. He leans in, his cock pressing into my ass, and I dream of moving slightly so he can slip inside me. He nips at my neck, and my pussy throbs. His hands slide over my shoulders and my nipples pebble further the moment his fingers find them.

"I'll tell you one thing, though," he says under the base of my ear. "I'm pretty sure I should've won an award for self-control when Troy called you his wife." When he plucks at my nipple and then swipes his thumb over it, I whimper.

"I-I never took you to be the jealous type," I taunt in a whisper, my face pressed against the cool tile wall turns up in a grin. I secretly like knowing that he's possessive of me.

Rowan growls into the base of my neck.

"The way I feel at the thought of you ever belonging to another man isn't jealousy..." He slides his hand down my center. "It's anger, love," he continues in a whisper. "It's wrath."

Rowan's teeth graze the space under my chin again, biting a little harder this time. I moan as his lips trail across my jaw. He slides his hand up to my throat and turns my face to hold his gaze. His dark, stormy eyes are on mine, his voice gravel.

"It's...fucking anarchy." His mouth comes down to meet mine and his hands tour my curves. Rowan spins me around and pins my shoulder blades firmly into the shower wall. One large hand traces my waist and then slips down the front of my hip to my already aching core.

"I spent years wishing I was the man who was touching you, Violette," he says in a low voice. "Years wishing I was the man with his face between these pretty thighs. Burying myself in this tight little cunt every single fucking night."

Two fingers slip inside me and my head falls back. My breath is ragged and my mouth begins to water at the sight of him like this; his blue eyes hooded and dark, his body strong, his huge cock begging to claim me. I run my fingers through his hair, gripping tight as he slowly fucks my pussy and then begins to stroke his cock simultaneously.

"The way I feel about you isn't just love, it's obsession. Every part of you is *mine*," he says as his mouth moves to my breasts. Rowan rolls his tongue against my nipple.

Fuck, that feels good.

I can barely speak because I'm about to come all over his still working fingers. Eleven days without him felt like an eternity, and I know I have a long way to go until the end of fire season.

"I want to be clear. The only thing I care about now is being the man who loves you. The man who takes care of you. The man who makes you come as you cry out my name." Rowan turns his free hand to my throat, using his thumb against the center to stroke. His lips come down to mine. "And you're so fucking gorgeous when you cry my name, Violette."

"Rowan..." I can't manage anything else as my legs feel like they're about to give out at any moment.

"Just like that." He crooks his fingers into me, and I fall apart over them as his mouth comes down on mine, swallowing my moans and cries.

Before I'm even finished riding out my first orgasm, he pulls his fingers from me, leaving me hollow and sensitive. He raises his hand and pushes the two fingers that were inside of me into my mouth. I moan in response and suck my arousal from him, letting my tongue trail between them. I watch as he drags them back out before kissing my lips. Water runs over us, dripping from his lips to mine, and the tile wall bites into my shoulder blades as he grips my jaw and pulls me in for a scorching kiss. Sliding his hands to my hips to keep me steady, he lifts me up, squeezing my hips tight as he does.

"It was always this body I wanted." He whispers. My legs wind around him, and he notches the head of his cock to meet my entrance, sliding eagerly into me without a word. After almost two weeks everything feels brand new. We both huff out a breath as he fills me. These are the moments I'm whole. Safe. Exactly where I'm supposed to be.

"I love you." I can't help the words; they fall from my lips before I can think about them.

Rowan circles my throat with his hand, lightly pushing against it with his palm while his other arm holds me up. The feel of his hand around my throat does something to me I can't explain. My pussy clenches around him.

"I love every single part of you, Violette." He takes my bottom lip between his teeth. We both breathe out little huffs as he begins to fill me to the hilt, and I mewl into him as another thread of control snaps.

"Now…" He grazes his thumb over the center of my throat. "I'm going to show you what being my obsession for years really looks like."

I force myself to keep my eyes open as I answer him with a tiny whisper of *"please."* I want to drink him in, his eyes are unhinged and he's animalistic as he begins to move. I love to see him like this. I want to push him like this forever, to see him wild, dark, out of control, in love with *me*.

"Fuck, I love watching your tight little cunt struggle to take all of me," he grunts as he thrusts into me, looking down to where we connect. I whimper as he stretches me and the hurt is bliss. "This beautiful body is mine, Vi, I'm the one who tastes you"—*thrust* —"fucks you"—*thrust*— "loves you."

He smirks an almost sadistic grin before he pushes deeper into me, hitting the spot inside me that makes me shatter.

"*Fuck,*" he groans as I clench around him.

Rowan pulls out almost all the way before driving back into me. Then he does it again, only this time he's slower. My lips fall open and my head tips backward to rest against the wall. He trades between slow and fast, setting a pace I can't get used to as each time he pushes into me I lose a little more of my soul to him. His hand slides from my throat to my center, resting between our bodies before his fingers find my clit and I lose the ability to function as my second orgasm begins to roll through me like a thunderous wave about to crash.

"Fuck, Rowan," I groan out as my head falls into his shoulder.

"That's my good girl, Violette," he coaxes me on with another vicious thrust. "Fucking take it all."

Shit. Those words just do me in.

My legs begin to shake around him, his eyes stay focused on where we connect while I come.

"Look at you my love, fucking soaking my cock, showing me who this pussy belongs to."

"Yes, it's yours, Rowan, always," I say, losing it entirely as he keeps his fingers working over my clit, stoking the fire in me that never seems to dim for him. Rowan kisses me hungrily and groans into my mouth. Driving into me over and over like he'll never stop. Somehow, some way, he brings me to the edge yet again as I feel him harden even more inside of me; his lips don't leave mine until he's ready to come.

"Gonna give me another? Show me that I'm the only man who can fuck you into this whimpering mess?"

"I can't…" I moan.

"Yes, you can. I can already feel this perfect cunt clenching my cock. Fuck, you're gonna make me come," he breathes out as his movements grow sloppy, un-orchestrated. "Make me, Violette. Come for me. One more time."

I'm helpless to fight it, his words, the brutal way he fucks me, it all comes to a head and the sounds I make when he wrenches one more orgasm from me would be embarrassing if I cared.

Rowan slaps a hand to the wall. *"Fuck,"* he groans as he spills into me, and I feel it all.

I pull him to me when he starts to slow his movements, wrapping my arms around him, feeling like the earth has shifted just a little around us.

"I love you, Violette," he says as he kisses my lips.

"I love you back, Kingsley." I savor where we are, knowing I don't know it all.

Knowing that it's taken ten years, but there's nothing left we haven't shared. Knowing that it's okay to be afraid, it's okay for the future to be unknown, because we'll face it *together.*

Knowing I'm in the arms of the man I'm meant to be in for the rest of my life.

It just took me a little longer than I expected to get here.

I smile as the steam rises around us, still in each other's arms, tangled together, the way we're supposed to be—twin flames. Brought together by fate, some science, and maybe a little help from the protective spirit who forever lives in my heart.

CHAPTER 60

Violette

OCTOBER - THREE MONTHS LATER

"Pancakes!" Rowan calls from the kitchen to Hollie, who comes running as fast as she can. She's gotten used to Rowan being here over the last few months whenever he's home. It's been a busy season and he's about to leave tomorrow to head to Arizona.

He's been gone quite a bit, and it hasn't been easy for me. Every time he leaves I struggle, but when he has been home, he's been here, which Hollie seems to love.

Lazy mornings on his days off before the afternoons at a park or the beach, visits to my parents or his for dinners are typical. Fire season is coming to an end, and this morning we're going to tell Hollie some news, so Rowan is making her his famous chocolate chip pancakes.

I come wandering out behind her having just woken up too. In a matter of weeks, Rowan will be home for the off season. He's already decided he'll be working as a part-time medic for those months and the rest of the time he's going to spend with me and Hollie while he can.

Those six months of the year where he's home are already something I know I'll look forward to every single year, but the months he has to be gone are just part of him. I've figured out through a shit ton of self-reflection, and through long talks with Teddy and my therapist, how to accept that and just be grateful for every day.

Rowan's unending love has taught me to live in the moment. I smile when his eyes meet mine. His hair is a little longer after a busy summer and he's wearing a white Seahawks T-shirt that fits tight on his upper arms, his sweats, and the icing on the cake? A dish towel slung over his shoulder.

What a fuckable man.

"Here you go, bud," he says, flipping two pancakes onto Hollie's plate and then spreading some butter on them. He carefully adds syrup and takes the time to cut her pancakes up. He's a natural with her and she can feel it. That's why some days I think she loves him more than I do. When he slides her plate over to the other side of the island and she climbs up on the stool, his eyes meet hers and he smiles. That same gooey warm feeling I've been having for months takes over. His eyes turn back to mine and he grins.

"Morning, Mommy," he says. "Pancakes?"

"Of course," I say, pouring myself a coffee then, taking a seat beside Hollie.

"Gotta eat up. Daddy is coming to take you apple picking this afternoon. Remember?" I remind her.

She nods. It's nice to say that to her, knowing he actually will show up, barring any real emergency.

Since Troy's car accident, he's actually turned over a new leaf. He settled on an agreement right away, and now he comes every single Saturday to see Hollie, without fail. He still works six days a week, but he hasn't missed one visit since the week he left the hospital and Hollie is blossoming with her new routine and all the people she has to love her.

Once Rowan has served himself some pancakes we eat in silence for a few minutes. I take a bite and look at him across the island telling him it's time.

"So, Hols…" I say to her. "You like it when Rowan is here with us?"

Hollie smiles at Rowan and nods.

"I like when the whole team is here," she says, meaning the three of us.

"I like being here with you and Mommy too," Rowan tells her. "So much that…I wondered if I came to stay with you and Mommy all the time, would that be okay with you?" he asks her.

Hollie looks at us in question. "Will you get into love?" she asks.

I stifle a laugh, she's way too smart for only having just turned four.

"Yes, we *are* in love, baby," I say to her. Trying to give her just the right amount of info.

"Daddy is always gonna be your Daddy, and Mommy is always gonna be your Mommy, but if you'll let me, Hols, I can be someone who loves you too," Rowan tells her, and I struggle not to tear up as I ask myself how this incredible man is all mine.

"Okay," she says. "Can we watch *SuperPets* every night?" she adds looking back and forth from Rowan to me, like it's of the utmost importance.

"Of course, baby, just like we do now," I say to her, kissing the soft top of her head.

"Will you make popcorn?" She looks at Rowan. "You make it yummy with the butter."

Rowan chuckles. "Of course I will, Hols," he says.

"Okay," she says, satisfied with that in her little mind. She leaps into Rowan's lap, catching him off guard and hugging him. He looks at me for a split second, realizing this is her approval, and his large hand strokes her curls for a second and he kisses her on the top of her head. She doesn't say anything, but she doesn't need to. It's obvious how much she loves him too. I smile at Rowan. He smiles at me as Hollie gets down from the island and scampers off to the living room and her toys.

"That was easier than I thought," Rowan says, coming around the counter to wrap his arms around me. "Was hella nervous, though." He grins, bending down to kiss me.

"She loves you," I tell him. "But you already know this."

"I do," he says, nuzzling his nose against mine. "And I love you," he adds, kissing me.

"Did you ever think we'd end up like this?" I ask him, feeling sentimental about our past, where we are now, and where we're headed.

"Yep, the moment I saw you when I walked into Shifty's, I knew you'd be mine again," Rowan says it as sure as the sun rises. "And I knew you wanted me, even when you wouldn't admit it."

I laugh and pinch his torso through his T-shirt. "Is that so?" I ask.

He pulls me tight to him and kisses my neck, right below my ear.

"It is, and I'm gonna spend the rest of my life making sure you always do," he whispers.

"The way I love you is as unstoppable as flames coming over a mountain. I could never fight it," he murmurs, his thumbs tracing my waist under my robe.

"Every hotshot knows you don't fight a fire." I grin as his lips dot my neck with kisses. "You can't stop it, only harness it and guide it right?"

"That's right, and with you, I'll stay as close to the flame as I can, Vi. Because, fuck, we burn so goddamn good together."

"Mmm," I mutter. "That is true."

"All right, I've convinced you to live with me, I've

convinced you to ink my existence into your skin…" Rowan slides his hand down my arm and lifts my wrist up. I glance down at the tiny symbols there that now match his. The symbols for protons and electrons under the wing of a hawk on my inner wrist, a much smaller, daintier version of his. My first, and probably only, tattoo. Rowan says those symbols no longer signal loss, but our fate and the common thread of Jacob's spirit that brought us back together. He leans down. "Now I've just gotta convince you to marry me," he says against my lips.

"You've got your work cut out for you." I laugh.

"Euchre later?" he asks. "I'll play you for it."

"Prepare to lose," I retort, knowing I'd marry him tomorrow if he wanted. "I can be very distracting," I add.

"Oh yeah?"

"Yeah, ever heard of naked Euchre?" I ask, my mind wandering as he sucks my earlobe into his mouth and takes it between his teeth.

Rowan chuckles then grips my face with both hands, kissing me so deeply I almost forget how to breathe. "Fight me all you want. You will be my wife. And naked Euchre? All I'm hearing is, either way I win."

"Fucking hotshots." I giggle, as he kisses me in my kitchen, soon to be *our* kitchen. "So cocky."

Rowan pinches my waist as his lips come down on mine again and everything around us becomes hazy.

My hotshot, I think I'll keep him.

EPILOGUE

ROWAN

ONE YEAR LATER

"Stop pacing, son, everything is taken care of," my dad says, his mustache turning up into a grin.

"You have the rings?" I ask. "I just want everything to be perfect. They deserve perfect."

My dad reaches into his pocket and pulls out the rings that Violette and I are about to put on to pledge our love to each other for eternity.

"Well, the bride's still here so I guess that's a win-win for you," Opp says with a wide smile, peaking around the corner of the covered porch where I'm standing with most of my squad.

We're at a resort in the valley at the base of the mountains where Jacob fell into that ash pit six and a half years ago, because this is where Vi feels close to him. I look around the corner of the cabin we got ready in and take in the scene. A hundred chairs face a natural wood altar, adorned with greenery and fall flowers, and the aisle is lined with white lanterns and rose petals. The valley itself is the showstopper. It's a wide open space surrounded by trees and the leaves are like flames that meet the sky with the fall colors. The sun is high, and the air is just crisp enough that it will be warm when we say our vows in front of everyone we love, a rarity for Washington in October.

Sup makes his way around the space and passes out a can of Jacob's favorite beer to each of us.

"A toast," Sup says, holding his can high. We all raise ours, and I smirk. I know he hates Corona, but he really loves us all and this is one of the ways he shows it.

"To King, for having the balls to make things right."

"And never letting up until Vi gave in," Cal chimes in, to which everyone chuckles.

"To health, to Rowan and Violette, to Jacob. I believe he's here with us today, even only if in spirit and he'd want us to give you this," Sup says with a smirk.

I look around at all of them for a split second before every one of them is closing in to manhandle me into a fucking bear hug. Patting me on the head, the shoulders, the back, laughing.

"Bunch of sappy fuckers." I laugh, fixing my hair after then backing away.

"Most importantly, to family," Sup adds.

"To family," everyone repeats as we take a swig.

"What the hell are you guys doing in here, making out?" my mother says, coming around the corner. She looks at me with a smile. "It's time, honey."

She gives me a squeeze and I hug her back. "Did I fix things to your liking, Ma?" I ask her.

Before she lets me go, she whispers, "You fixed it real good, baby. Now hold onto it and protect it with everything you've got."

I look out at the crowd filling the seats, and see the smallest glimpse of Hollie, the world's biggest and cutest smile on her face, the sun glinting off the little gold bracelet I gave her last night at our rehearsal dinner to show her she'll always be my daughter in my heart. She's at the end of the aisle, holding

Teddy's hand and her flowers, ready to walk down the aisle. She's practiced that walk to me ten times where she'll stand with her mother and me, but the fact that in just a few minutes I'm going to see it happen for real warms me in a way I just can't explain.

My mother doesn't need to worry. Loving and protecting my little family is exactly what I intend to do, and I'll do it with everything I've got.

Forever.

Violette

"If you were here, you'd be telling me to pull some kind of prank on Rowan at the altar, I know you would," I say, staring down at the picture of me and Jacob on my phone. "It might give Mom a coronary after all her hard work, though." I giggle.

I look out of my cabin near the end of the aisle we created. The aisle I'll walk down in just seven short minutes to Hollie and Rowan. The chairs are full of people we love, and Hollie is so excited to make Rowan her Daddy in her heart.

"You talking to yourself, Vivi?" my dad asks, rounding the corner in his tux, looking very dapper, yet older than he ever has.

"Talking to Jacob," I tell him with a smile.

"What's he saying?"

"I think he's saying I'm in the right place with the right person," I tell my dad, tears brimming in my eyes.

"He's always with us, honey, you know your mother thinks he brought you home to us."

I smile up at my dad as I pick up the handtied blooms Teddy and I put together in mine and Rowan's living room just two days ago.

"Maybe, but whatever brought me home again, I'm glad," I

tell him as he takes my arm into his and we make our way out into the fall sunshine around the back of the cabin.

Along the side is my mother, Scottie who's become such a good friend, and Teddy with Hollie at the front. Hollie looks back at me as the music starts and waves, I wave back and wait with anticipation.

Every moment of the last year is running through my mind. The struggles I've overcome in therapy, learning how to deal with my grief over Jacob's death, learning how to let go and have faith that Rowan will come home to me at the end of every roll. The way I've dealt with my fears and worries today instead of tomorrow, and showing Hollie how to be positive when Rowan goes to work so she doesn't live with the same anxiety that weighed on me as she grows.

And as the guitarist at the end of the aisle begins to play our wedding song, I remember everything else. The first day we spent alone, the first moment he kissed me, and all the smiles, tears, and moments of passion in between.

My dad reaches up and pats my hand folded into his arm as we begin our walk together. I smile as I take in my family, Rowan's family, his crew, and our friends from over the years. With every step my nerves settle and when my eyes meet Rowan's and Hollie's at the end of the aisle, I can't move fast enough toward them.

Rowan's eyes glisten with tears when he sees me and the smile I love so much breaks out across his face. Peace spreads through me like a wildfire through the trees. Looks like I wasn't meant to date a hotshot, after all.

I was meant to marry one.

The End

ACKNOWLEDGMENTS

To Dani and Sloane for asking me along on this unforgettable and incredible ride. I knew the moment I received Sloane's message of "Wanna write a book next year?" that this was going to be amazing. And amazing these books are. I'm so insanely proud of this series and these women that I was lucky enough to work alongside and get to know through this process. You're both beautiful, talented authors and I'm so grateful to be a part of this adventure! I can't thank you both enough.

Rowan and Violette's love story had my heart from the moment I started writing it! It was a journey that had me laughing, crying, kicking my feet and falling in love with a true golden retriever of a man!

To my amazing husband for taking a back seat to Rowan Kingsley as he always does with every MMC I write. For being my sounding board, offering advice and being my greatest muse.

To our own hotshot S, this series would never have happened without you. To take on three chatty AF women who have zero knowledge of what it means to be a hotshot and show us all the patience you did was incredible. You did this through months of countless texts and questions. You also took on reading chapters of romance novels just to ensure authenticity for us. You gave us guidance, extra reading material, photos, charts and stories. Because of you, we learned all about your world and it was one of the greatest pleasures of writing this book. (I will add you did it all while fighting fires like a boss-like I said, superhero.) Your expertise and experience was forefront in making Rowan Kingsley real, believable, heartfelt and human.

To Tabitha, for the incredible character development that comes so naturally to you. For having the perfect amount of first-hand knowledge for this book that made Violette the excellent nurse she was. For the deep dives into Violette's connection with

Jacob and the tiny little "embers" sprinkled throughout, I could not have made this book (or any books) what they are without you.

To Jordan, for always being honest, hilarious and encouraging as hell. Some of my favorite moments are waking up to your comments. Every author should have you in their back pocket to tell them when to turn the harlequin on or off and when the moment does or doesn't call for the fire of a thousand suns.

To Rose, for being my unofficial assistant with all things Paisley, your perfectly timed dad jokes, and for making sure I'm alive when I go deep into the writing cave.

To Caroline and Cathryn for taking one big word document and making it into a beautiful book. I couldn't do this without you.

To my BETA readers Rose, Katie, Kara, Trish, Jess and Mel, thank you so much for your incredible feedback and comments that had my cackling by myself in my living room at 6am.

A special note to Rose and Katie for always being willing to jump into any book I write at any time and giving it your all. I love you both and hope you're always the firsts to read my books.

To my ARC readers and all readers alike as well as my amazing street team, thank you! I may not do it better than anyone else but I pour my whole soul into these stories and every comment, like, share, edit, mention is noticed and loved wholeheartedly. Thank you for loving this series!

SERIES ORDER

Volume one **FIGHT** by Sloane St. James

Volume two **PROTECT** by Paisley Hope

Volume three **HONOR** by Danielle Baker

ABOUT THE AUTHOR

Paisley Hope is an avid lover of romance, a mother, a wife and a writer. Growing up in Canada, she wrote and dreamed of one day being able to create a place, a world where readers could immerse themselves, a place they wished was real, a place they saw themselves when they envisioned it. She loves her family time, gardening, baking, yoga and a good cab sav. For more information, you can follow her and/or reach out anytime.

@authorpaisleyhope – INSTAGRAM

@authorpaisleyhope — TIKTOK

authorpaisleyhope@gmail.com

MORE BOOKS BY PAISLEY HOPE

Wolf.e

<u>Silver Pines Ranch</u>
Holding the Reins
Training the Heart
Riding the High (May 2025)

www.ingramcontent.com/pod-product-compliance
Lightning Source LLC
LaVergne TN
LVHW051326180125
801527LV00012B/303